More praise for
NIGHTMARE, WITH ANGEL

NIGHTMARE, WITH ANGEL

Stephen Gallagher

BALLANTINE BOOKS • NEW YORK

Copyright © 1992 by Stephen Gallagher

All rights reserved under International and Pan-American Copyright Conventions. Published in the United States of America by Ballantine Books, a division of Random House, Inc., New York, and distributed in Canada by Random House of Canada Limited, Toronto. First published in the United States in hardcover by Ballantine Books in 1993.

Library of Congress Catalog Card Number: 93-3175

ISBN 0-345-38966-2

Manufactured in the United States of America

First Hardcover Edition: September 1993

First Mass Market Edition: April 1995

10 9 8 7 6 5 4 3 2 1

As always, certain thanks are due. In this case, to the following: In Hamburg, Polizeipräsident Dirk Reimers and Kriminaloberrat Michael Daleki. In Düsseldorf, Dr. Klaus Bielstein of the Innenministerium des Landes Nordrhein-Westfalen, Kriminalhauptkommissarin Edeltraud Wörz-Polachowski, Hauptmeister Liliensiek, Oberkommissar Bosimann, and Professor Dr. Jürgen Barz of the Heinrich Heine University's department of forensic medicine. In London, Michael Anft and Consul General Bernd Oetter for advice and liaison. And in the northwest of England, Keith Marsland, RGN, RMN at Whittingham Hospital, my wife, Marilyn, for her transcriptions of taped notes and interviews, and those police contacts to whom I've now turned on a number of occasions and whose generosity is no less appreciated for being off the record.

PART ONE

THE BALLAD OF THE JUNKYARD DOG

CHAPTER 1

Marianne, queen of the beach.

Marianne and her best friend, Rudi the dog.

But it would have to be said that right at this moment, Marianne hardly felt like the queen of anywhere. She was soaked and she was cold and she could see, with dismaying certainty, that their time on the sandbank was about to run out. The tide was rising, and the tide was rough. It was a bitter day, sky dark as a bruise and with banks of cloud pressing low; there had been rain in the afternoon, and the threat of rain again. This, on any day, would have been enough to drive most people away from the shore.

Everyone except for Marianne, and her best friend, Rudi the dog.

"Come on, Rudi," she said. "Rudi? Please, come on."

She was trying to encourage the dog to stand, but he wouldn't. Couldn't. He was looking game and he was beating his tail, but his back legs seemed to have completely given way. He'd moved no more than fifteen yards in the past hour and that had been with coaxing, with pleading, with pulling. . . .

"Rudi," she said with her arm around him and trying to lift, desperate now.

Rudi beat his tail even harder, and looked up at her with his big mongrel's grin, all teeth and tongue and hope in his eyes; but his ears were down flat to his head and this showed that he understood *something* of their danger, even if he didn't understand much.

Still crouched by him, she looked over her shoulder.

It was a rocky beach no more. Now it had become an array

of headlands and islands, with rapidly deepening shallows in between. Their own piece of ground, no more than a sandbar in the shape of a narrowing crescent, didn't even rank among the highest of them. Pretty soon it would be gone completely, the waves closing over.

It was a stupid, stupid way to die.

"Come on, Rudi," she said again, and this time she got a grip on his collar. She wasn't big enough to carry him. She wasn't even big enough to drag him by his leash if he really didn't want to move, but somehow she was going to have to try.

"Come on," she said. "Don't be scared, I won't let go." He was neither helping her nor fighting her, but it was taking all of her strength to pull him toward the water's edge. He was leaving a track in the sand as he slid.

As soon as the water touched his front paws he fought shy and scrambled back, breaking her grip. She couldn't hold on and she fell to her knees, hard. Rudi yelped a few times as he rolled over, and then righted himself looking ruffled and hurt.

"You rotten *bugger*, Rudi," Marianne said with tearful force, reaching deep inside her for the worst expletive that she dared.

Marianne was eleven years old. Rudi was ... well, she didn't know for sure, but perhaps even a year or so older. They hadn't been able to tell them his age when she'd gone along with her father to pick him out. All they'd said at the animal shelter was that he was gentle and he was house-trained, and that everyone who'd been along in the past couple of weeks had passed him over for the younger dogs or puppies. Two weeks was as long as the shelter ever kept any animal; after that, those unclaimed or unwanted took a last walk down the pens to the small room with the steel table, and then left via the back door in a black plastic trash bag. Her father hadn't argued with her choice. Whatever she wanted. His mind had been on other things.

That had been four years ago, almost.

Marianne took a deep breath of cold salt air, and let it out. Then she got to her feet.

Rudi watched her as she took another look all around. Hands clenched into pale fists, she walked the length of the sandbar. A dozen strides covered it and at the end she stopped, trying to gauge the depth of the water now. There was always a chance that she could do it alone.

She looked back at Rudi.

He beat his tail hopefully again, and then looked down in surprise as the rising tide suddenly washed up and over the end of the bar, swilling around him. Would he rise? she thought quickly. But no, he was scrambling to slightly higher ground with his front legs while his rear end dragged behind him like a sleeping thing.

She was starting to panic now.

She knew that she couldn't abandon him. And even if she'd felt able to do it and to live with herself afterwards, the time for that decision had already slipped on by. The waters between here and the mainland were running too deep, and too fast. The bay was a treacherous place, and was famous for it. For its great size and emptiness, for its tides, for its quicksands; there were numerous tales of travelers who'd set out to walk across its seven-mile width at low tide and who'd never been seen again, and almost none of the stories were legends.

The wash of seawater subsided, and air bubbled out of the sand at a thousand tiny points like a newly discovered gas field. Rudi was above it, looking back as if betrayed. He'd gone lame running after his ball and it had happened all of a sudden, scaring her badly. He'd peed at the same time, all over himself.

Well, at least the swell had taken care of *that*.

He wasn't old. Twelve wasn't old.

Marianne faced the shore and filled her lungs, and shouted as loudly as she could.

"Help!" she called. "Anybody, please, *help*!"

A couple of gulls turned over the low cliffs. The cliffs were of sheer dirt, undercut and overhanging with tree roots showing where the sea had undermined them. At the base of the cliffs there were shelves of rock that broke up the sea into a high spray as it came dashing in. Nobody was going to be scrambling around there.

She turned to look down the shore, in the direction of the wider sands and the distant town, and she took another deep breath and called out again. This time she tried too hard and the words seemed to catch in her throat, coming out at last like a fishhook pulling free. She wiped her eyes on her sleeve. Her call seemed to have been lost into the wind and the vastness beyond. Down the shore, miles and miles away, she could see a distant speck on the move against the clouds; a helicopter, probably, heading out towards one of the offshore oil platforms.

But it was too far away. Nothing like that ever came by here. Nothing ever happened down this part of the shoreline at all. That was exactly what had made it into one of her favorite places; but if she somehow got out of this, she was thinking, she would never come onto the beach again.

Not ever.

Rudi was whining now. She went back down the sandbar, and crouched by him and put her arm around him again. He was shivering against her.

"It's all right," she said. "We'll be all right. Somebody's going to come soon. Any minute now."

Any minute now.

As words of comfort went, they were pretty thin. But there had to be a way out of this for them.

There had to be.

Didn't there?

Their island had grown perceptibly smaller in the past few minutes. The sea's rise was less tentative now, more a steady surge. Her mind was a blank. Soon the waters would swirl in like a living thing, rising finally to claim this piece of territory, and then—that was the part she couldn't handle. It was an entire color outside of her spectrum, a big dark hole in the jigsaw.

"Any minute now, Rudi," she said, holding him tight. "Just you wait."

The day was closing down and the sea was closing in and no one, no one knew she was here. . . .

And nobody, whispered a voice in the most secret part of her soul, *nobody cares.*

She was hit by a sudden shock as the cold sea swamped all around her and instead of being crouched on the wet sand she was knee-deep in icy water that receded as quickly as it had come; in an instant she was up on her feet and so, just for a moment, was Rudi. As she grabbed for his leash and hauled on it he managed to stagger a few steps before his undercarriage went again and he sank onto what remained of the untouched sand.

Now both of them were shivering, and her clothes were dripping as well. The cliffs were more than a hundred yards away, and seemed to be receding even further in her perception. The swiftly vanishing beach seemed to run on for miles, with no one in sight. Behind her was the open sea, and the empty sky. She wondered if she might swim for it. But every time the sea moved in or out, the rocks under the surface seemed to set cross-currents boiling like a caldron.

Marianne hugged the dog harder.

She couldn't believe that something wasn't going to happen. She tried to think of a prayer, but the only prayers that came to mind were the ones that they chanted wearily in school assembly every morning. There was no form of words that could express the fear that she was feeling now. It was a terror so great that it was almost an ecstasy that threatened to lift her out of her body altogether.

"Oh, God," she said miserably, and then she threw back her head and yelled.

"Somebody ... please! Somebody ... help ... me!"

It roared in her own ears, so that she almost deafened herself. She could feel Rudi flinch and tense himself as if to bark, although he didn't join in.

And then someone called back to her.

CHAPTER 2

At first she couldn't believe it, but then she looked towards the beach.

It was a man, and he was over on the dry sand a couple of hundred feet away. She wasn't sure what he'd said, but it was probably just a *Hey!* He was standing there and looking at her and seemed to have appeared from nowhere, almost as if he'd been sent in answer to her call . . . except that any divine effect was undercut, rather, by the fact that he was in Wellington boots and a big ex-army greatcoat, with a khaki knapsack slung over one shoulder and his free hand holding a black plastic trashbag.

The bag was half-full. From the sound that it made when he let it fall, it seemed to be half-full of old tin cans.

"What are you doing?" he called out.

"I'm stuck," she said, confessing the obvious.

"How did you manage this?"

"My dog can't walk. There's something wrong with his legs."

He looked over the sandbar, as if measuring it in his mind, and then he looked out at the incoming tide. The sea was the color of newly pressed iron, constantly on the move. He said, "You'll both drown if you don't get off there."

"I know, but I couldn't just leave him."

"Don't move," the man said. "Stay back from the sides. You get a big wave, you'll be gone."

He looked around, as if to make one last check that he had no other option than the obvious one. And then he shrugged off the knapsack and his coat together, bundled them and threw both up the beach behind him, and started forwards.

8

He churned up the shallows like a speedboat. Within a dozen strides he suddenly pitched forwards and was in up to his waist. He forged onward and then, when his footing went, struck out in an overarm crawl. Marianne watched as he crashed his way through the water towards her like a barely coordinated seal. Within a few moments he was rising again, staggering up out of the waves and onto the sandbar.

His face was pinched and white with the cold of the sea, his eyes wide and the speech driven from him by the shock of it. As he reached Marianne he stopped and crouched down, half collapsing, before her. The water streamed from him as if he were some old piece of treasure newly dredged up from the deep.

She knew him.

Well, she didn't actually *know* him ... but she'd seen him before, a distant and lonely figure picking his way along the beach at low tide with one of his plastic sacks. He had a funny little place some way inland, between the river and the railway tracks; some of the boys from her school would occasionally go down there and pelt his roof with stones from the embankment and then run away. Nobody that she knew of had ever seen him close up.

Nobody, that was, until now.

He was gasping hard, struggling to recover. His dark hair was cut close, like a brush, and there was gray in it. He looked as if he hadn't shaved in a couple of days and there was gray in his stubble, as well. He had the look of someone who spent a lot of his time out of doors. There was a small, plain gold ring in the lobe of his pierced left ear. She couldn't guess his age. All adults looked about the same to her, and they all looked old.

"You're mad," he said as soon as he'd the breath to say anything at all. "Can't you read the warning signs?"

"I know it's dangerous," she said, and she looked down at Rudi. "I was trying to get him to move."

"You visiting?"

"I live around here."

"How far's your house?"

"You've probably seen it. It's the big one, out on the point."

"Right," he said, taking a breath as if it was time to buckle down and get practical. He looked at Rudi, and Rudi looked back at him uncertainly.

The man said, "Can he stand up?"

"Only for a second. Then he sits down again."

"How old is he?"

"Nobody knows. He's from the dogs' home."

There was something that she couldn't make out in the man's expression as he reached out and put his hand to the side of the old dog's head. He scratched behind its ear, and Rudi leaned his face into the man's palm with a sense of momentary bliss and gratitude. The hand was big and broad and battered, covered in tiny healing cuts as if he'd been digging through sand for razor blades.

And then he said, "Come on," and with his hand on Marianne's arm he started to rise.

She had to rise with him. She said, "Rudi's got to come with us."

"I know," the man said. "Where's his leash?"

"He's lying on it."

The man bent to tug the leash out from under the dog, and Marianne took another glance back at her narrowing island. Some way out on the water, coasting like a raft on the waves, a wooden fish box was going by. It looked as if it had been only recently lost, its corners battered but the black stenciling on its side still readable. A lot of stuff came in like that. Marianne had walked along the beach a thousand times and had never seen anything of value there at all, just weeds and dead shellfish and capped plastic bottles that, if they hadn't washed up where they did, would probably have cruised the oceans of the world for the next hundred years.

"Come on, boy," the man was saying. "Let's see you stand. Come on. Hup. Hup. Hup."

He was pushing the dog none too gently and the dog was trying to rise. Shakily and to Marianne's surprise, he succeeded. His tail was between his back legs and those same legs were trembling like the limbs of a newborn calf, but he was standing again.

Rudi's leash was a long one, more than five feet of well-stretched leather. Old and tame though he was, he couldn't be trusted around sheep and there could be plenty of those in the fields above the cliffs. The man clamped the leather between his teeth just below the loop of the handle, and then he bent and swept up Marianne into his arms.

"He'll drown," Marianne protested as they moved back towards the water.

"Not if he can help it," the man said through his clenched teeth, and with his head he gave a jerk on the leash. "No dog's *that* stupid."

Rudi stumbled, and started to follow.

"That's it," the man said. "Good boy."

They were already at the water's edge, and here he paused to hoist Marianne higher and then took the leather out of his mouth for a moment. "I'm warning you now, it's going to be cold. But don't mess around because there are all kinds of undercurrents to cope with as well. I know it doesn't look far, but it's far enough to be dangerous. All right?"

She nodded.

The man turned his head to one side, spat, and then clamped his teeth onto the leash again and waded out.

He must have taken a pretty good grip because Rudi was dragged after them, with a yelp. Marianne was being held against the front of the man's shirt and he smelled of nothing but the cold, cold sea. They plunged on and in and now he lifted her up high to keep her out of the water, holding her clear of himself. Already she could feel that his arms were quivering under the strain of holding her aloft as he waded out and descended to waist depth. She tried to turn her head to see how Rudi was doing, but this seemed to threaten the man's balance; whether in warning or just to keep his grasp on her, he squeezed a little harder and Marianne said, "That hurts."

"Sorry," he grunted, but he didn't ease the pressure. He was taking a slightly different line towards the shore, presumably to avoid the crossflow that had almost trapped him on his way over. It was happening, she was thinking excitedly; it was as if all of the clockwork of the world was turning, breaking up the alignment of those elements that had come together to form her danger. The beach would be the beach again, the tide would be the tide, and the biggest of her worries would be how to explain the lateness of her return and the condition of her clothes to Mrs. Healey.

Just a few more strides to go, she was thinking.

And then, without warning, she was plunged into the water and dragged straight down and under.

The shock of the cold was unbelievable. Literally unbelievable. It closed over her like the slammed pages of a book. She was battered and tumbled by the crosscurrents and when she opened her eyes she could see nothing but darkness and bubbles. She kicked and thrashed, and her fingers briefly touched sand that was sliding by underneath her at frightening speed; she gulped down salt and then gulped down more and tried to grab at something, and then for a moment she broke the surface. She was tumbling over like a log and in that moment she knew that this was it, she was gone, she was going to drown; the current was sucking her out like a pip and her last sight, if she was lucky, would be of the fast-receding lights of home.

Then a rough hand grabbed a piece of her coat collar and her hair together, and she was dragged up in an explosion of spray and held there, dangling like a puppet as the man plowed his way onward into the shallows. She could feel the submerged beach catching under her feet and she tried to get a footing, but he was marching her too fast and all that she could do was to bob around and kick at the water. But then he started to weaken and stagger, and he dropped her so that she was able to get her balance. Her weight seemed to return all at once, doubled, and with only the first couple of steps she almost stumbled and fell to her knees.

His hand was under her arm now, guiding her back up.

She looked around, disoriented. The landscape seemed to have changed completely in the few seconds since they'd gone under, and she realized that in that brief time they'd been swept some distance from the point at which they'd entered the water. To Marianne, it seemed like *miles*. A hundred yards, at least.

"Watch where you're stepping," the man said. "There's a hidden channel right about here."

She looked, and saw it. A thread of fast-moving darkness

under the shallows, another booby trap in the watery minefield that only hours before had been nothing more threatening than a handy space in which to throw a ball.

She looked around suddenly.

"Where's Rudi?" she said.

"Just watch where you're going," the man said as he jumped her roughly over the hidden stream with a jerk on her arm.

She tried to speak, but she'd already used up what little breath she had. Finally, as they sloshed their way up onto the sand, she was able to say, "Where is he?"

"I don't know," the man said, not looking at her.

She stopped. "You let him *go*?"

"He'll probably get ashore somewhere further along."

She pulled away. "No . . . !"

"It was him or you. What was I supposed to do?"

He continued walking up the beach towards his coat and his knapsack. They'd separated as he'd thrown them and the bag was already in the shallows, rocking with its own half-buoyancy under the to-and-fro action of the tide. The coat lay a couple of yards further on, like a tumbled scarecrow.

Marianne didn't follow him. She stood ankle-deep in the water and turned to face the open, and she called her dog's name. She looked for him, already in her mind seeing his bobbing head arrowing across the water. For one heartstopping moment she thought that she saw him for real; but it was just the black plastic bag, already some distance away and bobbing out to sea. It looked like a deflated balloon, and as it went it was spilling aluminum cans that floated in its wake like airliner debris.

There was nothing. Nothing but the big, wide, and empty bay. Nothing above it but the gray cloudy sky, with one pale streak of yellow late-afternoon sun breaking through somewhere close to the horizon.

The man was behind her now. He didn't touch her again.

He said, "He was swimming. I could see that much."

She turned and looked at him. He was soft-spoken, just a little hoarse. He went on. "I wouldn't lie to you about something like that. He was doing pretty well. Considering."

The shore breeze cut into her through her wet clothes. Her teeth were chattering.

"He *is* a good swimmer," she said hopefully.

The man looked out. "Well, there you are," he said. "Can he find his own way home?"

She nodded.

"Well," the man said, "then I'd wait for him there. If he can make it, that's where he'll head for. But listen," he said then, and there was a certain gentleness in his voice that called up in her exactly those fears that it was no doubt meant to calm. "I've got to say this to you. He's not a young dog, and when their legs start to go like that, well . . . sometimes it's better to say goodbye before things can start to get worse. Do you understand what I mean?"

"I've heard of dogs older," she said sullenly.

He didn't argue the point. Didn't seem to take offense, either.

"Come on," he said. And she felt the heavy weight of his coat descend upon her suddenly as he placed it around her shoulders.

So then Marianne turned from the sea and, with the tears running down her face and laying salt over salt water, she walked with the man towards the end of the cliffs. Beyond the cliffs lay the reclaimed flatlands. Across the flatlands ran the track that would take them from here to her home.

CHAPTER 3

Some of it was land proper, and some of it was land over which the sea had never fully relinquished a claim. The boundary between the two was marked by a flat-topped, man-made dike which the pathway mostly followed. The dike enclosed a wide acreage of low, green pastureland; outside of it were the drowned flats that ran out all the way back to the bay.

They followed the line of a fence—sheep fencing with a single strand of barbed wire along its top, and showing evidence of the sea's occasional inland forays in the form of rags and weeds that hung on the wire like fleeces. Beyond it lay a weird tracery of salt pools, great strange shapes chopped out of the turf as neatly as by any pastry cutter. The earth here was smooth and spongy, the grass as plain as baize. As they climbed up onto the dike, they passed one of the signs that the man had mentioned. It was cast in iron like the signs that they'd used years ago on the railways, and its lettering had been picked out in white; it read

DANGER

DEEP AND VARYING CHANNELS

and it leaned on its post. At the foot of the post lay a few pieces of driftwood, dried-out and bleached like prehistoric bones.

Marianne had to hold the coat up around her to keep it off the ground as she walked. She was thinking about Rudi. She'd convinced herself that he would be all right. She was even wondering if he might somehow get to the house ahead of them and be waiting there ... all logic said no, but it was a scene that she couldn't help replaying in her mind. If he wasn't there, he'd join them soon. And if it didn't happen right away, it would happen later.

She didn't care what anybody might say. She *knew* it would happen.

Her life had to be a charmed one. Hadn't she just experienced the proof of that?

At the end of the path, overhung by trees, stood the remains of an old copper smelting tower. Just the tower, nothing else, a twenty-five-foot stone stack with a hearth at its base and nothing to explain who might have used it, or when, or why they should have thought to site it here in the middle of nowhere.

Beyond the tower, a lane began. Here there was another

sign, only this one was handmade and it read PRIVATE PROPERTY. Behind this stood three cottages at the end of the lane, the start of civilization proper. Marianne and the man who had pulled her from the sea took a chance on the notice, and sat on the garden wall of the cottages to empty the water out of their boots. If anyone saw them, no one came out.

The man said, "The big house on the point. Is that by the road over the old salt marsh?"

Marianne said, "You can walk on the sea wall when the road's underwater."

He scratched his head, and then rubbed briskly at his hair. It came up like a brush again, as before. "I'd better walk the rest of the way with you," he said.

"There's no need."

He looked at the ground, and at himself. "If I could leave you, I would. But look at us both."

"I'm not so bad," Marianne said, but she could suddenly see herself through Mrs. Healey's eyes. She wondered how she might explain alone the mess that she was in. She'd be blamed for it, of that she was certain; the dangerous part somehow wouldn't be taken quite as seriously as it should because she was, after all, still in one piece, whereas the stupidity part could be used against her forever.

"You'll need someone to back you up," the man said, and she realized that he knew exactly what she was thinking.

"All right," she said.

The lane was overhung by trees, the path scattered with red berries that had fallen from the branches. It took them up by the big old rock quarry where sheep were often penned in bad weather. A couple of old railway cars off their wheels served as shelter for the animals; ironbound, plank-sided, the iron rusted to brown and the painted woodwork dirtied to more or less the same color. A couple of sheep bolted from by the gate as Marianne and her rescuer passed.

She said to him, "You live near the railway, don't you?"

"I've lived in all kinds of places," he said.

"But that's where you live now."

He didn't actually say yes. He just inclined his head, as if to concede the point. He seemed to be avoiding looking at her.

She waited a moment, and then said, "Some of the boys call you Grizzly Adams."

He looked up at the sky, as if checking for rain.

"Whatever they call me," he said, "I can bet I've been called worse."

He didn't exactly smile to himself as he said it; it looked like a smile, but it wasn't one.

All dogs are good swimmers, Marianne was thinking. And on the occasions when he'd wandered off from the house on his own, Rudi had always found his way back again.

The lane turned some way ahead of them, and beyond it the land dropped away once more to the level of the salt marshes. They'd effectively cut across a headland and were about to come back down onto the coastline.

The man said, "Where's the path from here?"

"I'll show you," Marianne said. She checked the lane behind them, in case—just in *case*—somebody or even some dog might happen to be following.

But the lane was empty.

They reached the house by way of the sea wall, because the tide was in and the regular causeway was under water. The distance was about the same. There had been three dwellings out on the point, but one was now a ruin and another was halfway to it and only her own stood, isolated as a beacon, where the early-evening sky and the land seemed to meet.

Her father's car wasn't in the place where he usually parked it on the rough ground outside. But there were lights in some of the lower rooms.

The man said, "Is your mother there?"

"Only Mrs. Healey," Marianne said. "She'll probably have seen us coming by now."

Mrs. Healey was their housekeeper, and she came over most days of the week from the village. She shopped and cleaned and took care of the evening meal. Sometimes when Marianne needed clothes, she'd go with her into town. These visits, it had to be said, were never the high spots of Marianne's year. She'd always been vague about the exact nature of their arrangement, but in practice it seemed to be that Mrs. Healey

was always around when her father wasn't . . . which meant
that Mrs. Healey was around for a lot of the time.

The house was tall and dark and gloomy; she thought of it
sometimes as a real House of Usher like the one in the story.
The FOR SALE sign nailed up by one of the bedroom windows
had become so weathered and flaking that it seemed like a permanent part of the place. Mostly Marianne gave its appearance
no thought at all, but to approach it now was to see it through
a stranger's eyes as well as her own. Mrs. Healey couldn't
have become aware of them, or she'd no doubt have appeared
to meet them by now. Marianne led the man around the side,
to the kitchen door. There had been a kitchen garden once, but
the soil here was little more than a thin covering of dirt over
shale and now even the weeds were having a hard time of it.

"I'll ask Mrs. Healey if we can find you some dry clothes,"
Marianne said as she unhitched the latch.

But the man said, "Don't worry about that. I don't plan to
be staying."

The kitchen was big and high-ceilinged, and as depressing
as most of the other rooms in the house. It had belonged to
some great-uncle that she'd never seen, and her father had in-
herited it. The great-uncle had lived here alone for his last four
decades, and had changed the place little in that time. Since
Marianne and her father had moved in, the changes had been
even fewer. Oilcloth covered some of the floors, threadbare
carpet the rest. The decor was long out of date even for an old
person's taste, and was moldering. The upper rooms were in a
permanent twilight, those downstairs were just downright
gloomy. Marianne felt more than a little self-conscious as they
stepped inside. She'd never brought anyone home to this house
before.

The man was glancing around. "Bendix," he said, but only
as if for the sake of something to say. "Good machine. Reliable."

She looked at the washing machine in its alcove beside the
walk-in pantry. To her it had always looked like an antique,
and it still did. In the alcove by the Bendix were Rudi's beanbag bed and his water bowl. Of the dog himself there was no
sign.

The man was standing there. He was trying to seem at ease, but she could sense that he felt awkward; and if his wet clothes were anything like her own, he'd be desperately uncomfortable, as well. He'd commented on the Bendix, and that was the extent of his small talk.

"Would you like something to eat?" she said, but the man was already shaking his head.

"I'm going to hand you over and go," he said.

There was a creak from the ceiling above them, followed by the sound of someone descending the stairs. A woman's voice called out down the hallway beyond the kitchen, "There are such things as mealtimes, young lady."

Marianne looked at the man and mouthed, *Mrs. Healey*. And he nodded, as if this was reasonably interesting news.

"I've had a bit of trouble, Mrs. Healey," Marianne called back to her.

"And if you can't be bothered to turn up for them," Mrs. Healey went on as if Marianne hadn't spoken, "why should anyone bother to—my God."

Mrs. Healey had reached the doorway and here she stopped, on the threshold of the kitchen. She was staring at the two of them, taken aback at what she saw. Although whether this was because of the state of Marianne or a reaction to the unexpected presence of a stranger, it was impossible to say.

Mrs. Healey blinked behind her glasses. She was an uncommonly pugnacious-looking woman, with an appearance suggesting that it was her life's pleasure to argue with shopkeepers. She was never particularly unkind, but she had a bent for sarcasm. She called it speaking her mind.

She wasn't speaking it now. She wasn't saying anything. She was just gaping like a goldfish. Not at Marianne, but at her rescuer standing beside her.

Marianne said, "I got into a bit of trouble . . . the tide was coming in and Rudi wouldn't walk and I got kind of stuck . . . and this man helped me and we both got wet, and Rudi swam off but we think he's all right, don't we . . . ?"

Marianne's voice trailed away. Mrs. Healey and the man were watching each other. Something was going on here, something grownup that she couldn't quite grasp. Mrs. Healey was tight-lipped, and saying nothing. The man was meeting her stare without flinching.

Marianne said again, "Don't we?"

And the man said with simple sincerity, "I really don't know."

"He *is* all right," Marianne insisted, and then added, for Mrs. Healey's benefit, "He's making his own way home."

It was sounding exactly the way that she'd feared it would, like a stupid scrape, a lame excuse for her condition rather than a situation of any real peril.

Mrs. Healey finally broke her silence. She said, "Where did this happen?"

"By the place they call Black Rake. I was going by, and I saw her just in time. It wasn't her fault—the sea comes in so fast along there, you can be trapped before you know it. She did well. She kept her head."

Mrs. Healey looked at her. And then she looked back at the man and said, with a sense of detachment as if her heart wasn't really in it, "Well, I'm sure Marianne's father will want to thank you, Mr. . . . ?"

"Most people just call me Ryan." He glanced down at himself. "And I'd really rather just head for home, if that's all right with you."

Mrs. Healey made no attempt to argue, or to persuade him otherwise. The man called Ryan nodded to Marianne, and then hesitated as he reached for the door. Not one of life's great socializers, was Marianne's guess.

"Thank you, Mr. Ryan," Marianne blurted out.

But Ryan had already gone.

Mrs. Healey was standing there, watching the door as if she couldn't quite believe or come to grips with what had just happened. Then, without meaning to, Marianne shivered once in her wet clothes, and Mrs. Healey seemed to remember herself.

She looked at Marianne in something of a daze. "You'd better get upstairs and out of those wet things."

"Can I have something to drink?"

"Hot bath first, and drink after. Go on, now."

Up in her bedroom, Marianne peeled out of her layers to the thunderous sound of the bath being drawn just down the hallway, and the usual low-pitched complaining of the plumbing from various places all over the house. Her clothes felt awful. Everything stuck to everything else, and the innermost layers stuck to her. Sand had found its way into every crease and fold.

Grownups, she was thinking. You just couldn't read them at all. They could be like another species, sometimes. It was scary for her to think of ever actually becoming one ... what would it involve? It was as if you'd have to forget so much, and leave so much behind. Almost like the prospect of dying within yourself, so that someone else could come in and take over.

Not something she felt that she was looking forward to, at all.

Mrs. Healey called to her then and so she went down the cold hallway in just her underwear, padding quickly on the thin carpet. Mrs. Healey was kneeling ready on a folded towel by the enameled clawfoot tub, the sleeves of her dress rolled up to her elbows. The bathroom was tall and narrow and full of steam. There was no curtain at the window, which was made out of leaded stained glass sections and probably had been quite something in its day. Now it seemed spooky, and a little depressing.

She had to put her arms up in the air so that Mrs. Healey could strip the wet underwear from her. "You'll get pneumonia," Mrs. Healey said. "What were you thinking of?"

"I didn't get stuck on purpose."

"Nothing you did would surprise me. You could have drowned. Enough people have, out there."

"Rudi couldn't walk."

"So you keep saying."

She had to turn and hold onto the washbasin with both hands in order to keep her balance as Mrs. Healey pulled off her cotton pants; facing the window like this and rising onto tiptoe, Marianne suddenly realized that she could see through the clear part of the glass and right along the sea wall from here. She could see Ryan, a distant figure following the defences back to the headland. Were he to look back, he might even see her.

In fact, was he looking back now? She started to wave.

"Stop it!" Mrs. Healey snapped, and she grabbed her arm and jerked her away from the window. "Stop making an exhibition of yourself."

Marianne let out an involuntary sound, because the grab had pinched her right on the soft flesh of her upper arm; Mrs. Healey seemed to catch herself, and made an effort to be more calm.

She said, "I'm only thinking of what your father's going to say."

Marianne might have said that she was waving because Ryan hadn't heard her thanks, and none from anyone else had been forthcoming; but she said nothing.

He'd been turning his head to look back. Or he'd been about to. The more she thought about it, the more she was convinced.

She wondered if he'd seen anything of her wave at all.

The bath was hotter than she'd ever had one before. Mrs. Healey told her not to be ridiculous because it was almost cold. She sat there spluttering while Mrs. Healey dumped scalding water over her head from the old milk pan that was kept by the bath for that very purpose, and then worked up a lather of Coal Tar shampoo on Marianne's head with fingers that felt as gentle as steel rods. All the way through this, she was muttering something about being employed as a housekeeper and not as a nanny, but not so that it sounded like much more than habit. After rinsing Marianne off and leaving her for a while to lie there and get warmed up, she came back with a coarse towel almost big enough to bury her in.

Wrapped in the towel, Marianne was shepherded back to her bedroom. There she found that the small electric fan heater from her father's study had been set out and left running so that the room was stiflingly, welcomingly warm. It was almost dark outside by now, and her bedside light had been switched on. Her night-dress and dressing-gown had been laid out on the bed ready for her.

She sat on the bed, and Mrs. Healey sat beside her and used a corner of the towel to rub dry her hair.

Marianne said, "I don't want to go to bed yet."

"Bed's the best place for you," Mrs. Healey said. And then there was a definite shift in the air. Mrs. Healey seemed to unbend a little; something came into her tone that was less distant, less abrupt than anything that Marianne had previously been used to.

"I'm not just ordering you about," she went on. "Sometimes I *do* actually know what's best. You've been soaked and it's cold and that sea's not as clean as it used to be, either. You can read your book, or I'll bring you the radio. Your supper can go in the oven for a while and then you can have it on a tray. Is there anything else that you want?"

"A drink."

"All right."

Marianne's hair was as dry now as toweling was ever going to get it. Mrs. Healey smoothed it down with a gesture that was almost an affectionate pat.

And then she touched a finger to Marianne's chin, and turned her head so that she could look her in the eyes. There was a kind of a clarity and a sadness in her gaze that Marianne had never seen there before.

She said, "Now, listen to me," and Marianne folded her hands on her lap and listened. "That man who brought you home. He's probably harmless. But stay away from him anyway."

"What do you mean?"

"Just . . . make sure you remember. If he ever tries to talk to you, just tell him you have to be somewhere and walk the other way."

"But he's the one who rescued me," Marianne protested, unable to comprehend.

Mrs. Healey did no more than smooth aside a stray lock of hair that was threatening to drop across Marianne's forehead, and said, "Then let's just say you were very, very lucky."

Marianne lay in bed, propped up on a spare pillow and reading her Narnia book, until Mrs. Healey brought her supper on a tray about a half-hour later. The cocoa smelled as if it was off; it wasn't, it had brandy in it that Mrs. Healey wasn't telling her about, but the effect was more or less the same because it made it too awful for her to drink. When the housekeeper had gone back downstairs, Marianne slid out of bed and tiptoed to the bathroom to empty the mug. She knew which boards didn't creak, and which to avoid.

It was while she was in the bathroom and quietly running cold water to rinse out the dregs from the basin that she saw the approaching headlights of her father's car. The tide must have dropped back now because there he was, coming out over the causeway. There was a moon tonight, and it picked out the wet road in a line of silver. The causeway wasn't as dramatic as it could sometimes sound. It wasn't even always covered at high tide, except at certain times of the year; a single-track concrete road a quarter-mile in length, it cut across an inlet to the point and disappeared for rarely more than a few hours out of every day. And when it disappeared, there were plenty of other tracks and pathways across the fields behind the house; nothing you could easily get a car over, that was the only problem.

The lights of his five-year-old Vauxhall swept by underneath the window, and she heard the crunch of its wheels on shale as he swung in by the house. Marianne turned off the tap, and headed back to her room.

He was usually late. Sometimes he was later than this. And on those nights he wouldn't even look in on her, probably assuming her to be asleep. But often she waited anyway, drifting along in a kind of daydreaming twilight until she heard his tread in the hall and, seconds later, the closing of his bedroom door. Then she'd turn from wakefulness and, like a sea bird from its ledge, spread her wings and slide off into the depths.

He didn't exactly have a job. These days he called himself a salesman, she knew that much, but he didn't seem to work for any particular company and the money that he made came in bits and pieces from all different places—when it came. He spent most of his days on the road, driving from one engineering firm in some big mill town to another in some far-flung corner of the region, and in the evenings when he got home he'd say little about what he'd been doing; instead he'd slump in a chair before the TV and stay there with a dark look on his face, his eyes on the screen but his mind focused somewhere else.

She set the mug on the tray by her plate, and climbed back into bed. She heard the kitchen door close downstairs, and voices through the floor—nothing that she could follow or even make out, mostly just the rumbles like those of far-off underground trains.

She wondered what was being said about her. It was taking longer than she'd expected and, as she waited, the suspense of it all began to ebb. She sank back into the double pillows, and sighed. She didn't want to read any more. She didn't want to sleep, either. She was exhausted and her mind was racing, and she didn't know how to reconcile the two states.

But she must have dozed, because she never heard him coming up the stairs.

He said from the doorway, "Well, I just heard all about this afternoon. You gave us all quite a scare."

She was awake all at once. She pushed herself up in the bed to sit with the pillows behind her.

She said, "Has Rudi come back yet?"

He shook his head. His dark hair was thinning on top, but either through intention or neglect he'd let it grow longer everywhere else. He didn't look so old; other girls' fathers looked a lot older than him, even if they weren't. Only in his eyes did he seem to have aged of late. Sometimes she'd look into his eyes, and she wouldn't recognize the person that she saw there at all.

She said, "Well, will you leave a door open for him tonight?"

He pushed a hand through his hair as he came over to sit on the bed. He wore his one good suit to go out to work, but whenever she saw him in it the tie was always undone and the back of his shirt was always halfway out of the trousers. She drew up her knees so that he'd have a space to sit.

"Look," he said, lowering himself down. "I know I'm not here as much as I'd like to be. But ... I thought I could trust you to be sensible. You know the beach can be a dangerous place, with the tides and the quicksands. All those stories, they're not just made up. People have died. Some have never been found. Is that what you want to happen? Is it?"

"No," she said. What she wanted to happen was for him to leave a door unlatched so that Rudi, when he finally got home, wouldn't have to wait outside in the cold until morning.

He said, "We're a team, here. If I go away, I need to know that I can leave you with some kind of confidence. Otherwise I'll just have to say, you stay in the house and you don't go out."

Quick to pick up on a nuance, she said, "*Are* you going away?"

"For a few days," he admitted. "It's business."

"When?"

"Next week. I've asked Mrs. Healey if she'll stay here with you. I know you don't like her too much," he added quickly, anticipating her objections, "but either she comes here or you'll have to go and stay at her house, and I think you'd probably like that even less." He put his hand on her knee, and squeezed it through the covers. "I'm sorry, Marianne. It's the way it is."

Then he started to stand.

Should Marianne ever have been asked to describe a spectrum with a trip to Disney World at one end, a stopover with Mrs. Healey would surely have to be at its opposite other. The one topic of conversation that seemed to animate her was that of inheritances and the duplicity of close relatives, particularly her own. Mention a piano in that context, and she was apt to veer close to bursting point.

What Marianne wanted to say at that moment before she lost his attention again, and had wished she could have said so many times before, was that her one desire was for everything to be as it once had been. Long ago, and far away; with no big gloomy house, no Mrs. Healey, and her mother back with the two of them again.

But as always, she couldn't bring herself to say it. Because she knew that the times had changed and the tides had run, and the possibility had by now receded too far to be anything other than abandoned.

And so instead she said, "*Will* you leave a door open for Rudi?"

"It sounds pretty much like Rudi's gone," her father said; not harshly, but not dressing it up too much either. "And leaving doors unlocked at night isn't exactly a good idea."

"He's finding his own way," she persisted.

"Look," he said. "It happens. He had to be at least eleven years old, he had a pretty good run. I know you'll miss him. And I'll miss him too . . . but they don't go on forever."

"He isn't dead," she said with complete conviction. "He was swimming for the shore."

Her father was in the doorway now. "Well," he said. "Who knows?"

And with those words of comfort, he stepped out and pulled the door closed after him.

I know, Marianne thought with desperate assertiveness. Having lost so much of everything else, the prospect of losing that final link with happiness was just too much for her to bear. *I* know. And she conjured Rudi in her mind, so real to her that there couldn't be the remotest possibility that he really could be gone forever.

And then, inexplicably in the face of such certainty, she turned her face into the pillow and began to cry.

CHAPTER 4

She woke in darkness.

She was still wearing her dressing-gown under the covers, and she was too hot. Perhaps that was why she'd been dreaming. In the dream she'd been in one of those fairground mirror-mazes, where some walls were mirrors and others were plain glass and you could never be sure which were which. Trying

to find her way through, she'd kept on glimpsing her own reflection; but instead of coming towards her as a reflection usually did, this one was always heading away. A trick of the mirrors, she was sure. But then, through several layers of glass,
she saw it find the exit and leave.

She knew that it was late. Her father must have looked in
again and had turned off the reading lamp for her. She rolled
over and tried to make out the luminous hands on her wind-up
Westclox alarm, but the dots were too faint to make out. She
rolled back and sighed, and stared up into the darkness.

There was nothing to see, but after a few moments her mind
began to call up shapes and patterns out of the grain. This
would often happen when she woke in the night, and couldn't
get back to sleep. Sometimes, she'd start to be able to make
out faces. And sometimes the faces would make her switch on
the light.

She switched on the light.

There were times when she thought that to live anywhere
else would be better than living here. It was an old man's
house, it even smelled like one; nothing since they'd moved in
had made it feel anything like their own. The plan had been
for them to live in the place until it sold, and then they'd use
the money to buy something more suitable inland. But as far
as Marianne was aware, they'd never even had anyone come
out to look it over. At first, she'd thought it could only be better than the succession of one-room flats and cheap hotels in
which they'd had to spend almost a year; but the novelty had
begun to pall even at her first sight of it across the salt marsh,
and the coastline and the countryside had offered little com-
pensation until she'd been given Rudi to explore them with.

Her father wouldn't have left the door open. Of this much,
she was certain. He didn't believe as she did, he didn't *know*. As
far as she knew, Rudi could be waiting out there right now; shut
out and wondering why there was no one to let him in, innocent
and stupid and trusting just like he'd always been. What if he
didn't wait around until morning? What if he saw the closed-up
house as a rejection? He might turn around and go in his dismay
and then be lost to her forever, never to be seen or heard of
again.

She threw back the covers. Her supper tray had gone from the bedside, as well. By now she'd convinced herself that it was essential for her to go downstairs and open the kitchen door *right now*, and that the life-or-death question for Rudi would be decided not on the beach but right here. Either in her action, or in her failure to take any. Perhaps he'd made a sound out there, and she'd heard it in her sleep and that was the reason for her certainty; it was faith without evidence, but she felt it was valid all the same.

She stepped out of her room and, avoiding the noisy boards as before, tiptoed down the hallway. The light was still on in her father's bedroom. Marianne knew that he didn't sleep much, but then he *said* that he never slept at all and she knew that this was wrong, because sometimes he snored. There was no clear indication of whether he was awake or sleeping now, but at least the slice of light from under his door allowed her to find her way to the stairs and down.

I'm coming, Rudi, she whispered.

There was a deeper darkness below.

She didn't dare to risk the hall light, that would be too much of a giveaway. But at the foot of the stairs she groped around and found the switch that put on the cellar light instead. The cellar door didn't fit too well in its recess under the stairs, and enough illumination came leaking out for her night-tuned eyes to pick her way. The cellar wasn't used too often. In a house so low and so close to the sea, it was always damp and had a tendency to flood.

She crossed the kitchen, feeling her way around the big table. She could see the windows in here, big squares of moonlight like sheets of opal glass. When she reached the kitchen door she found that, exactly as she'd expected, it was locked and the bolt had been shot. She felt resentment. What exactly was her dog supposed to do? It wasn't as if she'd asked for the door to be left standing wide open, just unlatched so that he'd be able to push it with his nose. It wasn't beyond him, he knew how to do it. And it was hardly a risk; who ever came out here? And what could they be wanting if they did?

She worked the bolt as quietly as she could. Then she took the key from its high nail and put it in the lock, and turned.

The door popped open. She swung it back and stepped forward, facing the night.

"Rudi?" she called in as loud a whisper as she dared. *"Rudi, are you there?"*

The cool air made her shiver. She could hear the near-distant sighing of the sea, and catch a sparkle of moonlight on far water.

"Rudi," she said. *"Come on in."*

She took a step out.

There wasn't complete darkness, at least not in the immediate area around the house. Long, pale bars of yellow light shone out across the ground from the cellar window. They picked out every feature in the rough ground, and threw long and jagged shadows from each clump of weed or sea-thrift in their path. But they also served to intensify the darkness that lay beyond, and in that darkness Marianne could see nothing.

She listened.

A birdcall, almost certainly an owl. But not close by. Something was out there, she was sure. If it was Rudi, she knew that he'd never ignore her. But what if he was unable to respond? What if he'd crawled so far, and was too weak to crawl further?

Still she listened, and became even more certain.

Something was there. And it *had* to be him.

If only she could find him, get him inside, where it was warm. The worst would be over then. She could persuade her father to call in the vet to do whatever it would take to get him fixed up again; injections for his arthritis, vitamins, whatever he needed to put the bounce back into him. Get him lithe, get him running, get him back the way he was. . . .

Eagerly, she took another step and almost stumbled; she'd been moving right out from the house and she hadn't even been aware of it, and she'd almost reached the point where the land began to drop towards the marsh. A break in the clouds let down moonlight, and she peered around her.

Something moved and she looked, but already she'd missed it. A night creature, perhaps, scared up by the sound? Or Rudi, doing the best that he could to respond?

She stopped again and listened—*more* than listened—and now she became certain of it.

There was a presence.

"Rudi," she whispered with more confidence, and took another step forward and held out her hand. "Come on, boy. It's me, you're home. Come inside out of the cold."

And then she turned her head as she heard something slither behind her.

She was a dozen or more strides from the house now; something was there, all right, but it didn't sound like any dog. She scanned the overgrown kitchen garden, but even as she looked, the moon slipped behind a cloud again and the scant details of the scene quickly faded from her sight.

And then she heard, quite distinctly, a measured footstep.

She started to panic. Nobody ever came out here. *Nobody.* Even the newsagent wouldn't deliver this far out, and that was by daylight. If someone was moving close to the house and in darkness, he was either lost or he was prowling. And he must have made a strenuous effort to get himself lost, if he'd wound up around here.

Marianne started to move back towards the open door. It was heavy going. All that stuff about seeming to have twice your weight and to move at half your normal speed, like in a dream, came home to her now. She was running, but it didn't feel like running. It felt like a long, slow ballet; the kitchen door swung to after her like the door of a big safe, and it was as if a herd of zebra could have stampeded through in the time that it was taking to travel. She threw herself behind it, but it seemed to make not a scrap of difference. It finally shut with a bang.

She took a piece of skin out of her finger in a hurry to shoot the bolt, but she felt no pain. She felt it happen, but that was all. She ran her hand down the door to find the key, and she turned it in the lock and pulled it out. She reached to hang it on its nail, and missed. She heard it hit the floor.

She bent and felt around, but couldn't find it. Not that it mattered. She was safely locked inside now.

No more than four feet away from her, something scraped loudly across the kitchen floor.

She spun, her back to the door. The scent hit her, the odor that she'd already once scrubbed and steamed and soaked away; the scent of cold, the smell of the sea. The smell of the drowned, and it was back in the room with her now. Her hand shot out, missed the light switch, and then found it.

The light blinded her for a moment. Then shapes burned in, and took form. She wasn't alone.

She looked down.

The dog looked up with dripping jaws, as if caught in some guilty act. His nose had been in his water bowl which was out in the middle of the floor now; Rudi always knocked it around with his muzzle when he'd emptied it and wanted more. It made a racket, but it got results.

Marianne's heart was hammering. She couldn't move. Rudi cocked his head, puzzled, and made an effort to wag his tail; not a lot happened, but it was there. He looked utterly spent, but his eyes were bright.

She fell on her knees beside him and threw her arms around him and said his name, but only in a whisper. She didn't want to bring her father downstairs; if the slamming of the door hadn't awakened him, it must have come fairly close to it. Rudi tolerated her attention for a while and then nosed his bowl again. She got up and wiped her eyes and refilled it at the sink. When she put it down again before him, he put his face in and drank greedily until the bowl was almost empty. Then he plodded over to his corner and dropped onto his beanbag with a heavy, heavy sigh. His leather leash, black and stiff and half dried-out, trailed across the floor behind, and she hurried to catch up with him and unhook it.

His fur was spiky and salty, and a little greasy-feeling. As she stroked his head, she could hear the water gurgling away inside him as if in a set of heating pipes. Suddenly he sneezed five explosive times in quick succession, looked bewildered, and then settled again.

Marianne laid herself down on the cold floor with her arms around him, and he was too weary to mind. He worked his head around a little to get comfortable, and then subsided with a long grunt of pleasure. Dog and beanbag, each felt as loosely connected as the other.

She laid her head alongside Rudi's. Nothing else moved in the house.

"Er sagte dass du zurück kommen würdest," she whispered close to the dog's ear. *"Er heisst Ryan und für mich ist er ein Held."*

His name is Ryan. And he's my hero.

CHAPTER 5

She woke in darkness.

Without making a sound, Jennifer McGann slipped out of bed and then out of the bedroom. There was a streetlight almost directly outside the window of the upper landing, and its clear yellow wash was more than enough to see by. Someday, they'd put up a curtain there.

Someday soon.

It was an old house, Victorian. Half-refinished, with a long way to go. The room next to the bedroom had been stripped right down to the boards and plaster; emptiness made it seem twice its real size, which was already considerable. Barefoot on the floorboards, Jennifer moved to the window. There she stood, looking out. Something was troubling her. She couldn't exactly pin down what.

As she watched, the moon broke through again. It silvered the rooftops of the houses opposite; big, well-kept old residences, half screened by mature trees. A very desirable area. Good investment potential.

She sensed his presence before he touched her.

"I might have known I'd find you in here," Ricky said in a low voice, his breath fanning her skin as he put his hands on her shoulders and started to massage them, gently.

"I couldn't sleep," she said. "You didn't have to get up."

"I wondered where you were. What's the matter?"

"Nothing. Just a bad dream."

"Want to tell me about it?"

"It was about you."

A car went by on the street. No sound reached them, but its passing lights threw bogeyman shadows along the facing terrace.

Ricky said, "And that's what you call bad? I'm beginning to be sorry that I asked."

"I mean, the dream was that you'd died."

"Ah," he said, and he moved in closer and put his arms around her shoulders. He'd pulled on his bathrobe, the one that was halfway to being a kimono. He said, "Well, as you can see, I haven't." And he hugged her close from behind as if to prove it, as he looked out with her into the night. Jennifer gave no response, and after a moment Ricky said, "Is there any specific reason for all this?"

"No," Jennifer said. And then, "Really, no."

There was a longer silence. And then Ricky said, in a low voice, "I wish you'd look for some other line of work."

She started to stir wearily, as if being forced to rise to some old, old kind of bait; and Ricky didn't press the issue, but backed off quickly.

"I'm not pushing for it," he said. "Don't get that idea. But if this is what it does to you, what can it be worth?"

She took his hands, but only to disengage herself from his embrace. "It's what I wanted," she said. "I've never wanted anything else. And there's really nothing more that I can say about it." Turning to look at him, she added, "You go on back. I'll be along soon. I just need a while to think."

He wasn't offended. Or if he was, he didn't let it show.

He said, "You know . . . I heard that if you dream something like that, it's certain not to happen. Old wives' tale."

"I don't believe in old wives' tales."

"Then," he said with a sense of triumph as if he'd chased down a quarry and finally pinned it, "you shouldn't believe in dreams either." He leaned in, closer to her ear. "Think about *that*," he said. With a parting pat on the shoulder, he left her and headed back to bed.

The house stood in silence.

She knew that he'd meant to reassure her. But she wondered if anything could. Specific worries could be shot down because they often had specific causes; but hers was a disquiet that had no particular form at all.

She ought to go back to bed. She knew that she'd probably feel dismal in the morning if she didn't, and she wanted to be sharp. She always wanted to be sharp. She wanted to keep the sense that every single day was *the* day that would define the life that would follow. The way she saw it, this was the only way to be. Like an athlete, in the most serious of games.

She ought to go back.

But she leaned by the window, and looked out at the moonlight.

CHAPTER 6

It was almost a week later, in the last hour of the last day of school before the midterm break, and Tony Gibbs had watched the last of his pupils skipping out through the gates in the certain knowledge that not one of them, not *one*, felt quite as much elation at the prospect of release as he did himself. The weather had cleared. There was sunshine, making the grass so green that it was almost dazzling. He'd checked the cloakrooms and the downstairs lockers as per his rostered duty, he'd picked up a forgotten Sony Walkman and handed it in at the school office before lighter fingers than his own could make it disappear altogether, and then he'd secured the pottery studio and the photographic darkroom before dropping off the keys and heading down towards the new building extension where the language labs were located. Isabella Weber's small Italian car, bright blue and hardly bigger than a roller skate, was one of the few remaining in the staff parking area. And he knew that Isabella herself was in one of the labs, because he'd glimpsed her through the window on his way around.

What the hell. He'd ask her out. There wasn't an unattached male teacher in the school who wasn't trying to limber up to do exactly that, and quite a few of the attached ones too. It was the sight of her through the window that had finally decided him. Unaware of being observed, head bent to her work with her dark hair pinned up, the graceful line of her had reminded him of one of those Dutch interiors, all pale skin and delicate lighting in the simplest of settings.

Seriously, now. No kidding around. He was going to go for it.

Tony's problem had always been that the women he'd found easy to approach were the ones he knew he wouldn't much mind being rejected by. So his successes, though many, had always been qualified ones, and as a result they tended not to last. Twice in his life, he'd been so intimidated by his fear of a rejection that he'd been able to do nothing. Two occasions, two major regrets. And two women who'd moved along and got on with their own lives and probably barely even remembered Tony Gibbs at all.

But he hadn't forgotten them. Sometimes, on the street or in a crowd, he'd find himself half looking for one or the other—separated, divorced, or widowed, or otherwise somehow free. It was a fantasy, he knew that, but he couldn't help it. The upside of his one-time reticence was that the doors had never been firmly closed. The downside was that he knew how much of an idiot he was being.

But only in his own eyes. And as long as it was only in his own eyes, then at least it was bearable.

The door to the language lab was slightly open. Isabella was still in there, seated at a table working her way through a stack of papers. She'd come to the school newly qualified; this was her first teaching job. There was the chop-chop-chop sound of a distant lawnmower drifting in through the window.

She sensed his presence before he spoke, and she looked up. He smiled.

"Hey," he said. "What's all this? Work on the last day of

school? Even God took a break at the end of the week." And then he saw her expression, and some of the forced breeziness went out of him. "What's wrong?" he said.

She glanced down at the paper that she'd been studying. "I don't know," she said. "Nothing." She reached down and opened the desk drawer as if to put the paper away.

"Come on," he said, moving around by the table. "Tell your uncle Tony."

"I'm sure you've got better things to do."

"Not on my own, I haven't. What's the problem?"

She sighed, retrieved the paper from the drawer, and handed it to him. Her hands were long and slim, her nails short but perfect.

Tony sat on the edge of the desk and studied the handwriting. It was an essay written in a firm, childlike hand. The essay was in German. The writing style altogether had an off-centered, unfamiliar look.

"It's Marianne Cadogan," Isabella explained. "This is what she just handed in. All I really ever have to do is give her the grammar. The rest of the time I let her write what she wants. It's pointless making her go through exercises. She's a damned sight more fluent than I am."

"Wochenende?" Tony said, scanning the essay hazily for some point at which he could make contact with it. He read no German at all. "I do believe that's some kind of a car."

"She's writing about her weekend," Isabella said.

He studied the name on the front. Marianne Cadogan? He couldn't put a face to it.

"Listen to this," Isabella said, and she retrieved the paper and turned it around so that she could translate.

She read:

I was alone. The sky was dark and the sea was all around me and nobody knew where I was. I called and called, and nobody came. I thought I would drown. But then he appeared out of nowhere, and told me to be calm. He put me on his shoulder and he carried me through the tide. The tide was deep enough to swallow us both, but I felt safe there.

When he took me home the house was empty, and when I turned around he had gone.

Tony waited, but that was all of it. He put on what he hoped was an interested expression and said, "So?"

Isabella's face was serious. "It bothers me. *She* bothers me. You always see her alone, she doesn't seem to have made any friends, in a crowd she just disappears. The one time I've ever known her to open up, this is what comes out."

"That's standard stuff for a kid her age," Tony said. "They all go through the same kind of phase, they're drowning and nobody loves them."

"She isn't even twelve."

"So, what are you saying? What do you want to do?"

"If I knew that, I wouldn't just be sitting here."

He leaned forward. "A suggestion, right? From one who's been around. You can take it somewhere if you want to. But be certain of your ground, and watch your back as you go. Because what lies ahead can be a total minefield."

Her face was expressionless. "You're saying do nothing."

"Monitor and observe, is what I'm saying. She comes in one morning with a fat lip and a black eye, you can save your conscience for then."

She looked down. She started to rise.

"Thanks," she said.

He could see that she was less than impressed, and quickly he said, "Hey. This is serious advice. Don't go in with all guns blazing because the girl sometimes gets depressed. If anybody was doing that for me, I'd spend my entire life looking over my shoulder for the Lone Ranger."

She gathered up her papers into a ragged armload, and started to head for the door.

"You've been a big help, Tony," she said as she bumped the door open with her hip and backed out. "Have you ever considered a career with the Samaritans?"

After which, she was gone.

Tony stared at the empty doorway.

Then he said, to the equally empty room, "I suspect this means that a fuck's out of the question."

Damn.

Damn.

Damn.

He left the language lab and went back through into the old building, where he trudged upstairs through empty hallways towards the art studio where he'd left his bag and his scarf. Damn.

Of course he could have handled it better; he could have thought before he'd opened his mouth, for a start. Try as he might, he couldn't quite call Marianne Cadogan to mind. He could call up a space that was more or less her shape, but as for a person to put in it . . . well, some kids were like that. And so many went through, and for so many of them the art class was just an opportunity to mess around or generally do nothing serious. How was he supposed to get across to them that art was observation, art was the captured stuff of life? They thought they had eyes, but they didn't. They saw nothing. Back at the end of the previous term, he thought that he'd maybe struck a glimmer of understanding in one or two; he'd set a class to draw from memory an old-style telephone booth, of which there was one right outside the gates. They passed it every day. Some of them had probably even vandalized it. But nobody could get the shape of it, or get the windows right. One boy even put a light on the top of his, like the police box in *Doctor Who*.

Damn.

The art studio was a big area, three classrooms wide at the top of the building, with huge cathedral-like windows supplemented by the usual dismal school fluorescent lighting; for all the acreage of glass, the room was always strangely dim. There were deep sinks stained by generations of poster paints along one wall, and tables that could have been used to cut out a morning suit for King Kong. Tony went to one of the cupboards and opened it up. This was where work was stored for assessment, big sheets of cheap crinkly paper in stacks separated by classes. He pulled out one stack, dumped it on the nearest table, and started to go through it.

He found her name in a corner. The same writing as the essay. Probably didn't look at all odd to a native German-speaker. Flakes of dried-out impasto paint fell to the table as he drew the sheet out and took it over to the window for a look in better light.

Now he could remember, now that he had a real image to work with. She was small, she was dark, she was quiet ... bright enough to have jumped a year, but yes, she *did* always seem to be apart from the others. As all of this was running through his mind, he lowered the picture and looked out the window into the parking area below. Someone had just slammed a car trunk; it was Isabella, walking around her little Italian roller skate to open the passenger door for someone. She was smiling.

And for whom? Tony blinked in disbelief. Roy *Bateman*? The sight drove all other thoughts from Tony's mind as he watched the two of them climb in like a couple of contortionists levering their way into a fish tank, and then heard the Fiat start up and putter its way out of the gates like a little dodgem car.

He stared out, emptily, for a while longer.

Then he returned his attention to the picture. It was a swirling mass of purple and black. And somehow, right now he knew exactly what the child had been trying to express.

But then he gave himself a shake. Don't go overboard, he told himself. Kids did stuff like this all the time; they made up stories or they painted pictures, or they wrote poems that could give bad dreams to Edgar Allan Poe. These were years that they would later remember with envy, most of them, and they were spending the time brooding on the awfulness of being alive.

It was natural. He put Marianne Cadogan's black nightmare back on top of the others, and returned the pile to its shelf in the cupboard. If she wanted to know what it was *really* like to feel down, she ought to come to an expert; fact of it was, there was nothing fundamentally wrong with kids like her. And it was healthy that they should get it all out of their systems. Better on paper than stuck inside, growing and spreading and getting darker and darker.

And wasn't that what it was all for? To deal with the nightmares? So Marianne wrote a story about drowning on a beach. She was getting out the demons, that was all.

He locked the cupboard, picked up his bag and stuck his scarf inside it, and made for the door.

Getting out the demons.

It was hardly as if she was writing her autobiography, or anything.

CHAPTER 7

Ryan lived in one of the strangest-looking places that Marianne had ever seen.

He had a workshop and yard over on the far side of the reclaimed flatlands, overshadowed by an embankment where the railway crossed a dirt track and a drainage canal. He had no neighbors other than the cattle on the fields, and a few ducks that lived out in the reeds and bobbed for tidbits under the bridge. The yard was an irregular shape, fenced around with a continuous six-foot wall made mostly out of old doors; interior doors, street doors, garage doors, four-paneled or hardboard-sided or ledged-and-braced, no two of them in the same style or color and some with their glasswork and letterslots still intact.

"Hello?" she called. "Is there anybody there?"

She'd tried the gate, but there was a big padlock on the outside of it. So then she'd stood with the envelope in her hand and looked all around, only to realize that out of the many letterslots in the fence there wasn't a single one of them that worked. Without exception, they'd all been nailed up or patched with pieces of timber or corrugated iron.

She supposed that she could simply stick the envelope into the door frame for him to find when he returned. Or reach up and flip it over into the yard, hoping that it wouldn't land somewhere out of sight and that the rain wouldn't decide to come back before Ryan did.

But neither solution seemed much use. Stuck in the door, anyone could take it. And if she threw it over and he didn't see it, he might walk right over it.

So she stuck the letter in her teeth, and jumped for the top of the gate.

The padlock and hasp gave her a foothold, and she scrambled over the top and dropped down on the other side. Now she was trespassing, but the envelope was her excuse. She held it in plain sight. If God was watching her, he couldn't miss it.

Feeling like a tourist, she looked around.

Over against the far wall with the railway embankment rising behind it there was a little lean-to shed, and leaning against the lean-to were a couple of doors that hadn't yet found their way into the scheme of the fence. There was plenty of other junk as well. A handcart on wheels, its frame rusty and the wood sodden and damp. The carcass of a blue rowing boat, full of rot and totally unserviceable but standing up on bricks as if rescue and restoration weren't entirely out of the question. Stepladders and chicken wire, lengths of plastic drainpipe, half-burned tires and cable in an open brick fireplace. Enameled shop signs, forty years old at least and most of them more rust than enamel.

The central part of the yard looked as if it had been laid aside for a piece of garden at one time; the earth had been tilled and planks had been hammered edgewise into the ground as a kind of border, but it didn't look as if anything had ever been planted. Clover and weeds had sprung up. Ryan's workshop overlooked all of this, a low building of wood and tarpaulin that resembled something knocked together on a survival course and then made permanent. Its roof had been patched with sheets of yellow plastic pinned down by nailed wooden slats, but either a fierce wind or a flock of birds had pulled it all apart so that the plastic flapped as jagged edges in the breeze. Its windows were tiny, and dark. Its door was padlocked, just like the outer gate of the yard.

She picked her way through slowly, taking her time, missing

nothing. This was the best and perhaps the last excuse that she was ever going to have, and she wasn't going to waste it. She saw a disused greenhouse that looked as if it had once been thrown up in a hurry and which now had no glass; inside, some long-abandoned plants had run riot and were now growing up through the open roof. By it were bags of sand that had split open, the spilled sand green with mold. And by the workshop wall, protected under clear plastic sheets weighted down with bricks, two second-hand washing machines in what looked like usable condition. One of them was very like their Bendix at home.

Ryan's actual house was in a divided-off section at the far end of the yard. As far as she could see, the house consisted of two antiquated mobile homes joined together down the middle and with a porch tacked onto the front. The building looked rickety, the porch looked solid.

On the side of the porch was a mailbox.

Well, that would have to be the end of it. She put her envelope through the slot and then lowered the spring flap to trap it with a corner showing, just in case Ryan didn't get much in the way of mail and wasn't in the habit of checking the box too often. Because the entire structure had been raised clear of the ground on pillars of brick—more junk underneath, including what looked like a complete set of windows removed from some other building and stored flat—it was too high for her to take a peek inside. She wanted to, but without something to stand on she couldn't. And there was such a thing, she supposed, as pushing it too far; much as she wanted to stay and keep on soaking up detail after odd and interesting detail, it was time for her to be going.

But when she tried, she found that she couldn't get back over the gate.

There was no foothold on the inside to use the way that she'd used the staple and hasp on the outside, and she couldn't scramble up far enough on her own. She tried, but all she did was to kick hell out of the woodwork for half a minute before dropping back.

Breathing hard, she looked around. If she'd been walking on eggs before, now she was feeling scared, of nothing and of no one in particular, but with the sense of having entered the labyrinth only to find that the way back was no more than a memory betrayed. She didn't want to be found like this. She rattled at the gate, but of course it didn't give.

She listened. Was somebody coming? Ryan on his way back, perhaps? She waited and listened for a while longer, wondering what she'd do if it was him, what she'd say. She could hear the ducks under the iron bridge. She could hear the wind stirring the grass out in the fields beyond. She could hear a cricket, God only knew where.

So then she went and got one of the blue plastic drums from over by the lean-to, and walked it on its edge across to the gate. It was awkward, but it wasn't heavy. She got it into position against the fence and then climbed up onto it and used it as a step; she had to go off it sideways and them clamber up onto the top of the gate and there was one moment where, with the ridge digging into her waist, she thought she was going to tip forward and fall headfirst to the ground, but she held back and did it right and, after swinging her legs over, landed in a breathless heap.

He'd know that she'd been there, of course. But only for the delivery, that would be self-evident. The nosing-around part he probably wouldn't even think about. And she could hardly have done it blindfolded, could she?

She followed the dirt track out under the bridge. On the other side she climbed up the embankment to the railway lines. Four trains a day came through on a more or less regular schedule; she'd sat with Rudi on a distant hillside and counted them, once. They were all freight services, anonymous container cars and tankers and the like, and they always seemed to be about a mile long and to take forever to go through. Here by the bridge there was a siding, and in the siding there were always half a dozen or more pieces of the rolling stock that had been shunted and left in the middle of nowhere.

Marianne crossed the tracks to the siding, and climbed up into the brake van that stood against the buffers. It had a roof but was otherwise open, no doors to close and no glass in the windows, just a bare wooden floor and a big iron wheel in the middle like a ship's wheel laid flat. Marianne's red rucksack was in the corner, where she'd left it about twenty minutes before. In the rucksack was her lunch.

She sat cross-legged on the dusty floor, and undid the ties. Rudi ought to be with her now; shared lunch was a tradition with them on weekends and holidays, but when she'd tried to encourage him just after breakfast, he'd stretched out on his beanbag and looked apologetic and given her a couple of token beats of his tail, making it pretty clear that he preferred to stay home and continue his recuperation. That was fine by Marianne. Whatever it would take to get him better.

From the rucksack she took some crisps, an apple, a fun-size Crunchie bar and an inch-thick cheese sandwich, more than half an inch of it cheese. Marianne made her own lunches. She wasn't exactly thrilled about the cheese, but it was all they ever seemed to have in the fridge. She'd brought her Narnia book along, as well. She was reading it for about the fourth time, now.

After a few minutes, she raised herself up to look out the brake van's unglazed window. From here, one could see for miles in any direction; and she could easily see down onto the yard, across a banking lined with brambles dense enough to stop a chainsaw. Ryan's yard was as she'd left it, the long lane beyond was empty.

A short time later she checked again. Again, the yard was as she'd left it.

But this time, a figure was heading down along the lane.

He was walking, and he was carrying something. As he drew closer, Marianne could see for certain that it was Ryan although the big coat and the slight forward-leaning stoop had identified him for her already. Over his shoulder was something that looked like the frame of a motorcycle; no engine, no wheels, just the basic frame like a rib cage without head or limbs. As he reached his yard, she lost sight of him behind the fence; but then she saw the gate open, and he stepped inside.

He stopped. Marianne tensed. He was looking at the blue plastic drum against the fence behind the gate.

Slowly, he let the gate close.

Marianne had hoped he wouldn't notice the change. With so much junk all over the place, who'd see any difference? But

Ryan had. She saw him move forward, cautiously now, scanning the yard from side to side but never looking up in her direction; he got out his keys one-handed and opened up the workshop, checking back over his shoulder all the time. *Go to the house,* she was thinking. *Go to the house, then you'll know.*

He was in the workshop for several minutes. When he came out he stopped in the doorway and stretched, as if trying to work a kink out of his shoulder. The bike frame must have been pretty heavy; she couldn't help wondering what use he was going to make of it, given that there was a negligible amount of bike left attached. Scrap metal, probably, like the aluminum cans. Or maybe there was a market in stuff like that. . . . Who but an expert could say?

Keys in hand, Ryan left the workshop and made for the house. Marianne craned her neck to watch him go, shifting position slightly to keep him in her sight. He passed by the boat, through the break in the fence that divided the yard, and climbed the steps of the porch. A few seconds later he was in the house with the door closing behind him, and she hadn't even seen him glance at the mailbox. She watched and waited for a while, but that appeared to be it.

Disappointed, she hunkered down again. She'd wanted to see him finding it; she'd have liked to have watched him opening it and reading the contents, if at all possible. Was it so much to ask?

Apparently it was.

She brushed absently at her jeans. The floor might be dusty here, but it was nothing that was going to kill her. She dug in her bag and brought out another fun-size Crunchie. She couldn't understand why they had to make them so small, if you always had to have more than one or feel cheated. She realized that she'd brought nothing to drink. There always seemed to be something that she managed to forget.

"Now, what's this?" a quiet voice from behind her said.

She almost hit the roof. That was what it felt like, anyway. Ryan was standing at the other end of the wagon, a big shape of darkness that seemed to suck in all the light and to fill the place with his presence. The card and envelope that she'd de-

livered were in his hand; the latter had been torn open messily
as if slit by a thumb.

"You made me jump," she complained.

She couldn't make out his face too well at the shadowed end
of the carriage. There was daylight, but it was all behind him.

He said, "I'm sorry. But what's the idea?"

"It's a thank-you card," she said. "I made it."

"For what?"

"For saving me."

Now that the shock of his sudden appearance had subsided,
there was a certain indignation in her tone. You'd have to be
pretty obtuse not to be able to spot a thank-you card when it
had THANK YOU written on the front in two-inch cutout letters.

He looked down at the card. It was yellow, and decorated
with stuck-on lace and a piece of red ribbon. She'd made it for
the biggest envelope she could find—she hoarded the unmarked ones from old birthdays and the like—but still it
looked small in his fist.

He said, "You shouldn't have done this."

"But I wanted to."

"I mean, you shouldn't have come to where I live. People
can get the wrong idea."

"Nobody saw me."

"No? You left a trail like a tank. We're out in the middle of
nowhere, here, and you don't know me at all. That's not a very
bright way for a girl your age to behave, is it?"

She couldn't understand why he was making such a big
thing of it; she'd thought that he'd be pleased, but it was fairly
plain that he wasn't. She said, "All I did was bring you a
card."

"Look," he said, lowering his voice as if to make a point of
not intimidating her but trying to press his message all the
same. "I can't explain it to you. I understand what you're trying to say. But do me a big favor and don't ever come out here
again."

With a sudden flash of inspiration, Marianne said, "Rudi
came home."

That stopped him. She could see his surprise; so he hadn't really believed that it would happen, after all. But in that same moment, she forgave him. Rudi had shown them all, hadn't he?

"That old dog?" Ryan said. "You're kidding me."

"It was just like you said," Marianne went on eagerly, sensing that the mood had turned and determined that she was going to make the most of it. "He found his own way."

"How is he?"

"He's sleeping a lot, but that's probably because he's tired. And I think he got a cold from being in the water, but he's shaking that off. My dad says he's going to be fine."

"Well," Ryan said. "What do you know. I'm pleased for you."

"Do you like it?"

He didn't follow her. "What?"

"The card. Do you like it?"

Ryan remembered the card, and looked down. "Yes," he said, "I do. It's very nice. And stop trying to get me off the subject. Thanks, but no more cards. No social calls, no dropping by. You go your way . . . you understand?"

Reluctantly, she nodded. This wasn't the way she'd planned for it to happen. This was almost a reprimand . . . and would have been, if only Ryan had known how to deliver one. He seemed embarrassed, as much as anything else. As if gestures like this weren't made in his direction very often.

He said, "Play with your friends. Not around here. It's nothing personal, it's just . . . a precaution. Now tell me you understand."

"I understand," she said.

He nodded. He didn't seem to know what else to say.

So then he turned and climbed down out of the coach, leaving her there alone.

CHAPTER 8

But she didn't leave him alone.

It was nothing that he ever knew about, but she continued to observe him from afar over most of the next week. She sat in the fields above the cliffs and watched him moving along the beach with his big plastic bag, walking along on the inside of the sea fence and checking the debris. The weather held, and continued to get better. She watched how he worked. He picked up and bagged all the aluminum cans that washed in. He picked up odd pieces and inspected them, bagging some, abandoning most.

Rudi often came out with her again now. Not every day and not with quite the same energy that he'd once shown, but she had his company again. There was someone to listen when she talked, and it didn't matter to her how much he understood. They both got what they needed. She wouldn't take him far, and when she could see that he was starting to tire she'd take him home. Then she'd set out again and, sometimes after an hour or two of searching, get Ryan into her sights once more.

Meanwhile, Ryan worked on and went about the business of his life. He seemed unaware that he no longer spent his days alone.

Monday was an exception. Monday was the day she had to go into town on the bus with Mrs. Healey to buy a pair of new shoes. As the day dragged by, Marianne found herself looking forward to the housekeeper's stopover less and less. She didn't even get the shoes that she'd wanted most, and they hadn't looked *that* ridiculous. And when they got back it was too late to go out, so she played a few games on her Amiga console instead. That night she heard her father going down into the cellar only to return and switch the light off after a couple of minutes. She got the idea then that there might be more to his impending trip than just business as usual.

"Will you be going far?" she asked him at bedtime that same evening.

"No, not far at all," he said in a tone that was supposed to convey surprise at her asking and which didn't convince her.

On Wednesday Rudi showed some reluctance at getting started, and so she left him snoozing on his beanbag and went alone. It was getting to the point now where she could predict Ryan's movements with reasonable accuracy, given that he tended to follow the tides; as high water receded he'd be there, combing through the newly washed-in rubbish and sorting out anything that he might be able to use. She could track him from the hills and the woodlands without any risk of being seen; as he passed out of sight behind one headland or another she could race across the fields and perch at the next lookout point and wait for him to come into view. It almost always worked, and she wasn't breaking anybody's rules.

But on Wednesday when the tide rolled back and Ryan wasn't there, she got over to the other side of the hill just in time to look down across the flatlands and see him walking off up the lane towards the road. Ryan was about a quarter of a mile away from her, and the road was about a half-mile further on. She climbed onto the wall by the side of a stile, and as she sat watching him go she could feel a sense of companionship slipping away from her.

She could see everything from here, the drained lands and the marshes spreading out below. She could see the ramrod-straight lines of channels that formed a pattern that was invisible at ground level, but from here looked like a landing strip for some expected civilization that had never arrived. And then out beyond the line of the containing wall there were those odd cutout water pools in the turf, precise shapes of sky color on green exactly like the ocean pictures in her school atlas but formed more like the marks of some unknown written language.

So much space.

So little that ever seemed to happen.

She went down to the beach, and walked along inside the wire fencing. The tide had been a high one, and in stretches the wire was hung with lengths of seaweed that looked rubbery and bleached, as if they'd spent time in the belly of some enormous creature and been half-digested. Otherwise it was the usual range of plastic bottles and cans, bird feathers, oil drums, orange shreds of fishermen's net tossing in the wind, and a solitary Reebok running shoe.

She wondered about the life that Ryan had led. Some of the places that he'd been. In her mind she could see him as an ex-soldier—mostly, she'd have to admit, because of the coat, but also because of his aura of self-sufficiency and his solitary nature. If not a soldier, she couldn't think what. So a soldier it had to be.

When Ryan got back later that afternoon, he didn't return alone. The first that Marianne knew about it was when she heard the sound of an approaching engine from her hiding-place in the railway car; she put her Narnia book into her rucksack and sat up to look out. That was when she saw the blue flatbed truck bouncing its way through all the ruts and water-filled potholes down the lane towards Ryan's yard. As it pulled up by the gates, she could see that he was on the passenger side of the cab. On the back of the truck there was a load of some kind, covered and secured by ropes and tarpaulins.

She recognized the driver. He left the engine running as the two of them got out, and Ryan moved to open the gate. The driver was a skinny bat-eared boy; she knew him from her school. He'd dropped out a couple of years ago and then for some months had hung around outside at lunchtimes with a group of his old friends until they'd started to get jobs or had otherwise drifted away. This boy had gone to work with his uncle at what passed for the local refuse dump, actually little more than a cabin and a wire-fenced enclosure off the road a few miles inland. There, half a dozen huge open hoppers were lined up in a row; people brought their waste along to be sorted, and as each hopper became full it was hauled up onto the back of a transporter and taken off for disposal somewhere even further inland. Marianne didn't know where. Perhaps it just kept on being moved around from one place to another, forever.

The boy undid the lines and the two of them rolled back the tarpaulin, uncovering various household appliances that had been lashed down with even more rope. She could see a couple of washing machines, a freezer, two regular refrigerators, and a number of vacuum cleaners all tied up together. All used, all with the melancholy look of defunct throwouts about them. Ryan brought out the wheeled handcart, and the two of them began to unload onto it.

Ryan did most of the work. He lifted the washing machines down single-handed and they were heavy, Marianne knew; they were supposed to have blocks of concrete in them to stop them from shaking around too much. He used the handcart to get everything to the workshop, and when the last machines were off the truck she saw Ryan look at them, and frown, and then do a quick calculation in his head.

"This wasn't the deal we made," she heard him say. "Where's the Zanussi?" But the boy shrugged and said something that didn't quite carry to her over the sound of the idling engine. Ryan went back into the yard to do a quick count on the delivery. As soon as he'd moved inside, the boy hurried around to the cab of his wagon and got up behind the wheel and slammed the gears into a noisy reverse. He was already accelerating backwards up the lane when Ryan emerged and called after him. The wagon bounced and danced over the ruts again, and was well out of range by the time the boy was able to turn it around in the opening to a field.

Ryan stood out in the middle of the lane with his fists doubled, powerlessly watching it go; then he turned and slammed a fist into one of the refrigerators on the handcart. It made a dull boom like a thunder machine.

He took a deep breath, let it out, and ran his hand across the dent. It was a dimple in the white panel. He shook his head. Something seemed to hurt, was Marianne's guess, but he wasn't going to let it get to him. Had he damaged his hand? she wondered. But he picked up the handles of the loaded cart, moved it into the yard, then closed the gates.

He stayed in the workshop after that, so there was little to see. Smoke began to come out of the tin pipe with its coolie-hat cover on the roof, so he must have lit the stove. Marianne hung on a while longer, but the late-afternoon chill started to get through to her. She gathered everything together and put it back into the rucksack. She brought the red rucksack out every day now, and slung it over one shoulder just like Ryan did with his. Being honest with herself, she had to admit that it wasn't so comfortable. But she was assuming that she'd soon get used to it.

She climbed down the steps from the brake van, picked her way across the tracks, scrambled down the embankment on the side away from the yard, and then set out across the flatlands for home. The light out over the bay was starting to deepen into the beginnings of a sunset. She'd no doubt that she'd be able to find him again in the morning.

Or maybe, if the timing was right, maybe *he'd* find *her*. And then he'd have to say hello just to be friendly, because that's how people did things.

People did that all the time, Marianne reckoned.

Didn't they?

CHAPTER 9

"I don't know what to do about it," Jennifer confessed. "Sometimes I think he's the best thing that ever happened to me. Other times I feel like we're living on two different planets."

"I've got news for you," Angela told her across the cafeteria table. "I was married six years and that's about as good as it ever gets. How deep are you in?"

"We both sold our flats and we're buying the house."

"Together?"

"Not wedding-bells together. It's more like a business deal."

"Yeah," said Angela cynically, pushing her empty sandwich plate to one side and drawing her coffee over. "With one shared bedroom and no lock on the bathroom door."

"The personal side of it's a completely separate arrangement," Jennifer said, already aware that it didn't sound anything like as convincing as she'd hoped that it would. "But one of the problems now is . . . I keep wondering. Are we going to stay together because we want to? Or because we're stuck with each other and neither of us can face all the effort it'll take to go out and start again?"

She glanced at Angela, who was looking around. Angela had cropped her blonde hair short and she'd taken to wearing tight jeans and a denim jacket—all part of the look for the current job, but Jennifer still wasn't used to it yet. The cafeteria was light and modern and more than two-thirds full; the service counters stayed open for most of the day, but now was the time when nearly all the clerks and secretaries took their lunch hour. It wasn't bad, as such places went. The food was standard, but the seating was pleasant and the views along one big-windowed side were of open farm land. It always reminded Jennifer less of a staff canteen than of the restaurant of some smart and progressive zoo.

Angela said, "Wait until he starts pushing for you to change your line of work."

"We had that already."

"It always comes up. What did you say?"

"I let it go."

"Wrong move. You should put a wire on his dick and every time he raises the subject, run mains voltage through it, because that's the only way you're ever going to kill the topic. We've got enough going against us already without having to bring along that kind of luggage from home."

"Is that why you two broke up?"

"No. Me coming home early and finding him trying on my underwear, *that's* what broke us up."

With her index finger, Jennifer idly drew lines across the faint wipe-down marks on the tabletop. Her diet Pepsi had gone flat but was no great loss, because it hadn't even been cold. One day, she'd work out why that was always the case; the cold drinks here were never cold, and the hot drinks . . . well, they came out of a machine and they were never all that hot.

She said, "I just wish I knew myself better. I can't seem to match up getting what I want with wanting what I get."

"It's a tightrope act," Angela said, "the whole thing. If you get nothing worse than bad dreams out of it, then all I can say is, say nothing and feel lucky. I've been on a surveillance for six weeks and I'm getting migraines like somebody sprung out my eyeball and put nutcrackers on it. But you know how it is . . . give them one whiff of weakness, and you might as well be setting course back to peewee corner."

Jennifer glanced across the canteen. Over in peewee corner right at that moment, a big uniformed sergeant who looked like a heart attack waiting to happen was leaning too close over three young Woman Police Constables and saying, "How's it hanging, girls?"

"In your case," one of them said, "there's not very much of it."

"And it doesn't hang so far," added another.

Jennifer and Angela exchanged a glance as the sergeant, who to Jennifer's eyes was about as sensually appealing as used mouthwash, grinned and glowed and sauntered on over to the counter with a tray under his arm.

Jennifer checked her watch. Lunch was just about over.

She said, "Time to run."

On the walk from the cafeteria to the communications building, Jennifer decided that she *was* feeling better after all. It had been some time since they'd worked together in uniform and their careers had taken different directions since then—Angela into the Drugs Squad, Jennifer into the CID and then the Serious Crime Support Unit—but they still met every month or so and swapped notes on life, love, and the pursuit of some kind of happiness. Angela knew things about Jennifer that she'd never been able to tell to any other living soul; only Angela knew about her weeks of nightmares after a brush with a rogue and psycho named Johnny Mays. Angela's life, by contrast, seemed to be a series of false starts and letdowns that she took in her stride as if she'd never been expecting anything else.

The new County Police Headquarters had been located on a green-field site in the farming belt to the west of town. It was five or six miles out of the center and with its all-new buildings and an open, rambling development, it had the look and some of the atmosphere of a university campus. The only incongruous touch was the tall radio mast on top of the communications building; the building itself resembled a state-of-the-art sports complex and stood with a view across a cricket pitch and the bridle paths where the nearby mounted unit brought their horses for exercise. Known as New Comms when it wasn't being called The Bunker, it was the operational heart of the headquarters layout. The rest of it—two long office blocks and several other buildings—was given over to administration, fleet vehicle maintenance and site services.

Serious Crime Support was actually based in a big old house two miles away, but Jennifer had to report to New Comms once a week to tape the links for the unit's video roundup. Down in the New Comms basement was a tiny one-man studio with a Betacam setup and the most unflattering lighting that modern science had been able to devise. The half-hour show—pending cases, wanted persons—was circulated on cassette around each of the stations in the region. One small outpost down at the other end of the county sent her regular fan mail, signed Jez and the Lads. She didn't like it much. She didn't like the notion of being known to people whom she didn't herself know; sometimes, the gaze of the camera could feel too much like that of a gunsight.

These sessions were the price, she supposed. The price of her acceptance into a toughly contested squad at a level where you used whatever you had going for you to get an edge over the competition, and did it without shame. Her boss had as much as told her; it's down to you or Benny Moon, he'd said, and Benny's so ugly that he couldn't get a fuck in a nurses' home on his birthday. Jennifer had smiled tightly, and she'd said nothing. She'd stick at it for as long as she had to, but she'd get out of it when she could; whatever handhold offered itself to her next, she'd be there and reaching for it.

She crossed the parking lot for blue passholders and presented herself at the door to New Comms; she hit the bell and waited before the flattened square glass lens of an observation camera. After a few seconds' wait she got the buzz of a door release and went on through. This process was always unnerving in its way, as well. No one ever spoke back to her. She'd no idea who was at the other end of the line, or even where they were located.

Once through the doorway, she was at the bottom of a stairwell that had been turned into a small waiting area by the addition of some low seating. There was no desk or reception window, and she'd never seen anybody waiting there. She descended to basement level and stepped first into the Ladies' lavatory to check on herself in the mirror. She'd never met anyone in here, either—except for a plumber, once, and he'd been lost. New Comms was the strangest-feeling building that she'd ever worked in, and she was glad that she didn't have to come here more often. Smart, subdued, windowless, and airconditioned, for Jennifer it had the sense of a place where everything happened quietly and just around the corner out of sight. The top floor was where the action was, with the big lighted map of the entire county and the duty officer's desk overlooking all the radio positions; but even that had the chilled hush of a museum reading room.

The studio's part-time technician wasn't alone when she entered, two minutes before the start of the booked time. She was surprised to see that the duty officer was there as well; halfseated on the reading table, he slid off and onto his feet when he saw her and said, "Here's Charlie's Angel now."

"Job's yours if you want it," she said.

"No thanks," the duty officer said. His name was Calcutt and he was in uniform shirt sleeves. "Check your pager, can you? Your boss has been trying to get hold of you."

And with his message delivered, he nodded to the technician and left. Jennifer took out her pager, a smooth block of dark gray plastic with the size and appearance of an electronic stopwatch, and pressed to test it.

Nothing.

"You've got to excuse me," she said to the technician, and

she picked up the phone on the desk to call Ray Stapleton's number. He wasn't in his office, but on the second attempt she got him on his mobile. She heard him speak through what was starting to become a familiar acoustic, the chunky, faraway sound of a call to a car on the move.

"Where've you been?" he said.

"My beeper died," she said. "What's the problem?"

"I've been handed two new suspicious deaths and no more officers to cover. Any reason why you can't get out this afternoon?"

"I'll be finished here within the hour," she said. "Where do you need me to be?"

"Post mortem on a hanging at two. Hope you had a decent lunch."

She knew that Stapleton wasn't ribbing her. Well, probably not, anyway. She'd done her share of PMs, and they'd long ceased to bother her; she dreaded the prospect of ever having to attend a child's autopsy, but that was more or less universal. So far, her first had been her worst. That had been a rape that had turned into murder. The perpetrator had broken into a house where his victim had tried to barricade herself in; he'd chased her upstairs where she'd jumped from a first floor window and then, despite some serious bruising and a broken ankle, had been trying to run when he'd brought her down. He'd dragged her back into the house and when she'd continued trying to fight him off, he'd beaten her senseless before committing the act. Then he'd beaten her some more, causing the hemorrhages from which she'd later died. His defense on the rape had been that anyone could see how she'd been asking for it.

"I can warn you now," Stapleton added. "This one's been up for almost a week."

"Lunch was fine," Jennifer said. "Where's it all happening?"

CHAPTER 10

Well, this was it. Today was the day. Mrs. Healey was coming to stay, and wasn't *that* just worth a big cake and a parade?

Marianne was the first to rise. She got out of bed in a cold bedroom, and pulled on her jeans and a sweatshirt in a hurry. She knocked on her father's door and then went downstairs into the kitchen and switched on the electric kettle. She set out the milk and the sugar and the cereal ready for when he came down. She put on the radio for the morning news, which he said that he liked to hear but then never seemed to listen to. Some days he didn't even bother with breakfast, but went straight on out, leaving her alone to get herself ready for school or, in the holidays, like now, to wait for Mrs. Healey's arrival around ten.

By the time she'd got everything ready, she could hear him moving around upstairs. Water sloshed in the old pipes behind the walls, telling Marianne that he'd reached the bathroom as she went over and crouched by Rudi.

Last night's dog food lay more or less untouched in its dish. The water bowl, by contrast, was almost empty and she took it over to the sink to refill it. Rudi's eyes half opened as she set it by him, but those pale inner lids stayed down and he didn't really wake, even when she stroked his head. He was a friendly-looking dog, even in sleep. She'd never seen him bare his teeth or snarl, ever. Heard him growl a few times, but never seriously. Once she'd tried to work out what breed or combination of breeds he might be, just so she could make a guess as to where his temperament came from, but she'd had to give up. Old English Hearthrug was the best description she could devise for him.

"Good boy, Rudi," she whispered, and left him to sleep on. She went upstairs.

The bathroom door was open. Her father was still in there, dressed for the road in suit and tie and leaning over the basin to stare into the shaving mirror. At first, he wasn't aware of her, but then he seemed to sense her presence. He turned and looked at her, and for a moment she hardly recognized him; his eyes were dead and his skin was gray and sallow, but then it was almost as if he hauled up a mask and fixed it into place. It was a brave face, and mostly faked in the manner of all brave faces.

Marianne said, "Rudi won't eat. Even the stuff he likes best he won't touch. I think he might be ill."

"I looked at him last night," her father said. "He seemed all right then."

"He looks all right, but he hardly moves. He won't come out with me or anything."

"He's an old dog," her father said. "Just let him have some peace and he'll be fine."

"He's *not* old!" Marianne said with a loudness and sudden passion that startled even her. Her father blinked at her almost in shock for a moment.

He sat on the side of the bathtub, and beckoned her to him. She moved closer, feeling awkward. He was making an effort, she could see that.

He said, "You think a lot of him, don't you?" She nodded, and he even gave her a little wry smile. "More than you do of me?" But then, seeing the panic rising in her eyes at the prospect of having to answer a question that she didn't know how to cope with, he added quickly, "I know, it's not a fair question. You don't see me, I don't see you, I don't give you anything like the attention I should. But I want to. And I will. Just as soon as I get us ... I mean, just as soon as I can ..." He couldn't quite find the words. He frowned and hesitated, as if the sense of his failure was almost physical. Then he tried again.

He said, "I mean, things are so difficult. You wouldn't believe it, and they don't get any better. It's ... it's grownup stuff, I don't even want you to be worried by it. But I've got to make this trip today, and it's going to clear something up and then after that I can guarantee that it's going to get one thousand percent better. So look, what we'll do is . . . you stick it out with Mrs. Healey for the next couple of days, and I'll do what I've got to do, and next weekend we'll put Rudi in the car and we'll go somewhere nice. Anywhere you want. While I'm away, you can be thinking about somewhere. Deal?"

It was embarrassing, more than anything. He'd made her such promises before, and almost without exception they'd been forgotten. Marianne nodded, hoping that she didn't look too unconvinced, and her father levered himself up from the side of the tub and gave her shoulder a squeeze.

He said, "We'll cheer him up, eh? That's what he needs most. Dogs are like people. They're up, they're down. It doesn't last."

"If that doesn't work, can I take him to the vet?"

"Of course you can."

He went to his bedroom, and Marianne went downstairs. He joined her in the kitchen a few moments later. He'd brought down his overnight bag, and he set it by the table. Then he glanced at his watch, and picked it up again.

"It's later than I thought," he said. "I'll get something to eat on the way."

He gave her a perfunctory kiss on the top of her head, and made for the door.

There he stopped. "Listen," he said, turning to her one last time before he went. "Try to be more careful, all right? And stay off the beach."

And then, with this advice, he was gone.

Rudi made a small sound, but it was only in his dream. He was twitching the way he always did when he dreamed, ears and paws and facial muscles, as if someone was running a mild current through him. Marianne patted him again, and then went upstairs.

From the window, she watched her father loading his bag into the car. It took him three slams before the trunk stayed closed. Back in Germany they'd always had a big company car, never more than two years old. She'd heard him say that cars aged fast because of the sea and salt air around here and, judging by the state of the Vauxhall, he was right. Were it to hit a good bump at speed, she wouldn't be surprised to see the headlights fall out.

She kept on watching through the window as he drove away. It was just after nine. She could hear the radio still playing in the kitchen down below her. When the Vauxhall was well out over the causeway, she turned from the window and headed downstairs.

The cellar door was always locked, but the key was hidden in the pendulum case of the wall clock right alongside. She wasn't supposed to know that it was there. She took out the key and opened the door, put on the light, and went down.

The steps were steep, and made out of brick. The cellar felt damp, and was dank. It wasn't very big, just two linked rooms and an L-shaped passageway that went nowhere but whose walls presumably served some structural purpose. One side of one of the rooms, the one with the window, had been fitted with rough shelves on iron brackets; nothing much stood on the floor except for some rusty garden tools and a broken chair and a few lengths of pipe. Two feet up from the ground, there was a tidemark on the whitewash marking the last level of flooding. Marianne didn't know how long ago that had been.

She dragged the broken chair over and climbed onto it. On the shelf, she moved some boxes. She knew that there was nothing much in any of them. Her great-uncle had apparently been a great hoarder, from used parcel string to unfinished candle stumps. Having made space, from behind a hat box she pulled out an old leather attaché case with a broken handle and scuffed corners. She opened it.

All the key papers of the household were kept in here. Photocopies of the deeds, birth certificates, insurance policies, a handful of premium bonds in her name. It took her no more than a couple of minutes to establish for certain that her father's passport was no longer there.

Marianne had been keeping track. You didn't always get a stamp on a passport these days, that was the problem. She was fairly sure that he'd made at least two trips back to Hamburg in the last year, but that was something she'd had to deduce mainly from the German lawyers' letters. Some of those letters seemed to be missing now.

The photograph had gone too.

Her mother's photograph. The only one, as far as she knew, that he'd kept anywhere in the house, and unless he'd chosen this moment to throw it away like the others, it seemed likely that he'd taken it with him. But why?

Setting everything back inside the case as she'd found it, she closed the lid and returned everything on the shelf to the way that it had been. Then she carried the chair back across the floor, and kicked out the marks in the dirt where its legs had stood. Sometimes she'd come down here and look at the picture just because it helped her to keep an image of her mother fixed in her mind. And now she felt its loss. It was only a snapshot taken in their garden with the sun behind her, but by chance it had turned out to be the best one of her ever. There had been no warning, no posing—just a call and a turn and a click of the shutter, and in that fraction of a second it was as if a trace of something indefinable had flown to the camera and been pinned for all time. Marianne would have taken the print somewhere for a copy if she'd known where to go, and if it could have been done on the same day to avoid the chance of the original being missed. If there was a negative, it was probably lost. But the fact that her father had kept anything at all had always seemed encouraging. As if the links hadn't been broken completely, as if there was still a chance, however slender, that life might return one day to the way it had been.

Wouldn't that be something? she found herself thinking. But under that thought was another, less bright one.

Times had moved on. Ground had been lost. Things could never be as they were, whatever she might hope; that happy self was someone else now. Whatever he'd gone away for, it wasn't to find them a way home. The drift of the lawyers' letters had told her that.

No reconciliation was coming.

More likely, he'd gone to make the parting absolutely final.

CHAPTER 11

"Rudi?" she said. "Do you want a walk, Rudi?"

There had been a time when the mere mention of the word in conversation would have brought him to his feet with his head cocked, ready to go. But right now, he seemed happy enough lying out on the bare ground. He was about a dozen feet from the back door of the house, and disinclined to move; not in pain or anything, just perfectly contented where he was. As if all he had in this moment was all that he could possibly want—home, somewhere to lie, and the afternoon sun on his face.

Marianne scratched his head between his ears, and he stretched himself right out with a grunt of pleasure before subsiding again.

She didn't know what to think. He'd tried a few trips out with her, but now he seemed to have found the strategy that suited him best. Here she was with this big training program in mind to get him back as he'd been, and he didn't want to know. He showed it pleasantly, almost apologetically, but he really didn't want to know. Perhaps her father was right. Perhaps she was rushing the dog. Because his eyes were clear and his nose was wet and his breath didn't smell any worse than usual; and even if his appetite was down, he was drinking lots of water and the dog book seemed to indicate that this was no bad thing. He could move when he wanted to. He'd get up and plod over to his customary toilet spot about fifty feet from the house, and then he'd amble back and fling himself down with a grateful sigh.

"All right, then," she said. "Be good, and I'll see you later."

As she was walking away from the house, it was as if

she could sense Mrs. Healey watching her from the sink at the kitchen window. Marianne half-turned and waved, but she couldn't see if Mrs. Healey was waving back or even, for certain, if she was there. The housekeeper had the knack, like certain teachers, of forever making her feel uneasy. She always had the feeling that Mrs. Healey disapproved of what she was doing, even when she was doing nothing at all. If she watched television, she was rotting her mind. If she read a book, she was ruining her eyes. If she did neither, she was daydreaming and getting no fresh air . . . but then if she went out, she was running wild.

So, running wild was to be the order of the day. As always, it was a relief to cross the saltings and to leave the house behind her.

She climbed the hill to the sheep fields above the coast. On a drystone wall of whitish lime, she stopped to get her breath; the air was close today, as if there was a thunderstorm in the offing, but the skies were clear. Later in the week, perhaps. She climbed down by a big galvanized water tank that had been pressed into service as a trough. A makeshift wooden rail had been nailed up around it to keep the sheep from falling in, and their hooves had churned up the grass into mud for yards around. Marianne skirted around it and took a diagonal line across the long, sloping field to the next stile. The sheep, most of them down in the far corner, paid her no attention at all.

From a rock on the slopes just outside the next field, she scanned the beach for Ryan. But he didn't seem to be about. Somebody was walking down there, but it wasn't him.

So then she sat on the rock, and wondered what to do next.

The days were so long.

She thought about the weekend, and wondered if this time her father might follow through on his promise. He'd told her to think of somewhere to go. What would she say? A park, a zoo, or go into town and see something at the multiplex? There was usually a Disney or some kind of cartoon playing whenever the school holidays came around. She was torn between trying to come up with something where they wouldn't have to make the effort to talk, and some venue where they'd have no choice. The long silences when they were together these days only tended to make obvious the divide between them. But if he had to talk to her and there was no way to slide out of it, perhaps she'd learn something of significance at last. Like where her mother was now, what was she doing, was she ever likely to see her again ... and that one, all-important, never-addressed question.

Why?

Like an impending fatality in the family, it had been talked around, but never talked about. Knowing, not knowing ... over the years, she'd come to the point where she didn't know which prospect scared her more.

They could go for a burger, perhaps. One of those places where the food was like shit but they gave you a balloon.

Some of the biggest butterflies she'd ever seen were dancing in the air around the rock on which she was sitting. Way down on the shore, the bright dots of far-off ramblers in fluorescent parkas were crossing more or less where she and Rudi had managed to get themselves stranded. Sometimes on weekends she would see them in their hundreds, trooping out en masse right across the full width of the bay with guides to keep them out of the quicksands. Back in the old days, people were supposed to have crossed at low tide by coach and horses. Some had raced the incoming sea, and some had lost. When conditions were right, you were supposed to be able to hear their ghostly hoofbeats and the jingle of their harnesses drifting in over the sands.

Marianne clambered to her feet, and set off again across the fields for a look at Ryan's place.

The first thing she found was that her observation platform had gone. Sometime in the last twenty-four hours the freight cars and brake van had been shunted away. The siding now stood empty, just the open rails and the weeds growing up between the tracks and a few patches of leaked oil on the timbers. She stood on the tracks and looked down on the yard, aware that she was now a conspicuous figure against the empty sky.

Nothing moved.

She could see that the workshop door was open about a foot and she watched it for a while, but nothing happened. Inside, the workshop seemed to be dark. After a while the open door started to look like a trap for some small animal, waiting to be sprung. And still nothing moved.

She started to worry a little. What if he was lying on the floor in there, hurt? It could happen. She looked towards the house but there was no sign of life in that direction, either. She wondered if she should call out his name. Anyone who might be down there couldn't help but hear her.

She didn't call out. But she scrambled down the embankment, and went under the bridge to the gate.

The gate was closed, but this time it hadn't been padlocked. Perhaps he *had* gone out, but in a hurry.

She knocked.

Out in the open air like this, the sound was nothing.

She pushed at the gate, not too hard, and it started to swing inward.

Marianne hesitated. He'd sent her away once, but . . . well, she'd been able to sense that he hadn't really meant it. So that was all right. And if he was in there and he *was* hurt, then who was going to help him? He obviously had no neighbors, and she knew from her own observations that no one ever visited. If she didn't look out for him, it seemed to her that no one would. The story was that her great-uncle had lain dead in the house for three days until the visiting home help had finally discovered him. It was horrible for her to think about; not the dying, which she couldn't really imagine, but the dying alone, which she just about could.

This made her hesitate. She didn't want to find anybody *dead*. But then again her great-uncle had been old, and Ryan wasn't; well, he was old to her, but not old as in *old people*. She'd prefer it if he'd collapsed, or hit his head on something, or just fallen. Something that a wet cloth might cure, and nothing more technical than that.

The fact of it was that she was bursting to take a closer look around, and she would gladly have imagined Ryan pinned under the weight of a falling wardrobe if it would provide her with a valid excuse. She wondered what the inside of the house would be like. Something bare and functional like a prospector's log cabin, she imagined.

She looked both ways along the lane. Empty, as ever.

"Mr. Ryan!" she called out.

The ducks under the bridge flapped and squawked, but that was the only reaction she got.

The gate scraped inward, and Marianne went through.

Everything in the yard was more or less as it had been before. The plastic drum that she'd used in her exit had been returned to its place among the weeds. Otherwise, nothing seemed altered except for the inviting yawn of the workshop door. She glanced around. No one was observing her.

She went over and pushed the door open.

The workshop was one big, badly lit room with no ceiling other than the rafters of the roof and an overall sense of being barely indoors, like in a garage or a barn. Everything was wood or tarpaulin except for the floor, which was concrete. All the household appliances that she'd seen being delivered were now crowded in here, stacked two-deep and taking up most of the free space; one of them stood in pieces on the spread-out pages of a copy of *Exchange and Mart*.

Ryan wasn't here.

But there was lots of interesting stuff for her to examine.

There was a workbench, chopped and worn like a butcher's block, and on it stood the motorcycle frame that she'd seen him bringing home a few days before. He'd been straightening it out and cleaning off the rust, and now he'd wrapped rags around some of the joints which he'd then soaked in oil. Marianne looked around, fascinated. Everywhere that her gaze fell there was something different; it was like being inside a junk sculpture conceived by an obsessive mind of disturbed originality. There were chains of all lengths and sizes, hanging like monster plaits from iron hooks on the wall. Half-used cans of paint. Tea chests on the floor, each of them filled like a machine-age grab bag: pumps and motors, rotors, nuts and bolts, doll parts, and Japanese toy cars and robots with their paint all mostly scoured away by time and mistreatment. Hung up like a Christmas stocking was a plastic trash bag filled with those aluminum cans from the beach, only now they'd been hammered flat and took up a fraction of the space. When the bag was filled, presumably he'd have it weighed for scrap.

A tricycle like something seen in a distorting mirror, looking as if it had been run over by a truck.

An engine block from something or other, seemingly too rusted and incomplete ever to be of any use at all.

Every time she picked up something, she'd uncover something even more interesting underneath. Lead soldiers. A gas mask, the rubber all perished. A stack of magazines at which she looked, and then looked again—not the kind of stuff that they tended to put within reach of the little kids at the news-agents'. They were in clear plastic bags with the flaps taped down, and paper labels had been stuck over the ladies' rude parts on the covers. She was intensely curious, and they made her uneasy. But she didn't dare to pick at the tape to look inside.

Marianne suddenly realized that she'd lost track of the time. She might have been in here for two minutes, or twenty. What kind of a Samaritan was she supposed to be? There was Ryan, supposed to be stretched out and groaning somewhere, and here she was with her nose into all this material that was, she'd suddenly realized with some embarrassment, very personal. Not without some reluctance, she backed out.

A couple of blackbirds flew up startled as she emerged, but there was still no one around. Something crunched underfoot as she walked towards the house.

She looked down. She'd stepped on a slug.

"Uuurgh!" She scraped the sole of her sneaker across a clump of grass to clean it off. The slug did nothing, having no further interest in the affairs of the world.

And then, limping for no serious reason, Marianne went on towards the house and called out, "Mr. Ryan! Are you there?"

The house stood in silence. She knocked on the door of the porch, and heard a faint echo coming back through what sounded like the emptiest of empty rooms. She listened, hopefully, for some kind of a feeble cry, but nothing came.

He wasn't lying hurt.

He wasn't even there.

Which, she couldn't help feeling, was kind of inconsiderate of him. But then, turning from the house, she brightened, because it left other days and other opportunities for him to find out how he might need her help, and left today's explorations to stand as a bonus. She'd moved nothing this time, there were no witnesses, she was leaving no trace, so he wouldn't even know that she'd been there.

She pulled open the gate to leave, just as the low-loader from the local dump drew in alongside the yard. The cab stopped level with the open gateway. Ryan, on the passenger side of the cab, was looking down at her in some surprise. It wasn't the kind of surprise that came with birthdays or unexpected meetings with long-lost friends. It was more in line with accidental damage, or bad news over the telephone.

She gave a little wave and waited, her mouth suddenly dry and her heart pumping in her chest.

On the other side of the cab, the boy who'd been driving was now climbing down. As before, he'd left the engine running. Now she remembered his name from school: Brain-Dead Fishwick. It probably wasn't his christened name, but it was the only one she'd ever heard him given. She wondered for a moment if he might recognize her, but the glance that he sent in her direction was flat and incurious. He moved around to the back of the vehicle, and started to uncover the load.

Perhaps there could be something in a name after all.

Ryan stepped down before her.

"What are *you* doing here?" he said, letting the cab door fall shut behind him. He didn't seem pleased to see her.

"I was just passing," she said lamely.

"No one 'just passes' this place. How did you get in?"

"The gate was wide open," Marianne said, embroidering a little. Ryan glanced towards the gate, and it was clear, from his momentary hesitation, that he wasn't one hundred percent sure whether he'd remembered to secure it or not.

"Whether it was or it wasn't," he said, "you know that's still trespassing."

"I was wondering if you were all right."

"Why shouldn't I be?"

There was a rasp of rope across canvas, and they both glanced towards the back of the low-loader. A solitary second-hand washing machine stood revealed, lashed down with ropes like a witch to the stake. The missing Zanussi, was all that Marianne could assume.

She looked at Ryan; Ryan was looking at the boy, and she could see a definite anxiety there. As if he was worried about what the boy might think or, perhaps even more important, what he might say.

Ryan turned to her and said, "Look. I've told you this before. Don't come here, don't hang around. I've got a living to make."

"I didn't move anything."

"I just don't want kids getting in the way. There's paint and battery acid and all kinds of dangerous stuff here. Do you understand me?"

She looked him in the eye. He was raising his voice more than was necessary, and she knew that this outburst was at least as much for Brain-Dead's benefit as it was for hers. His eyes seemed to be telling her a different story. *Go along with this,* they seemed to be saying. *Please.*

And she said, "I understand."

"I mean it," he said. And then, less forcefully but with what she was sure was a recognizable streak of sincerity, "I don't want you coming around here."

"I'll go, then," she said. She didn't move.

"Please."

She held her ground for a moment longer but then, when it was plain that nothing more was going to be said, she abruptly turned to walk away.

Before she went under the bridge and out of sight she turned and called back, "I trod on a slug!" Her voice echoed under the low rivet-studded roof but the two of them were lifting the Zanussi down from the back of the van, and neither seemed to hear her. If they did, neither looked her way.

So then she walked on.

CHAPTER 12

There was no real reason why the house should feel any emptier than usual that evening, but it did. Marianne sat across the kitchen table from Mrs. Healey, quietly dreading the hours that stretched ahead. Rudi lay on his beanbag. Mrs. Healey was making conversation and had strayed, with grim inevitability, to the usual topic of acrimony. The roots of it were simple; out of three sisters, one had died and named the other two as co-executors of her estate. Mrs. Healey was one of the two. Open warfare had ensued. Marianne was sure that it was only a matter of time before the subject of the piano was due to come up again and when it did, she was afraid that she would scream.

She wondered how long she could decently leave it before making some excuse to slip upstairs and stay there. She could read, or perhaps she could play on the Amiga with the sound turned down low. Or then again, she had schoolwork that she'd been given and which she'd have to complete sometime before the end of the holidays ... but on the other hand, there *were* limits.

Suddenly, something that Mrs. Healey said broke through to her. Marianne didn't know whether she'd made an abrupt change of topic, or whether the wandering of her own thoughts had prevented her from registering the lead-in. But after feigning an interest and actually taking in nothing for almost half an hour, Marianne's mind was re-engaged with a crash of gears.

Mrs. Healey was saying, "If that man ever follows you again, you be sure that you tell somebody."

There could be no doubt as to whom Mrs. Healey had in mind. But Marianne said, "What man?"

She couldn't know about that afternoon, not already. Or could she? As far as Marianne knew, Mrs. Healey hadn't been out of the house, but had somebody phoned and told her?

Mrs. Healey said, "We both know who I'm talking about."

"He's never followed me."

"Well ..." Mrs. Healey said meaningfully, determined to make her point regardless of the facts of the situation, "it could have been a coincidence that he was down there on the beach at the same time as a child on her own. But on the other hand we'll never know that for certain, will we?"

"He's *always* on the beach," Marianne said. "It's part of what he does, collecting things."

"Very convenient for him, I'm sure."

"What's he supposed to have done?"

"It's not necessarily what he's done. It's what he *might* do that we have to watch out for."

"Like what?"

"Stay away from him, and the question won't even arise. And that's exactly the way it ought to be. What are you doing tomorrow?"

It was impossible. Everyone around her spoke in half-meanings, and no one would ever explain.

"I was going to meet some friends from school," Marianne said.

And that, for the moment, seemed to satisfy Mrs. Healey.

Of course, she wasn't going to meet anyone from school at all. They all had their own gangs and groups of friends, and she wasn't a part of any of them. Nobody picked on her—not often, anyway, and then it was usually only threats and empty words—but most of them had known each other from early childhood, gone through the village schools together, and carried those tribal ties intact into the secondary school that served the entire area. Marianne had come from outside, and she'd joined late. She was a loner and would ever be so.

Besides which, she rarely made much of an effort. Some people are born to be loners, she reckoned. Some people are happier that way.

And she supposed that she must be one of them.

She was lying in bed and reading when Mrs. Healey looked in to say good night. As Marianne might have expected, Mrs. Healey didn't seem to approve of what she found.

"Why aren't you asleep yet?" she said.

"I always read first," Marianne told her.

"Don't you know what time it is?"

"It doesn't matter as long as I'm lying down."

Reasonable as this seemed to Marianne, it was apparently less so to Mrs. Healey. "And I'm supposed to fall for that one, am I?" she said, and moved forward into the room. "It'll matter in the morning. Come on."

She was reaching for the book. "I haven't finished the chapter yet!" Marianne protested, knowing already that it was a battle lost.

"Finish it another time," Mrs. Healey said, and took the book from her.

"Don't forget the bookmark," Marianne said, but Mrs. Healey seemed not to hear. She was studying the cover of the paperback with some bafflement.

"What's this?" she said.

"*The Lion, the Witch, and the Wardrobe.* It's my favorite book. I've read it three times."

"But this is . . ."

"*Der König von Narnia*'s the German title. I've tried it in English but I like the German better."

Mrs. Healey turned the book over and looked at the back, but it was obvious that nothing she saw there meant anything to her. She looked at Marianne. "And you can understand it?" she said.

"I'm bilingual. It's just the same for me either way."

Mrs. Healey seemed dazed. "Really."

"It's nothing special. Anyone could do it."

"I'm sure."

Marianne could see that she'd at least given Mrs. Healey something to think about. The housekeeper set the book down on the bedside table and switched off the lamp, so that the only light now came in from the doorway. Mrs. Healey was a silhouette against its spill.

"Well, good night," she said, and then she surprised

Marianne by bending over and giving her a dry, scratchy kiss on the forehead.

After she'd gone, Marianne listened for a while. Mrs. Healey seemed to spend forever in the bathroom, but then she heard the housekeeper's tread as she went down the passageway towards the spare bedroom. The chink of light around Marianne's door went out, and the closing of the door to Mrs. Healey's room could be heard a few moments later.

The house was dark and silent now. It creaked as it settled. Marianne waited for several minutes, and then she reached over and switched on her lamp. At first it all seemed startlingly bright and unreal, but her eyes soon readjusted as she retrieved her book and pushed up her pillows.

Once more, she started to read. After only a few lines, she broke off and rubbed at her forehead.

Then she carried on again.

CHAPTER 13

By the third day of her father's absence, Marianne was no longer bothering to look for excuses to get out of Mrs. Healey's company. She'd simply go, and sensed that the relief was equal on both sides.

That afternoon, she found Ryan back on the beach again with his knapsack and collecting bag. She watched him following the wire along as usual, and then she saw him stop and set everything down. He crouched, and seemed to be working on something that had been caught on the barbs. As far as she could tell, the work was careful and patient and it went on for some time.

Marianne wasn't watching from the hills today. She was down on the sea wall, at a spot overhung by a salt-dried and dead-looking tree that somehow just managed to cling on to life. The tree gave her some cover, but not much. Assuming that Ryan was following the same pattern as always, he'd come along by here and pass within a few yards of her. He couldn't miss her, not even deliberately—well, not convincingly so, anyway.

What could be more unremarkable? Her sitting under the tree looking out at the bay, and him walking by. Except that he seemed to be taking forever to get here. Marianne craned her neck, but she couldn't make out what he was engaged in. He was still a couple of hundred yards away, out along the sweeping curve of the sea wall.

She got to her feet, and watched him for a minute or so longer. He'd see her now if he should glance her way, but he didn't. What was he *doing*?

She started to walk towards him.

He'd paused at a spot where a drainage channel came out through the wall. The outflow of water had cut deep into the turf below, and some rocks and an old tractor tire had been dumped into the trench to prevent further erosion. The fenceposts leaned inward and the wire between them was a tangled mess. It was here that he'd hunkered down, and seemed to be trying to unpick something out of the snarl.

Marianne was on the grassy top of the sea wall. A slight breeze was blowing in from the sea. Further inland, one of the day's freight trains rolled along the line with a sound like distant thunder. Or perhaps it *was* distant thunder.

Ryan had paused in his work, and was searching in his knapsack. She stopped, looking down at him. He took out some pliers and turned back to the wire, seeming not to have registered her presence at all.

But he said, without looking at her, "There's no telling you, is there?"

"It's a public beach," Marianne said. "No one can say I've no right to be here."

"Whatever you say," Ryan said. And he worked on, ignoring her.

Or at least, he did his best. Kicking idly at the scrub on the lip of the wall, she moved to get a better view of what he was doing. A little figure hung in the wire. A child's doll, and in hardly the finest condition; its rag body was black with filth, and its stuffing hung out at the seams.

Still without looking at her, he said, "I wish you wouldn't do this."

"Do what? I'm not doing anything."

"I get nervous if people watch me. And I can tell you now, it doesn't get any more interesting than this. So just go off and play. Go home."

"I'm only trying to be friendly. What's so terrible about that?"

"It isn't right."

"Why not?" she said, but he didn't explain.

She said, "You're as bad as Mrs. Healey. Everybody's always telling me things and then not explaining what they mean."

"That's not just you," he said. "That's life."

He put two-handed pressure onto the pliers, and a length of the wire snapped. The entire fence quivered like a spring. The drab-looking doll had taken one step closer to freedom.

Marianne said, "My dad thinks my dog might be getting better."

Ryan shifted the pliers along to another part of the wire on the other side of the doll and said, "Good."

"Would you like to come and see my dog?"

"No."

"You could come when there's nobody there."

He turned to her at last. "No!"

He went back to his work, not quite muttering under his breath.

Marianne said, "I never realized you were so miserable before."

She sat down on the lip of the wall, swinging her heels to bump against the dressed stone. It looked as if Ryan was going to have to cut the wire in several places just to get the doll away without tearing it. She couldn't see why he'd want to bother. It was hardly more than a mass of mildew. Squeeze it hard, and it would probably disintegrate with a stink like a blocked-up toilet.

"You're ruining the fence," she said.

"The fence was ruined before I came here."

"Is it worth the trouble?"

"I don't know that, yet. The head's porcelain, it could be Victorian. I'll have to look it up in a book at the library and if I'm right, there are people who'll pay money for that kind of thing."

"Why don't you just pull the head off?"

"It might break," he said, cutting through one final strand and then lifting the doll free. Short lengths of chopped and rusty wire stuck out at angles from its body, giving it the air of some miniature Christian martyr. "You've got to take more care than that."

From his knapsack he now took a plastic bag, and after carefully folding down the wire ends he wrapped the doll in it before stowing both package and pliers and getting to his feet. He looked at Marianne, his face set and dark. He seemed to be about to say something but instead he picked up his bags and started to walk, making a point of not acknowledging her any further.

She tagged along but he simply put his head down and walked on, as if this was something that he was going to have to weather so that, as with taking stitches or having a bone set, he could look forward to it being over. The sea wall stretched on ahead of them. The path followed it for some distance and then veered inland towards the railway. There was nowhere else to go.

"Think it'll rain?" she said. He didn't answer.

And then he said, curtly, "No."

That was when she knew that she had him, because he wasn't ignorant enough to ignore her completely. He couldn't do it. Like in the story they'd been told about the young Mozart dragging himself out of bed every morning because he couldn't lie there after hearing a scale on the piano that was one note short of complete, Ryan couldn't let a straight and honest question hang forever.

"Are you a beachcomber?" she said.

He sighed. Looked at the ground, as if in despair. Shook his head a couple of times.

And then he said, "I'm a scavenger. I pick up stuff that nobody's interested in and I try to turn it into something that someone could want."

"Can you make a lot of money doing that?"

"Well," he said, spreading his arms in a look-at-me gesture as much as his baggage would allow. "Obviously."

"I could carry one of those for you," Marianne said.

"No thanks."

Marianne skipped along beside him for a while. Then she said, "My father sells machine parts. Whatever they are."

"Well, I'm sure that's better than this."

"I don't know. We've got bills he hasn't paid in months. Last winter they were going to take his car away because he was so far behind. But then he must have worked something out."

"This isn't stuff you should be telling people. What would your father say if he could hear you?"

"I wouldn't tell just *anybody*. We're friends, aren't we?"

"No, we're not."

"Why'd you rescue me, then?"

He stopped suddenly, and turned to face her; he'd caught her by surprise. He said, "Look. I'm not saying I don't like you. This is nothing personal. But for the last time . . . don't follow me. Don't hang around where I live. You'll give people the wrong idea, and then *I'll* get all the trouble."

He'd rammed home the point, and now he moved on.

Marianne followed again, but gave him a little distance. When he sensed that she was still behind him he faltered, but then he pressed forward.

"Who needs to know?" she said.

"Please," he said. "Don't. Don't follow me."

"I'm not following you. This just happens to be the way I was going. You don't want me to stay on the beach again, do you? The tide's coming in."

He set his shoulders. She couldn't see his face, but she could guess that he was glowering.

She kept on chatting, thinking that this was probably the best way to lighten his mood and bring him around. She told him one of the stories that she'd heard about the bay; the mod-

ern version, in which the coach and horses was replaced by a
busload of children and instead of the hoofbeats, it was the
horn and their singing that would drift inland through the fog.
Ryan kept his head down, and said nothing. Then she said
look, she thought she'd hurt her leg back there, and she started
to limp. But he didn't look, so she had to abandon the limp
and run to catch up with him again.

"Those bags do look heavy," she said. "Are you sure I can't
carry one for you?"

He turned on her.

"For God's sake," he shouted, only inches from her face.
"Go away!"

She could feel herself turn white. It was almost as if he'd
spun around and slapped her. He pulled himself away, almost
with a growl, and stalked off.

She felt stricken. Betrayed, almost. But even then, there was
something in his anger that made it so she couldn't quite believe in it. Something plaintive. Almost despairing.

Marianne kept her distance now. Still dogging him, but not
so close. Out of reach, even out of conversational range. He
left the sea wall and followed the footpath inland, and she
scrambled down after him. The distant rumble came again; real
thunder, not a train, and it had moved some way closer. A
dozen or so young calves grazed the reclaimed fields, scattered
widely over several acres. Ryan unhooked a gate to cross a
footbridge, and closed it behind him. Marianne climbed over
the gate a half-minute later. Now they were almost at the railway embankment. Beyond the embankment lay Ryan's yard,
and the lane out to the road.

When she came through under the railway bridge, he was
standing by his gate and watching her. The gate was
unpadlocked. His face was expressionless.

"It's a public road. You can't stop me walking on a public
road if I want to."

He said nothing. He turned and pushed his gate open, and
went inside. She could hear the click of the latch and the inner
bolt being drawn.

Marianne took a run at the gate, and jumped. She got hold
of the top and, as once before, hunted for a foothold on the

hasp and staple which would enable her to scramble all the way up. At the top she swung one leg over, and got enough of her balance to perch upright. And there on the fence she stayed.

Ryan clearly hadn't been expecting this; he was halfway to the workshop and had stopped to look back at the sound of all the noise she'd been making. Now he gazed up at her, his mouth half-open.

He shut it with a click, and straightened up.

"Right," he said. "Now, this isn't a public road and it isn't a public beach, it's mine. I pay rent here. That's my fence and I'm telling you to get off it. And don't even *think* of climbing down on this side. Go on, or I'll have to throw you off."

She said nothing, but stared back defiantly.

He glanced at the sky. "It's going to rain soon," he said. "You want to get soaked up there, that's your problem."

Marianne didn't move.

She was wondering if he'd do it, if he'd carry out his threat and come over and throw her off the fence. Or drag her down and throw her out, at least. She seemed to have annoyed him enough. The fact was that she didn't believe that he'd actually go through with it, but she also knew that life could be full of surprises.

After a few moments' standoff, Ryan turned and opened up the workshop. He dragged the day's haul inside.

For a while he came and went between the workshop and the house, studiously paying no attention to her at all. Then he disappeared into the workshop and for some time she didn't see him. Even though she kept shifting around on the top of the fence, it quickly grew uncomfortable and after not too long it started to hurt.

She looked up at the clouds. She wondered if he was right, and if it would rain; she hoped that it would, because then she could really show him. She'd show him what determination was.

It started to rain.

It didn't come for a while but when it came, it arrived with clear and serious intent. This was the thunderstorm that had been promising itself for most of the week. The first drops were so big and hit so hard that they made her wince. Then, as if the warm sky had been slit from end to end in a slaughterhouse, it birthed its payload in one huge and sudden torrent.

But instead of pumping and then abating, the torrent went on. Marianne screwed her eyes shut and hunched herself down and did her best to stick it out. In less than a minute, it was hammering like hail on the roof of Ryan's workshop. It was coming down with the kind of force that drove cars off roads and flattened crops. Less than a minute after *that*, the downspouts on the yard's outbuildings could no longer cope. Marianne hung on, soaked through, drenched, pounded, tears running and mingling with the rain. The worst of it passed but the rain carried on, and a flash of lightning went to earth somewhere out across the bay. Thunder followed, barely a heartbeat behind.

She opened her eyes. Ryan was standing there in the workshop doorway. And she knew then that she'd won.

He made a brief, defeated gesture for her to come over and join him. She clambered down from the fence, into the yard. In places it was ankle-deep in water, which had fallen too fast to drain away. She didn't run. There didn't seem to be much point, because she could hardly get any wetter than she already was.

She knew that when she stopped being so numb, she was going to start hurting. But with all the dignity that she could muster, she walked stiffly across the yard and into the workshop.

CHAPTER 14

The workshop roof was leaking, and Ryan had already set out a few pails and buckets to catch the worst of the drips. Marianne sat on a cracked vinyl typist's chair in front of a two-bar electric heater and watched as he positioned a plastic basin under another leak that had started up by the window. She was wrapped in his ex-army greatcoat. The rain itself hadn't exactly been cold, but once indoors she'd started to shiver.

He looked at her. His shirt had no collar and the sleeves were rolled up. He wasn't big, not muscle-builder big, but he looked solid and hard like a fairground worker or a Gypsy. She hadn't noticed before, but his hands were tattooed. Not words or pictures or anything, just little x's and o's across the fingers. They looked as if he'd done them with needles and ink on himself.

Ryan, at home.

He said quietly, "You're a stubborn little thing, aren't you?"

It didn't sound as if he'd actually intended to say *thing*; he'd started to say something that began with an f but had caught himself just in time. She shivered again, and didn't reply.

He said, "Why are you doing this?"

She shrugged.

He said, "I can't believe you don't have better places to be. You should be out with your friends."

"I haven't got any."

"I don't believe you."

"It's true. The other girls call me The Kraut."

He folded his arms, and leaned back against the workbench. He was frowning. "Why?"

"Because I'm half-German. I lived there for most of my life and everything was fine. But I've been to four different schools since I had to come over to England."

"Why did you have to leave?"

"No one's ever told me."

Hunched in his coat and with an accompaniment of dripping water in buckets all around her, she gave him her story. Her father had worked for an American electronics company whose European center of operations had been sited just outside Hamburg. There he'd met and married Anneliese, her mother, and they'd settled in a big house in the suburbs. Marianne had come along two years later. She'd grown up among company families and she'd attended an expensive school. She could speak unaccented English but she'd visited England only twice, and had clearer memories of the boat trips than of the country. That had been her life until about five years ago; and it had changed completely in the course of a single day.

"He came and got me out of school one afternoon," she explained. "I can remember being really pleased to see him. He almost never came to pick me up like that. Usually he was always working."

He'd been early, and he'd given some reason for needing to take her away. As he'd walked her out to the car she'd noticed that he seemed distracted, and that he dropped his keys twice getting the car unlocked. As they were driving away from the school, Marianne had seen her mother's little VW runabout coming down the street. Her last memory of Anneliese Cadogan was of her mother's bewildered look as she'd registered them driving by in the opposite direction. Her father had been staring straight ahead.

He drove them straight to the ferry dock, midway between the *fischmarkt* and the old harbor. There were bags in the back of the car, hurriedly and unmethodically packed. It was June, but he'd gathered all her winter dresses and not a single T-shirt. "Some of the stuff that he'd picked up came out of a pile from next to the wardrobe," she said. "It was all stuff that didn't even fit me any more. It was supposed to be given away."

He'd told her that it was a surprise holiday at first, and for those early weeks in England they'd stayed in reasonable hotels. Then they'd moved between a number of cheaper places, and that was when he'd had to give up the car. It wasn't his to keep, he'd explained to her then, and he'd had to let it go back. It was around this time that she'd begun to realize that something big and irreversible had happened in her life.

She wasn't exactly sure how he'd planned for everything to be. All she knew was that those plans seemed to go wrong. After the cheap hotels they'd lived in a succession of rented flats, and then finally they'd moved out to here. It was as if her life had stopped in its tracks, without explanation. She could remember riding lessons, swimming lessons, ballet class. Here she had an old dog and a second-hand computer and an empty beach to play on.

Ryan said, "Nothing ever happens without a reason. And your father must have had a good one."

"Like what?" she said.

"I don't know. Stopping you from being unhappy."

"But I *am* unhappy."

"More unhappy, then. I don't know. He's the one you should be talking to, not me."

"But he's not like you," Marianne said. "Any time I try to tell him anything ... it's as if I can see his mind going off somewhere else and I'm not even there. I told him I was lonely once, but he never asked me why. He just got me Rudi. He wasn't like this before. And I don't know why he's like it now."

Ryan looked out of the window.

"The rain's finished," he said. "Go home now. Please."

She slid off the chair. "I only wanted us to be friends," she said.

"That isn't possible," Ryan said, taking the big coat from around her shoulders. He said it as gently as he seemed to be able. "I'm sorry, it just isn't. Don't ever come here again. You wouldn't understand why and I wouldn't ever want you to. One day you will. And you'll know I was right."

He went out with her across the yard to the gate. In those places where the rain had flooded, it was like walking across a mirror of the sky. The air was fresher and cooler, as if the storm had washed it clean.

By the gate he said, "Wait here a minute." He slid the bolt and put his head out to check the lane in both directions before opening the gate wide.

What else was there to say? She'd said it all, and now he was sending her away. He wasn't being unkind about it, but he hadn't been swayed by her story either.

Marianne started to walk towards the bridge. After a few yards, she looked back.

He was still in the gateway.

"Go on, now," he said. "Run home."

And so she did.

CHAPTER 15

When she reached the house she saw that her father's car was back in its usual place and in spite of everything, she felt her heart leap a little. She found him in the kitchen, going through some of the bills and the junk mail that had arrived during his absence. Mrs. Healey, it seemed, had already gone home. Her father looked up at her with a good try at a pleasant smile, and then as the state of her registered with him he looked again, only now with faint dismay.

"What happened this time?" he said.

She went around the table. "I got caught in the rain."

"What were you doing?"

"Just walking."

She bent and scratched Rudi's head. His fur was bone dry, so she supposed that he'd sensed the rain coming and moved into the house. He put up with her attention for a few moments and then resettled himself.

Her father said, "But Mrs. Healey told me you've been seeing some friends every day."

"That's where I was walking to," she said.

"Oh, Marianne," he said wearily. "What am I going to do with you?"

"I'll go and get changed," she said.

She went upstairs, leaving him to open more envelopes and flyers. Even the bills seemed to come with junk mail added, these days. When she reached her bedroom, she found that he'd already been there and left something for her; there was a W. H. Smith's bag on the bed and it contained three new games for the Amiga. One of them he'd already bought for her on another trip about six months before.

She changed out of her wet jeans and top into her denim dungarees over a long-sleeved T-shirt that was striped like a burglar's jersey. She put her sneakers on top of the radiator to dry and dug out her second-best pair from under the bed.

As she was sitting on the bed and lacing these, she heard her father coming up the stairs. She thought he'd go on past, but instead he came into the room. There was an opened letter on pale cream stock in his hand.

"Thank you for the presents," she said.

He said, "I just opened this letter from one of your teachers. Miss Webber."

"Miss *Weber*," Marianne corrected him without thinking. "She says it the German way."

"What does she do?"

"Languages. Spanish as well as German."

"Have you any idea why she might want to see me?"

Marianne looked at the letter, but the wrong side was towards her. "Doesn't she say?"

"I wouldn't be asking you if she did." He sat down on the bed beside her. Marianne folded her hands in her lap, and waited.

He said, "You'd tell me if anything was wrong, wouldn't you? I mean, we've always been straight with each other, haven't we?"

He was handing her a problem of diplomacy here, in that he seemed to believe what he was saying. And mostly because it was what he seemed to want, she nodded.

He said, "So, I'm not going to get any nasty surprises if I see her."

"I don't think so."

"Good. She'll probably want to know why I missed the last parents' evening. What's she like?"

"She's very nice."

He smiled. He always seemed tired when he smiled, these days. He said, "I'd better go along and take it like a man, then."

The bed creaked as he got up to leave. Marianne was trying to think of some reason why Miss Weber should want to call her father in to see her. And why now, when there wasn't even any school? She wondered if she might be able to get a look at the letter, sometime later on. To ask to look at it now might seem like the reaction of the guilty.

"Listen." Her father had stopped at the doorway and seemed to have remembered something. But he had that overcasual manner of someone who hadn't forgotten anything at all but who was pretending that he had because it was an awkward matter to raise.

"There's quite a lot of stuff backed up from when I was away," he said. "It looks like I'm going to have to work through the weekend after all. Is that a big problem?"

Marianne shrugged. What did he expect her to say?

"I know what I promised, but ... nothing changes, we just move it all on down the calendar. Deal?"

"All right," she said.

Satisfied, he turned to go. But then he stopped and added, "These friends of yours. Why don't you invite them around? Rent some videos, whatever you want to do."

She didn't actually say anything in answer to this, but he took her silence for agreement and then, with the matter apparently settled, went out. He was moving in the direction of his own bedroom, perhaps to finish unpacking his overnight bag.

Marianne stayed seated on her bed for a moment. But she couldn't contain herself. She jumped up and rushed to the doorway.

He was at the far end of the landing, about to go into his room.

Marianne said, "Did you see her?"

Her father stared. "What do you mean?"

"I know where you really went. Did you *see* her? What did she say?"

There was a long pause. Her father's face gave nothing away, but she sensed turmoil beneath an unmoving surface.

He said, "No. I didn't see her."

And then he went into his room and closed the door, too hard.

CHAPTER 16

Mrs. Healey didn't believe in pandering to children's moods. She'd never had any children of her own, but she'd spent a lifetime being annoyed by the way other people mishandled theirs in public. Letting them laugh and giggle, waste food, ask questions all the time, run riot and talk too loudly. All in all, she'd come to feel that she rated her own lack of issue as a blessing. Even Mr. Healey, when he'd been alive, had tended to clutter the house up with his presence. She'd only had to straighten the covers on a chair and there he'd be five minutes later, sitting in it.

Marianne was a quiet type, but could clearly be a handful when it suited her. Although she *had* displayed a surprising maturity in the interest that she'd shown over the saga of the piano. She'd sat there and listened without a peep, too fascinated to interrupt.

Mrs. Healey arrived at her usual time the next morning to find Marianne with her head in the refrigerator and her red rucksack on the floor beside her. And much as she didn't believe in pandering to moods, sometimes she did feel that Marianne was perhaps being hastened into her maturity; so she put a little brightness into her voice as she set down her bag on the table and said, "Who's raiding my kitchen?"

"It's for a picnic," Marianne said. "I'm taking Rudi, if he'll come."

Mrs. Healey unbuttoned her coat. She'd passed the dog on the way in, lying outside the house in his usual spot; he'd worn the grass down and the earth bare over the past few weeks.

She said, "Do you really think he's up to it?"

"Dogs are like people," Marianne said, pulling the drawstrings on her rucksack and then standing up to close the fridge door. "They're up and down all the time. Something like this could be just what he needs."

Mrs. Healey hung up her coat in the broom cupboard. "Well," she said, "remember to keep away from the beach. We don't want a repeat of what happened last time." But when she turned around, Marianne had already gone out.

She went over and stood in the kitchen doorway. Marianne was out there, crouching by Rudi. Mrs. Healey noticed that last night's German paperback was sticking out of one of the rucksack's side pockets. Rudi had raised his head and was looking keen and beating his tail, but he didn't rise.

"No?" Mrs. Healey said.

"He's nearly there," Marianne said confidently. "See? He wagged his tail. Perhaps tomorrow."

"Can't be too much wrong with a dog like that," said Mrs. Healey.

Marianne stroked the dog's head as he settled back. "Good boy," she said. "Good boy, Rudi."

Mrs. Healey said, "Was that his name when you got him?"

"He didn't have a name then. So I called him after my dad's old boss."

"Why did you do that?"

"Because he was nice to me and I liked him. I liked everything back then. Especially school."

"Does that mean you don't like anything here?"

"I like Rudi," Marianne said, and she stood up.

Mrs. Healey didn't go in straight away, but stayed in the doorway and watched Marianne's departure. As Marianne walked out over the saltings, she was checking the fastenings on her red rucksack. She was such a small figure, striding out with such confidence. The kind of confidence that could walk straight into harm and not see it coming.

But how to warn against that without destroying the innocence that you were seeking to protect?

As Marianne walked on, she slung the red rucksack over a shoulder and held it there one-handed by the strap.

Just like that Ryan man always did, Mrs. Healey realized with a chill.

Ich war ganz allein. Der Himmel war schwarz und ich war vom Meer umgeben und niemand wusste wo ich war. Ich rief nach Hilfe, aber niemand war zu sehen. Ich war sicher dass ich ertrinken würde. Aber dann erschien er wie aus dem Nichts und versuchte mich zu beruhigen. Er nahm mich auf seine Schulter und trug mich durch die Flut. Die Flut war tief genug dass sie uns beide verschlingen hätte können, aber ich fühlte mich trotzdem sicher. Als wir zuhause ankamen war das Haus leer und als ich mich umdrehte war er auf einmal nicht mehr da.

CHAPTER 17

Patrick Cadogan, father of Marianne, lowered his daughter's German essay and said, "You'll have to forgive me for being so slow. My German's a little bit rusty."

"I'm a language teacher," Isabella Weber said. "Slow's what I'm used to. Can you follow it?"

"I can follow it."

They were in the language lab. The school was empty but had been opened up over three days so that senior pupils could call in to get their exam results; according to the teachers' rota in the office Miss Weber's stint of duty had ended at midday and she appeared to have gone, and so Cadogan had asked the school secretary if there was anyone else around who could talk to him about his daughter, Marianne. The secretary had been unable to place the name. She'd smiled in embarrassment and apologized as she'd checked the records, saying that she'd worked at the school only since the beginning of the year. Cadogan had gone a little cold inside at this, although he couldn't have said why; there were hundreds of pupils here, and it was a natural and human mistake.

Out of all Marianne's teachers, no others were scheduled for duty that afternoon. He'd been walking out through the empty hall, the letter still in his hand, when he'd heard someone tentatively calling his name; he'd turned and there she'd been, walking towards him. Apparently she'd stayed on for a while to catch up on some preparatory work for the new term, and had been about to leave when she'd spotted and half recognized him. They'd never met before. She seemed absurdly young to be a secondary-school teacher, but then, so many of them did nowadays. They weren't so young that they couldn't do the job. He was simply getting older.

He'd never been in one of Marianne's classrooms before, either. It had a battered but pleasant look, unlike those in his own memories of school, which he recalled as one long spell in jail. He finished picking his way through the short essay and then lowered it again, saying, "Why exactly did you want to see me?"

"Well," Isabella Weber said, "among other things, I thought that we might talk about Marianne's writing."

He looked down at his daughter's script. "Seems clear enough to me."

"I don't mean the quality of the work or the way it looks, I mean the content."

"Well," Cadogan said, "that's easy enough. It's something that happened to her a few weeks ago. She got herself stranded on the beach, and someone brought her home." He saw Miss Weber's look, and in fact had been anticipating it; he said, "Wait a minute. You're thinking that she made this up and that it's a cry for help, or something? No. It's factual. It's exactly what happened."

Miss Weber said, "It's not only this. If it was only this, I wouldn't worry."

"Worry?" he said, sliding the paper back across the table to her. "What's to worry about?"

"We could have gone through it all on parents' evening, if only you'd been here."

"Yeah, well, I know about that," he said. "I work hard and I work late. I'm building up my own business and it doesn't leave much time. I'm not making excuses, but that's just the way it is."

"Is the business going well?"

"Yeah," he said darkly, "it's a success. It gets better and better."

"But you don't see much of Marianne."

She was watching him intently and, young as she was, she was making him nervous. Perhaps it was because of her profession. He knew of plenty of grown men who became awkward boys again in the presence of schoolteachers. Or perhaps it was even simply because she was a woman—for him, after Anneliese, that alone might be enough.

He said, "Slow down, here. What's this all about? I thought you were supposed to have asked me to come in today so that you could tell me something."

"You're a one-parent family, isn't that right, Mr. Cadogan?"

He looked around the room, for nothing in particular. "Oh, wait a minute," he said. "A one-parent family? Whose book did *that* come out of?"

"It's just an expression."

"It's not just an expression, it's a label. And you can keep it. I work bloody hard for Marianne, and she wants for nothing."

"Except a father's interest."

He leaned forward, starting to get angry now, knowing that he shouldn't, but feeling it rise in him anyway. He said, "And what am I?"

"I don't know, Mr. Cadogan. What are you?"

There was a moment in which they faced each other across the table, neither trying to push the confrontation further nor back down; Cadogan stung to something approaching belligerence, and Isabella Weber betraying only a flicker of her own nervousness by the involuntary twitch of a muscle close to her eye.

She really did seem *very* young.

He sat back. "Jesus," he said wearily, as if it was nothing personal against her, but she ought to realize that her grasp of the truths of this world was less than complete. "This, on top of everything else. I'm going to be making a complaint."

"That's entirely up to you. But right now can we please talk about Marianne?"

"What's to be said? She's got a roof over her head, she's fed, she's happy. And if I don't see so much of her, it's only because she's out with her friends all the time."

"Can you name any of them?"

"No, I can't name any of them. You see them every day, you tell me."

"As far as I know, Marianne hasn't any friends. I know that

some of the other girls have tried to include her, but she has
a tendency to stay on her own."

"I've got to go," Cadogan said, checking his watch. He had
nothing lined up, but the teacher wouldn't know that. "Make
your point."

"I think she's desperately unhappy and you can't or won't
see it, that's my point. I was hoping that together we might be
able to do something about it."

"I'll tell you what, Miss Weber," Cadogan said. "You concern yourself with my daughter's education. Anything beyond
that is my department and I can assure you, we've got no
problems that we can't sort out on our own. We're a close
family," he added, getting to his feet now. "There's nothing she
can't tell me. We talk. We talk all the time. I get a fucking
headache just *listening* to her, sometimes."

His voice had risen in volume and he realized, almost too
late, that he was looming over the teacher and close to shouting. She hadn't moved or dropped her gaze, but her face had
grown pale and tense, and he turned away from her because
this was nothing like what he'd intended at all.

He said, "We're off somewhere this weekend. It's all arranged. There's nothing wrong that I can't fix, so stick to your
schoolbooks, Miss Weber."

He didn't look at her again, and she didn't speak.

"Nice to have met you," he said.

CHAPTER 18

"Where's Marianne?" he said. "Is she here?"

He'd driven straight home, almost. This hadn't been his
plan, but his original plan for the day was now something that
he could only vaguely remember. On the way back he'd gone

down one of the lanes that led to the beach and then, leaving his car by the row of three cottages at its end, had walked on to reach the shore. He'd had some mad idea that he'd be able to find her but once he was out there, he'd had to concede the impracticality of it. The empty coast stretched in either direction. The wind had whipped at him, and even as he'd called her name he'd known that he was wasting his time. So then he'd driven back up the lane and through the village, which stood on a muddy inlet with a few boats high and dry on tidal moorings; some were almost wrecks, others were fair-size fishing boats half-tilted onto their sides like dead dinosaurs waiting for the mud to rise and claim them. He passed Mrs. Healey's house on the end of its row, neat and buttoned-down with its foot-wide strip of garden behind iron railings, then he passed the parish hall and the little mission church with the area's one public telephone standing outside, and then he was on the final track down to the saltings and home.

Mrs. Healey had emerged to meet him. Marianne's dog was over on his usual outdoor spot, lying with his head between his paws.

In answer to his question, Mrs. Healey said, "Marianne's out. And there's something you've got to see to before she gets back."

Cadogan was about to charge on past her and into the house, but he stopped and said with a sudden intensity, "You've seen her friends around, haven't you?"

"If she's got any, she never brings them home. Are you going to listen to me or not?"

"I pay her attention. You've seen us. It doesn't matter how busy I am, I'm always there for her, aren't I? How could anybody say that I'm not?"

"Mr. Cadogan!" she said, more sharply and loudly than she'd ever spoken to him before.

"What?"

"Your own dog's dead in front of you, and you haven't even noticed *that*."

For a moment, he didn't understand her. It sounded almost as if she'd said something about the dog being dead. He looked, and Rudi was lying where he always did. Just lying, that was all. Nothing unusual.

Not moving.

He went over and crouched down before Rudi, and he spoke the dog's name, and saw then that it was true. He wasn't breathing. Gently, he put his hand under Rudi's head and lifted, and the head came up with the unresponsive weight of a bowling ball. The dog's eyes were half-closed and dull, and there was fresh blood around his nostrils that looked as if it had been delicately touched-in there with a makeup brush. About the equivalent of one burst bubble of the stuff on each side, no more.

Mrs. Healey said, "He came outside just after Marianne left. He lay down in the usual place, and that was it. I don't know how long he's been like this."

He laid the dog's head down carefully, without jarring it.

"Oh, Rudi," he said wearily, and sat down on the bare ground beside him.

Poor old dog. Age indeterminate, breed equally so, but even-tempered and faithful and ever eager to please. He was about to run a hand over Rudi's coat but then he checked the gesture in midair and let his hand fall. All of a sudden, his heart felt like a heavy stone. He couldn't remember a time that he'd shown the animal any affection at all. Some nights, he couldn't exactly remember when, he'd maybe patted Rudi's head in passing and said a few words. And that was about it. He'd longed for his own dog, when he was a boy. But that boy was someone whom Rudi would never now get to know.

He felt as if he'd been hit from an unexpected direction. Rudi lost at sea, that was one thing, almost a convenient completion of the process, the final act of slipping from Cadogan's mind where there had never been much of a place for him anyway. But Rudi dead before him, that was something else. He felt a complex weight of guilt that he couldn't explain, and he knew that the death of the animal was but a tiny part of it. They'd gone to the shelter looking for a puppy, but he was the one that Marianne had chosen; and he'd responded with the utter devotion found in so many rescued dogs, to the extent that there had been a time when Marianne only had to walk out of a room for him to scramble to his feet and follow her.

Mrs. Healey said, "You'll have to move him before Marianne gets home."

God, yes. Breaking it to her was going to be hard enough; he wouldn't want her to see the dog like this. Getting back up onto his feet and dusting himself down, he said, "I suppose I'd better bury him."

"Not around here, you can't," Mrs. Healey said. "There's a place you can take him to."

"Oh," Cadogan said. But he didn't move and just stood there, looking at Rudi, until Mrs. Healey said, "I'll see if there's a sheet or something," and went back into the house.

It made sense, he supposed. You couldn't dig a proper grave around here; the soil was too thin and the sea was too close. The tide might suck his body out of the earth and then spit it back onto land somewhere further along the coast. She might even find it as she walked along. Waiting for Mrs. Healey to return, Cadogan ran a hand through his hair. He still felt guilty. About the only real attention that he'd ever paid to Rudi over the past twelve months had been to step over him whenever he was lying in the way. Well, it was too late to improve on that now.

Too late.

He'd let all kinds of things slide. He could see that it had been happening over a long period, now . . . the months since he'd walked out on Anneliese, in fact. Months? It was years. That showed how much of a grip he had. The idea had been to put together a fast and bright new life among the ruins of the old, but it hadn't been that easy. Somehow he'd become stuck in the rut of trying.

And in all that time, he was beginning to realize, he'd been steadily losing sight of his daughter and it had needed some squirt of a teacher barely out of her training bra to pinpoint the fact. Just like the dog, he'd come to notice her only when she got in the way.

Perhaps, he thought suddenly, Rudi's dying was a sign. A warning shot, even.

Mrs. Healey was emerging from the house now, unfolding a

peach-colored bedsheet that he'd never seen before. They spread the sheet out by Rudi and then Cadogan rolled him over onto it, after which the two of them picked up the corners and carried the bundle hammock-fashion around to the Vauxhall. It was heavy—*a dead weight*, was the thought that Cadogan was doing his best to avoid. When they'd lifted it onto the back seat of the car, they folded over the spare material to make everything look neat.

"I wrote down where you have to go," Mrs. Healey said, and handed him a piece of paper torn from the memo pad in the kitchen. It had about a dozen lines of her writing on it, in the pale blue ink she always used for shopping lists.

"Thanks," Cadogan said, and he closed the car's rear door. As he was walking around to the driver's seat, he added, "Don't mention this to Marianne, all right?"

"What if she asks?"

"Just tell her Rudi's with me. I'll talk to her when I get back. I know I ask you to do a lot of things for her. But if this is anybody's job, it's got to be mine."

Mrs. Healey nodded.

The Vauxhall's engine was still warm and, for once, it started for him on the first try.

Cadogan drove back through the village and then inland, on minor roads through green fields until he picked up the main route about five miles beyond the village. This was the way that he followed almost every morning, and he covered it without having to think too much. His briefcase and his parts catalogues were on the passenger seat beside him. Just under the dash was the bracket where the car phone had been, until he'd had to let it go back to the renters.

A Nissan showroom, one of those high-tech modern buildings with glass walls and a big parking lot and a dozen flagpoles, marked the end of the countryside and the beginning of what wasn't quite the outskirts of town. There were fields here still, but there were also stretches of derelict industrial ground served by spurs of brand-new road that led, as yet, to nowhere. Car-culture land, waiting for the tarmac and prefab warehouses that would give it all some purpose.

When he'd passed the motorway intersection he referred to Mrs. Healey's directions, but then after veering over the center line a couple of times he had to pull off the road and into a lay-by so that he could look at them properly. Her writing was cramped and backward-sloping, and hard to make out. From the order in which she'd explained everything, she was clearly no driver herself. Two lorries were already in the lay-by, and a third joined them as he was reading. As he pulled out to rejoin the traffic he saw that a small white van serving as a snack wagon was doing business at the far end, having been screened from him by the two sixteen-wheelers. The van didn't look big enough to stand up in, but a hand-painted sign leaning against one corner read SEATS INSIDE.

Two miles further on, an arrow pointed him along a lane. The lane was hardly more than a dirt track, but it was hard packed and full of potholes and obviously saw heavy use. On top of the hill at the lane's end he could see the tall aluminum stack of the disposal point, the lower buildings screened by trees. White smoke was coming out of the top of the stack and dispersing itself into the sky.

He felt his heart sink. It was an incinerator plant. But then again, what else could he have been expecting?

At the top of the lane there was a chain-link fence with a gate, and the gate had been propped open with a traffic cone. Beyond the gate was a weighbridge with a sign that read ALL VEHICLES MUST REPORT TO THE SITE MANAGER, but there was nobody in the weighbridge cabin. Cadogan drove on over the metal deck, which clanked under his front wheels and then again at the back, and then turned into the open area beyond.

He stopped the car and got out. There didn't seem to be anyone around. He could hear muffled sounds of machinery and a hum like that of generators, but he could see no one. He wasn't sure what to do next.

The asphalt on which he stood had a slick and greasy feel. Over against the boundary wall, seagulls were picking and arguing over domestic rubbish that had been bulldozed into a more or less compact hill. The incinerator plant towered above them, bigger than a bus garage and with the same kind of wide, tall entranceway; as Cadogan crossed over and went inside, he felt as if he was entering some oversized prop from a tale about giants.

A deep trench—thirty, perhaps even forty feet to the bottom—ran the entire length of the building. Compactor rams stood ready to clear it when it had been filled, pushing everything down to the open furnace at its end. The trench was about half-filled already, with sloping sides made up out of every imaginable kind of garbage. About halfway along, a van had reversed in with its doors close to the edge and a man was heaving out tied plastic bags and throwing them over. They tumbled down, end-over-end, and as some of them tumbled they split. The air was stale. Down in the trench itself, the air would almost certainly stink to the point of unbreathability.

Cadogan walked towards the van's driver. Overhead there was a crane track with a grab running the length of the trench, but like the weighbridge, it was unmanned. Another sack landed and split with a thud like the blow of a boxing glove. In the vastness of the interior, the sound was almost nothing.

As soon as he was within earshot of the van driver, Cadogan called out, "Is there anyone in charge around here?"

The man stopped, barely. He was wearing blue overalls and heavy gloves.

"I dunno," he said, and then he reached into the van for another bag. "Ask at the office."

The site office turned out to be a portakabin around the corner; nothing much, but at least it was on a more human scale than the rest of the building. There was a radio playing inside and at first Cadogan wasn't sure that his knock had been heard, but then a brawny man in a greasy pullover opened the door and climbed down.

"I've got a dog in the car," Cadogan said.

"Hope it's a ratter," the man said. "We could use one."

"I mean, it's, er . . ." Somehow, he couldn't bring himself to say the word *dead*, but the man seemed to pick up on his meaning.

"For disposal?" he said. "How big?"

Hesitantly, Cadogan held his hands apart to indicate Rudi's size.

"He's in a sheet," he added.

"Yeah," the man said. "Go on."

Cadogan glanced back in the direction of the entranceway, and the trench beyond. "In there?" he said.

"That's how we do it if you want to bring him here," the man said. "I mean, we're not one of your fancy pet cemeteries or anything. Go for that if you want. But it's all going to be the same to your animal now."

Cadogan hesitated. The man was right, of course, but ... God, what a way to end up, even for a dog. Stiff-legged and turfed into a pit of filth, to lie buried under it until the furnace was ready; no headstone, no ashes, just down there with the baked-bean cans and the vegetable waste and with the daylight gone forever.

But what was the choice? Anything else would cost money. And as the man had said, it would all be the same to Rudi now.

Cadogan said, "You couldn't do it for me, could you?"

The man looked at him without expression. Then he nodded, and took the car keys that Cadogan was offering.

Cadogan turned around and walked away as the man overrevved the Vauxhall and drove it into the plant like a stock car. There was a squeal of tires that echoed from the huge interior as he braked and slammed the gears into reverse. If Marianne asked, he'd tell her something other than this. He wasn't sure what, yet, but he'd make up something comforting and when she asked if the dog had gone to heaven, as he was almost sure that she would, he'd say yes. When Cadogan had been Marianne's age, he'd believed in heaven too.

Sometimes, he wished that he could believe in it still.

There was a big wagon coming in over the weighbridge now, a skip carrier with a full load of what looked like metal scrap. Cadogan stuck his hands in his pockets and watched as the middle-aged, heavy-set driver climbed down and pressed a buzzer by the window on the weighmaster's office. A bell like a fire alarm rang out loudly. The driver's mate was climbing down on the other side of the cab, a skinny teenaged boy in work gloves that made his hands appear to be several sizes too big for his body; and the odd thing was that the boy was looking straight at Cadogan, and he seemed to expect to be recognized.

He waved and called out, "Mr. Cadogan! Remember me? Brian Fishwick. I used to bring your milk on Saturdays."

Cadogan shaded his eyes and peered at him. "Of course you did," he said, not remembering him at all but not about to show it.

"I'm working for the council now," the boy said, walking over to him. He indicated the driver who was standing by the weighmaster's office. "I'm down at the skips with me uncle Billy."

"Glad to hear it," Cadogan said. Uncle Billy stuck his thumb on the bellpush again, and this time held it down for a dozen seconds or more.

When the ringing had stopped, the boy said, "As soon as I saw you then, it clicked. I saw your little girl the other day and I've been trying to place her ever since."

"You saw Marianne?" Cadogan said. "Where?"

"Well, that's what I thought I'd better tell you. Have you ever heard of someone around your way called Ryan?"

"What about him?" Cadogan said.

"He lives near the beach on his own. He's a bit creepy. There were all kinds of stories told about him when I was at school."

"I know the man. What of him?"

"Well, your Marianne was down at his yard."

"When?"

"Two or three days back."

"Doing what?"

"Nothing I could see, but she was there. I just wondered if you knew about it."

"No," Cadogan said. "I didn't."

"I didn't think so. He tried to look surprised and he was acting like he'd warned her off, but she didn't look worried." With a nod towards the driver, Brian Fishwick added, "Uncle Billy said I should tell you."

"Well," Cadogan said, "now you've told me. Thanks."

"Even if half the stories aren't true ... there's got to be *something* behind them, hasn't there?"

Cadogan's Vauxhall came up alongside with a skid -like a boy on a slide of pavement ice. The engine was left running as the man from the office got out and, leaving the driver's door open, headed over towards the weighbridge. The back seat was now empty.

"Keep yer fuckin' hair on, Billy," the site man was saying pleasantly. "You haven't got that much to spare."

Cadogan got into his car and drove away.

Leaving the disposal plant behind, he drove like a machine. He was doing everything right behind the wheel, but he felt dead and somehow cut adrift on the inside. But then suddenly it all caught up with him, and he had to pull off the road. He plunged his face into his hands and he knew that he was crying, but it came out more like a series of barks of surprise. He beat himself hard on the side of the head with his closed fist and then he sat there, gripping the wheel. The blow had left him with a stupid pain that wouldn't go away, but at least he felt back in control of himself again. He'd never realized it until now, but he was operating dangerously close to the edge. He felt as if he was being pushed towards it, scooped up and carried forward as if on a tide of bulldozer refuse back there by the pit.

He set out to drive the rest of the way home as sedately as any old lady. But as soon as he hit the straight open road, he began to pick up speed.

CHAPTER 19

It hadn't been one of the great picnics of all time. She'd been bitten by bugs and she'd found some birdwatchers occupying one of her favorite spots on the hill. The cake had been stale and she hadn't taken enough of it. The only yogurt left in the refrigerator had been black cherry flavor, which looked and tasted like pink disinfectant. Marianne had never met anyone who liked black cherry yogurt and yet she found one in every pack of four, without fail. She was convinced that they stuck them in only because there was no other way to get rid of the stuff. Like when they did selection packs of specialty tea, and there was *always* a tin of Earl Grey, which was the worst tea in the world.

As she was dumping the papers and the rubbish out of her rucksack into the bin under the kitchen sink, she noticed that Rudi's water bowl had been washed out and stood upside down on the draining board. She refilled it, and set it down in the usual place. The cover was gone from his beanbag, as well; Mrs. Healey must have decided to put it in the laundry.

Marianne had expected to find Rudi here when she hadn't seen him outside, but she knew that when the beanbag was uncovered like this he wouldn't lie on it. Sometimes he'd sneak upstairs and lie on one of the beds instead, almost invariably her own, but he always looked tense and guilty when she found him doing it.

She found Mrs. Healey in the hallway. She was putting on her coat, getting ready to leave. Mrs. Healey always wore the same tan raincoat with a headscarf out of doors, the same blue nylon coverall inside. It might be high summer with a temperature in the eighties, but the raincoat stayed on.

There was something in her manner now that Marianne found odd. But she couldn't have said why.

Mrs. Healey said, "Your father will be home soon. He has some things he wants to tell you."

Miss Weber, Marianne thought, her heart dropping like a safe. Miss Weber had obviously told him something unwelcome. But what? Surely there could be no worse feeling than that of being in big trouble and not having even an idea of the crime.

Mrs. Healey said, "I have to leave now. But what I wanted to say first was . . . not everything's always as dark as it seems. Sometimes you look back on the worst times and realize, that's exactly the moment when it all began to get better."

She set off for home without saying any more.

Well, great. That *really* told Marianne where she stood. Now she didn't know whether to expect bad news, or good news, or good news out of bad, or what. She wanted to grow up right then. She wanted her father to come home and find this grown woman waiting and finally realize that the days of gnomic utterances and deferred truths were over.

She went out and called to Rudi, but it seemed he'd wandered off somewhere. Wherever he'd gone, it wouldn't be far. On her way back in through the kitchen she checked the oven and, as she expected, she found one of Mrs. Healey's all-purpose unidentifiable casseroles running on a low heat inside.

The living room was huge with a high ceiling and almost no furniture. There had been a walnut sideboard and an elegant but threadbare sofa, but both of these had disappeared one day around the time of the difficulties involving the car. Marianne switched on the TV, and sat on her floor cushion with the remote as she watched *Blockbusters*. Every now and again when the questions got boring she would take a quick wander through the channels, but she always came back. Outside it was beginning to get dark, but she didn't switch on any lights.

She hadn't heard the car draw up.

She didn't know how long he'd been watching her from the doorway.

Marianne jumped a little when she glanced over and realized that he was there. He was a dark cutout shape on the dark side of the room with the gray fading light of the hallway behind him. He was just standing there.

She said, "You gave me a surprise."

But as soon as he spoke, she realized that the wrong was something worse than she'd been able even to imagine.

Her father said, "Your mother was a little tramp. And now I'm beginning to realize that perhaps you're no better. I'm trying to hold it all together and I ask for your support, and what do I get? You ignore everything I say and do the opposite of what I ask. I don't know what I'm going to do with you, Marianne. All I know is that right at this moment I'm very angry with you. I might even hurt you, and I wouldn't want to do that. So go upstairs. Go in your room. I'm going to fix your Mr. Ryan for good."

"What are you going to do?" she said.

He moved aside from the doorway, to give her space to pass.

"I think you heard me," he said.

On the TV, the audience began to applaud and the music began to play. Cadogan was moving towards the telephone by the window, and Marianne took a few hesitant steps around her side of the room in order to maintain the distance between them. Now he was picking up the phone, and she was by the door.

"He's done nothing to anyone," she said.

But Cadogan didn't answer her. He dialed a three-figure code, waited for a few moments, and then said, "Have you a number for the local police, please?"

"No!" Marianne said, and he flashed her a look of warning.

"No!" she said again, and she turned and dashed out.

She went down the hall, through the kitchen, straight out of the house by the open back door. She could hear him crashing through after her.

"Marianne!" he was shouting. "Come back here! It's too late, there's nothing you can do!"

But Marianne was lighter and faster and she cut through the air like a switch. She ran across the open ground, barely seeming to touch it. She bounded up onto the sea wall and kept on going. He couldn't follow her this way in the car and, by God, she'd be sure that he would never catch her on foot.

She heard him calling her name.

But she didn't look back.

She kept on running.

CHAPTER 20

When she got to Ryan's place, breathless, gasping so much that even the roots of her teeth seemed to hurt and with a stitch in her side like a long, long needle, it was to find the padlock on the gate and no signs of life around the yard. She'd run, she'd walked, she'd picked up and run further. In all the distance that she'd covered to get there, she hadn't stopped once.

And for nothing.

She crossed her arms over her chest and crouched down with her back to the gate. It banged inwards on its latch about a quarter of an inch when she let her weight fall against it. Her legs felt weak, and her heart was in overdrive. Where was he? And how could she warn him now? She didn't even have any paper to leave him a note.

She hadn't seen him all day. Not around the yard, not on the beach, not from any of her usual lookout points on the high ground. It was almost as if he'd gone away. But he couldn't have done that. This was his home. Where else would he go?

Wearily, she got to her feet. She didn't feel as if she was being much of a friend. Perhaps she could find a soft stone and write BEWARE on the gate for him to find when he got back . . . but beware of what? Beware of my father, beware of the police, watch out for the fact that they're talking about you? When it came to specifics, she was stuck.

But at least if he wasn't around, there was nothing that they could do to him right now.

Marianne looked down the lane. A long way away, almost as far out as the point where the lane met the road, a figure was walking in the fading light of the day. She had no doubt at all that it was him, probably just off the bus and heading for home. She waved, but there was no response; he probably didn't see her. So then she started to run towards him.

Before she'd covered any distance, she saw the lights of a police car making the turn into the lane.

She stopped, ran on, stopped again and called his name, but he didn't hear her. He was looking back as the police car came up behind him. The knapsack was on his shoulder, but that was all the luggage he had. The patrol car pulled in alongside him and two uniformed men got out. While one of them was talking to him, the other walked around the car. There was one man before him and one behind him now, so that if things started to go wrong he couldn't turn and run.

But he didn't try. One of the policemen indicated for him to get into the back of the car, and he went without argument or protest. Despite Ryan's lack of resistance, Marianne could see clearly that one of the officers placed his hand on the top of his head and pushed him down firmly into the vehicle.

The policemen got in, they slammed the doors, the car made a turn in the narrow lane and then sped back towards the road.

Marianne was left alone. No one had noticed her.

With the car gone, the lane was empty.

She turned, and slowly started the long walk home.

He was waiting.

He hadn't switched on the lights and he hadn't switched off the TV. He was sitting by the phone with the window behind him, and didn't look as if he'd moved since he made the call. That must have been an hour ago, almost.

She stood in the doorway and said, "What did you do to him?"

There was no reply. Unless silence counted as a reply of a kind.

She said, "He never hurt anybody, what did you do?"

"There's no way you can understand," Cadogan said. She couldn't see his face in the shadows, now. "I've done what was necessary and I did it for you."

"You didn't do it for me," she said, surprised that her voice was firm although the rest of her was almost trembling with anger. "You've never done *anything* for me. It's always been for you, like when you brought me here. I was happy before, but this is just like being dead. I don't know what she did to you ... but I bet you asked for it and if I knew what it was, then I'd do the same thing as well."

She was almost shouting by the time she'd finished, determined to get it said but rushing because Cadogan was rising now; and as he came to his feet she turned and she ran. She hit the stairs and they slowed her; he was coming up behind her taking them two at a time, and as she reached the top he almost managed to catch her by the hair.

But she could move. She always could; even at the age of three she'd been a demon to pin down. Cadogan was bigger and stronger, but clumsy. He couldn't turn as fast and he couldn't dodge things. A table went down with a crash behind her. There was a bolt on the door of her room; nothing elaborate, just a thumbslide that was a part of the old-fashioned black metal latch, but she'd tried it and it worked. The bathroom was closer and had a real lock, but a bathroom was no good for a long siege. She was going to get inside and lock herself in and then stay silent through every effort to get her out until he was *really* sorry.

And if that didn't happen . . . well, what then would be the point of ever coming out at all?

She dived into her bedroom and turned to slam the door. But he was closer than she'd expected, only inches behind her. He was already coming through and she squealed because it was too late but then she'd started to throw the door shut anyway and it hit him; it must have hit his foot because it rebounded like a ricochet and her last clear memory for a brief period of time was of a hundred pounds of solid Victorian timber springing back to hit her squarely in the face.

She wasn't aware of the pain. She wasn't aware of falling. The force of the blow seemed to knock her a step outside of herself and the next sensation to come through was of being lifted.

He was hugging her. He was saying something. He was saying he was sorry as he carried her over to put her on the bed.

That was about when it started to hurt.

All of one side of her head felt as if it had swelled to the size of a pumpkin and was about to burst. She tried to raise a hand to touch it, but didn't dare. Her bedside light had been switched on but her father wasn't there; the door stood open and she could hear the sounds of running water from the bathroom.

He returned a few moments later, folding and refolding a damp washcloth. In the light from the reading lamp, he looked pale and scared.

As he moved towards her, she pushed herself up on the bed and away from him. The pillows behind her rode up the headboard as she squirmed back. He stopped where he was.

"Oh, God, Marianne," he said. "I'm so sorry. What can I say?"

She glowered at him. She said nothing.

Hesitantly, as one might approach some spooked and wary animal, he moved to sit on the end of the bed. Her radar tracked him every inch of the way, but she didn't move. He said, "I know it's not like it was. But that's not because I wanted it this way. Things happened and . . . this is how it all turned out. I wish I could explain it all to you. . . ." He started to reach out as if to smooth back a strand of her hair but she flinched, and he gave up the attempt.

"I don't know," he said, and after looking around for a moment he put the damp cloth down on the table by the lamp, where she'd be able to reach it for herself. "You may even be grownup enough to handle it now. But I'm not sure that *I* am. All I knew was that I had to protect you, even if it cost me everything else. But I don't seem to have done a very good job in any department, do I?"

Downstairs, the phone began to ring.

He said, "You're going to be looking for him, so I've got to tell you this now. Rudi's died. It didn't hurt him and it was all very peaceful, he just closed his eyes and went to sleep. I was trying to work out some better way of breaking it to you, but now I have to tell you like this."

The phone was still ringing. "That's probably the police again," he said. "I'll have to go and talk to them. This *is* all for you, you know. I'm sure you don't think so, but it is."

He got to his feet, but reluctantly. Marianne, knowing that silence was her best weapon now, continued to glare at him and say nothing. He paused and almost said something more, but then he abandoned the attempt and turned to go, waving it down and shaking his head as if to concede that he had no better case to make than the one he'd already given her.

She could hear him going downstairs. She tried to rise, and it hurt. She didn't move for a few moments but that hurt, as well. But she wasn't going to use the washcloth compress, as a matter of principle.

She could hear him talking on the phone as she tiptoed along to the bathroom, but she couldn't make out what was being said. Under the stark light of the bathroom's unshaded bulb, she tilted the brass shaving mirror to study her face.

The edge of the door had caught her at a three-quarter angle.

There was a cut on her brow and a big raw skid on her cheek-bone directly below that. The entire area was starting to stretch tight and swell but there was no bruising, as yet.

Before going back she stopped by the top of the stairs and tried to listen, but there was nothing much to hear. Whoever was on the other end of the line seemed to be doing most of the talking now. When she heard the phone being hung up, she hurried back to her room as quickly as she dared.

Silently, she closed the door. The bolt slid across with a click after some hard pressing that threatened to leave her with a permanent dent in the end of her thumb. She listened for a while after that, but nothing seemed to be happening.

Then she pulled her linen chest over and set it behind the door, and piled a lot of other stuff on top of that to make a barricade.

He came back and knocked gently and called her name. She sat watching the door, and didn't respond. He tried the doorknob then, but of course to no effect. And then he went away.

A couple of hours later she had to go to the bathroom again, but she treated the visit like a raid and then didn't pull the chain so that the plumbing wouldn't betray her presence. Back in her room she rebuilt the barricade, and then pulled the cover off her bed and dragged it over. Some bolts you could open from the outside with a screwdriver or a penny, she knew; it was supposed to be a safety feature to guard against the possibility of children or old people getting themselves locked in. The locks on the toilets at her school were all like that. She couldn't tell if the one on her bedroom door could be opened in the same way, but she wasn't going to take the chance.

She slept on the cover, after folding it double to make a bed.

This way, he couldn't enter and look down on her without her knowing.

CHAPTER 21

He came again in the morning. He tapped on the panels and called to her, but she lay still and wouldn't reply.

He said, "I've got to go, now. I'm going into town."

And then he waited.

After a while, he added, "They're expecting me first thing, so I have to leave right away."

Another wait.

He said, "I'm not going to tell them that you went out to the place where he lives unless I have to, do you understand that? If they don't ask me straight out, we can pretend that part of it never happened. Be good for Mrs. Healey when she gets here, will you? I've called her and explained. We'll have a real talk later."

Still no response.

"Marianne?"

She sat with her back to the linen chest, waiting for him to leave. When she heard him go she stayed there a while longer, almost as if she lacked the will or the energy to move.

She'd been thinking about Rudi. About how he was gone, and how she felt nothing. It was as if she'd shed her tears and said her good-byes already, days and weeks before when she'd first thought him drowned. He'd come back, but that had just been—what was the phrase?—borrowed time. A few last hugs, a few more afternoons in the sun, but all the way through it his bus had been waiting.

Her father had sounded rattled, uncertain. And had that been a hint of despair in the way that he'd called out her name at the end?

If it had, then, good.

She'd slept in her clothes so now she changed them and, in her clean underwear, went back to the bathroom for another look in the mirror.

The side of her face was more spectacular now. She had a real black eye. It looked even worse on the mirror's magnifying side and so she kept turning it over to compare the effects. It wasn't like the black eyes they got in her comics. It was bruised and ugly.

While she was downstairs getting her red rucksack, she picked up a box of sugar-coated cereal and a carton of milk and took them back up to her room. As she picked out the best things to pack, she munched on the dry squares and took swigs of milk to wash them down. She was going to need to keep her strength up. The problem with the red rucksack was that it was fine for a day's picnic but too small for anything more ambitious; but then again, anything much bigger would be a problem for her to carry.

From her bedroom, she went down to the cellar.

Her kit was almost complete now, but there were just a few more items that she needed. The post office savings book in her name was only one of them. When she'd finished in the cellar, she locked up after herself and returned the key to its place inside the pendulum clock.

She put on her coat, and slung the rucksack over her shoulder. She was ready. She paused for a minute in the hallway; the house felt achingly empty.

There was nothing here that she'd miss, not now.

Then with a sense of leaving only ghosts behind her, she set off.

CHAPTER 22

"I'm just going to run through this, right?" He'd introduced himself as Detective Inspector Tomelty when he'd ushered Cadogan into the interview room about a half-hour before, but Cadogan had heard one of the other officers calling him Frank. He seemed well-spoken but with the common touch. Earnest. To the point. He wore a gray suit and a tie, but his manner wasn't too formal. He reminded Cadogan of some of the department managers that he knew, family men and weekend footballers. He had a form pad on the table before him, on which he'd been making careful handwritten notes as they'd talked. But it hadn't been like an interrogation. More like an ordinary conversation, if anything.

Tomelty went on. "Stop me if it gets too wide of the mark at any point."

"Right," Cadogan said. He folded his hands on the table before him as Tomelty looked over his notes.

"Ryan O'Donnell brought your daughter home from the beach on the twenty-fifth. She was soaked and he said she'd been in the sea. Your suspicions weren't aroused at that time."

"No reason to be."

"Did he say how he'd come to be alone with your daughter?"

"I didn't actually see him or speak to him then. My housekeeper did."

"Did he explain it to her?"

"Not that I know. She said he seemed anxious, and he didn't want to hang around."

"Perhaps because he was wet, as well?"

"I suppose so."

Tomelty was nodding, as if everything was fitting together just the way that he'd expect. He said, "And the next time you saw him was . . . ?"

"Two days later, about half a mile from the house."

"But you don't remember the time of day."

"No."

"And you weren't suspicious then, even though you now think that he was probably watching the place."

"No."

"How did you know who he was?"

Cadogan opened his mouth, and closed it again. Tomelty's delivery hadn't varied, but there was a sudden sense of something amiss in the air and Cadogan didn't want to risk a stumble. His mind raced, looking for the snag.

Tomelty looked up from his notes, and said, "If you hadn't actually seen him yourself, the first time that he came out to the house."

"Everyone around here knows him," Cadogan said. "From a distance."

The DI kept his eyes on Cadogan for perhaps a fraction of a second longer than was comfortable. Then he looked down at his notes again, and ran his ballpoint down the lines to find his place.

"Then around nine o'clock on the night before last," Tomelty said, "you heard a sound and went outside, where you saw the same man running away. You reckon he'd been trying to climb in through a window."

"That's how it looked."

"Any idea for what purpose?"

"Well, you tell me. He was on the same side of the house as my daughter's bedroom."

"You got a clear look at him?"

"Very clear."

"Was there a moon that night?"

Was there? Cadogan said, "Enough of one."

"And you're positive that it was Ryan O'Donnell."

"One hundred percent."

"Right," Tomelty said, setting his ballpoint down on top of the pad and nodding to another officer who'd just looked in and made some kind of signal over Cadogan's head. "Just come with me for a moment."

"Are we finished?"

"Not yet."

Tomelty led the way out of the interview room. There was a waiting area outside with a few hard chairs and a lot of traffic passing through—people carrying file boxes, an overall-clad painter with his buckets. Cadogan followed Tomelty out of the waiting area and down a quieter back corridor.

Tomelty waved to someone as they passed one of the open offices. There seemed to be a move of some kind going on. Cadogan was feeling nervous, but not too much so. He'd be glad when it was over, that was all. It wasn't exactly as if he'd *lied*, he was thinking . . . he'd just leaned on the facts to make them fit the truth a little better. When a man with the reputation of Ryan O'Donnell started to take too much of an interest in a girl of Marianne's age, action had to be taken. You didn't wait for a man like that to make his move, whatever the law might say. If you could skip the crime and get straight to the punishment, you'd save a lot of innocent grief for the same end result.

That made sense, didn't it? He'd given it a lot of thought. No one was going to be able to challenge him—apart from O'Donnell himself, whose credibility wasn't exactly going to cause many problems.

And whatever Marianne might think, he *was* doing it for her.

They went down some steps to a floor of painted concrete. There was a hum of air-conditioning somewhere nearby, and there were double doors like those of a loading bay that gave out onto daylight. They were marked FIRE EXIT and opened by crush bars from the inside. Tomelty leaned down on one of the bars, and the bolts lifted with a sound like the breech of a rifle being opened.

"This way," Tomelty said.

Less certain, now, Cadogan followed him outside.

The bright daylight made him wince. It was a vehicle yard, overlooked by offices on three sides and with a gated entrance-way at the far end. The entranceway was controlled by cameras and a stop light, and was closed. Four police vans and a dozen private cars were parked there.

In a line in the middle of the yard, watched over by a young officer in uniform, stood seven indistinguishable strangers.

Cadogan felt his heart sink. Was this right? They were going to ask him to identify Ryan O'Donnell.

And he couldn't, because he'd never actually seen the man.

Tomelty said, "Just walk down the line and pick him out for us. If you're not completely sure, don't guess."

Cadogan nodded. He'd better not panic. He'd never imagined that they'd do this to him. He'd assumed that they'd simply pull O'Donnell in and then take it from there.

But he walked to the end of the line, ready to start. He didn't know how he was going to handle this. The men stood and looked all ways other than at him. Their heights varied, a little. Their clothes varied. A little. Two of them had shaved that morning, the others hadn't. They were all different, of course, but in the most mundane and unspectacular ways. There really wasn't any useful basis for choosing between them.

Cadogan started to walk. Nobody met his eyes. They stared through him, they stared past him, they glanced over his head. One studied the ground, but straightened at a word from the uniformed officer in charge. Cadogan looked at this man with particular interest, hoping for some sign. But there was none.

Somebody coughed.

"Take all the time you need," Tomelty called to him.

Had he passed O'Donnell already? Cadogan was beginning to sweat, and he wondered if it showed.

He seemed, entirely by his own efforts and by anybody's definition, to have been thoroughly shafted, here.

He paused by the sixth man, as he had by all the others. He wanted to glance back at Tomelty just so that he could see what was on the policeman's face, but he didn't dare. It would be a giveaway. He could walk on to the end of the row and then he could walk back, and then unless divine inspiration should strike him somewhere along the way he'd have to take a chance. The odds weren't good, one in seven. But he didn't see what else he could do.

The sixth man met his gaze.

And held it.

Cadogan was the one who had to look away. He looked down at the man's hands. They were folded before him, but too tightly as if he was self-conscious about his tattoos. They were big hands, a working man's hands. Cadogan turned to look at Tomelty.

"This is the man," he said, not looking at him again.

"Right," Tomelty said, and indicated for the two of them to go back inside.

Walking back towards the interview room, Cadogan felt as if he'd just stepped away from the ultimate in white-knuckle rides. He took a deep breath, but not so that Tomelty would notice. For a few minutes there he'd been in serious danger, and not just of making himself look like a fool. But he'd come through. He'd kept his head, and it had turned out all right.

They sat at the same table in the same room as before. There was recording apparatus at the end against the wall, but they hadn't used it then and they didn't use it now. Tomelty asked Cadogan if he wanted coffee, Cadogan said no thanks. He waited as Tomelty glanced again through the handwritten notes that he'd made.

Then Tomelty said, "Now, if I get this typed up, you're ready to sign it as a full and accurate account of what happened."

"Yes," Cadogan said.

"And you've formally identified the man that you know to be Ryan O'Donnell."

Cadogan nodded.

Tomelty detached the top sheet of the pad and took one last look at the notes.

Then, slowly and deliberately and holding them up for Cadogan to see, he tore them from one end to the other and dropped them into the wastebasket under the table.

"I'm going to give you a while to sit and think this over," he said, rising. "Then I think we'd better start again."

Jennifer had just come from a final check of the borrowed office space that now stood empty; the terminals were out, the

National Police Computer link had been closed down by the systems manager, and the active part of the past week's investigation was now officially over. The drafted-in officers of the major inquiry team had gone back to their regular duties and those from Serious Crime had all headed off to new assignments. She saw Tomelty standing outside the interview room, looking pained and with his eyes screwed shut as he pinched the bridge of his nose like a man trying to fight off a migraine.

She said, "What's all the action this morning? I haven't seen a lineup in ages."

"I don't know," Tomelty said, exasperated. "I've just had a week's holiday, and I'm beginning to feel sorry I came back in."

"Why?"

He indicated the door behind him. "From in there I'm getting a drama in three acts about a local character with a certain reputation. And what scares me is that I'd probably gag it right down like a bad oyster if I didn't know for certain that it couldn't possibly have happened the way this man's telling it. I took him out in the yard, and he just identified the window cleaner. Ever have one of those days?"

"I have them all the time."

"Well, go down there and have a look at a man called Ryan O'Donnell, first. Then I'll tell you the best part."

She went along to the next door, and worked the slide that opened the spyhole. It wasn't actually a hole, but a panel of glass with mirrored stripes on the inside. A man was sitting alone in the room, hands folded on the table before him as he stared into space with almost bovine patience. Ryan O'Donnell. It was almost as if he'd trained himself to this kind of thing. Then Tomelty stepped aside from the next doorway as she moved along and took a look at Cadogan. Also alone, he was biting his thumbnail. He glanced sharply at the lookthrough, as if he'd sensed that she was there. Jennifer didn't flinch. She stared for a while longer, and then she closed the slide and moved away.

Two mirror-image men, in two mirror-image rooms.

"All right," she said to Tomelty. "What's the best part?"

"O'Donnell's supposed to have been spotted trying to climb

in through an eleven-year-old's bedroom window," Tomelty said. "Except that at the exact time when he was supposed to be doing this, he was also playing cards with one of the nurses and two of the patients on his old hospital ward fifteen miles away. Now, I've heard of schizophrenia, but that's fucking supernatural. He has to check in regularly with his community psychiatric nurse, and he's no car so he gets the last bus home. He's known to all the drivers. Meanwhile, I'm checking around and I find that there's a note on the girl in question in the at-risk register. It was placed there yesterday at the request of a teacher who'd just met her father."

"Yeah," Jennifer conceded. "That *is* pretty good."

"But even that's not the best part. You want to know why he goes back?"

"No," Jennifer said, "but you're going to tell me."

"It's one of the terms of his release," Tomelty said. "The place that he goes back to is a low-security unit attached to a high-security mental hospital. In which Ryan O'Donnell spent fifteen years for the murder of an eleven-year-old girl."

CHAPTER 23

It was late in the afternoon when she saw him. New rolling stock in the siding had given her somewhere to hide in the form of a wooden freight car with a sliding door. It wasn't too light and it wasn't too clean, but it provided her with cover whenever the wrong people came. She sat on the dusty floor and waited; didn't play, didn't read, didn't do anything other than bob her head out to check the landscape every now and again.

The sun was low. He was walking along the lane towards home like some weary pilgrim. A car had taken him away, but nothing had been provided for his return. It seemed to take forever. When he finally reached the yard gate, she saw him stop.

The gate had been kicked off its hinges, and hung at an angle like a broken drawbridge. Ryan stared at it, trying to take in the meaning of the sight. She expected him to go rushing onward then, but he didn't. He stepped carefully over the gate before he went through into the yard.

Nobody was inside there now. She'd been watching, so this was something that she knew. If it had been otherwise, she'd have run down to warn Ryan already.

The yard had been a mess before, and it was a mess now. The big difference was the difference between scrap and wreckage, or between an interesting sense of disorder and outright vandalism. Wherever there was glass, it had been smashed. The wooden boat had been overturned. The workshop door had been broken down and a lot of the stuff from inside had been flung out. Some of the refrigerators and one of the washing machines had been brought out and bounced around, making them fit for no purpose ever again. They lay upside down or on their sides now, doors wide open and gutted of their works.

Ryan showed no emotion as he picked his way through. He looked about him, taking in a detail here and there, but his face gave away nothing. Not even when he reached the house and saw, as he must have been expecting, that it hadn't been spared. He stood on the porch steps looking up at the splintered door for a while, and then he pushed it all the way open and went inside.

Marianne got to her feet, and climbed down out of the freight car. She pulled her red rucksack after. It was grimy where it had been standing but mostly with plank dust, and that would clean off. Slinging it onto her shoulder, she started down the embankment.

She took the same route through the yard. No sound was coming from the house. Wherever she stepped, something crunched or broke underfoot. She could see places where small fires had been set, burning themselves out before they could spread; charred wisps of newsprint still drifted whenever a breeze came.

Climbing the porch steps, Marianne felt a sense of excitement. This would be her first time inside the house.

But if she'd wanted to see how Ryan lived, she'd missed her chance. The inside of the house had been wrecked. The first thing to hit her was the stink of urine, and worse, in the hallway. Pieces of the wallpaper had been ripped from the wall, exposing some kind of insulating foil underneath. Watching her step even more carefully now, she went through and found Ryan in the devastated sitting room.

It had been a plain room with a gas fire and a threadbare sofa and an ex-rental television set. He was just standing there. He hadn't even taken the knapsack from his shoulder; he wouldn't have found anywhere to set it down if he had.

The doll's head had been nailed to the wall. The six-inch nail was wider than the eye socket through which it had been driven, so the head had cracked. Red paint had been thrown at it and had mostly missed, making a big arc across the wall in the shape of a dripping scythe. The empty paint can lay in a pool on the floor. Other colors had been used to draw swastikas and obscene graffiti. The word VAMPIRES had been written in black over the fireplace, by someone who'd made a bad estimate of the space that he'd need; half of the thin and ratty carpet had been torn up to expose the fiberboard beneath, and what looked like engine oil had been dumped onto that. Spent matches lay on the oil, but they hadn't been able to get it to light. The TV, oddly, hadn't been touched.

Marianne said, "I knew they'd have to let you go. You'd done nothing wrong. I'd have told them if they'd asked me."

He looked at her once, just about registering her but otherwise not reacting to her presence. Then he moved on into the next room.

Marianne followed. In here, they'd tried to tear down the actual walls and they'd partway succeeded, pulling off some of the lining boards so that the glass wool insulation bulged out. Paperback books lay on the floor, torn from their covers. Old Christmas cards, cheap ones, from the emptied drawers—about two dozen of these.

Marianne said, "Some men came first in the afternoon. They

stood outside and called for you and then they kicked the gate down. Why would they do that?"

Ryan didn't look at her, or reply. He gave no sign that he'd even heard her.

She said, "They looked in all the windows, but once they knew you weren't here they went away again. It was some boys who came later and did all this. I could recognize some of them."

He turned over a book with his foot.

She said, "They hung around outside whispering until they were sure there was nobody home. Then one of them kicked in the workshop door for a dare and then they all went mad."

How the word had got around so fast, she couldn't say. Some of the boys she'd known, some of them she hadn't. From up in her hiding place she'd been able to make out only a part of their conversation, and that was the part that had sounded more or less like *EyblahfokkinblahfokkinEyfokkin*. There had been a few other words in there to modify the meaning every now and again, but otherwise that had just about covered it. When they'd finished, they'd pulled down some of the yard fence and headed up the embankment at a run and she'd retreated to the darkest corner of the wagon out of fear that they might see her. Something had hit the wooden side of the carriage as they'd passed, but they hadn't stopped.

"I suppose you'll think this is all my fault," she said.

The next room was the kitchen. It wasn't large, but it hadn't been overlooked. Anything that couldn't be opened with a can opener, they'd smashed or otherwise emptied. Then they'd used the can opener on the woodwork. Then they'd pulled the wiring out of the walls.

He hadn't spoken a word to her yet.

"Ryan?" she said.

"Go home," he said quietly, without looking at her. "How many times have I got to say it before it sticks? Isn't all this enough for you?"

"I can't go home," she said. "Look at me."

He looked at her. With awareness, this time, and she could tell that much from the change in his eyes.

She said, "This is what he did to me last night. And he said my dog was dead, just like that. If I go back now, he'll do worse."

"I wouldn't worry yet," Ryan said. "The police don't like being lied to. They've kept him there."

"But they won't keep him forever. *Then* what will I do?"

"That's not my problem."

"And neither of us can stay here. Have you got any money?" Something seemed to occur to him then. He suddenly pushed past her and moved into another room. She followed him into his bedroom, which had a line of rising damp on the walls like a tide mark on the embossed wallpaper. The mattress and bedding had been pulled onto the floor and befouled. He crouched by the fireplace and levered up one of the tiles on the surround, uncovering a hole behind it. Stuffed into the hole was a plastic bag, and inside the bag was a folded wad of what looked like money. To Marianne it seemed like a lot; hundreds, even. Ryan probably didn't make much, but then, living the way he did, he didn't seem to spend so much either.

Whatever the amount, he was clearly relieved to find it intact. Still crouched by the fireplace, almost as if he'd suddenly found that he no longer had the energy to rise, he said, "I knew it all had to be going too well. I had my own place, a kind of job ... I bothered no one, and no one bothered me. Then you had to come along."

"How much have you got?" she said. "I brought my savings book."

"For what?" he said, on guard.

"I brought my father's birth certificate as well. We can't use his passport because it's got his photograph in it and you don't look the same. But with the certificate we can get you a cheap one at the post office. It'll only be a visitors' passport, but it'll do for what we need."

"You're mad," he said. "What are you talking about?"

"I'm not mad. You've got to get me to my mother. I can't do it on my own and there's no one else I can ask. I think he's going to kill me if I'm still around when they let him go. And if he doesn't and nothing changes, then I'm probably going to kill myself."

Ryan looked bleak. He stared at the floor. He ran his hand through his hair.

She added, "I mean it."

"You don't mean it," Ryan said.

"And the men said they'd be coming back."

"They won't come back," he tried to say, but his voice cracked in the middle of it. He closed his eyes and put a hand over his face. The hand shook, a little.

He said, "Why me?"

"Because you're the only friend I've got."

He was shaking his head. But he couldn't deny that much, because it was the truth. She went over to the fireplace and, deliberately, she put her hand on his.

He froze.

"Please," she whispered. His gaze went from her hand, still on his own, to her face.

Had she won? She didn't know.

Looking at his face right now, she realized that she didn't know anything at all.

PART TWO

THE CUNNING LITTLE VIXEN

CHAPTER 24

One day early in her CID career, Jennifer had participated in a dawn raid on a pedophile's home. There had been three of them in the team, two of them staying out of sight while the senior officer had rung the doorbell. The householder was a widower, retired and living alone, and he must have known the purpose behind the visit as soon as the senior man had identified himself. He'd stood trembling in the doorway as the officer had asked if he could have a word, and once they'd all moved inside and into the hall he'd been informed that there was a warrant to search his premises under the Protection of Children Act. The senior officer had been Ralph Bruneau, known to all as Bruno, and Jennifer had always remembered the way in which he'd conducted the operation. He'd been scrupulously polite as he'd explained that he was looking for indecent photographs and said that it would save a lot of time if, should any such material be present in the house, the man would produce it now.

He'd gone upstairs, and Bruno had gone with him. They'd returned with an envelope containing five Polaroid shots involving underage boys. Then the team had proceeded to search the house anyway, taking more than an hour to get through everything. The householder, still in his threadbare plaid dressing gown, had seemed desperately eager to help but also seemed to have a few convenient blind spots, because without his guidance they'd turned up another envelope of photographs and some imported magazines and a Polaroid camera which they'd bagged and marked for taking away.

They couldn't make an arrest. As the law stood, they could only remove the offending items and inform the man that he

133

would be summoned to make an appearance in court. And that, as Bruno had complained out loud in the car as they'd been driving back towards the station for breakfast, was the most frustrating part of the whole process; because now the man was free to get out and warn contacts and make any phone calls that he wanted to, which meant that he could act to burn up any trail that might have led to other practicing child molesters or their lines of supply.

While still in the car, Jennifer had asked if she might see the photographs. Bruno had passed them to her without comment, and then he'd looked the other way. She'd seen similar material before, so the subject matter was nothing new to her. But these weren't magazine shots. They were one-off images and, as such, were direct physical links to an event of pederastic foreplay and they seemed to have a charge associated with them, a kind of dark and negative form of charisma that reached beyond the content alone.

She'd reclosed the envelope and handed them back and Bruno had said, with a trace of suspicious concern, "Are you all right?"

And Jennifer had said, "He was one of my teachers."

Mr. Glick, mathematics and geometry. A name that they'd had some inevitable fun with, outside the range of his hearing. Maths had been Jennifer's all-time weakest subject, a total no-hope area until she'd entered his class, but then over the next three years he'd helped her to a passing grade. She'd scraped through at the lowest possible level, but for her this had rated as a major achievement. All through the raid, she'd been waiting for him to recognize her. But he hadn't, and for this she was grateful. He'd talked too much and he'd seemed terribly small, and he'd looked straight at her several times although he'd never actually met her eyes. But she'd come out of it without him ever realizing who she was. The briefcase in which he'd kept the pictures at the back of his wardrobe, unless she was mistaken, had been the same one that he'd carried into school every morning.

She supposed that she ought to have been feeling betrayed. Outraged. And she did, for the children; all had been staring into the camera flash with that same rabbit-in-the-headlights look, except for one who'd been in tears.

But for old Mr. Glick, sick Mr. Glick, worthless, perverted, life-in-ruins Mr. Glick, she'd felt desperately, desperately sad.

Barely twenty-four hours after supervising the breakup of her unit's temporary incident base in borrowed offices, here she was, helping to put it all back together again in the same location. But then, when a child disappeared, everything tended to move at speed. Stapleton himself was the senior investigating officer on this one, and a team of thirty detectives had already been assembled. The incident log was open and running. There was an office manager to check all the documentation, a statement reader to assess the information as it came in, an action allocator to relay new requirements to the detectives in the field, a receiver to take their feedback, and four civilian secretaries to input the whole mass of detail into the computer system in an indexed and retrievable form.

Tomelty was standing by the coffee machine and watching, with a vague air of despondency, as his normally quiet premises were once more taken over by the purposeful circus of the Serious Crime Support Unit.

When Jennifer stopped to use the machine, he said to her, "Doesn't seem like five minutes since all of you lot moved out."

"It isn't," she said. "Have you seen Bill Stark around?" Bill Stark was the unit's systems manager.

"He was, but he said he'd be back in twenty minutes."

"Isn't HOLMES on-line yet?" HOLMES was the acronym for the National Police Computer. No one could ever quite remember what it stood for.

"Not if the look on his face was anything to go by. How much more space are you going to be needing?"

"Same as last time plus one extra desk and a modem for the fraud squad," Jennifer said.

"How many of them?"

"Two. They're going to be running a financial profile on the girl's father while we're getting the rest of it into place."

"Right," Tomelty said gloomily.

Jennifer lifted the little door on the front of the machine and took out her coffee. At the end of every day for the past three weeks she'd been determined that she was going to bring along her own jar and a plug-in kettle, and every morning she'd rushed out of the house without remembering.

Too many late nights.

Too many bad dreams.

She said, "Is Cadogan here yet?"

"He's being collected," Tomelty said, and he levered himself away from the wall where he'd been leaning and started to wander off.

"I knew last night that this wasn't going to be simple," she heard him saying as he went.

The missing girl's father was brought in about twenty minutes later, by squad car into the inner yard that had been the scene of the previous day's lineup. The squad car's driver wanted to know what to do with him, so Jennifer took over.

Cadogan seemed pale and shaken, somehow diminished. Tomelty had kept him until late into the evening and finally let him go with the promise that a charge of wasting police time was to be given some serious consideration. He'd have released Cadogan sooner had it not been for his doggedly sticking to the same story, despite a credibility rating of somewhere around sub-zero. He'd turned sullen, he'd gone silent, but he'd never recanted even in the face of the facts. So how do you account for these discrepancies? You explain them. I know what I know. Cadogan didn't seem like a man who made admissions of wrong easily, to himself or to anyone else.

"Mr. Cadogan?" she said. "I'm Detective Inspector McGann. I'm part of the team who'll be looking for your daughter."

He looked at her dazedly.

She went on, "We're going to get her back as soon as possible. How effectively we do that is largely going to depend on you."

"I was already on my way," he said. "You didn't have to drag me in like this."

"But you haven't been straight with us so far, have you, Mr. Cadogan? How do you think that looks from our end of it?"

His skin was gray and there were dark circles under his eyes. He said, "If you'd listened to me the last time, this wouldn't have happened."

"Well, we listened, but you lied, didn't you? O'Donnell never tried to get into your house, on that night or any other. But then you never told us that your daughter had been visiting O'Donnell's yard on her own."

"All I was trying to do was keep her out of it."

"And look where that got you."

"Yeah," Cadogan said darkly. "You sent him home, you kept me here most of the night, and that's when he took her."

"*Did* he take her?" she said, looking at Cadogan levelly.

He returned the look, warily. "What do you mean?"

Jennifer said with care, so that Cadogan would have to think as he listened, "What I'm saying is that if there's anything else you want to tell us . . . it's better if you do it now, rather than later."

Cadogan was blank.

"*Do* you want to tell me anything?" she said, and then gestured towards the activity that was going on behind her. "Before all of this goes any further?"

He looked. He blinked. He began to understand.

"Am I being arrested?" he said. "I mean, nobody's said that I am."

"You're not under arrest."

"Because," he said, his voice rising now as if he was trying to reach a wider audience that included everyone within earshot, "if you're trying to point a finger at me while he's out there with Marianne, and then something happens to her . . . then you can take *this* down and use it in your fucking evidence, I'm going to kill somebody."

"Calm down," she said. Cadogan was rattled, and people were looking their way. It would hardly do to be seen losing her control of a one-to-one situation when Cadogan wasn't even her own interview subject. Down the corridor behind Cadogan, she could see Detective Inspector Somerville and his sergeant, Benny Moon, heading towards them.

Cadogan said, "You're telling me to calm down? Have you got any kids?" He didn't give her time to answer. "No," he said, "or you'd know. It's love and war from day one. No one else understands. Nobody even tries."

"Two officers are going to be talking to you now," Jennifer said. "Don't try to mislead us again, Mr. Cadogan. You've already seen what can happen when you do."

Somerville and Benny Moon took him back into that same interview room in which he'd spent much of the previous day and night. Jennifer's last sight as the door was closing was of Cadogan looking dazedly down at the tape recorder on the table. It hadn't been used on him before.

But they'd be sure to be using it now.

Most of the next half-hour she spent with the office manager. Uniformed branch was organizing a search of the beach. O'Donnell's closest relatives were being traced. A call came through for Jennifer, but by the time she got there someone else had already taken and dealt with it. During all this she became aware of Tomelty, who was ... well, *hanging around* was the only way she could think of to describe it.

As the station's duty officer, Tomelty wasn't actually assigned to or directly involved with the missing-child investigation. His concern was to see that the regular day-to-day business of the station went on as normal alongside the major inquiry that happened to have been based within his premises. But something seemed to be troubling him.

While she was making some notes, he came and leaned over the desk alongside her.

He said, "I don't suppose you know what the word is."

"About what?"

"About us letting O'Donnell walk out of here yesterday."

"What's to say? There wasn't a scrap of a reason to hold him any longer."

"You know that, and I know that. But history gets rewritten sometimes, doesn't it?"

"Only in the Sunday papers."

"Yeah," Tomelty said dispiritedly as he straightened up and started to move away. "The ones that everyone reads."

Then she had to go out for an hour and when she got back, it was to see Stapleton's big silver-gray Jaguar parked out in the vehicle yard. Two dog vans were setting out, presumably for the beach to join in the search. She found her boss in the main office where all the desks had been pushed together and there was a write-on, wipe-off board on which they'd keep an updated summary of progress. So far, the board was blank. A stranger could have picked Stapleton out immediately. His was the best suit in the place.

When he'd put the phone down, she said, "I've just come from arranging a surveillance on the house of O'Donnell's sister. The one time he absconded from the open unit, that's where he went. He could head there again."

"Cancel it," Stapleton said.

"Why?"

"We've been too slow off the mark. They're already out of the country. Hull to Zeebrugge on the night boat, both of them traveling on a visitors' passport under Cadogan's name." He held up his hand with his finger and thumb about an eighth of an inch apart. "We missed them at the other end by *that* much. Any idea on what Cadogan's been able to give us up to now?"

"As far as I'm aware, Somerville and Moon are still working on him. I get the impression he's not going to be easy."

"And the mother?"

"That's one of the things we're trying to find out. The mother lives somewhere in Germany, but we don't seem to be able to establish where. O'Donnell could have told the girl that they were going over to look for her."

Stapleton was unimpressed. "Alternatively," he said, "he could be fucking the kid with a rope around her neck in some foreign ditch right now. You were here when O'Donnell and Cadogan were both in yesterday, weren't you?"

"I was here, and it was exactly the way Tomelty's telling it," Jennifer said. "Cadogan spun a fairy tale and Tomelty blew him out. I don't see anything else he could have done."

Stapleton sighed, and shook his head. "I don't know," he said. "Maybe the border police will grab them and we'll have a quick result with no damage. But it's like everything else, you know what I mean? If you get the chance to stop something right at the beginning and you don't take it, then it always ends the same way."

"Like what?" Jennifer said.
"Like one big mess," said Stapleton.

CHAPTER 25

Peter Heym, a uniformed patrol-car officer with the freeport division of Hamburg's police department, pulled his green and white Opel onto the shoulder of the road and reached into the glove compartment for his binoculars. They were his own pair, a present from his parents when he'd been in his teens. He'd used them for bird-watching, star-gazing, and occasional hopeful surveillance of the bedroom curtains of seventeen-year-old Pauline Meier who had lived in the apartment house opposite. Now he kept them in the car because they could be handy when he was working.

The freeport was vast, a city outside a city, and he'd never known anyone who'd failed to be impressed by its scope when first they saw it. Tourist buses came here, just to drive around. What they saw on their circuit was an endless spectacle of container yards and warehouse units, rail tracks and canals, ship terminals and cranes, coal heaps and ore mountains, and a network of autobahn-standard service roads that looped over and through it all like a skyway system in some science-fiction landscape.

He was at one end of the highest of the high road bridges. He'd just had a radio call, relaying a report from a signals controller on the railway down below who'd seen two people crossing the tracks about a kilometer along from his box. But nobody walked here, ever, unless it was to find a phone when a vehicle had broken down. Leaving the blue light flashing as a warning to the traffic, Peter Heym walked around the patrol car with the binoculars in his hand. Big container transport lorries roared by as he leaned on the side of the car to steady himself.

The misty-green spires of the town itself could be seen from here, but only across an expanse of dock buildings, stretches of water and then wide areas of terminals and cranes again. He adjusted the glasses, and started to search.

Down below the road, in the shadow of its concrete support towers, there was a veritable undercity. There were jetties and linkways, barges and houseboats. The houseboats were brightly painted, but not gaudy. No activity around them at all. He went on scanning, looking for the railway lines. A big lorry went by at speed, rocking the car and him along with it for a moment.

He found them.

One was a man, the other was a child. He couldn't tell at this distance whether the child was a girl or a boy; they were figures in a landscape, hardly more than far-off dots. They were leaving the railway tracks and crossing an asphalt parking area that had been marked out into a hundred car spaces with not a single vehicle in them. He saw the man put his hand out, the child take it and scramble over a low barrier. Then they walked on.

Well, they didn't *look* like Red Army Faction saboteurs. But they didn't exactly look as if they knew where they were going, either.

He got back into his car, waited, and then pulled out into the first gap in the traffic. He went over the bridge and then left the road by the next exit. He knew where he was going, and that there was no quick way to get there. But it didn't matter. The two wouldn't have much chance to wander far.

He drove by the ore yards, with their dead mountain landscapes and their big cranes and conveyor hoppers rising above them like alien presences. Out on the main waterway, a solitary tug was arrowing its way along with a listing barge hitched to its side like a lifeless twin. A couple of radio messages came through, but nothing that concerned him.

As Peter Heym's days went, today didn't seem like anything special. Just ahead of him, on this much quieter access road, the two of them were walking.

He overtook them, and pulled in. Glancing in the mirror before he got out, he saw that they'd stopped. They were both standing there, expressionless.

Both were dressed for the road. Both carried knapsacks, the old-fashioned kind. The man had a hard look, the girl much less so. She was about ten or eleven, still on the skinny side of adolescence. They waited as Peter Heym walked towards them.

"Where are you going, please?" he said.

It was the girl who answered. "We're trying to get into town. A man gave us a lift and he said we were almost there, but then he dropped us in the middle of nowhere. We've been walking for an hour."

Peter Heym looked at the man. "From where?"

The girl chimed in again. "We were in the Netherlands," she said. "We're here to look for someone."

"I was talking to you," he said to the man.

"He doesn't speak any German," the girl said.

The man's face hadn't changed. His eyes were small and dark and they gave nothing away. Then Peter Heym looked down at the girl, who said, "We haven't done anything wrong."

Perhaps that was so. But nevertheless, there was something here that didn't feel right. The girl sounding like a local, the man saying nothing at all. The man shifted slightly, resetting the weight of the knapsack on his shoulder, but his face didn't open up any more.

On the high arch of the overpass, someone in the fast traffic leaned on his horn.

Peter Heym said to the girl, "Is he a deaf mute, or something?" But the girl shook her head.

So then he said, "Tell him I want both of you to get into the car. And if he's got any identification, I'm going to want to see it."

CHAPTER 26

Jennifer had spent more than an hour on the phone, first to various offices of the prison service and then around the Health Authority in an attempt to put together as much information on O'Donnell's time in the system as was possible. They already had all the juvenile court papers and his records from the adolescent unit within Broadmoor. They'd details of the assaults that had been made or attempted on him by certain other inmates, and files from the interim secure unit and then the open ward that had been his way station on the route to supervised housing and eventual freedom. She'd compiled what she referred to as a chase-down list and was working her way through it, ticking off some items and marking others to be pursued, when she saw that Detective Inspector Somerville was out of the interview room and talking to Stapleton by the main office doorway. She grabbed a sheet of paper from the desk and went over, reaching them in time to hear Somerville saying, "He's bloody heavy going. He's dodging all over the place."

Stapleton said, "Refusing to answer?"

"Nah, but . . ." The big detective grimaced and shook his head as if he'd spent too long trying to pin down something that was both simple and subtle at the same time. "None of the answers gets us anywhere. He doesn't even know where his own kid went most of the time. Doesn't know what she likes to do best, doesn't know if she ever thought about going to visit her mother. Says he doesn't even know where her mother *is*."

Someone jostled Jennifer from behind, and mumbled an

apology as he passed by. Jennifer moved around a little, but she didn't back off.

"Needle him a bit," Stapleton was saying. "Try to get him angry."

"We're trying everything. I'm bloody sure there's something there, boss. We're going all around the outside of it and we're not touching it at all."

"Well, keep at him. Make sure he understands that he doesn't come out of that room unless it's to piss or say good-bye."

Rubbing at one eye as if there was grit in it that he wanted to clear, Somerville headed out of the main office and back towards the interview room. From where she was standing, Jennifer could see through two doorways to where a uniformed woman officer was backing through with a tray carrying three coffees and, before Somerville moved across and blocked her view completely, she got a glimpse of Cadogan looking up from the table. He looked bent, he looked haggard, he looked stubborn. And she couldn't understand why. He ought to be bright-eyed and desperate, giving them everything that he could, not having to be pressured and to have information teased out of him as if from a reluctant witness. It was his own daughter who was in danger, for God's sake.

"Well?" Stapleton was looking at her.

Jennifer said, "I got hold of O'Donnell's doctor over at the unit."

"What does he sound like?"

"He says he wants to help."

"Because some of these doctors live in a little world of their own, you know. Is anyone going over to see him?"

"I am, unless there's something else you want me to be working on."

"No, that's fine," Stapleton said. "Get over there and turn on the charm, see how much you can get him to spill."

"Stick your tits out," a voice from behind Jennifer advised. "That never fails to impress."

Jennifer looked behind her in the direction of the voice, first to the right and then to the left because he'd already passed by;

it was Burke, the red-haired detective sergeant who was deputy to Stapleton on the investigation.

"Oi," Stapleton called across to him. "If you're here, who's talking to the CPP?"

Burke was pushing open the teak-effect door to the Gents'. "They're calling me back."

"Well, get by the phone, then."

But as he disappeared backwards through the doorway with a grin, Burke held up the cellular phone that he'd been hiding down by his side.

"Oh, the sound effects in there are *really* going to impress the Crown Prosecutor," Stapleton said as the door swung shut behind his deputy.

Jennifer said, "You're going for a *Commission Rogatoire*?"

"Soon as we can nail down Pearson."

"Who's going over?"

"I haven't decided, yet."

The *Commission Rogatoire* would be the key document in securing international cooperation in the pursuit of O'Donnell. Specific to the case and therefore specially written, it would allow local officers to be sent over to work with the police on the ground. They'd be advisory only, with no legal powers of inquiry or arrest. But they'd bring background knowledge and a continuity to the investigation that would throw the whole thing into a much more urgent focus.

She said, "I've got A-level German." And then, when he looked at her, she added defensively, "That's more than most around here."

"It's not six months since you went to Antwerp."

"I know, but we're not talking about treats and outings, are we?"

Stapleton took a moment and seemed to be sizing her up, as if there was something about her that he was noticing for the first time.

He said, "Quite an ambitious little tyke, aren't you?"

She glanced around. She was nervous about this being overheard, but in spite of the crowd that was either working in the office or constantly on the move through it, everybody seemed to be into his own business and nobody was paying any special attention to her.

Without any trace of reluctance or doubt, she said, "Yes."

Stapleton nodded thoughtfully.

"I don't know if I like that in a woman," he said, and then he moved on.

CHAPTER 27

The procedure was straightforward. Suspicious-looking persons who couldn't account for or identify themselves could be taken in and made the subject of a report. Details could be put on telex to all other departments and the subjects could be held for a maximum of two days. After that, they'd have to be charged or released.

But life was never as straightforward as procedure. And besides, as Peter Heym soon found, the two of them *did* have identification; it was a British temporary passport in the name of Patrick Cadogan and it carried the man's photograph and details. The girl was on record as his daughter, Marianne. The two of them sat in the back of the Opel as he read through the document. The photograph had the look of a rush job in a photo booth. The passport had been issued within the past couple of days.

But there were birth certificates, as well, for both of them. And some letters from a law firm in Hamburg, addressed to the man by name. In addition, the girl was able to give an address that they were heading for. He wasn't so certain of her accent now; for a moment at first it had seemed perfect, but now it wasn't. Now it was like any other British child's of school age.

Bloody awful.

Peter Heym refolded the documents and held them out over his shoulder. "Take them," he said.

The girl took them. The man didn't move.

As he started the engine, Peter Heym looked at the man in his rearview mirror. He was stone-faced as before. No fear, no friendship; no sign of anything from him apart from that one moment, glimpsed through binoculars, when he'd put out his hand to help the child over a wall.

In the mirror, the man's eyes met his.

Peter Heym felt a chill.

He drove them to the waterfront at the edge of town and dropped them by the freeport gates, where barriers and fences controlled the traffic over a series of waterway bridges. This was the site of the old harbor with its narrow alleys and redbrick warehouses, and of the quays where pitchmen for boat trips worked the ice cream and restaurant crowds. Before he let them out of the car, he turned and said to the girl, "You see the city railway, over there?"

She looked. Above the main east-west road, an elevated section of the S-bahn ran parallel for a way before making a landward turn and then disappearing among office buildings.

He said, "You can pick up a train on the front, here, or you can follow the line into the middle of town. It isn't far. From there you get a Number 286 bus and it'll take you to the place you need to be. Do you think you can manage that without getting lost again?"

"We weren't lost before," the girl said.

"Go on," Peter Heym said. "You're free to go."

The man looked at the girl. The girl nodded, and the two of them started to get out of the car.

Peter Heym swung the Opel around and watched them as they reached the busy east-west road and waited for the lights to change so that they could make the long crossing. A strange pair. As if the man were the passive one, and the girl in command, but with undercurrents and tensions in the relationship that couldn't even be guessed at. The lights changed and the two set out, the man reacting with just a moment's delay as, again, he took his cue from the girl. They weren't like any father and daughter that Peter Heym had ever seen. More like a child with her big, slow brother, the one in the family whom strangers preferred to avoid.

A train passed overhead, making the ironwork sing and the ground shake. The traffic under the railway started up again and the two were lost from sight, absorbed by the city already; two people among two million, and with little about them now that might single them out.

But, all the same . . .

All the same, he was inclined to make a report and drop it into the system at the end of his day. It couldn't hurt, and it would allow him to shed the uneasy memory of the wise, wise child and her dancing bear.

The child, wise beyond her years.

And her dancing bear—unmuzzled, unchained.

CHAPTER 28

Jennifer knew of the Wilmington Hospital, but she'd never had a reason to drive out to it before. Formerly a Victorian asylum in its own extensive grounds, it stood several miles out of town in an area of farmland and small villages. It was the kind of institution that people joked or told stories about, but didn't really know. The many roads in and out of the estate could be used by anyone, and it had no high walls or gates. There was a staff-organized concert every Christmas and a church-run summer fête each August, open to all. There couldn't be many in the area whose family histories hadn't been touched by it at least once.

But as far as most people were concerned, it was still that weird place where the lunatics lived.

The driveway was about a quarter of a mile long, straight

and tree-lined; only when she was almost at its end did she get sight of the complex of redbrick buildings with their high roofs and solid, hint-of-gothic design so characteristic of old schools and workhouses. But the potential grimness of the architecture was offset by the grounds surrounding the buildings; where there were no roads there was the neatest of neatly cut grass, and where the grass stopped the gardens began.

There was plenty of room to park, but she got as close to the main building as she could. There didn't seem to be anyone around apart from one elderly man who was picking up dead leaves from one of the verges and stuffing them into a plastic sack; she asked him for directions, and he pointed out the entrance that she'd need. Some of the outlying buildings had been boarded up, she'd noticed. Not because they were derelict, but more as if they'd been mothballed.

"Detective Inspector McGann?"

A man was coming down the steps towards her, his hand outstretched. She took it and said, "Dr. Wallace?"

"Call me Roy. You're not what I was expecting."

"What *were* you expecting?"

"Well, bear in mind that I deal with more hairy-arsed prison officers than most. That can start to warp your view of the world."

They went inside. First impressions of Roy Wallace were of a pleasant-looking man in his forties whose tailored blue suit was in a constant war with his shape, with the suit on the losing side. He wasn't tall, but he was solidly built. His beard was graying. The same might have been true of his hair, but there wasn't enough of it left to tell.

Jennifer said, "I thought this place was attached to a high-security unit."

"On paper, it is. The secure unit's more than five miles down the road but administratively, it's all treated as one. There's not really enough that goes on here to justify anything else."

They were crossing the entrance hall now, all marble and fluted columns and a big oak staircase. Jennifer said, "It seems huge."

"It used to be," Wallace said. "Now it's being run down to

nothing, and the site's to be sold. We're down to three dozen patients and most of them not a day under sixty. Did you see Terence out in the gardens? Quite tall, very straight, never takes his cap off?"

"If he's the one who gave me directions to you, yes I did."

"Terence has been here since he was a boy. Now, *he's* absolutely amazing. He can remember when the place had its own farm and workshops and everything. Did you ever hear anybody say how it even had its own railway line?"

"No," Jennifer said, wishing that they could get to where they were going so they could drop the small talk and get down to business. "I never did."

They went through a double set of doors and into a corridor whose tiled floor would have been worth thousands in architectural salvage alone. The walls were whitewashed, and peeling slightly. From somewhere further along echoed the transistor-squashed sounds of Radio One.

"Well," Wallace said, "that was the Victorian asylums for you. Now we've got care in the community. Last week I bumped into one of my ex-patients outside a pub in town. He'd no shoes on, and he was asking for pennies." He glanced around before making the turn into an offshoot passageway that had five closed doors and very little daylight at its end. "It's going to be a conference center, I think. They'll turn the old farm into a golf course."

They went into his office. It had the sense of a squeezed-up corner that he'd made into his own with books and houseplants and some inexpensively framed sixties psychedelia posters; almost as if, with all the space that surely must be on offer around the slowly emptying building, he genuinely preferred this claustrophobic den with its high narrow window and low ceiling and painted-over fireplace. There was a white coat, not so new but not so worn either, on a hanger behind the door; otherwise, nothing to identify it as a medical man's office at all.

"Is that his file?" Jennifer said, nodding to a heap of interleaved folders at the center of a big desk that was more like a table.

"That's everything we've got here," Wallace said, gesturing

for her to sit, "but I can probably save you some reading time if you'll just tell me what it is you need to know. I mean, to start with, what's he supposed to have done?"

"He's taken an eleven-year-old girl out of the country and he's posing as her father. There was an accusation against him regarding the same young girl ... we believe that the accusation's false, but we don't believe it to be entirely groundless. Our main concern right now is for the child."

"My God," Wallace said. For a moment Jennifer wasn't too sure whether he was shocked or impressed.

She said, "Does this surprise you?"

"Are you sure we're talking about the same Ryan O'Donnell?"

"Absolutely. The two main questions I've got to get answers to are, exactly what did he do before and what might he be capable of now?"

Wallace thought for a few moments, scratching nervously at his beard while he rescaled his outlook to take account of the new situation.

Then he said, "You understand that I've had dealings with him only over the last five years. Nothing that predates the time of his release."

"I understand that."

"For what he did, I can only read you the record. And for what he *might* do ... I can give you an informed guess at the most, and in the light of what you've just told me, I wouldn't be inclined to have too much confidence even in that."

"You don't think it's in character?"

Wallace shook his head. "I don't know. I really don't know what to say."

"Would you say he was mad?"

"No. He's a marginalized individual of limited social skills. People will think him odd because of that. But he isn't mad."

There was silence for a moment. Jennifer waited. Wallace seemed to be on the point of saying something, only to find his thoughts diverted onto some parallel track from which the words wouldn't quite come.

She said, "Dr. Wallace, time's short." She nodded towards the file. "Please?"

Wallace snapped out of it, and put his hand on the stack of folders.

He said, "This is what I can gather. As a child, Ryan always had a fertile imagination. Overfertile. He couldn't easily distinguish between fantasy and reality. He was a bright little kid from a working-class background, and as far as his parents were concerned, he was always telling lies. He didn't call them lies, he called them visions."

"Are we talking about schizophrenia?"

"That was the diagnosis in his pretrial assessment. I can't go on record as disagreeing with it, because I wasn't there at the time."

"Off the record?"

"I've never yet seen any clear signs of the schizophrenias in Ryan. There's a classification of simple schizophrenia that involves nothing much more than loss of will and drive and affect, but the picture can be so close to normal adolescent bloodymindedness that it's hard to tell the difference. Misdiagnosis can't entirely be ruled out."

"Even with visions involved?"

"Schizophrenic hallucinations are usually auditory. Plus the fact that he knew what the visions were. He's not mad, and he's not at all unintelligent. It's perfectly possible that he was a more or less normal child who was coping with a difficult situation in his own way. Didn't you ever lie there in bed and look at the faces moving in the wallpaper? You can think back and know that it was just a trick of the light and your imagination and they couldn't have been anything real. But even now . . . isn't there a small place in your mind that won't ever be convinced otherwise?"

Jennifer knew what he meant. There had been one particular chair that she'd dragged out of her bedroom and onto the landing every night after her parents had gone downstairs. Her father had insisted that the carving was supposed to represent fruit, but for her the shapes of the fruit made a face. Whenever the lights went out, the face would wait for a while and then start to grimace at her like a hundred gargoyles, one after another.

Wallace said, "My opinion's always been that the only big

difference between Ryan and the rest of us is that he could be so overwhelmed by the things he'd seen that he couldn't resist telling other people about them. For all I know, if he'd been born five hundred years ago he might even have been a saint by now. This is what led to it, anyway, and because he told the other kids, he got a reputation. They'd wind him up about his ghosts and his angels. One time, this younger child asked him to show her one of them. They went off together and she was found on some waste ground later the same day."

"Any sexual element?"

"Apparently so. She hadn't been undressed and there was no sign of any attempt at penetration, but when they searched his home they found traces of semen in some underwear that he'd tried to hide in the bottom of the dustbin. What the sequence was is anybody's guess, because Ryan was never able to talk about it. The girl wasn't precocious and she didn't have a reputation of any kind, so nobody could try to say that she'd asked for it. She was eleven years old, for God's sake. What he did, he did."

Jennifer said, "This is all nearly twenty-five years ago. But what about now? Could he do the same thing again?"

"In the light of what you've just told me I'd have to say, possibly yes. I mean, I don't believe from what I know of him that he ever had a genuine mental dysfunction, whatever the records and the release board might say ... which means that I can't tell you that everything's fine because of some miracle cure."

"You're saying he was more or less normal, but still he killed someone."

"And then we watched him for long enough, until finally we had to call him sane and let him out. But bear one thing in mind. He's an adult now, he isn't fifteen years old. He's outgrown a lot of his problems just like all of us do. But then again, he's capable of more. So ... I don't know, I can't give you any guarantees either way. I can say that, on balance, I wouldn't have believed it of him. But all that time ago, he crossed over into a country that neither you nor I have ever seen. There are people in my profession who'll tell you with great confidence what the landscape's like over there. But the simple fact of it is, none of us have been there and none of us know. And if I'd been Ryan's doctor on the day before it happened, I couldn't have given you any better answer than the one I'm giving you now."

"You seem to like him," Jennifer said.

"He can be very plausible," said Wallace.

The interview over and a set of photocopies under her arm, she headed back towards her car. The parallels were disturbing; O'Donnell giving no clear signs of danger, the girl taking the lead, O'Donnell following like something big and tame and unsuspected . . . and then something happening out there from which only one of them would return.

It didn't *have* to go the same way twice. Could all the years between count for nothing at all? Jennifer knew that the physical and sexual drives of a fifteen-year-old could be comparable to a loaded gun on a hair trigger; most of her boyfriends around that age could have raised an erection by staring for too long at a doughnut. But O'Donnell was no fifteen-year-old, now. He was nearly into middle age.

She thought of the sex offenders she'd encountered in the past.

Most of them had been nearly into middle age, too.

But most of them had also had continuous records; they'd reckoned that Mr. Glick, her one-time maths teacher and almost seventy years old when caught, had a history of abusing that went back at least over two decades. Ryan had one, apparently unrepeated offense counting against him. And with his visions now just memories and with an adult's more limited imagination, surely the situation was no longer the same. He would no longer dream such vivid dreams, and if ever he did, he'd know them for what they were.

Fantasies. Just fantasies.

Not visions at all.

As she reached her car she saw Terence, the elderly patient who had given her directions when she'd arrived. His sack of leaves lay on the grass verge behind him and he'd produced a yellow dustcloth from somewhere, and now he was polishing the door mirror on the driver's side of the vehicle. He smiled as she approached. He had four teeth, none of them together.

He stood there with the dustcloth in his hands, waiting. For a moment, Jennifer was uncertain. Was he waiting for money?

She said, "Are you Terence?"

He nodded, still smiling; a black hole, with wickets.

Jennifer said, "I'm a friend of Ryan O'Donnell's. Do you know him?"

"Everybody knows Ryan," Terence said. He had a strong local accent, and the lack of teeth made his speech indistinct. He took a step back as Jennifer opened the car door and reached in to drop her papers onto the back seat.

She said, "How is he these days, do you think?"

"I've been here longer than anybody else, you know," Terence said.

"I know. Did Ryan have much to say when you saw him last?"

Terence pointed. "There used to be a farm over there."

"I know, and a railway line. Did Ryan say anything about going away?"

"No."

"Because we can't find him, and I'm worried about him."

"He wouldn't go anywhere else. He likes it where he is. I like it here, but they say they're going to close it. I came when I was twelve. I used to work on the farm."

Jennifer decided that it was time to capitulate, and gave up hope of getting any useful information. He meant no harm. Didn't even seem to expect money, as she'd first thought; he was being friendly, that was all.

"Thanks for doing the mirror," she said, and he shrugged as if it was nothing, although she could see that he was pleased.

And then she said, "Why did they send you here?"

"I was a handful for me mam," he said. "And she was getting married again, and *he* didn't want me. She liked lavender scent." He leaned forward slightly, as if to tell her something that couldn't be shared with the wind and the birds. "D'you know," he said, "whenever I smell it now, I still think of her."

"Good-bye, Terence," Jennifer said, and got into the car.

Just as she was about to close the door, Terence said, "He told me he saw the Devil, once."

Jennifer stopped, all senses on full alert, and stepped out again. "Who did?" she said.

"Ryan did. He saw him in town. Sitting in a cafe, reading a paper. He had to tell someone about it but he didn't want to tell the doctors, so he told me instead. That proves I'm his friend, doesn't it?"

"When was this? Was it recently, or a long time ago? Take your time, if it isn't too easy to remember."

But Terence didn't even have to stop to think.

"This were last week," he said.

CHAPTER 29

As soon as she saw the road beside the river by which they were leaving town, Marianne knew that they were in business.

It was called Elbchaussee and it headed out into the prosperous suburbs. Its sides were densely wooded in some places, gave views over the river in others, and featured big houses in a variety of styles. She had a clear memory of coming along here by car. She'd traveled just about everywhere by car in those days, mostly driven by her mother. When they all went out together they'd go in her father's big company car but usually, on weekdays and on the way to and from school, she'd be in the back of Anneliese Cadogan's VW with her lapstrap and booster seat.

Marianne wondered if she'd still have the VW. If it would be parked there, in its usual place just off the concrete driveway that plunged at such a steep angle into the basement garage under the house. Their house hadn't been as big as those overlooking the river, and hadn't stood on as much land; but it was in an area almost as good, and only a little way further out. Lots of company people lived around there. Lots of her friends.

Her mother would be amazed at how she'd grown. There would be no call for a booster seat in the back of the car for Marianne now.

She glanced at Ryan. He was sitting on the bus seat beside her, knapsack between his feet and one hand holding onto the strap. His face was slack, and he wasn't looking out of the window. As far as she knew, he hadn't slept on the boat. He'd been too sick. Now he had the look of a man who was doing nothing more than listening to a dull buzz inside his own head, but then after a moment he seemed to sense something, and he looked at her.

She knew what it was. He was scared. He'd never been so far from home and he didn't know the language, so it was natural. Dump Marianne in the middle of France or Finland and she'd probably feel the same. But this was different. For her, this *was* home. She'd known it as soon as their ride had crossed the border.

She put her hand on Ryan's, to reassure him.

He shook it off.

"Don't do that," he said.

She shrugged, and returned her attention to the window.

They were passing a dark stand of trees, and for a moment she could see her reflection. The swelling had mostly gone down. The bruising she'd managed to cover up with an inexpensive pancake stick from the shop on the ferry, the kind of thing that the older girls were buying to paint out their spots before going to the on-board disco. Marianne had wandered by and watched for a while, but it had been like the dance floor of the living dead.

But, all the same ... was this an adventure, or what?

That policeman hadn't noticed the marks, anyway, so they *had* to be fading. Policemen were trained to notice things like that. When she'd sensed that he was curious about her fluency, she'd slipped into a really crap accent like Kevin Dinsdale's at the school back in England. Kevin Dinsdale thought that learning languages was stupid and a waste of time. He thought the same thing about history, geography, maths, computer studies . . .

She tensed.

For a moment, there, she'd thought they'd arrived. But she'd been thinking the same thing every half-kilometer for the past fifteen minutes. She was certain that she remembered everything that she was seeing along the way—buildings, bridges, views across the Elbe—but the certainty came only once she'd seen them. Even somebody walking with a dog, she'd think *Yes, yes, I remember him too.*

They had to be there soon. Oh, God, she prayed, don't let me go past. Don't let me miss it. *Have* I missed it?

When this part was over, she could show Ryan all the tourist places before they bought his ticket home. He hadn't been enjoying the trip much so far, she could tell. In fact, she sometimes marveled at her own ability to persuade him along. The couple of times he'd balked and held back, the solution had been simple; she'd simply gone on alone. Soon enough, he'd be with her again. Like when they'd argued and she'd left him so that she could start hitching, and the man in the green truck with the load of tar and stones on the back had pulled in to pick her up. Ryan had jumped into the cab and slammed the door at the last moment. The driver hadn't seen him coming, he'd moved so fast. The driver hadn't liked it and there had been an atmosphere for the rest of the ride, as if there was something unspoken between the two men. Ryan had glowered across the cab for the entire distance, never once taking his eyes off the driver. After dropping them off, the other man had spat out of his window as he'd driven away.

Her mother would want to thank Ryan properly, she was sure, and they'd work out some way to repay him any money that was owed. Any trouble, they'd smooth it out then.

Nothing would be impossible in this bright new future that now stood only just out of reach.

Her mind had been wandering. Suddenly, she looked back down the road.

And her heart leapt.

She scrambled to her feet. "Come on," she said to Ryan. "Come on, we just passed it!"

It was the strangest feeling she'd ever known. She didn't even hear the bus as it pulled away. Ahead of her, making a junction with the road at a slight angle, stood the street on which she'd spent more than half her life. Wide, tree-lined, quiet. It struck her like some lost place from a dream. In her memory, it had started to blur and fade into some thing of the imagination. But here it was once again, hard-edged and real.

It was all just the same. It was all somehow different.

She started forward.

Ryan was behind her somewhere, almost forgotten. She heard him call something to her, but she didn't hear what. She was running, now.

These were nice houses, all different styles. Five or six bedrooms at least. A Victorian type with portico columns and fancy gables stood next to a high-tech white block that gave way to a Dutch-looking place with a mansard roof. Then a place that looked like a pocket-size manor house or an American mausoleum.

Then her own.

Now she was flying. The ground was under her, but she wasn't even making contact. She could hear her own breathing and the blood pounding in her ears. There it was: white walls, red tiled roof, waist-high chainlink fence on the street side. In her mind she could already see her mother rising from her chair, her magazine falling to the floor, moving now to meet her as she swung in by the gate.

The path to the door. The door about to open.

The big dog, running to greet her.

Wrong.

Marianne's dog was dead. Rudi belonged to another time, another country, and he was gone. This one was dark and sleek and had saliva spraying from its jaws as it arrowed across the lawn towards her with wild eyes and bared teeth. As if from a great distance, she could hear Ryan shouting.

Marianne! Stop! Get back from there!

and just as he did, the dog was jerked up short on the end of its twenty-odd feet of line.

Marianne had slammed to a halt in her tracks; another couple of strides and she'd have been within the Doberman's range. It was up on its hind legs and straining away at the stretched loop of its collar, barking loud and fast and at a deafening pitch. She couldn't move. Couldn't do anything other than stand there, flinching. She felt some of its spit touch her cheek as it flew by. It was showing the whites of its eyes and almost choking itself in its eagerness to reach her and do harm.

The door opened as she'd envisioned. But a man came out, newspaper in hand, and stood on the covered porch. He was no one that Marianne knew. He called a few sharp words to the dog, which the dog ignored.

Marianne managed one stumbling step backwards.

Then a firm hand steadied her from behind.

"What do you want?" The man on the porch called out. He was middle-aged and he had a mustache. He was wearing a big baggy button-up cardigan, the kind that nobody would ever wear outside of his own home. There was a pair of reading glasses in the hand that held the newspaper.

"I want to see my mother," Marianne said.

"You're in the wrong place," the man said, and he waited.

Marianne looked around. Her head moved jerkily, as if responding imperfectly to command. There was no VW in the driveway, but there was a new-looking mailbox that had no right to be there. And the windows looked different, she wasn't sure how. New shutters, perhaps.

But it *was* the same house.

It was.

Ryan, who could have understood none of the exchange between Marianne and the dog's owner, began to guide her back towards the street. He was breathless himself, and must have run to catch up with her. At first she didn't turn, but took a few uncertain steps backward. He continued to steady her all the way until finally she turned, and went with him out of the gate.

"Are you all right?" he said.

She managed to nod.

"I know," he said. "I know just how you feel. Come on."

He put his arm around her shoulders, and they headed back towards the road.

It was getting dark by the time they got back into the middle of town. They'd waited for a city bus and nothing had come, so they'd started to walk; and of course, a bus had then passed them less than five minutes later when they were midway between stops.

It was too much of a distance to cover on foot, but they walked more than half of it anyway.

Marianne was in a daze. She didn't know what to do. Everything had been so simple, so perfect, a neat jigsaw that locked where it fit and which now fit nowhere at all. Closer into town they picked up the S-bahn and rode in on the train. Marianne sat with her head leaning against the cool glass, staring out.

"I give up," she said.

"You can't give up," Ryan said.

And that was the extent of their conversation until the train reached its terminus in the Hauptbahnhof.

They came up from the S-bahn by escalators and tunnels into the main railway station. The station was vast, the biggest building interior that Marianne had ever seen in her life, big enough almost to have its own weather, the high arcing roof of the place so lost in darkness that it might as well have been the night sky. They crossed on one of the broad street-level walkways, looking down onto the open tracks through power lines. With all the trains and the noise and the masses of people, the sense was of being inside some immense living thing—half biological, half machine, a thing of steel bones and blackened ribs and vaulted chambers, the trains moving through on their prescribed courses like oiled pistons.

There was such a crowd in the square outside that it was as if every club, theater, restaurant and cafe had emptied onto the streets at once. The atmosphere was electric, like getting an adrenaline shot. By a twenty-four-hour snack stand at the station's entrance, three policemen were arguing with a bunch of youths. The policemen were wearing padded jackets and white riot helmets, and they carried long batons. The youths could be best described as scruffy, a couple of them with skinhead hair-

cuts and all with the loud, strutting manner of no-hopers everywhere. Most people were cutting on through, finding the scene
anything but remarkable. Two girls were the loudest and least
cooperative of the group.

"Come on," Ryan said, and he pulled Marianne along.

"I was only watching," she said.

St. Georg was the district to the north of the station. All she
knew of it was that she'd once been warned never to go there.
It proved to be an area of inexpensive jewelry and electrical
stores, Turkish restaurants, cheap hotels, and quite a few late-
opening shops of the kind that set rummage baskets out on the
pavements with marked-down goods in them. On the bigger
avenues there were also a number of sex cinemas and peep
shows and in the side streets, about every fifty yards or so,
women in fake furs and bright, tight Lycra pants stood alone
with an air of waiting for nothing in particular. Marianne knew
what they were, even if she was rather vague about what it
was that they did.

She started to stir, a little. It wasn't so bad, being with Ryan.
At least Ryan took you to places that your parents never
would.

At every street corner he'd stop and look around, thinking,
calculating. He'd no idea where he was going, but he seemed
to know what he was looking for. Nobody looked at Marianne
with any special interest. She asked him what they were supposed to be doing.

"We're looking for somewhere to stay," he said. "Somewhere they put the price on a board outside. They're always
the cheapest, and they can't pad the bill because it's up there
for everyone to see."

"We passed three like that already," Marianne said.

"Where?" said Ryan.

"We're standing in front of one now."

The hotel that Ryan eventually chose had a backlit yellow
sign out over the street and a walk-up entrance between two
ground floor businesses. The reception desk was little more
than a window in a corridor, and they paid cash in advance.
Marianne had to do all the talking, what little there was. They
were given a key to one room with two beds in it. They went

up two floors by a narrow stairway, and Marianne waited as Ryan had to fiddle around a little to make the key work. The bathroom was one floor down. She hadn't expected them to be sharing a room. She wondered how they were going to work this out.

The carpet was cheap and the curtains were dirty, but the bed linen was clean. There was a washbasin in the corner with a couple of thin and ratty towels laid out by it, but they'd also been well laundered. The window was open a few inches, and looked out onto the back of another building.

"Hey, this isn't bad," Ryan said, brightening.

They had a curtained alcove with a few hangers in it instead of a wardrobe, a low coffee table with a book of matches and a bottle opener, and a big radio. Ryan slung his knapsack onto one of the beds and tried the radio. It came on, but it didn't seem to pick up anything.

Marianne was still standing by the door. She didn't know what to do.

Ryan gave up on the radio, straightened, and turned to her. He said, "I'm going to go downstairs while you get yourself into bed. Switch the light off when you're done, I can manage in the dark. Will ten minutes be enough, or did you want to use the bathroom?"

"I'm on holiday," Marianne said. "You don't have to have baths when you're on holiday."

He picked up his knapsack and went out, taking the key with him. The door closed behind him with a click. Marianne took a big, deep breath, and let it out.

She was alone in the room.

She sat heavily on the bed, and pulled off her Reeboks. Her feet hurt. Her shoulder was sore and her back was stiff from the hours that she'd been carrying the red rucksack. But worse than any of this was a feeling of sick hopelessness that lay in her chest like something that she couldn't quite swallow. She hadn't eaten in ages, and didn't want to. She didn't know what she was going to do now.

Hardest to handle of all, she felt stupid.

If it hadn't been for Ryan, she'd have been scared as well, a lost child on the road on her own. It didn't matter that he was nervous himself and away from familiar territory, because his presence alone was enough to support her and keep her going. She'd never have had the nerve to book herself into a hotel, even one as horrible as this. She'd probably just have hung around the station all night, or walked the lighted streets until her Reeboks rubbed so much that her feet would start to bleed. And things could happen to you on the streets. That much she knew.

Perhaps it would all seem different tomorrow. Perhaps they'd get some new ideas.

But why had he taken his knapsack if he was only going to wait outside?

She'd got her woolen sweater pulled halfway over her head when it occurred to her that he might have decided to leave her there. What if he had? What would she do then? She started to panic. What if he was phoning her father right now and telling him where to find her?

However limited their options might be, that was the unthinkable one. She struggled out of the pullover and dropped it on the bed, and moved to the door in her stockinged feet. She flipped up the button on the catch so that she wouldn't lock herself out, and went onto the landing.

The landing was in near-darkness, the timer on the hall light having cut out. Illumination came from the next floor down, through the banister rails and casting long shadows like bars up the walls. Ryan wasn't there. Somewhere down below, there was the muffled sound of a toilet flushing. Was *that* him? She moved to the rail and looked down the stairwell.

Somebody was leaving the bathroom. She couldn't see who it was, but she knew that it wasn't Ryan. She knew because she could see him, sitting on the stairs where the light was better on the middle floor. He'd opened his bag and he'd taken out some papers, and he was looking through them. Even at this distance she could recognize the lawyers' letters. He wasn't actually reading them; she knew that he couldn't because they were written in German and were such heavy going that she'd given up on them herself a long time ago. It was all legal stuff about assets and joint property and trusts, whatever they might be. He seemed to be shuffling through, scanning them, looking for some hint of an idea or some clue that might leap out at him.

He didn't look up, didn't know she was there. She stepped back from the rail and returned to the room, where she undressed to her underwear and climbed into bed. She'd left on the small striplight over the washbasin mirror so that Ryan would be able to find his way around. She pulled the bedding up to her chin and waited, an anonymous shape under the covers in that part of the room where the light didn't reach.

Ryan came along a few minutes later. She heard the key scratching around the lock and then he came in, trying to be quiet but making the floor creak wherever he moved. The first thing that he did was to pull the cord to switch off the washbasin light. Then she sensed rather than saw as he set down his bag in the darkness, took off his coat and slung it over the back of a chair, and then pulled off his boots. Then he dropped, still mostly dressed, onto the other bed.

Her eyes started to adjust. She could see the shapes of the room, as in a cave by starlight. She could hear Ryan breathing. Grownup breathing, heavy and exhausted-sounding. He turned over once, and the bedsprings complained. He hadn't said anything to her, so he was probably assuming that she was asleep.

He sighed then, and started to settle.

Marianne was wondering exactly where her mother might be, right now. Her father hadn't ever talked about her. He hadn't even let Marianne herself say anything about her. Anneliese Cadogan had become a taboo subject, as if she was a criminal who'd shamed the family or something. But why? What was she supposed to have done?

Ryan made a long, low groaning sound meant for nobody's ears, but of course Marianne was immediately straining to listen.

There was silence for a few moments.

And then she heard him mutter something.

"Ohhh, God," she heard him say, mostly into his pillow. "What the fuck am I *doing*?"

CHAPTER 30

For the police, it was Day Two.

Jennifer was down early and grabbing breakfast on the hoof when Ricky finally appeared. She could hear him descending the stairs, then a pause as he stopped to pick up the newspaper from the mat. Then he came shuffling in, yawning and scratching himself through his bathrobe. Ricky always insisted that he was a morning person, but he spent the first hour of every day looking as if he was fighting off an overdose.

"Christ," he said blearily. "You're up early."

"Lots going on," she said.

She'd got the table mostly covered with notes and papers, and she had to scramble them into a more coherent pile to make some space for Ricky. She'd been reading through copies of old statements from Ryan O'Donnell's schoolmates, questioned about O'Donnell himself and about his victim. The rest of it was her own work from the previous afternoon. After talking to Dr. Wallace she'd been to see the schoolteacher who'd put on record her concerns about Marianne Cadogan. Then she'd returned to the incident center and had been spending the early part of the evening writing up the two interviews, when more of the historical stuff had started to come through on the fax.

Ricky said, "Looks like your child molester made the papers."

"Really?"

He passed the newspaper over. There was O'Donnell, in a smudged-looking photograph in a lower corner of the second page. The piece alongside it was no more than two column inches, the bare facts in bold type with no names given other than O'Donnell's own. Sought by police for questioning in connection with the disappearance of an eleven-year-old girl, believed to be traveling together somewhere in Germany or the Netherlands.

"I wonder where they got the picture," Jennifer said, handing the newspaper back. "Ours are even older."

She left Ricky looking deathly over his Sultana Bran, dumped all the papers into her briefcase, and took the briefcase out to her car. An early start would mean an easier drive, and she had to get right across town and then pick up the motorway. She'd be leaving him a clear run at the bathroom, anyway, so he'd have no excuse if he turned in late today. Ricky worked in local government, setting up training programs for school dropouts and out-of-work adults; the job was supposed to be covered by a flexitime scheme but he was always having to use it to catch up on his late appearances instead of making it work to his advantage. If Ricky was a morning person, Jennifer was thinking as she pulled out of the end of the street and into the seven o'clock traffic, then so was Count Dracula.

Most of the police station was still dormant apart from the all-night charge desk, the cell block, and the Support Unit's borrowed suite of incident rooms on the inner corridor. Staffing levels had dropped overnight, but the phones and the terminals had been manned all through. There would be a full briefing for everyone at some stage in the morning, but as soon as she got in Jennifer asked around for the news. It appeared that the Hamburg police had picked up the two of them, checked them out, and had no reason to hold onto them, as details were still in the process of being circulated via the Interpol office in Wiesbaden. Another hour, perhaps even less, and they'd have been held. Marianne Cadogan had been in good health and under no apparent pressure. O'Donnell had said nothing.

It was a frustrating near-miss, but at least it was a sighting and it narrowed the search. The *Commission Rogatoire* was now in hand for Hamburg, and officers were almost certain to be traveling out later in the day. Rumor had it that Somerville and Moon were favored as the chosen team, although at the moment it seemed that the pair of them had become stuck in a rut over their questioning of Patrick Cadogan. According to Detective Superintendent Burke, one mention of Cadogan's wife and the man turned into Marcel Marceau. Meanwhile, the two financial specialists had been working on his profile. He'd been borrowing money to pay off interest on the big sums that he'd borrowed to pay off his debts, and those debts were increasing all the time. But this hadn't prevented him from running up charges with an expensive Hamburg law firm, as Jennifer learned when she joined a small group of detectives who'd gathered to listen as Benny Moon recapped their findings for Stapleton's benefit.

"But ask him about the lawyers," Benny Moon was saying, "and he goes all thick and says he can't remember. We know it, he knows it. But that's as far as we ever get."

Jennifer said, "Can I try?"

Benny Moon looked at her. They *all* looked at her. Benny Moon said, "If it's anything worth knowing, we'll have it out of him."

But Jennifer was concentrating her attention on Stapleton, shutting the others out and trying not to imagine what they'd be thinking. She said, "Let me have ten minutes with him. No tape and no one else present."

"What are you going to do," Benny Moon said, "show him your underwear?"

A couple of the others smiled, but this was too much even for Stapleton. *"Benny,"* he said with a note of warning in his voice; but Benny Moon had now been either stirred or stung to argue, it was hard to say for sure which.

"One officer and off the record," he said, "it wouldn't even be admissible."

"We're not trying to mark his card," Jennifer said. "We need what he knows. It's obviously something delicate, and you're going after it with a crowbar."

They waited as Stapleton thought it over. Neither Somerville nor Moon would like it, she knew. And then Stapleton looked at Jennifer and said, "Go on, then. Show him your knickers. Ten minutes maximum."

She could feel Benny Moon's stare burning into her back as

she headed off towards the interview room. But she tried not to let it worry her.

DI Somerville and Patrick Cadogan were facing each other across the interview room table in silence, like a couple of bareknuckle fighters too exhausted to continue but with their antagonism undiminished. The tape machine wasn't running, but a stack of sealed and dated cassettes alongside it was evidence of several hours of questioning. Each was duplicated; one copy for reference and transcription, the other for the record.

Jennifer said, "The chief wants a word."

Somerville looked from her to Cadogan and then back again, uncomprehending. She made a small motion with her head, indicating for him to leave.

Somerville stood abruptly, and left without comment. He didn't close the door behind him. Jennifer went over and closed it herself before returning to the table and taking the other officer's place.

"How's it going?" she said pleasantly.

By way of reply, Cadogan let his head drop forward so that his forehead hit the table with a hollow thump.

"*That* well?" she said.

Cadogan raised his head again. His eyes were still red-rimmed, but now they weren't so dull. They looked at least halfway human.

"Why?" he said.

"You're not helping," Jennifer said with a shrug. "That's how they see it."

"I've told them everything they need to know."

"You can't *say* what we need to know. That's why they're being so persistent."

"I had to sleep in a cell," he said. "The door stayed open, but I still had to sleep in a cell."

Without changing her tone, Jennifer said, "You know he's going to kill her."

Cadogan stared at her in silence. She'd no doubt that something similar must have been said to him before. But perhaps now she could make him believe it. Here in this room, right at this moment.

She said, "It's only a matter of time. And God knows what he'll do to her first. You know they're in Germany now? We think that Marianne's trying to find her mother."

Cadogan put his elbows on the table and held his head in his hands. His face was screwed up as if in pain.

"No," he said.

"That bothers you even more than the thought of her being with Ryan O'Donnell, doesn't it? Something set you against her, and you've been taking it out on your daughter ever since. But look. It's just you and me, now. We're off the record and no one else is going to come in. We're going to get it one way or another, and I can tell you ... it's never going to get any easier than this."

She waited.

Hands folded on the desk, head down, he looked at the floor.

Then he straightened.

And Jennifer said, "So how about it, Mr. Cadogan?"

When she emerged five minutes later, Benny Moon was standing by a doorway with his arms folded and showing all the signs of having nothing better to do. Stapleton was beyond the doorway, talking to Somerville in the main suite. Almost the entire team had turned in by now. She'd left Cadogan on his own for a while, on purpose.

"Jezebel," Benny muttered as Jennifer passed by him. "We'll have you for this."

"Only in your dreams, Benny," Jennifer said.

Stapleton looked at her and she indicated for the two of them to move through into one of the other rooms. Anything said in here would immediately become general knowledge. What she was going to say would soon filter through to everyone anyway, but at least this way it would be at the right time and through the appropriate channels.

Stapleton led the way into the fraud squad's little side room. Somerville and Moon followed her. Benny Moon pushed the door half shut, as a gesture towards privacy.

Jennifer said, "An unlabeled video arrived at Cadogan's office in Hamburg one morning. It was home-made. He ran it, and saw that his wife was on it. Two men beat her and made her eat shit. It was a ritual humiliation and she was a willing participant. The envelope containing the tape was addressed in her own handwriting. It had been posted three days before. During that time he'd thought that she was ill and couldn't concentrate on anything, but she'd said nothing that could have made him suspect this. He snatched his daughter from school and they were out of the country by the end of the day. He's never seen or spoken to the woman since. He's been using the lawyers to try and trace her now because he's close to bankrupt and he'd abandoned all of their joint property; there's some money, but it's in a trust that it will take both of their signatures to release. He doesn't want to meet her. He'll be happier if someone tells him she's dead."

Benny Moon whistled.

Somerville nodded and said, "Good one."

Jennifer said, "We've been working on the assumption that Ryan O'Donnell's lying to Marianne about helping to find her mother. But perhaps we ought to start worrying about what might happen if he isn't."

CHAPTER 31

The building containing the lawyers' offices was barely more than a dozen strides from the city hall square in the middle of town. The square was huge and cobbled, and the streets off it were cramped and narrow. The city hall itself was major-league Gothic: huge, spired, soot-stained, lions at the side entrances, everything. The frontage onto the square before it was so powerful and ornate and forbidding that its main function seemed to be to scare everybody out of the area. By contrast, the entrance to the lawyers' building was through a minor stone-arched doorway between a hairdresser's and a bakery. The doors, of black cast iron and glass, had been pinned open for business hours and would close like fortress gates at night. The entrance hall contained only mailboxes and brass plates. According to the plates, everyone here from the ground floor up practiced some kind of law—some in partnership, some on their own.

The firm named on the letterheads in Cadogan's correspondence occupied all of the topmost floor. Ryan and Marianne sat in the waiting area. The walls and carpet were beige and cream, the seats were low and black and might have been real leather. Ryan perched on the edge of his.

Across from them was a receptionist's desk in expensive-looking black ashwood. Beyond the desk was a door with a three-figure punch-coded lock that presumably led to the lawyers themselves. The receptionist had disappeared through this a few minutes before. Her phone had buzzed in her absence, but the call had been picked up elsewhere within a half-dozen rings.

Now she came back. She didn't even glance towards Ryan and Marianne, but sat down at her desk and began to leaf through a big leather-bound diary. Marianne sat up as Ryan leaned towards her and whispered, "Do we get to see him now, or what?"

"It doesn't look that way," Marianne whispered back.

Awkwardly, struggling to keep his balance, Ryan got to his feet. The woman looked up. She had a blonde rinse and a boyish haircut, a serious and businesslike look. They'd seen quite a few like her on the streets as they'd walked here, most of them carrying slim attaché cases and wearing good clothes and heading for somewhere that they most definitely had to be. Ryan had said that they all looked like Michael J. Fox in drag.

Ryan said, "Excuse me. Do we go in now?"

"I'm afraid that I don't seem to be able to make an appointment for you," the receptionist said in perfect but slightly accented English. "Herr Boshammer is extremely busy for the rest of this week."

"We don't want to make an appointment. Just an address is all we need."

"Then for that, perhaps you should try the phone book."

She closed the diary and turned to her typewriter, where a half-finished letter waited. Marianne could see that she clearly expected them to go now. Marianne stood up, seeing no other option, but Ryan moved forward until he was standing right at her desk. He put his hands out and leaned on it.

"Look," he said, "you've a client who's been using this place to try to trace his wife. That's how we read it, anyway. All we want to know is, have you found her and where is she?"

The receptionist looked up at Ryan. From her point of view, he must have been looming right over her and Marianne reckoned that, if you didn't know him like she herself did, Ryan could probably be an intimidating sight.

But the woman didn't waver. She said, "The business of clients is confidential. Now, I'm going to have to insist that you leave."

"This is the client's daughter," Ryan said, indicating back towards Marianne. "She's looking for her mother. Doesn't that count for something?"

The woman said nothing. She continued to look up at him stony-faced, and unswayed.

Ryan said, "Look, we've got nowhere better to go. So why don't we just sit around here while you think it over?"

She started to reach for the phone as Ryan turned but somehow, his hand caught it first and swept it off the desk and out of her reach. He stooped quickly, and caught it just in time and with a loud clatter of plastic before it could hit the floor.

"Sorry," he said. He put the phone back on the desk and the receiver back onto its cradle. He smiled pleasantly at the woman. Then he turned and went back over to rejoin Marianne, and Marianne saw him wink at her.

The woman got to her feet, and quickly tapped in the code that would let her through into the inner offices.

Ryan had barely touched the seat. As soon as they were alone he was rising again, and he crossed the office in two strides.

"What's the name of that detective?" he said. "Come on, make it quick."

She hadn't been expecting this. She fumbled out the correspondence from inside her coat as Ryan reached over the desk and flipped open the lid on the receptionist's Rolodex. Suddenly Marianne's fingers seemed about as supple as unripe bananas. Ryan was watching the door for the woman's return. Marianne had read out the name in the letters for Ryan only that morning, but what had the name *been*?

She found it.

"Schlesinger," she said. "Johann Schlesinger."

Ryan spun the Rolodex to the approximate section. He didn't bother to search any further but instead began to rip out the cards in batches of half a dozen or less. When he had them all, he spun the remaining entries to cover the gap and then closed the lid.

"Come on," he said, pocketing the cards. "Let's get out, before we're thrown out."

The stairway was well worn but scrupulously clean. The elevator ran down the middle of it in a caged shaft of brass rails and iron mesh. It was rising as Marianne and Ryan took to the stairs for their descent; they were only one flight down when the lift doors opened above them and two uniformed security men emerged onto the topmost landing. They looked like no great threat from down here. They looked as if they'd taken the job only after retiring from something else, and then not before time.

"Problem dealt with," Ryan called up to them. "We're leaving."

"I don't think they understood you," Marianne said.

"Don't worry about it," Ryan said. "Just keep walking."

Which they did.

CHAPTER 32

Cadogan had been brought in with no car the day before, so Jennifer volunteered to drive him home. He looked a mess, and almost certainly would be feeling like one too. He didn't have much to say. She'd had another half-hour with him in the interview room, this time on the record and with the twin cassettes running, and she reckoned that they'd covered everything that was essential. The biggest hurdle was behind them now. After the shock of that first incision, everything else was just post-operative pain.

The road petered out, and became the causeway.

"Is this really the way?" she said.

"Yes."

"What happens when the tide comes in?"

"It doesn't often come in this far."

She'd driven around the back and into the police yard to pick him up, because there had been press people hanging around at the front. Not many because it wasn't big news yet and the focus of the action had already moved overseas, but enough of them to be able to give Cadogan a hard time. He was the father of the missing girl, which meant that there was a public role that he'd be expected to play. But God only knew what he'd come out with if he was to open his mouth in answer to a provocative question right now.

He sat low in her passenger seat, face somehow dark and drained at the same time, staring out of the window.

Jennifer could see the house, now.

Cattle were grazing out here on the marsh flats. They were tough-looking, shaggy, and young. Nothing else moved, apart from the birds that had come down to pick worms out of the mud and that flapped up and away as the car went by. Every now and again the causeway boundaries were marked either by black and white painted posts or, here and there, by more substantial concrete blocks that appeared to have been cast in oil drums. The tide might not come in too often, but when it did, it clearly came in with some force. Some of those blocks had been tipped right over, and lay yards from the roadway.

The house drew nearer. To Jennifer, it looked like the loneliest place on the face of the earth.

Carefully, she followed the dirt track up onto the point. This was no place to get stranded. She pulled in beside Cadogan's own car, and switched off the engine.

She glanced at him. He was sitting there with his hand to his forehead. He seemed too weary and broken even to move.

She said, "Now, look. What happened to you may have been devastating at the time. But by any realistic scale of human suffering, it's not the worst thing in the world."

"Really," Cadogan said without expression.

"Yes, really. And you can't keep picking at it like an old sore that you're never going to let heal. You've still got a daughter, in case you'd forgotten, and we're working flat out to bring her back . . . but to what?" She stuck out her thumb towards the house. "This could be heaven or hell, depending on what you make it for her. I'd have loved to have grown up in a place like this, but I'll tell you something: I wouldn't have wanted to have to share it with a miserable bastard like *you*. Quite a few people have seen Marianne and O'Donnell together now, and nobody's suspected a thing. You know why? Because she seems to be fairly happy in his company."

Cadogan's eyes were on her, and his face was a bloodless mask as she started to get out of the car.

She paused and said, "One last thing. If you're still feeling sorry for yourself and you need something to brood over, think about this. When Marianne needed to turn to someone, some criminal deadbeat who picks over rubbish on the seashore offered a more encouraging prospect than you. Come on."

A woman in a blue nylon coverall had emerged from the house and was waiting, uncertainly; Jennifer worked up a look of concerned sympathy and said, "You must be Mrs. Healey.

Mr. Cadogan and I have just been discussing this awful business about Marianne."

Mrs. Healey looked, bewildered, from one to the other. Cadogan was climbing stiffly out of the car. He moved as if shell-shocked.

"Mr. Cadogan!" she said. "What's been happening? The police came here last night with court papers and they went through everything. No one would tell me why."

It seemed to be working. He seemed to get a definite grip on himself and then, like a man taking his first unsteady steps out of a wheelchair, he said, "Marianne's missing, Mrs. Healey." He looked at Jennifer. "I'd have thought they'd at least have told you that."

Mrs. Healey said, "They wanted to know what had happened between her and that tinker. But no one explained anything."

"I know. I'm sorry. That seems to be the way they like to work. Let's go inside."

Jennifer followed them in.

Cadogan sat at the kitchen table, and Mrs. Healey filled the kettle and set it to boil. The table was cluttered with file boxes and papers and old correspondence, stuff that the boys last night had obviously gathered and sifted and then left for the owner to put back into order. There were a number of big lever-arch files and, lying open, an old leather attaché case with a broken handle and scuffed corners. Jennifer looked at Cadogan across all of this and said, "One other thing. Don't even *think* of going out there."

Cadogan didn't react in any way that would tell her anything. But he said, "Could anyone stop me?"

"There's nothing you can achieve. You could even make the situation worse. What you've got to do is stay available and be more cooperative. Today was a start. It may not be me that you have to talk to next time, but whoever it is, you've got to be just as straight with them."

"*You're* going out there," he said.

"No one knows who's going yet. Now, you may have to deal with the press at some stage. I don't mean talk to them, I mean cope with their attention. Marianne's name won't be released, but there are always leaks and there's always gossip. We can go for a ruling to prevent them identifying her in print, but that doesn't mean there's no story, so they may still come around. You understand that?"

"Yes," Cadogan said.

"It's best to say nothing. Don't be drawn. They won't be here out of sympathy, they'll be doing a job." She looked from him to Mrs. Healey. "That applies to both of you."

Cadogan took the warning with a nod. Mrs. Healey seemed too dazed by it all to respond. Her mouth opened once and then closed, with no sound coming out.

With nothing more to say, Jennifer said a brief good-bye and then left them.

He felt Mrs. Healey's hand on his shoulder. It was a hesitant touch and she said nothing, but it was the most demonstrative that he'd ever known her to be. He raised his head from where he'd been letting it rest on his arms and said, "Thank you."

He'd never felt so weary. He felt like a man who'd just completed an impossible journey, only to find himself at a set of tremendous gates that opened before him and gave him his first sight of the *real* journey to which all of his efforts had been but a prologue.

But to fall to his knees now would be to waste what he'd learned. And the learning had been anything but easy.

He pushed away some of the papers from on top of the attaché case. His passport was underneath. He sat looking at it.

Mrs. Healey said, "She told you not to go."

"I heard her."

He didn't move.

"But you're going to, aren't you?"

He said, "They had a thousand questions for me, and I couldn't answer half of them. All about Marianne. You know, on the day she was born, I think I was more proud of her than of anything that I'd achieved in my entire life. I used to bore people rigid with all those stupid little stories that parents tell. Last night they asked me when her birthday was, and I couldn't say. Couldn't remember the date. Which means that this year it came and went, and she never said a word about it. I just forgot. Fucked up nicely there, didn't I?"

"Mr. Cadogan!" Mrs. Healey said, but her shock was only half-hearted.

He started to get to his feet. "If I don't go, what's the best thing that can happen? Strangers find her, strangers bring her home. And I'll just be here with this stupid look on my face and it'll be okay, nice to have you back, business as usual." And then he slammed his hand on the table. "She's *mine. I've* got to go for her. Me, more than anybody else. I've got to be the one she sees coming for her."

He went upstairs. The door to Marianne's bedroom stood open; the police had been through everything in there, too, but then it was always such a mess that it was hard for Cadogan to see any difference. He stood there for a minute, looking in. Then he went to his own bedroom and pulled the suitcase out from under the bed.

Mrs. Healey moved into the doorway after a few minutes, and watched for a while as he packed. Everything in the drawers had been disturbed. They'd obviously been thorough.

Mrs. Healey said, "Can you afford to do this?"

"No," Cadogan said, "but the credit card people can come for my hide when it's over."

With some delicacy, Mrs. Healey said, "I've ... got some money. Not a huge amount. And I tend to keep quiet about it."

"Don't tell me they finally settled the insurance." He stuffed a couple of shirts into a space down the side.

"There were one or two things around my sister's house that the others never got to see."

He stopped what he was doing, and stared at her. "Why, Mrs. Healey," he said. "You old dodger. I bet you were back there from that funeral like a Ferrari."

"If you're going to be insulting," she said, "I might just withdraw the offer."

He brought down the lid of the suitcase, and she moved around as if to give him some help as he made to squash it shut on the contents.

He said, "The offer's appreciated. We'll see how it goes."

"Fine," she said, stopping the lid. "Now, you go and phone about a flight, and I'll redo this for you properly."

CHAPTER 33

Marianne had said that she was hungry. Down by the expensive shopping streets they found a Burger King that had been built within the shell of what looked like a town center war memorial; the outside was a Greek temple in miniature while the interior was exactly like that of every other American-owned fast-food chain. There was a lunchtime crowd, but they found a corner table. Ryan said that he didn't want anything, but then he kept stealing her fries. He'd pulled the sheaf of Rolodex cards out of his pocket and he was leafing through them, checking them one at a time.

Marianne said, "That was really sharp, the way you got hold of those."

"I'm not sharp," Ryan said. "But once or twice I've had the chance to watch people who were." There was nothing on the backs of any of the cards, but he turned each one over and looked at it anyway before he laid it down.

Marianne said, "Were you in the army?"

"Well ..." She couldn't be certain whether his hesitation was due to embarrassment or modesty. "I *have* been in uniform," he said, and he stared at one of the cards as if on the point of making out some hidden meaning; but then he set it down with the others and, picking up the next with the same intensity of interest, said, "What's the man's name again?"

"Schlesinger."

He turned the card to show her. "Is that what this says? I can't read the woman's handwriting."

Marianne took a closer look. "That's him," she said, "and I

think I recognize that address, as well. It's not too far from here."

"Are you sure?"

"Of course I'm sure."

"Only, I don't want another tour of the coal yards with a ride back in a police car."

"We could take a taxi."

"No taxis. Those things cost money."

"I told you I'd pay you back."

"Have you ever heard the expression, *jam tomorrow*?"

"I might," she said warily. "What's it from?"

"I don't know," he admitted.

"What does it mean, then?"

"It means we're not going anywhere by taxi. How long will it take to walk?"

"Ages," she said.

"We'd better get a move on, then." He dumped the rest of the unwanted Rolodex cards into her empty bag before nodding towards the bun and the few fries she had left. "Choke that down and let's go."

"You're rotten to me," she said.

"I got you this far, didn't I?"

She stuck her tongue out at him by way of an answer.

He said, "And clean yourself up, you've got lettuce on your chin."

She picked up the paper napkin and scrubbed the lettuce off, and then she stuck her chin out for inspection.

She sat there with it stuck out for several seconds, while Ryan looked at her and said nothing. He was looking better today. Her jaw was starting to ache and she was beginning to feel stupid, but then he said, "You're enjoying yourself, aren't you?"

She let her face relax, and sat back. "Is that wrong?" she said.

But he shook his head.

The streets were busy, and no one gave the two of them a second look. Sounds of an oompah band were coming from one of the plazas, but it was a taped playback from some tent promotion for Austrian wines and it seemed oddly out of place among the department stores and big sportswear shops. They'd left their bags in a locker at the station that morning, so they were traveling light. It was a pleasant day, not too warm. Marianne's feet no longer hurt.

As they walked along, she said, "You know what I used to pretend? I used to pretend that my dad had gone away and that some stranger had taken his place. And my real dad would come back someday and he'd see the stranger off and everything would be all right again. He used to be nice. But that's all so long ago, I can hardly remember. Since we left here, he never took me places. This is the first holiday I've had."

Ryan said nothing.

They walked on.

At first, it looked as if the address for the Johann Schlesinger Agency might be wrong. It appeared to be for an old-fashioned redbrick market hall on a two-way section of the town's inner ring road, that part of the road that ran down from the center to the harbor. The building's ground-level windows had been painted black and screened with wire mesh, and its entire length up to arm's-reach height had been posted with handbills for political rallies, jazz clubs, movies, and rock concerts. In places these had been pasted in layers so thick that they were lifting away from the wall at the bottom, like sheets of curling cardboard. There was one main door, painted gray under the graffiti and looking so solid that one could probably run a tank at it and still not get in.

But there was another entrance as well, at the far end and just around the corner. This was shared with an antiques center in the next building and had the look of the back way into a run-down toilet. It wasn't encouraging, but they went in to take a look anyway. Through the glass doors of the antiques center, Marianne could just make out the shadows of piano legs and other kinds of furniture.

The posters carried on up the stairs, floor-to-ceiling on the walls to either side. The stairs had been painted once, but the paint had now been worn or had flaked away to uncover the old concrete beneath.

Ryan said, "Looks like you have to *be* a detective just to find yourself one."

At the top of the stairs they took a left turn, went through a set of swinging doors, and emerged into something like daylight.

In fact it *was* daylight, but softened to the point of opalescence by an all-glass skylight roof about a hundred feet above. The interior space of the hall was one long, three-balconied arcade with a wooden block floor and the kind of interior ironwork that every modern shopping center in every European city was trying to imitate. But this was low-rent and original, and was showing its age.

Counting the units, they climbed the iron stairway to the second level. There weren't quite shops, they weren't quite offices; hardly bigger than booths in some cases, they housed tailors and watchmakers and mail-order bookdealers, coin traders and stamp dealers and wedding-stationery printers, each of them crammed into a minimum of space and many of them with the blinds down. They found Room 258, Johann Schlesinger's premises.

But they didn't find Johann Schlesinger.

The door was locked, the room beyond it was dark, and a yellow Post-It note had been stuck on the glass at eye level. Ryan tried the door anyway. "What does the note say?" he said.

"All packages to go to Room One-Eighteen," she read. "What does that mean?"

"That there'll be nobody here to take them in, I suppose."

"There's got to be a secretary, or something."

"I don't see much room for one."

A phone started ringing somewhere inside. Ryan put his face up against the glass in an attempt to peer in through one of the slight gaps in the vertical blinds. Marianne did the same. She couldn't see much, just an office in darkness. The phone stopped ringing abruptly, but now she could see the tiny red point of an answering machine operating light amid the clutter of a disorganized desk.

"We could leave him a message," she said.

Ryan's grunt sounded like it might be intended as agreement, but seemed to contain little enthusiasm. He let his fore-head rest against the glass for a moment, banging it a little too hard.

Then he straightened up and said, "Let's go and see who knows anything."

Room One-Eighteen was a kiosk space occupied by a photo retoucher. He worked at a high desk on a high stool like a turn-of-the-century bookkeeper, with his materials on shelves that ran all the way up to the ceiling and all of them reachable without even a stretch.

Marianne questioned him and then translated for Ryan.

"He says that Herr Schlesinger's working out of town. It could be for days or it could be for a week, but it's rarely for much longer than that."

"How long since he left?" Ryan said.

She asked.

"He doesn't know."

"Tell him thanks," Ryan said.

Ryan didn't say much for some time after that. They walked for a while and then they sat for a while, looking out across the Alster lake that was the heart and the pride of the city. She could remember when her father had talked of them moving to a bigger house, one that overlooked the lake instead of the river. There hadn't been a time in Marianne's life that she hadn't been able to look out of her bedroom window and see open water—unless one were to count her time in the cheap hotels, which she didn't. It was strange. All that time in the house on the point, she'd been homesick for here. And now that she was here, it was almost as if she could sense the first glimmerings of—

But she put a stop to that thought, before it could get any further.

Ryan said, "I don't see anything else to do. We're going to have to hang around until he gets back. Today's Friday, we could be stuck for the whole weekend."

"Can we afford to?" she said.

"I can't afford not to. Don't ask me to explain it."

She shrugged, and they got to their feet.

They picked up their bags from the station and went back into St. Georg to get another room. St. Georg by day was a tamer, duller place, even respectable in those sections that were given over to unpretentious working-class apartment houses. But while they were picking up some supplies for the evening in a Turkish-run grocery store, Marianne heard shouting on the street and looked out to see a gang of about twenty or thirty young white men going by. They were chanting like a football crowd, pointing at the traffic in the street, punching the air and stabbing their fingers to all points of the compass. They were sticking out their chests like gorillas and as they moved on past they left a wake of nervousness behind them that was almost tangible. Old men came out and stood on the street, watching them go.

She looked at Ryan. Ryan's back was turned to the door. He seemed to be studying something, and he didn't look up.

They got back into the same hotel. It wasn't the same room, but it might as well have been. Ryan sat heavily on one of the beds, and Marianne began to unpack their shopping. The bed creaked more loudly than the last one and the carpet had a kind of jaguar-spot pattern.

Ryan said, "Where'd the beer come from?"

"I picked it out for you," she said. "The Cherry Coke's for me."

"When did you do that?"

"Right in front of you. I thought you were watching."

"Well," he said, reaching over and picking up one of the two cans for a closer look, "thanks for the thought, but . . . you see, I don't really drink that much."

"Are you a Jehovah's Witness?" she said.

Ryan set the can down again, puzzled.

"No," he said.

"There was a girl at one of my schools, her parents were Jehovah's Witnesses. They didn't drink or anything. They wouldn't even let her watch television. Can you imagine that? She knew *nothing*. Except for what's in the Bible, and she knew all that backwards."

"There's nothing wrong with that."

"My dad always said that stuff's too far-fetched to be believed."

"But it doesn't matter what it says. What counts is what it means."

"What does it mean, then?"

She waited, politely; and he looked blank for a moment as if this was the last question in the world that he'd actually expected her to ask.

Then he seemed to give up, and said, "That's something I wish I could tell you."

"You haven't only got one kidney, have you?"

"What?"

"I heard of someone who had an operation and had a kidney taken out, and he didn't drink either."

"No, it's just . . . I never got used to it."

She'd laid just about everything out for them now, arranging it on the wobbly coffee table. The bread, the processed cheese, the vacuum-packed slices of ham, the little packet of fancy cookies to follow. If he didn't want the beer she'd picked up for him, hard luck. He wasn't getting any of her Cherry Coke.

He was searching around in his coat, probably for his pocket knife, when she said, "Have you ever had an operation?"

"Once," he said.

"What was it like?"

"I don't know. I wasn't really watching."

"What kind of operation was it?"

"It was after an accident. Well, is wasn't really an accident. Someone knocked me down and kicked me in the head. They had to let the pressure out or I would have died."

"You nearly died?" she said. This was impressive stuff.

"So they say."

"What was that like?"

He'd found the knife, and now his eyes narrowed as he looked at her. "What do you want to know stuff like that for?"

"Because it's interesting. My uncle died. He died in the house in one of the rooms near mine. He was there for two weeks before anyone found him. I've only been in the room once. I still get bad dreams about it."

"You don't need to have bad dreams about something like

that," he said. "People die, it's nature. It's been happening forever."

"So," Marianne said, "what was it like?"

He rubbed his face and then scratched around the back of
his head, as if he'd never been asked to describe it before and
now found that he didn't quite know how.

He said, "Well, it was strange. I saw strange things. But
there was a kind of beauty in it as well. It left me with this
feeling that for a minute I'd understood everything that I'd
ever wanted to know, but then I'd forgotten it again. I was always scared of dying until then. But never since."

Outside, it was beginning to get dark. The nightlife of St.
Georg would be starting up on the narrow streets below them
soon. With the window open they'd be able to listen to the
cars, listen to the arguments.

Marianne said, "What did you see?"

"Hey," Ryan said sharply. "Enough." He reached for a piece
of the bread and opened up his knife to cut the plastic wrapping. It had a long blade, much longer than she'd expected to
see.

"Aren't you going to tell me?" she said.

"Yeah," Ryan said darkly. "I can just see us down at the end
of the line and the police wanting to know what we talked
about all the time, and you telling them this. Well, I'm going
to have enough explaining to do as it is." With two neat
slashes, he ripped open the packs from end to end and then
closed the knife and put it away.

Marianne said with some curiosity, "You don't think my
mother's died, do you?"

"Oh, God," Ryan said bleakly. "That would be all I'd need.
Anything but that."

"Do you think we're going to find her?"

"I know we are."

Marianne said confidently, "I know we are, as well. But I'm
glad I've got you until then, all the same."

She gave him a few moments but he didn't say anything, so
she added, "Are you glad you've got me?"

He wasn't looking at her.

"Shut up and eat," he said.

So that was what she did, and there was a silence that lasted all of a minute.

Then she said, "Jehovah's Witnesses can't have operations. They can't have blood transfusions. So they can't have operations because they'd bleed to death."

Ryan stopped in mid-bite, stayed that way for a moment, then carried on.

"You can open that beer for me," he said when he was able. "I think I'm going to need it."

CHAPTER 34

The newly arrived British officers met Werner Odendahl in the Police Praesidium building at nine o'clock that evening. A uniformed driver had picked them up at the airport and brought them straight to the concrete and blue-steel tower on Berliner Tor; they'd had fifteen minutes with the section head and the sections head's commander, and then had been passed along to Werner. Along with another of his fellow officers, he'd be their main contact in the *Landeskriminalamt*, the State Bureau of Investigation and the local equivalent to their own CID.

As soon as they were out of the eleventh-floor office, Werner said, "I'm going to apologize in advance, because my English isn't all that good."

"Good enough for me," Jennifer said, thinking of her own hesitant stabs at a few words of German compared to Werner's fluency. Benny Moon said nothing.

They took a fast elevator down to the second floor. The building was largely deserted at this hour. Her immediate impression was that the place itself was more formal than what she was used to, the people slightly less so. Werner's boss wore a jacket and tie, but Werner himself looked more like someone whom Werner's boss might arrest.

Jennifer said, "What's supposed to have happened at the lawyers' offices?"

"O'Donnell and the girl went there this morning," Werner said, "but we were never called. We only found out about the visit when *we* called *them*, on the information you'd given us."

"Damn," Jennifer said.

"I know," Werner said, "but look at the encouraging part. They're using their own names and they seemed to be making a real effort to find the girl's mother. I'm not saying that your man's intentions are pure. But perhaps he's realized what he's started and he's having second thoughts."

"Do you know where she is?"

"Not yet. But we expect to know soon." The elevator slowed, and an electronic voice announced their floor. As they stepped out into the corridor, Werner said, "What exactly are your fears for the girl?"

"Well," Jennifer said, "the man she's with is a convicted murderer, a long-term mental patient who's broken the terms on which he was released, and he's a suspect in a sexually-motivated breaking-and-entering that may or may not have some substance to it. If you're going to tell me that the girl appears to be going along with him without pressure and he's helping her in what she wants to do, then I'm going to tell you that it's all a part of his act. Last week he saw the Devil reading a newspaper in a coffee bar. The crime is abduction, and I don't care if neither of them happens to see it that way . . . I want them found and separated before she comes to any harm, and that's why I'm here."

They stopped by one of the office doors. Werner produced a bunch of keys and searched through to find the one that would let them in.

"All right," he said, "I'll do what I can to be of help."

He went in first, and switched on the lights. This was the robbery squad section, from which they'd be working. It was a series of linked offices running parallel to the corridor, with a shiny blue floor and white walls buried under the usual mass of maps and mug shots and memos.

Benny Moon said, "Say it turns nasty or develops into a hostage situation. What can we call on?"

"I'm afraid you can't actually call on anything," Werner said. "You have only advisory status here."

"We understand that," Jennifer said.

"But you do have some kind of rapid-response unit?" Benny Moon persisted. "Weapons-trained officers who can go in hard if it's called for?"

"Go in hard?" Werner said, puzzled.

Jennifer said, "He means if O'Donnell has to be shot down to stop him, can it be done with maximum efficiency?"

Werner understood. "For armed operations we have the SEK," he said.

"Thanks, Benny," Jennifer said dryly. "But I think we'll try to take them back alive."

Benny Moon's reply was a loud, honking blow into his handkerchief.

Then he said, "Don't bet on it."

CHAPTER 35

The next morning, Benny Moon looked no better than he had on the plane. There he'd been red-eyed and dopey-looking, and Jennifer had put it down to the unsuccessful day and night that he'd spent trying to squeeze some truth out of the tightly closed shell of Cadogan's shame. He'd dozed in the seat, and they'd hardly talked at all. But that might have been deliberate on his part, for all kinds of other reasons.

The taxi had taken no more than ten minutes to bring them back to the Praesidium from their hotel, and most of that had been spent in negotiating Saturday traffic on the busy intersections of roads and railway bridges on the east side of town.

Now that she'd seen it by daylight, Jennifer reckoned that she could probably walk the distance in about the same time. She'd do it, too.

She only hoped that she wouldn't have to be doing it too often, or for too long.

They met the weekend detail of the robbery squad at eight-thirty and then got down to the business of planning the search. The matter of liaison was a delicately balanced one. As visiting officers they had no statutory powers at all, and the local men with whom they were dealing had workloads of their own. Apart from theft the squad also handled all the city's blackmail, kidnapping and weapons offenses, a mixed bag of crimes that didn't quite fall within the remit of any of the bureau's other departments. Ryan O'Donnell and Marianne Cadogan might be on the agenda now, but they weren't necessarily at the top of anyone else's list.

They didn't have an office of their own. They had two chairs around a communal desk in an office used by five investigators who, fortunately, rarely all turned in at exactly the same time. Benny went off to beg the use of a coffeemaker while Jennifer phoned Stapleton in England to confirm their arrival.

When Benny Moon got back, he was still looking like death warmed over.

"Are you fit for this?" Jennifer asked him.

"I'm fit for anything," Benny Moon said, and sat down heavily.

Jennifer said, "I left the hotels list for you. Most of the reception staff are going to speak English, so you should be all right. I've been working off the mother's maiden name to see if I can get a fix on any grandparents. I'll cover the hospitals, as well."

Benny looked around. "Where's that hippie?"

"By that, do you mean Werner?"

"Who else?"

"We're not at home any more, Benny. They do things differently here."

"Obviously."

Jennifer said, "The lawyers hired an enquiry agent to trace

Anneliese Cadogan. Now Werner's trying to trace *him*. He went off to Brussels and he's been there for two days, and that's all that we know."

Benny heaved open the fat commercial directory that she'd set out for him, and reached for the phone. The hotel list was one of the longest in the book, but there was no way of cutting it down; nothing in the names or the numbers distinguished the four-stars from the flophouses. Benny looked about as eager as a bullock on its way to the gelding shed.

"Hello," she heard him saying into the phone as she ran a finger down her own list photocopied from the regular city phone book. "Is there anybody there who speaks English?"

Cold-calling wasn't exactly Jennifer's idea of a good time either, but it had to be done and at least it was something that they could legitimately handle. Werner would be back with them in about half an hour, and by then might have come up with something that would allow them to target the search somewhat better. The problem with good policework was that it didn't travel well; at least not at the hands-on, nuts-and-bolts level. It involved knowing your area, and having a sense of the interlocking networks made up of the people within it. She and Benny were off their ground, and Werner was dealing with strangers on his.

But at least they were dealing. And with two near-misses in as many days, could a result be so far away?

So far on her could-be-grandparents list she'd eliminated ten of the names and drawn no reply from three, marking them for another try later on. At first she'd been hesitant, but her confidence was growing. By the fourteenth call she was almost on automatic pilot, running off her opening and already anticipating the likely reply.

But her alertness returned at the sound of an elderly woman's voice.

All that the woman did was to give her surname and then, as Jennifer was identifying herself as a police officer, hang up the phone. In just those few words she'd sounded hesitant, a touch frail, and definitely apprehensive. Jennifer was left with a dead line and a stupid feeling, but also a sense of something to pursue. She dialed again, and the phone at the other end rang and rang. Nobody picked it up. She tried once more, but this time it was off the hook.

She glanced at Benny Moon on the other side of the desk. He'd tilted his chair back. Feet up, he was looking at the ceiling. "Hello," Benny was saying, "is there anybody there who speaks English?"

Jennifer opened her spiral-bound notepad, and began to copy the address.

Patrick Cadogan stopped for a moment in the doorway of the hotel's coffee lounge. He'd been there before—years before—but now he felt nervous. This was the hotel where they'd always put up their trade visitors from out of town, and he'd had many a business meeting over untouched coffee on silver trays in this very room. The hotel was big, anonymous, modern, discreet. Its character was that of the gold Amex card, the corporate report. Cadogan had taken a corner room on the sixth floor, and perhaps because he'd turned up at the desk with no reservation they'd made him feel as if they were letting him have the last available room in the city. He'd charged it. His card credit was good because he'd paid off his bill with a long-term loan about six months before and hadn't dared to use the plastic again since. The company had been threatening legal action until he'd settled. A few weeks after he'd settled, they'd extended his limit.

Though it was early in the day, the room was tastefully dark. The decor was themed in black marble and gold. Seating was on low settees around even lower glass-topped tables.

Cadogan squared himself.

He walked over to one of the settees and sat down.

A red-jacketed waiter came over and said, *"Was möchten Sie mein Herr?"*

"Einen englischen Tee bitte," Cadogan said.

"Mit Zitrone?"

"Nein, mit Milch. Nein, warten Sie einen Augenblick ... bringen Sie mir einen Kaffee, aber schwarz."

The waiter moved away with the order, and Cadogan sat back. That hadn't been too bad. Not as bad as he'd feared, anyway. Ever since he'd arrived, he'd had a sense almost of settling into a shell of his old self that had been waiting to receive him. It wasn't exactly a perfect fit—a few pounds had been added here, he'd spread a little there—but there was a definite sense of belonging, and of having been away too long.

The previous evening, he'd taken the hired car into town and driven past the old house. It had been a company-owned property back then, but looked as if it had since been sold; the outside decor had been changed, and on the small front lawn a tethered Doberman had watched him cruise past with eyes of iced milk.

They'd been happy there, he supposed. If you could call anything happiness when there was something so bad waiting patiently around the corner. Cadogan had left school at the age of sixteen, worked in a warehouse for three years before realizing that he was going to be shifting goods forever and it wasn't enough, and then reenrolled in a technical college as the beginning of a journey that had brought him, then aged twenty-five, to the main European sales division of a Japanese-American company called Masako Electronics. He'd been as proud of his dropout origins as he had of his achievements. Married a local girl, daughter in a private school, the embodiment of the bourgeois trans-European dream.

And then, after the dream, had come the awakening.

His black coffee arrived. He said to the waiter, *"Könnte ich bitte ein Telefon haben?"* The waiter nodded briefly and disappeared again.

Only now was he beginning to see how he should have handled it. There had been worthwhile things in their life here that he should have tried to hold onto. And not just the material things, either; he'd managed to lose it all because he'd chosen devastation over damage limitation. One might say that he hadn't been so wise. One might say that he hadn't been so bright.

But then, one hadn't experienced the shock of that hand-labeled tape, arriving at his office on a routine workday morning.

The telephone brought to his table was a radio remote. Now, *there* was something new. He dialed a once-familiar number, and a few moments later was saying, "Rudi? It's Pat Cadogan."

There was a stunned silence at the other end of the line. And then: "You're kidding me."

"I'm not kidding you, Rudi. I got into town last night."

"I don't know what to say."

"How about, welcome back?"

"Well, of course, but ... Jesus, Pat, it's been *years*! What happened?"

"I more or less dropped out of sight."

"We actually thought you were dead for a while. We couldn't imagine that you'd disappear without even getting in touch, but then Anneliese called."

Cadogan was surprised. "She called you?"

"She called Christina. She said that the two of you had broken up and it was all her fault, and she was going away so that you and Marianne could pick up the pieces. I was supposed to give you the message, but you'd vanished."

"Did she say where she was going?"

"No. Christina said the way she talked, she sounded almost like a dead person. We were worried about her. We were worried about both of you."

"I know, I'm sorry. I just went home."

"You always said your home was here. It must have been quite a row that you two had."

"It was."

"But you still don't want to talk about it."

"Talking won't help it, Rudi."

They stayed on the line for a few minutes longer, but the conversation was effectively over. Cadogan wondered whether to tell Rudi that Marianne had once named a dog after him, but he didn't. Friends could talk about that kind of thing. But there was a distance between them now, a space forced by his own unpredictability and by the passage of time. Rudi knew nothing of Anneliese, he'd seen nothing of Marianne.

Finally, and with the usual promises, they both rang off.

Cadogan kept the phone. He'd more calls to make. Other friends. The school, if he could get hold of anyone today. He'd make the calls, and then he'd get out onto the streets.

Starting in a moment.

He sat there, holding the receiver. The waiter appeared and hovered on the fringe of his vision, but Cadogan shook his head.

The tape. He'd seen it only once in reality, but he'd rerun it countless times in his mind since then. He'd no choice or control in the matter; whether his guard was up or down, whether he wanted to dwell on it or not. It was like being pursued around every room in the house by someone singing him a song that he didn't want to hear. You can assume that you know people, he was thinking, but you don't. He'd thought that there was nothing left for him to find out about Anneliese but there it had been, a guilty appetite hidden from the beginning and growing out of view until, finally, it had consumed even her. How could someone conceal so much inner emptiness so effectively and for so long? And how could he have failed to sense it?

Had he sensed it? Had he sensed it there but turned away?

He wondered if he might ever come to pity her. He didn't feel as if he would; but then again, there had been a time when he wouldn't even have considered it as a question.

Anneliese had been a secret stranger in his life. And so, he was now beginning to see, had his daughter Marianne. For one it was too late, for the other . . .

He *hadn't* lost her. He hadn't lost her yet. His eyes had been opened for him just in time.

He'd seen the darkness in the depths. Now it was time to begin a rise towards the light.

Marianne said, "Do you think it's worth waiting?"

"For what?" Ryan said. "He's either here or he isn't. And he isn't, right now."

They were back in the arcade and once more standing on the railed balcony outside the offices of AGENTUR JOHANN SCHLESINGER. A man of remarkable consistency, Johann Schlesinger was still somewhere else. For a moment they'd thought otherwise when they'd climbed the stairs and seen, from a distance, that the yellow Post-It note on his door was no longer in place, but they'd found the door still locked and the office beyond it dark and then, stooping, Marianne had picked up the fallen note from the floor. The tacky strip on the back had become clogged with dust and fibers. She'd tried to press it back onto the glass, but it wouldn't take.

"Perhaps he's out there looking for her," Marianne suggested hopefully.

Ryan was squinting through the gap in the blinds at the darkened office.

"I'd give anything for five minutes to dig around in that filing cabinet," he said.

He tried the door again, giving an almost savage twist on the handle and putting his shoulder into it, not exactly as if he was trying to break the door down, but more as if the threat alone might cause it to pop open. It gave its usual quarter-inch, whereupon it was stopped by the lock. It wasn't *much* of a lock. But it was there.

Marianne was watching him with an apprehension that was close to wonder. It always scared her a little when his anger came up like this. But, like fire in the wrong place, she found it as fascinating as it was disturbing.

He saw her expression and said, "What's the matter?"

But she shook her head.

As they were descending the stairway, Marianne said, "Perhaps he's already back, but he doesn't come in on Saturdays."

"Who knows," Ryan said woodenly.

"How much money have we got left?"

"Not enough to fuck around with," Ryan said, and then quickly, "Forget I said that."

She was silent for a while. She wasn't sure that she liked him so much in this kind of mood.

As they waited to cross the street, she said, "We could try looking at those churches."

"Churches," Ryan said. He didn't sound enthusiastic.

Lying there and trying to get off to sleep the previous night, she'd been telling him about how she used to go to her grandparents' place and it had been a flat somewhere close to a big church. But where, and which church, she wasn't able to say. She hadn't been there often. She didn't know her grandparents too well. Her German grandmother was a bit of a mouse, and her grandfather she remembered as being like a big old lion whom nothing could please. She'd told Ryan all this and then Ryan had said, *Please. Just shut up. Just for a while.* So she'd lain there not daring to speak, and then eventually they'd both drifted away. The strange thing was that in the morning she'd opened her eyes and found him sitting by her bed on the room's one straight-backed chair. He'd been watching her as she slept, she didn't know for how long. Waiting for her to wake up, she supposed.

"All right," he said.

"All right what?"

"We'll look around by some churches."

The lights changed, and they started to cross.

"And I'm sorry I swore," he said without looking at her.

CHAPTER 36

They were ringing the bells as Werner found a space to park the pool car just outside the church square. The square itself was impossible. Empty tourist buses on half-hour layovers were nose-to-tail on the cobbles and constantly being stop-started around to keep the traffic going. Like all the other public buildings in Hamburg, the church was huge in scale and was topped by a greening copper clock tower. Lines of people were trooping up and down the steps, some of them without cameras. They were half a mile uphill from the old harbor area, here.

Werner led the way. They had to stop for a sight-seeing tram that had been dressed up to look like a train, and then they were able to make for the apartment house that faced the church from the opposite side of the square.

Jennifer said, "What kind of housing is this?"

"It was built for sailors and their families," he said. "But that was a long time ago. Things change. All kinds of people moving in."

"Not a place to find a rich family, then."

"Not rich, not desperately poor. Just ordinary."

They entered the complex through an archway leading to an inner courtyard, stepped in levels to take account of the slope of the hill. The building was of red brick, but within the archway tunnel there was a running stone design of ships and anchors and curling vines. A number of doors overlooked the courtyard, which had been made into something of a garden area by the use of tubs of evergreens crowded together.

They climbed an airy stairway to the second floor, where Werner rang a bell. There was a long wait, and then the door opened a few inches. Werner spoke quietly and showed his identification. Jennifer couldn't pick up what was being said, but she did hear the name *Anneliese*. The door opened further and Werner glanced back at her, indicating for her to follow him in. It was clear from his look that their journey here hadn't been wasted.

The woman holding the door was in her seventies, at least. Her hands were like a bird's, thin and delicate and parchment-pale. They trembled.

There was a faintly sour smell to the place, like an empty thermos. But otherwise it was tidy enough. The apartment seemed too big for one, but as far as Jennifer could see, the woman lived alone.

They sat. Werner introduced her and she nodded to the woman, and tried to follow the conversation as Werner asked some questions. The woman's eyes flicked from one to the other of them, clearly apprehensive. When she answered, her voice was almost a whisper. Jennifer wasn't entirely sure of what was being said.

After a few moments, Werner turned to her and explained, "She's alone here. Her husband died three years ago. She says that she put the phone down on you because she thought that you were calling to tell her that her daughter was dead also."

"Why would she think that?"

Werner asked her. The woman replied, and then got up and

went over to an old chest of drawers in the darkest of dark wood. A clock and some framed photographs stood on top of it. Werner said to Jennifer, "She says she's had no contact from Anneliese since her daughter's husband left her and she disappeared. All she's ever had is one letter."

Closing one of the drawers, the woman brought the letter over. She handed it to Werner, who took it out of the envelope and read it at a glance before passing it to Jennifer.

It was very brief, and she had little trouble with the translation. *Remember me when I was happy, think of me now as one who has gone. Dear mama. I am so sorry. Anneliese.* Jennifer turned it over and looked at the envelope. It had a Düsseldorf postmark. She glanced up and met Werner's eyes. He'd noted it, too.

The woman asked a question.

Werner explained, "She says if we're looking for Anneliese, does that mean we know why she disappeared so suddenly? It as good as killed her father. What do you want to say?"

He was obviously going to leave it to her. The woman's eyes were on her, as well. Choosing her words carefully, Jennifer said, "Tell her I'm sorry . . . but it's a mystery to all of us."

As they were standing to leave, Jennifer glanced at the framed photographs on the cabinet. There were some old black and whites of a little blonde girl—Anneliese, presumably. A pretty child, at a distance of years. Nothing of her grown-up. The one adult photograph was of a man who she assumed to be Marianne's deceased grandfather. He'd been in his twenties when it had been taken, and he wore some kind of uniform. Perhaps the print had faded or perhaps it was just the way he'd been lit, but his eyes were dark pits and his mouth a grim, uncompromising line. *Dear mama,* Anneliese's letter had said. No mention of her father in it at all.

But you could read only so much into less than a couple of dozen words.

Werner gave the woman a number to call if she should hear anything from anyone, especially her granddaughter. She might get in touch, he told her, and it's vital that you call us if she does.

Then they thanked her and said their good-byes, and then they left.

"How's your hotel?" Werner said to her as they were reentering the robbery squad room after the drive back to the Praesidium. At a glance she could see that Benny Moon was no longer at the desk where she'd left him. Josef, the *Kriminalhauptmeister* who'd been assigned as their second contact, was two-finger typing just a couple of chairs along. She wondered if Werner had forgotten that he'd asked her the same question once already that morning.

She said, "I've been in and out so fast, I've barely seen it. Hotels always look the same anyway."

"If we can wrap this up quickly," Werner said, "perhaps you'll stay around and see some of the parts of town we're more proud of."

"I can just imagine my boss footing the bill for *that*."

Josef spoke up from his typing. "Listen to me," he said, "let me give you a warning. Don't get involved with this one—he's a one-man disaster area as far as women are concerned."

There seemed to be one of those team in-jokes in the offing here, and Jennifer didn't quite grasp it. "Why?" she said.

"Well," Josef said, gesturing, "look at him. They never know what to do with him. In the end they always have to give up and move on."

Werner just stood there and took it, albeit a little wryly. "Thank you for those kind thoughts, Josef," he said. "And do you know where the other English officer is right now?"

"He was gone when I got here."

"I'll check his desk," Jennifer said, moving around behind Josef to look. "If he's found anything, he'll have made some kind of note."

Werner picked up a discarded newspaper from one of the other work areas and, rolling it as if to stick it in his pocket, said, "I'll be in my office, talking to Düsseldorf. See you later."

He walked by Josef and, in passing, whacked him across the back of the head with the newspaper. It was obviously a friendly sparring gesture, but it seemed just a little bit harder than anything that friendship might call for. It left Josef wincing and rubbing his head ruefully.

He looked at Jennifer.

"I think that means he likes you," he said.

Jennifer gave him a pained look, and bent to check the notes on Benny's desk. The desk was a mess, but the notes were neat and straightforward. She saw Patrick Cadogan's name, along with a hotel and room number. As she was taking this in, the phone rang and she picked it up.

Benny's voice said, "You're back, then. Any luck?"

"Nothing worth knowing. Where are you?"

"Downstairs in the playroom. Come and see what we've been turning up."

She caught up with Benny one floor down, in an open-plan office area that was deserted apart from Benny himself and the woman police officer over whose shoulder he was looking. The woman—short-haired, and in a big pullover and jeans—was seated before a Siemens PC computer and was scrolling her way down a long list of names and data. There was a modem hookup alongside the machine.

Jennifer said, "I saw your notes upstairs. Do I take it this means that Cadogan's in town?"

"He is," Benny said. "And after you warning him off, as well."

"How did you hear?"

"I turned him up while I was phoning around the hotels. It's not O'Donnell using Cadogan's name again, it's the real thing."

"You know that for certain?"

"I spoke to him. He wasn't in his room, but I had him paged and caught him on his way out. He says he doesn't want to be involved, he just wants to be close for when we find her."

"And do we believe that?"

"I've seen ginger hairpieces more convincing."

Jennifer glanced at the computer screen. The data was still scrolling through, stopping every few seconds, moving on again.

She said, "That's not the ferry passenger list, is it?"

"No," Benny said, "it's a lot more interesting than that. Say hello to Renata." Renata glanced up briefly. "She's with homicide and sexual crimes. Josef told me what she does in the department and then phoned her at home for me. She came in specially."

Jennifer pulled over a chair, and seated herself behind the policewoman's other shoulder. "For what?" she said.

Benny said, "The vice squad here have started to do regular checks on electronic maildrops and bulletin boards. These are like the old contact magazines, only with a big dash of *Star Trek*. I've asked Renata if she can do us a trawl through the kind of scene that we know Anneliese Cadogan was into." He indicated the screen. "Just about every kinky subculture you can think of uses these things for networking now."

"Well, that's fine," Jennifer said. "But bear in mind that we're only trying to trace the mother in case it helps us to intercept the daughter. If she's buried as deeply as that, it'll make no difference."

Benny looked at the policewoman. "Tell her what you just told me," he said.

The woman named Renata took her hands from the keyboard, and the roll-through on the screen halted. She looked at Jennifer and said, "Through this we have access to information being passed between sadomasochists, neosatanists, and pedophile rings. An untraceable preadolescent child in this market would have a minimum value of fifteen thousand American dollars. Of that, seven thousand dollars would be refunded if she were to be returned to the vendor alive. Then she could be sold again and resold with diminishing value until the end of the line."

Somewhere outside and far away, a car alarm was set off and quickly stilled.

Benny Moon said, "Poor little Marianne, eh? She'll wish she'd stayed on the beach."

Jennifer said, "What have you found so far?"

"Well," Benny said, "it's a cagey market. Nobody gives their names and nobody ever says straight out what they're looking for. It's kind of like a lonely dicks column. You know . . . you send me a picture of yours, and I'll send you a picture of the horse's behind. What I'm thinking is, suppose O'Donnell *does* manage to keep himself on a leash for long enough to get her to her mother in one piece ... then we're still not necessarily talking about an over-the-rainbow ending. The kind of friends her mother's going to have will make O'Donnell look like a total amateur. Your man's been seeing devils in Wimpy bars, but he doesn't realize that he's on the express track to the genuine article. Anything could happen when he gets there. They might prove to be his kind of crowd. In which case, Marianne could be the price of entry."

"These networks aren't only local," Renata added. "We're talking about a worldwide exchange system. If she disappears into that, you can pretty well forget about ever finding her."

"Gets deeper and deeper, doesn't it?" Benny said.

"No," Jennifer said. "She couldn't. Not to her own daughter."

But the two of them sat looking at her, saying nothing.

"All right," she said then. "Stick with it."

CHAPTER 37

Saturday night in Hamburg.

The day had continued with no more success than its beginning. Despondent and footsore, they rode the U-bahn back into the middle of town. The train was clean and spartan, the rips in its seats stitched like old wounds. Across the carriage sat two young women carrying cello cases. The young women got off at Rödingsmarkt and the train carried on towards its terminus under the Hauptbahnhof, the mainline station to which all of their travels had so far returned them.

Marianne said, "I'm sorry."

"For what?"

"I thought I'd know. I thought I remembered everything. But nothing's the same."

"It never is," Ryan said.

"But I've been dreaming about it for years. About being back, and knowing I was home. But this isn't home. It isn't anything. So what was I dreaming about? I mean, what's the point of dreaming at all if it can't come true? That's just cruel."

Ryan seemed to hesitate, then he raised his hand and ruffled her hair sympathetically.

"Don't do that," she said, jerking her head away.

"Sorry."

They'd tried almost all the churches in town. Every time, she'd insisted that they'd found the place. And each time without fail it seemed that, despite her certainty, they hadn't. Eventually the light had started to fade, and the building floodlights had started to come on. Department stores all the way through town had emptied out and closed their doors but still remained brilliantly lit on every floor, like moth traps with only their killing power turned off. As some of the street noise and the traffic died back, masses of pigeons could be heard roosting up in their own secret city above the city.

Ryan and Marianne made their way through the maze of tunnels and underpasses beneath the Hauptbahnhof, heading once more for the lockers where they'd parked their luggage for the day. Ryan had said nothing about money, but Marianne knew that it was getting tight. She'd been wondering how much longer they'd be able to carry on. But she didn't dare ask, in case she didn't like the answer.

There were kiosks and odd little bars hidden away in unexpected corners down here in the tunnels. They were passing one just as a paramedic team was arriving with emergency bag and folding stretcher. Someone, it appeared, had collapsed in a corner of the bar. Everyone else had carried on drinking, but out of deference they'd dragged across a couple of empty beer crates to section off the corner where the man lay. The place was small and there was standing room only and at least this way, no one was going to forget and step on him.

They rose on the escalator into the evening of the station

square. It was even more crowded now than on the night of
their arrival. The usual bunch of slightly unsteady, slightly unshaven young men was there by the head of the stairway—
some sitting and conversing, some just hanging around. And as
they moved back into the St. Georg district, Marianne saw that
the women on the streets were out in force again. Their ages
varied, from late teens to one middle-aged woman who looked
as if she was dressed and made up ready to go to church. They
stood on the side streets at well-spaced intervals, staring ahead
and waiting for someone to catch their eye.

Their hotel was full. They'd have to find another. Marianne
was too weary to search, but too weary to protest. The one that
they eventually found had two lights over its entranceway,
green for free and red for occupied, like traffic lights. And
from the sounds that reached their room, the traffic in the corridor outside seemed likely to keep moving all night.

Compared to their last, this place was a rathole. The rooms
didn't even have locks with keys, just a sliding bolt on the inside of the door like in a toilet. Their room was a lot smaller
than the previous one, and the beds were much closer together.
There was a loud fan just outside the window, and a strong
smell of Italian food in the air. They had some fruit and half
a packet of biscuits left for supper. Marianne sat wearily on
one of the beds.

"So," Ryan said. "What are we going to do now?"

"I don't know," Marianne said.

"Time's running out. I don't know how they work, but
they're bound to catch up with us in the end."

"Who?"

"The police."

"He won't have called the police."

"Why not?"

"He doesn't care about me that much."

Ryan sat on the other bed. Their knees were almost touching. Someone lumbered past outside, heard through a plaster-
board wall that offered nothing in the way of soundproofing.

"He's still your father. That's got to count for something,
hasn't it?"

"He isn't like that," she insisted. "Not any more. Last year, he didn't even bother about my birthday. I got one card, and that was from Mrs. Healey. I put it where he wouldn't see it. If he couldn't remember it on his own, I didn't want him remembering at all."

"Well," Ryan said, "I don't know what else we can try. It's not just a question of time. The money's running out, too."

"I bet you're sorry you ever met me."

"Part of me is."

"Oh, thanks very much."

"I'm being honest with you. Who'd want to get stuck in a situation like this out of choice?"

"You could just leave me," she said.

"I could."

"Why don't you?"

"Say I were to do that, and something happened to you. How do you think I'd feel then?"

Marianne shrugged.

"I can tell you. I'd feel as badly as if I'd hurt you myself, and I wouldn't want to have to live with that. I once did something I had reason to be ashamed of, don't ask me what it was. I paid a price for it ... but then I found that this wasn't the same thing as paying off the debt."

"What's the difference?"

"The price is what everyone expects of you. The debt is the distance you know you still have to go. But I don't expect you to understand that."

"I don't."

"Well, perhaps that's just as well. You're young, and you've got nothing bad on your slate."

"I wouldn't be ashamed of you," she insisted. "Not unless you went to prison, or something."

Ryan smiled at this. But he seemed to be forcing it.

He said, "That doesn't do much to get us out of this situation, does it?"

"I've had another idea," Marianne suggested. "Somewhere we used to go on Sundays. It's a Sunday tomorrow. She might be there."

Ryan sighed, and spread his hands in an open gesture. "What the hell," he said. "What's to lose?"

He got up from the bed and went outside into the corridor, leaving her to get ready as usual. She hardly wanted to stand. She seemed to ache, all over. She kept glancing at the door as she undressed, nervously because she knew there was no lock.

"Are you there?" she said at one point.

"I'm right here," he said. From the sound of his voice, he was only just outside the door. Knowing this, she felt safe. She quickly changed into her last set of clean underwear and climbed into the bed.

"Ready," she called out, pulling the covers up under her chin.

He came back in and bolted the door. Then he took off his coat and pulled off his shoes and stretched out on the other bed. He reached for the pull cord on the wall between them.

"You'll ruin your clothes," she said, "sleeping in them like that."

"They're ruined already," he said, and switched off the light.

The room didn't go dark. There was too much going on outside, casting shadows of watery neon through the thin curtains and up the walls. They lay in silence for a while.

And then Marianne said, "I'm still hungry."

"Me too," Ryan said from the half-night. "We're just going to have to hold out until breakfast."

She heard him take a deep breath and then sigh, heavily, the way he did every evening as he ran himself down into sleep.

"Ryan," she said.

A pause.

And then: "What?"

"Even if you'd been to prison, I still wouldn't be ashamed."

Had she been able to see him in the darkness, she'd have seen his face close as if in pain.

"Go to sleep, now," he said.

CHAPTER 38

"I'm told that some parts of town can be dangerous," she said from behind Cadogan as he waited to pick up his room key. She saw him tense and half turn. "You shouldn't be out so late on your own."

He looked at her. He seemed weary, but unfazed. He said, "You're not on home ground now. You can't tell me what to do."

"I know it," Jennifer said. "So why don't we see if we can be of some use to each other, instead?"

The receptionist laid his key on the countertop. Cadogan scooped it off, and indicated for Jennifer to follow him. "I feel as if I've got no secrets from anybody, now," he said as together they walked across the marble floor towards some open-plan seating. "But if you want to come fishing for more, you're welcome to try."

It was a visitor waiting area, unused at this hour. The seats were vaguely antique reproductions from no particular period and were overlooked by glass-cased displays—one for expensive perfumes, another for even more expensive watches. As she seated herself and Cadogan let himself drop onto a sofa like a sack, Jennifer said, "You've got quite a taste in hotels for a man with your financial profile."

"The check bounces just as high for soup as caviar," Cadogan said. "Are you going to tell the management?"

"All I want to know is whether you found out anything useful today."

"If this is supposed to be a trade," Cadogan said, "then why don't you tell me your side of it first?"

Rather than argue, she told him. She didn't mention

209

Düsseldorf and she left out the alarmist stuff about the child sex networks, but otherwise she gave him a reasonably accurate picture of their developing strategy.

After hearing what she had to tell him, Cadogan said, "I've been looking for Anneliese, too. I've been checking the shops where she used to have credit."

"That's something we didn't think of."

"You never had to keep up with the money she could spend. But I got nowhere. She didn't close any of the accounts, she just hasn't used them. Did you contact the school?"

"The local police have done that for us. If Marianne gets in touch with any of her old friends, we ought to hear. But it's been a long time, and children can grow apart really fast. Unless something breaks for us tomorrow, I reckon our best chance is with the private detective your lawyers hired."

"Him? He's fucking useless. Ads in the newspapers, that's been *his* brilliant contribution."

So she explained that Cadogan was missing the point. It really didn't matter to anyone in the investigation whether Anneliese was reached or not. What mattered was that Ryan and Marianne seemed to be making an effort to find her, which brought an element of predictability into their movements. They knew by now about the theft of the Rolodex cards from the law offices, and she told him that this was as useful a signpost as they could ever hope to get.

"At the start of business on Monday morning," Jennifer said, "whether Schlesinger's back in town or not, there's going to be someone sitting behind his desk, waiting for a call or a visit from O'Donnell and the girl."

"One of your people?"

"Exactly."

"So, where *is* this office?"

"I'm not going to tell you. And don't waste your time with the phone book, it's an agency name. If O'Donnell turns up without your daughter, we'll play him along and then have him followed. If she's there, we'll separate them safely and take him in. Which is something that will take the grace and finesse of the Royal Ballet and which your presence, I can guarantee you now, would ruin."

Cadogan was looking at her. He didn't like it, she could tell, but she could also see that he'd grasped the fundamental delicacy of the situation and knew that he was going to have to accept it.

He said, "This Ryan O'Donnell. He may be insane. But he isn't stupid, is he?"

"No," Jennifer said. "I don't believe he is."

CHAPTER 39

It was ten past seven on the Sunday morning, and the daylight was now coming on with an opal clarity. Cadogan had turned up his collar, and still he shivered a little. His senses seemed to have been sharpened. He'd had to set out in near darkness, feeling like a monk or a knight setting out on some spiritual journey while the rest of the world slept on. Elsewhere in town there had been very little traffic, nothing to disturb the peace except for the faint cries of gulls out across the harbor. As he'd passed under the elevated track of the U-bahn, one of the early trains had gone over, a flicker of dashes and hyphens of light seen through the complex of supporting girders.

There were people on the train. And most of them probably had the same destination he did.

It was called the *fischmarkt*. Once exactly that, a quayside fish market, it had grown to become a kind of Sunday-morning carnival that fired up every week at the crack of dawn and had vanished by eleven, leaving only an empty ground and a lot of windblown litter. Eleven o'clock was the magic hour when church services began and trading, by ancient law, had to cease. Everyone came here. Whenever they'd had visitors, this was where they'd brought them. Marianne had always been the hardest to drag away. For the adults it had begun to pall after a couple of hours, but she'd been in Disneyland every time. Once she'd vanished and they'd had a panicky fifteen minutes until they'd found her at one of the stalls, staring at half a shark whose jaws had been propped open with a wooden wedge, blood leaking from its gills and eyes gone as if imploded from a sudden change in pressure.

The closer he got, the less empty the streets became. There were two young men just ahead of him, both of them tall and thin and wearing bomber jackets, jeans, cowboy boots, and gloves. One of them was knocking back a beer. The other had just finished one, and dumped the can in an overflowing trash bin as they passed.

He could hear music.

After the policewoman had left him the previous night, he'd gone up to his room and made himself some coffee and then stretched fully clothed on the bed for what he'd intended to be a snatched half-hour. His plan had been to go out again and start checking the city's late haunts and talking to the night people; he'd left the TV switched on to stop himself from drifting away, and then he'd drifted away. He'd woken about five hours later, the untouched coffee cold by his side and with the TV roaring static. He'd shed his clothes on the way to the bathroom and then he'd stood under the shower for as long as it took to revive himself. Afterwards, he'd contemplated himself in the mirror as he'd pulled on a clean sweater and combed his damp hair. He was thinking that he had the look of a down-and-out who'd been shaved and tidied up for some important appearance. In court, maybe. Or a family wedding. Or his own funeral.

Out across the harbor in the freeport zone, the ships and the cranes and all of the handling gear were studded with tiny lights. He was already late. It was seven-twenty and some people were already leaving the market, dispersing to their cars laden with cardboard boxes full of plants and ferns and palms and small trees. Beyond the bollards and the police-controlled barrier, the crowds were shoulder to shoulder.

He hesitated, but only for a moment.

The quayside bars were all playing loud music with their doors thrown wide open, and were crammed. Stalls opposite

were hung with smoked eels in bunches like bullwhip handles.
One pitchman was shouting to get attention, another was beating on the roof of his van with a fish. Cadogan went with the
flow, scanning as he moved. Further along, the old waterfront
opened out into a marketplace overlooked by restored warehouse buildings. How many people were there, crowded in for
as far as he could see? Five, ten thousand? He couldn't even
make a decent estimate. If O'Donnell and Marianne were
around, it would be easy to miss them. But it wasn't beyond
imagining that he might spot them, as well.

Cadogan pushed his way past a stall of junk and bric-a-brac,
with ice skates and old luggage and what looked like a Russian
army uniform hung out for sale. Alongside it someone was
selling a miracle car polish, boxes and boxes of the stuff being
offered out of the open back of a vehicle with an indifferent
shine.

He wondered how they'd spent the night. Didn't like to
think about it, but he had to. He'd read about people like
O'Donnell. Some of them had no guilt, because they didn't in
their hearts believe that they were doing anything wrong; in
their own minds they were persecuted lovers, misunderstood
by a world that couldn't see the beauty in what they were
doing. Others knew exactly what they were about. They
grabbed and they despoiled and then they covered their tracks
and came up with denials. Many held normal jobs, led unremarkable lives. Many got themselves into positions of trust,
where they could work with young children.

Let him get his hands on O'Donnell. He'd put him in some
kind of a fucking *position*, all right.

Someone looked at him. Had he made a sound?

He put his head down, and moved on.

At least, he tried to keep telling himself, it wasn't just a
straightforward forced abduction. O'Donnell didn't have her in
a crate, or anything. Unlike the birds and the rabbits and the
wildfowl in the section of the market through which Cadogan
was now moving. Under the shelter of a loading bay awning,
livestock was being sold. Doves, geese, day-old chicks for a
Deutschmark each. The chicks were milling around under an
infrared lamp. The geese were listlessly pulling out the feathers

from their own rear ends. They were in boxes, pens, cages stacked on top of one another so that their feces dropped straight through. Marianne used to like this part, as well. She'd thought they were all pets.

Cadogan shoved his way through the open entranceway that led into the big market hall. Someone called out in protest behind him. He muttered something halfway suitable, but he didn't look back.

As in the bars, the music in here was loud; but unlike that in the bars, this was live. The hall was a fair-sized space with a stage at its far end, and trestle tables and benches set for its full length. Stalls down the sides were selling food: pancakes, fried prawns, sausages drowned in mustard, raw fish sandwiches with onion rings the size of bangles. The entire place was in a haze of spotlight-pierced steam from all the cooking. People were eating, people were dancing, people were lining the gallery rails of the upper level and watching. The group was the usual continental four-piece combo of people whom Cadogan couldn't imagine ever getting together under any other circumstances. A blonde girl dressed in black, a middle-aged Johnny Cash wannabe on bass, a lead guitarist who looked like an undercover policeman in a leather jacket, somebody's grandfather on the drums. They were playing "At the Hop," and as the number ended, a good half of the audience began to whistle and shout and stamp.

Watching their faces, almost counting them off, Cadogan moved to the iron stairway and started to climb. He had to step over two teenage girls eating breakfast of fried potatoes and eggs out of cardboard trays.

No wonder Marianne had always liked it so much here. Fried food, loud music, and lots of weird things to look at. And you could sit on the stairs and eat with your fingers, and nobody minded.

Now they were playing "Wand'ring Star," from *Paint Your Wagon*. Cadogan moved into a space on the rail, and looked down. If there was any two-way influence between them at all, she'd probably have O'Donnell bring her here. And she'd probably clean him out, as well, if he let her, and he wouldn't realize it until the end of the morning when, after being bowled along from one of her enthusiasms to another, he'd find that there would be nothing in his pockets but his hands. There had been a time, around four years old, when Cadogan's name for her had been Marianne the Money Pit.

He looked for her. O'Donnell he still didn't know, but one glimpse of Marianne would set him off like an alarm and then, no matter what stood in his way, he'd fly to her and he'd grab her and he wouldn't let her go. That policewoman had been right, he'd looked at his daughter and he'd seen too much of Anneliese and he'd turned away. Maybe there was even more to it than that; he had to admit it now, because he'd been more honest with himself in these past few days than he'd had to be in a number of years. He could remember, because he'd forced himself to recall, how back in those early days in the cheap hotels he'd sometimes woken at four or five in the morning to find the weight and the warmth of Marianne against his side. She'd crossed from her own bed, and climbed into his; sleep-walking, perhaps, and seeking the kind of comfort she'd known as a much smaller child. He'd panicked then, aware of how easy it would be to dream and reach out, and only too conscious of the dreams he'd been having; and so without a word, without waking her, he'd crawled across to the other bed to sleep out the night alone.

There was no avoiding the fact that he'd grown to be afraid of Marianne. Afraid even to touch her. Afraid of what close contact might mean, in a world from which all innocence had been driven. And so instead he'd obsessed himself with the details of his going-nowhere business and failed to see what he was making of it, an escape. It was as if he'd simply put Marianne on hold, intending to return his attention to her on some vague and distant day. But you couldn't do that with people, he realized now. Time didn't stand still, she didn't stop in her tracks just because his thoughts were elsewhere. She couldn't stay the same forever. Only the dead could do that.

And then something struck him. Oh, God, he thought. O'Donnell was probably keeping her in some cheap hotel or a hostel now. What if she started to do it again?

Cadogan sobbed. It took him by surprise, like a hiccup. He realized that the people to either side of him had moved away.

He wiped his cheek. His face was wet. He sniffed. He wiped his eyes on his sleeve, and glanced around to see if anyone else had noticed.

And his eyes met Marianne's.

CHAPTER 40

It took more than a moment for Jennifer to adjust when she opened her eyes. The window of her room was slightly open, her curtains stirring in the breeze. She wondered if she'd been dreaming again, and she wondered about what. She had that sense of unease, as if there were things still waiting out in the darkness that she couldn't give names to.

But it wasn't dark. It was morning. As the heavy curtains moved, some light leaked into the room. Drowsily, aching a little as one might on the day after hard exercise, she got out of bed and went over to let in some more. She'd a feeling that she might have been dreaming of old Mr. Glick, but she couldn't be certain. He'd never made it to his court appearance. He'd been found in his car with the engine running and a rubber hose from the exhaust to the interior, five hours dead. Turning from the opened curtains, she saw that a large envelope had been slipped under her door at some time during the night.

It was one of the hotel's own envelopes, and it wasn't sealed. Looking inside, she saw that it contained a number of fax sheets. They were unfolded. She took them over to the table and drew them out carefully. These appeared to have been transmitted in sequence from the incident room at home, shortly before midnight the previous night.

She yawned, and sat, and started to skim through. More newspaper clippings from the time of the first murder. Police photos of the victim and the site where she'd been discovered; the transmitted quality of these was so dismal that they had a look of having been airbrushed in soot, and this somehow made them seem even grimmer. The girl's body rested on the kind of brick-strewn plain left behind in the wake of wholesale urban demolition, where entire acreages of houses had gone but developers hadn't yet moved in. She appeared to have been covered by some ratty piece of carpet that had been moved to one side for separate inspection. In the background was the sweep of an elevated concrete road, and a line of apartment houses beyond that. The child lay like a broken doll. There were closeups, as well, in the same overloaded blacks and whites. She didn't seem to be sleeping. Jennifer had never thought that the dead looked as if they were sleeping.

Some of the other stuff was medical, those parts of O'Donnell's file that had been missing and which had now been tracked down and returned to plug some of the holes. The attack on him by another inmate early in his detention; he'd been kicked about the head badly enough to require surgery, it seemed. Such attacks weren't unusual, where an offense had involved a minor. They were preventable by segregation, but not completely. Other sheets referred to a time much later when he'd absconded from the open ward and turned up at his sister's house some eighty miles away. She'd called the hospital, and the police had picked him up within half an hour. It was one of the few mentions of O'Donnell's family background that Jennifer had seen, and it told her nothing.

She checked her watch. And then she went through into the bathroom, and started to run the shower.

She had no clear picture of O'Donnell yet, and this worried her. Who could say what might have been cooking in his mind for all these years? Not his doctors, that was for sure. They hadn't even been aware of O'Donnell's two rumored liaisons with adult women, neither of them traceable. According to the sources, one drank and the other barely spoke English. The police had found a few skin magazines and six cameras in their search of his vandalized home, but the magazines had all been over-the-counter stuff and not one of the cameras was in working order. The only photographs they'd turned up were old family pictures, way out of date from a family that appeared to have disowned him.

What was the key?

Jennifer didn't believe in evil. Not in an absolute sense. Evil was a word too often used to dodge facing the reality of whatever you had to confront. To call it evil, to call it other, was to deny the common presence of those basic materials from which such horrors could be assembled. She didn't seek to make excuses; but she was sure that each time a denial was made, the way was prepared for some further atrocity. She could remember, as an example, the particularly vicious killing of a jeweler in the course of a robbery in his home. The thieves had been two know-nothing boys who hadn't even had any idea of how to unload what they'd stolen. They'd been caught trying to sell the stuff out of a suitcase to shopping crowds. She'd interviewed them in their cells, and she'd been unable quite to reconcile the two conflicting impressions that she'd received: such losers in life, but with such a creative streak in their brutality. She'd heard the same kind of thing said about concentration camp guards—give them a victim and take away the pressures of any moral framework, and in such darkness even the most ordinary could shine with the light of Lucifer himself.

Showered and dressed, she returned the faxes to the envelope and called Benny's room. There was no reply. Could he be up and out already? Down at the buffet breakfast, perhaps? If he was, he must have managed to shake off whatever had been making him look so rough the previous day. What she'd taken for tiredness had been starting to look like something more lasting.

The envelope in her hand, she left the room and went downstairs to Benny's door. She didn't expect to find him there, but when she knocked a voice called out a bleary, *"Come in. . . ."*

"I can't," Jennifer said, her heart sinking. "The door's locked. You've got to open it."

There was a long wait, and then sounds of fumbling around. And then the door opened onto a darkened room, where the curtains were still drawn. Benny Moon stood there blinking in

his pajamas, self-consciously trying not to be seen to be holding the fly together in his fist.

Jennifer said, "Do you know what time it is?"

"I know," Benny said. "I know."

"We're supposed to be meeting Werner at his office in half
an hour."

"Don't wait around for me," Benny said. "I'll see you over
there." He was red-eyed and unsteady. Worse than yesterday,
not better.

Jennifer said, "If you're not fit, Benny, don't try to soldier
on. Pack it in and let them send out a replacement."

"I'm fine," Benny insisted.

"You don't look it."

"I said I'll be fine," Benny insisted again, this time with an
edge.

So, what could she do? She handed him the envelope with
the faxes, and left him to it.

At least, she reflected as she went the rest of the way down
the stairs, she'd given him something with which to cover the
morning hard-on.

CHAPTER 41

His eyes met Marianne's.

He didn't move right away. For several seconds the significance of it hardly seemed to dawn on him. He just stared.

She was on the opposite balcony, the uncrossable space of
the entire hall between them; she was at the rail and, leaning
over to get a sight of the band, had looked up at precisely the
same moment as he. Was O'Donnell with her? If he was,
Cadogan didn't register him. He was locked onto his daughter's eyes and her pale, surprised-looking face.

She stared back.

But then she turned and dived into the crowd behind her, disappearing between two adults as if into the darkness of tropical undergrowth.

Cadogan bellowed her name, and started to move.

Immediately, he collided with someone. There was a grunt and then several yells of complaint, but he was already on his way and he didn't look back. He couldn't go across, so he'd have to go around. It was a long distance to cover. A big crowd to get through. He tried to glance across and see her, but already there was nothing to be seen. He shouted her name again and saw those around him wince and duck almost as if he'd fired a gun over their heads.

No matter.

He launched off once more without looking and slammed into someone else, a woman, and she fell but he didn't stop. He was still calling Marianne's name. But this was like fighting his way through a heavy sea. Someone grabbed at the shoulder of his coat as if to restrain him, but he raised his elbow and rammed it backwards. It connected, and the grip was gone. People around him were screaming now, something flew out over the balcony rail—upset crockery from the seventeen-mark buffet, at a guess—and seconds later there was a crash and a shout from down below, and then the band stopped and there was nothing but the roar of the crowd all around him.

And still he tried to fight on, calling Marianne's name but knowing that now it would be lost in all the racket that had sprung up around him, and he hadn't covered any distance at all and the heavy sea was now a tidal wall and it was fighting against him. . . .

And then something chopped him over the back of the head and he suddenly went down and it was a sea again, bearing him up and preventing him from falling, making him weightless and taking away his control. . . .

Someone was talking loudly about the police, but Cadogan saw a glimmer of an opportunity. He tried to push onward, but he was held back and held down. The opportunity was a glimmer no longer.

He fought, and called her name once more.

Then the sea closed over him.

"Are you sure it was him?" Ryan said.

They'd slowed to a walk, now, and both of them had begun to recover their breath. She'd found him and grabbed his sleeve and dragged him out with only a hurried explanation. With all the commotion still going on in the big hall behind them, they'd fled the market by heading through the crowd and then making a turn into a cul-de-sac between two of the warehouses. At the end of this was a set of stone steps set into the hillside. At the top they'd come out into an area of high-rises with open walkways and gardens between the buildings.

No one was around. Even the children's play areas, tiny, bright, and functional in their planned spaces between the buildings, stood empty.

Was she sure it was him? She gave Ryan a disbelieving look.

"All right," he said. "But maybe it means that he wants you back after all."

"You didn't see him," she said. "He went completely mad. I never saw anybody carry on like that before. He was worse than when he chased me and hurt me at home. You've got to keep me away from him. Please."

"We're nearly broke," Ryan said.

"We can sell something."

"Like what? Look at me!"

"Well, *I* don't know!"

There was a tense silence as they walked along for a while. Ryan moved with his head down, looking at the ground. Then he seemed to come to a decision.

"Come on," he said, and stepped up the pace.

She'd supposed that they were going to go straight back to that awful hotel, where Ryan had planned for them to spend a second night to wait out the time until Monday morning and another shot at seeing the enquiry agent. They'd even left their bags there, hidden under the beds to save the left-luggage money. But about half an hour later they reached the building where Johann Schlesinger paid his rent and seemed to do little more than dodge the office. "What are we doing here?" Marianne said. "Nothing's open."

"I know that," Ryan said. He stopped under one of the mesh-covered windows and held up a hand for silence. They listened. Marianne couldn't hear anything but the Sunday traffic on the street behind them, then she picked up the sound. A faint drone, like a distant motor.

"*Someone's* inside," Ryan said.

The contract cleaners were inside. Their van was at the back entrance and the doorway's roll-down metal shutter had been raised most of the way. The van's rear gate was open and Marianne could see all kinds of equipment in the interior, where industrial-size drums of disinfectant stood and long, looped electrical cables hung on wall cleats. The van was unattended. Ryan ducked under the shutter's edge and went inside. Marianne didn't have to duck as she followed.

They paused at the inner doorway, to check the scene ahead. The droning sound had stopped, but there was a radio playing. Stepping like a cat, Ryan headed up the iron stairs. On reaching the first gallery, he took a cautious look over the rail and then gestured for her to stay back; but as soon as he'd turned away she took a look, as well, and saw two big polishing machines standing idle out in the middle of the old business arcade's floor. Two men in white coveralls, possibly Turks, were taking a break with the radio on and a thermos between them almost directly below. The cables from the machines snaked out across the open floor like deep cracks in a windscreen.

Marianne followed him up to the next level.

She didn't know whether they dared to speak but, two floors up now and with the radio for cover, Ryan seemed to think that he might safely risk it. As they stopped outside Schlesinger's door he whispered, "I like you, Marianne. You're a decent kid and you don't deserve any of what you got. Maybe I started this for the wrong reasons. All I know is that whatever I try to do to get me out of it just gets me in deeper ... and as if the police weren't bad enough, now I've got the Terminator on my trail and one way or another, I think it's best if I get you off my hands."

She stared. He'd pulled a scarf out of his coat pocket and he was wrapping it around his right hand, again and again and again. She couldn't imagine what he was planning to do.

He said, "I don't want to spend one more night lying awake, listening to the sirens outside in the street and wondering which one of them's coming for me. I'm scared. And I don't mind who knows it."

Down below, the polishing machines started up again. Ryan moved as if on a trigger. Marianne flinched as he turned and punched through the glass in the door. His fist went through like a hammer. Then he knocked the louvers aside and reached around for the lock and let them both in.

It was dark in there, with all the blinds drawn. Ryan made sure that the door was closed behind them, and then he switched on the light.

Nothing improved much. The room didn't even look interestingly seedy, like detectives' offices in films always did. What she saw was little more than an undecorated dump for some second-hand furniture. The lawyers' letter had made it sound as if they were bringing in some hotshot specialist with lots of experience and thousands of contacts, but this was obviously a cheap one-man operation.

Ryan said, "You look through the stuff on the desk. See if you can spot a name or anything you can recognize."

"We'll be in big trouble if we get caught like this," Marianne told him.

"I think you're finally starting to grasp the situation."

There were three wire trays on the desk, one of them piled high with material waiting to be filed and that looked as if it had been waiting for some time. The tray next to it was full of aspirin bottles and cold remedies. The tray next to *that* contained a saucepan and a spoon and a single empty soup bowl. The other end of the desk was given over to a spaghetti maze of wiring in which sat a phone, a fax machine, an answering machine, and a line-switching box with a blinking light into which all of these had been plugged.

Ryan was tackling the filing cabinets. There were two of them, well battered but of different designs and both apparently locked.

She was annoyed at his attitude. She wanted him to know it

and suffer, so she started to empty the tray noisily by dumping the papers out in big handfuls. If that didn't work, she'd talk to herself so that he couldn't quite hear. She knew all the grownups' tricks.

But she didn't manage to get quite that far, mainly because she wasn't paying enough attention to what she was doing. Suddenly her stack was too big and the papers were sliding out of control and she had to make a grab to keep them all together, and her grab snatched up some of the wiring. The heavy fax machine stayed firm, but the phone receiver sprang up into the air and the answering machine slid to the edge of the desk and over. She dropped the papers, caught the machine. She hit every button at once and the machine squealed and went into rewind.

She looked at Ryan. Ryan was staring at her. A few more letters slid off the desk and plopped onto the floor. The back-winding tape gibbered away like a demented duck.

"I didn't know it was going to do that," she said lamely.

"Just put it down," Ryan said.

Then he turned away. If he'd shouted at her, then she could have shouted back, but he hadn't. He'd just sounded as if he was weary of her, and that was something to which she had no answer. She put the machine back on the desk and hung up the phone. Without her having to do anything else, the message tape completed its rewind and then started playback as she bent to gather up letters and memos from the floor.

Why couldn't people stay the way they were when you'd decided that you liked them? Nobody ever did, it seemed. Not even the Blues Brothers—the fat one died, and then the thin one got fat. Everything changed, like on the beach. You were high and you were dry, and then you were stuck out there in the middle of the tide and it wasn't even as if you'd moved. You didn't have to make things go wrong, they went wrong all the same. You couldn't rely on *anything*.

The phone messages ran. There was nothing worth telling him about, so she didn't bother to translate any of it. Ryan had his knife out and was trying to use the blade to trick the lock at the top of one of the cabinets, without much success. Marianne had sometimes wondered what it would be like to be a burglar. She'd imagined it might be kind of exciting, but it wasn't. It was frightening and felt a little bit degrading, if anything; should anyone catch them doing it, they'd look really stupid and they'd have no way to explain.

Ryan was rattling the cabinet in frustration now. One of the lower drawers slid out, and hit him in the shins. He looked down at it.

Marianne said, "I don't think it's locked."

"But I couldn't open it."

"That's a safety thing. Only one drawer opens at a time. Otherwise the weight could tip it over."

He pushed the lower drawer fully shut with his knee. Then the top drawer opened easily. Ryan was looking down at a series of alphabetically ordered sections, from A to F.

"Remind me of her full name," he said.

And the answering machine said, *"Anneliese Cadogan."*

CHAPTER 42

It was a message about her. It was a woman's voice, all right, but it wasn't anything like Marianne would have expected her mother to sound. Someone must have been making the call for her. The first couple of times they played it through, Marianne stumbled on the translation because her mind was racing off in every direction. Ryan dug up one of Schlesinger's pens and a notepad and told her to write it down. The opening was clipped slightly, but there was something about a newspaper advertisement, and then an address. She wrote down the address, but not the rest that followed.

Once more, Ryan started to rewind the tape.

Marianne said quickly, "I don't want to hear it again."

He looked at her, and saw that she meant it. He stopped the

machine and said, "Tell me what else she was saying. Don't leave anything out."

"She said ... she said the address can be used if it's an emergency, but don't expect a reply. She doesn't want anyone to remember her. She doesn't want to talk to anyone who might ever have known her. She wants to be forgotten by the world. She wants everyone to carry on as if she was dead."

"And that's exactly what she was saying?"

Marianne managed to nod.

"Why would anyone talk like that?" she said.

"How did she put it?" Ryan wanted to know. "Did she say it like, *I* want to be forgotten, or *she* wants to be forgotten?"

"*She,*" Marianne said. "Like she's talking about somebody else. So it can't actually be her, can it?"

"No," Ryan said after a moment, but he didn't sound as encouraging as she'd hoped that he might. "No, it doesn't sound like it can." He looked at the notepad. "I can't read your writing," he said.

"It's Düsseldorf," she said. "It's more than two hundred miles from here."

"Oh shit," Ryan said bleakly.

He didn't say much as they walked the streets heading back towards the hotel, but she could see that it was perhaps more of a setback for him than the advance for which they'd hoped. It wasn't hard to guess why. The depressing tone of the message, the widening out of the search when it ought to be narrowing down to its end. It hadn't even been a proper address, just a private box number in a bureau.

"We came this far," she said. "It's not so much further."

But Ryan said nothing to that.

The indicator light above the hotel entrance showed green, meaning that rooms were available. Although why they had to do it that way, Marianne couldn't imagine. Everywhere else, you just walked up to the desk and asked, and when they were full, they put out a board. This place seemed to fill up and empty every other hour.

As they climbed the steps to the door, Marianne said, "When we find her ... I thought perhaps you might want to stay with us for a while. I know you'd like her. And I think she'd like you."

"Nice thought," Ryan said. "But it's not going to happen." He pulled open the door.

"Ryan," Marianne said.

She'd stopped on the steps. He looked down at her.

She said, "I haven't seen her for years. I never thought I'd feel this way. But now I'm scared."

He checked the street, both ways, before looking at her again. His eyes told her nothing. It was as if he'd backed off, retreating somewhere into himself.

"You don't know what scared *is*, yet," he said.

CHAPTER 43

Jennifer looked at the clock on the wall. Werner was late, and there was still no sign of Benny Moon. The longer it took, the less likely it seemed that he'd appear.

Oh, great.

This almost certainly meant that she was going to be expected to carry him until he was fit again, and to say nothing about it. That was how the unwritten code operated, all the boys pulling together and covering for each other. He'd expect it, he'd consider anything less as a betrayal. The problem for Jennifer was that she somehow doubted that the same outlook would apply were their positions to be reversed. Then it would be proof that the girlie couldn't hack it, so best to send her home. And don't send a woman on a man's job again.

If the Praesidium had been quiet yesterday, then it was deadly silent this morning. The only sound within the past hour had been the clattering arrival of a metal canister in the passageway outside, brought by the building's compressed-air delivery system. She'd gone out, and taken it from the bag. It had contained a set of faxes identical to those she'd received at the hotel that morning.

She looked through them again, in case there was anything vital that she might have missed. But there didn't seem to be. She shuffled them together and went through eight of the fourteen linked offices to put them in Werner's *in* tray.

Werner was there already.

He'd just arrived. He was taking a couple of files out of his soft briefcase and throwing them onto his desk.

"I've an excuse for being late," he said quickly. "Your Mr. Cadogan."

"What about him?"

"He's being held at the police station down at the *fischmarkt*. I just got back from talking to him. Two of the pickpocket squad had to jump on him and take him in."

"Why?"

"Apparently he went berserk in a crowd after thinking that he'd spotted his daughter. Tried to charge down anyone who was in his way, which seems to have included more than half the people in the market. He's in there for his own safety, as much as anything else."

"*Did* he see her?"

"Even he's not sure of it, now. He was in the wrong, but I'm not sure that I blame him. If I had a daughter in the same situation, I'm sure I'd be on a pretty short fuse as well. We put officers to watch all the ways in and out, just in case. But if she'd been there at all, she was gone by then."

It was exactly the kind of reaction that Jennifer had feared were Cadogan somehow to find his way onto the scene when they set their Monday-morning trap at Schlesinger's office. She said, "I don't suppose there's any way you could just put him on a plane and send him home?"

Werner smiled regretfully, and shook his head. "That's hardly up to me," he said. "For now they're going to hold him for a while and then let him go. A few hours in a cell where he can sleep won't do his state of mind any harm."

"And locking him up is probably the only way you're going to achieve it. What's happening now?"

"I've got some people checking on all the church missions and hostels. But I think most of our hopes have got to be with them turning up at Schlesinger's office sometime tomorrow. That's all arranged, now. I'll be waiting for them myself."

"I suppose I'll just have to carry on with the phoning around, then," Jennifer said without much enthusiasm.

"Not the best way to spend a weekend, I know. If I could make it more interesting for you, I would."

"That's all right."

"I had a word with my lady friend. I suggested we should maybe invite you over for the evening. But then she reminded me, we've already an arrangement that we can't break."

Lady friend? Here was something new. She said, "Don't worry about it. It was a nice thought. Some other time."

Werner accepted this with a shrug.

Jennifer said, "So, all that stuff about you and your woman trouble, that was just—"

"Oh, that," Werner said with a dismissive wave of his hand. "That was just Josef. He likes to . . . what would you say? undermine people. He does this all the time. But I try to be understanding about his reasons for it. I'm told he has a *phenomenally* small penis."

She kept a straight face, and so did he.

But only for a moment.

Jennifer returned to her borrowed office. By the time she'd reached it, that momentary good mood had leaked away.

She couldn't explain why, not even to herself, but she was beginning to feel a hint of something resembling despair. Werner and his people had a systematic search under way, the regular *Schutzpolizei* were on alert. They had a plan to follow and a baited trap waiting to be sprung, and yet . . .

And yet she couldn't escape the feeling that she was losing sight of her quarry more with every day that went by. When she'd started, she'd had O'Donnell in her sights and a plain sense of danger for the child. But now she felt further from them, not closer. She felt like some runner who'd come pounding out of the city gates with confidence, only to find herself on a vast and empty plain with few landmarks, fewer paths, nothing of certainty to aim for.

She sighed, and reached for Benny Moon's hotel list. The groundwork might as well go on. She dialed the next unchecked number, and went through the procedure. Any booking of an English male accompanied by a German-speaking girl.

On her third call, the hotel clerk on the other end of the line said, "I believe that we have. One moment, please, while I check."

Jennifer waited. There was a stirring of excitement in her that wouldn't quite be held down. But then the clerk came back on and said, "Yes, we have a Mr. Moon and Miss McGann. They're with the British police."

And Jennifer realized that she'd just dialed the number of her own hotel.

"Ah . . . yes," she said, trying not to sound embarrassed and manifestly failing. "I understand you. In fact, this is Miss McGann speaking. Could you put me through to Mr. Moon, please?"

It took Benny a while to answer.

When he finally came on the line, he said, "Yeah?" His voice was almost a croak.

"You were asleep," Jennifer said.

"I'm shaking it off," he insisted. "It's some kind of a bug, that's all. I'm fighting it with bed rest and room service. If you hold the fort today, then I'll be fine. I mean, it's still only Sunday, and the big plan's for tomorrow. You've got to admit that it makes sense."

"God, Benny. You're pushing it."

"I'd do the same for you."

"Do you think I'd ask you to?"

"The way you've got your eye on the ladder? Don't doubt it."

"Sweet dreams, Benny. But if you're not here in the morning, you'd better be thinking of going home. There's enough set to happen without me having to handle it all alone."

"I knew it," Benny said. "You're annoyed with me. It must be love."

"Not for you, Benny," Jennifer told him. "You'd be second choice to press-ups in a cucumber patch."

She cradled the phone with a sigh. There was only so much

that she could say to him. She'd almost certainly have to be working with him again tomorrow, after all. The simple fact of it was that Benny was scared of being seen to crawl home ill and in need of replacement. He'd think it wouldn't look good, and who could really argue? But she told herself that were the pace to heat up and he became a liability, then she'd dump him without a backwards look. And then she wouldn't allow herself to care what kind of a bitch they'd make her out to be, back home in the police canteen.

The remainder of the list waited.

But instead, she dialed her home number on an impulse. It took a few seconds to get connected, but then the phone at the other end began to ring. What would Ricky be doing right now? she wondered. She'd know that soon enough.

She could hear him picking up the receiver as Werner came through the door from the next room. She was just opening her mouth to speak, when he interrupted.

"Urgent callout to a transient hotel," he said. "A girl's been found dead in one of the rooms. Right age, right description, and she was sharing with a middle-aged man."

Werner was already on his way out and Ricky was saying *Hello? Is that you, Jen?* when Jennifer had to say, "Sorry, Ricky, I'll call again later."

She hung up the phone, and dashed out after Werner.

CHAPTER 44

She caught up with him by the elevator bank. He was watching the indicator panel as he pulled his jacket on over his waistband holster. When it didn't seem to be moving fast enough for him, he hammered at the call button as if he could somehow hurry the elevator car along. As she reached his side, he snarled in his impatience and took off through the adjacent doors and into the nearby stairwell.

Jennifer followed. Here was an aspect of Werner that she hadn't had the chance to see before. He was heading down the stairs two and three at a time and she didn't catch up with him again until she'd emerged and saw that he'd waved down one of the green and white patrol vehicles from the *Schutzpolizei* building next door. He was beckoning to her, and as she went over he slid into the back of the car.

The car took off before she'd even closed the door.

"This will be faster," Werner said.

"How far is it?"

"Two minutes, no more."

The driver seemed to be intent upon shaving some time off even that estimate. As they came out under the barrier, they made a hard right, and then a hard right again. The driver touched his siren, the traffic ahead cleared. Holding onto the door handle to keep herself from being thrown around, Jennifer said, "Do we know what happened?"

"Somebody heard a cry from one of the rooms and the manager went in. He found the girl lying on the bed. Uniformed officers are on the scene already." Werner stopped, and then said something to the driver. The driver turned up the volume on his police radio. Some kind of an exchange was going on, but Jennifer couldn't follow it.

Werner swore. The driver floored the accelerator pedal and the car went lightspeed.

Jennifer was slammed back in the seat. They were in the side streets now with the howler going full blast, and she was aware of parked cars and dodging pedestrians flickering by in a stroboscopic blur. Werner had reached behind him and drawn his Sig Sauer automatic from its holster, and he was trying to keep steady as he checked it.

"Now what?" she said.

"They caught up with the man," Werner said, springing the clip and then slamming it back in. "He's taken one officer's gun and wounded him. It sounds bad. Everybody's on their way there now, but I think we'll be closer than most."

They had to slow to cut into the traffic flow at the end of

the street. But not much. There were shops, lights, colors, flash-photographs of surprised faces as the car shot by. Then they were out of the narrow street and into a square with high, narrow buildings all around and a railed garden area with a stone monument at its center.

Werner leaned forward and said with some urgency to the driver, *"Es ist dort hinten. Du bist gerade daran vorbei gefahren."* Jennifer was thrown forward as the driver braked, and would have hit the seat before her had Werner not caught her arm. Then they were going backwards, seemingly at the same speed as before; the driver had turned in his seat and was dodging from side to side in order to see around his passengers. He braked again, and Jennifer hung onto Werner and felt her stomach lurch in protest. It didn't help that the back of the car already bore the faint scents of disinfectant over vomit. She braced herself ready for the next roller-coaster swing as the Audi that had almost rammed them scooted hastily back and cleared the way, but then, as their driver revved to continue, he made a miscalculation and the engine stalled.

"Lass es hier stehen," Werner said. Leave it here. He reached to open the door and get out.

"Over there!" Jennifer said.

She was pointing across the square, to a dingy-looking building with a flight of steps leading up to its entranceway. Like all the buildings around here, it was ground-level tacky but with a kind of forgotten grandeur from the first floor up. From the top of the stairway, starting to descend, there came something that might once have been a man but which had somehow been transformed into a bellowing, lumbering beast; a beast with a deadly weapon in its fist which, even as she watched, it raised and fired up into the air twice.

Somebody screamed. Somebody down the street was running across, crouched low, and Werner was cursing and slamming the door handle up and down but nothing was happening.

Jennifer tried her own door, and it was the same. The car had childproof locks that could be opened only from the outside, and they'd been set so that no prisoner could make a sudden break for freedom.

Which meant, right at this moment, that until someone was to let them out, they'd be trapped.

She glanced up. The beast had seen their vehicle now, and was walking across the street towards them.

Jennifer looked around. She could hear approaching sirens, but there was no other presence in the square as yet. Their own driver was making a desperate effort to restart his stalled engine. Werner was hurriedly trying to wind down his window far enough to reach over and open his door from the outside. He shouted to someone in a doorway about fifteen yards away, but nobody moved.

"Oh, my God," Jennifer said dully.

The beast was looking straight at her.

Bellowing still in a rage of grief and anger, he came onward. Those few remaining people in the square who'd been slow to catch on were now diving for cover. The police driver uttered a dull curse and tried again to restart his engine, and still it wouldn't catch.

Coming closer.

"Werner!" she shouted.

The beast leveled out his gun arm and took aim at the car. He was right in front of them now, framed in the windscreen as if in Cinemascope and coming on twice as unreal.

Still walking, he fired.

She saw his arm jerk at the report and heard the shot go wide somewhere close above the car's roof. The driver was panicking now. The car's interior was filled with the stink of petrol from the flooded engine. Three rounds gone into the air, and one for the wounded man inside the building. The beast's arm came down again, only yards away now and with much less chance of him missing.

This time, he stopped and stood still before taking his aim.

Jennifer realized that she was looking straight out into the tiny ring of darkness that was the automatic's barrel. He clearly wasn't an experienced shot, but at this range that hardly mattered. She could crouch down, maybe even dodge the first round. But she couldn't get out, and there wasn't a thing that she could do to stop him shooting up the car.

She really ought to duck.

But somehow, she didn't seem to be able to move.

At which Werner reached forward and, with his hand spread wide and pushing with a strength that defied resistance, he forced the driver's head down and out of the way while his other hand leveled his own automatic over the seat back at the windscreen. Suddenly Jennifer found herself thinking about the petrol fumes and the instant danger of explosion but already it was too late, because Werner had fired.

The entire windscreen crazed, and burst outward in slow motion. She saw the glass spread and hit the gunman like a nuclear wind. Her ears rang with the noise of the blast; and as the flying cloud dispersed she saw the beast, the lower half of his face blown away, taking a surprised and staggering walk backwards with his gun hand swinging wildly. He got off another shot, surely no more than a reflex, and it went wide. From beside her, Werner fired again, a torso hit, textbook fashion—an aorta shot with instant loss of oil pressure as the beast's legs folded beneath him and he dropped from their view.

Jennifer's hearing slowly returned.

Someone was screaming. But at least it wasn't her. Werner slapped the uniformed driver on the shoulder twice, an all-clear signal, and the driver slowly levered himself to sit upright again. There was some glass in the car, but there was a lot more outside it. Someone was opening Werner's door for him. After a moment to gather herself—her heart was pounding like a steamhammer—Jennifer slid across the car and followed him out.

"Are you all right?" Werner said.

Jennifer nodded.

There he lay, a widening pool beneath his head and an even bigger one spreading from under his body. More police vehicles had pulled into the square, and more uniformed men were running over. Others dived into the building from which the gunman had emerged. How long had this taken? It felt as if an hour had passed, but it couldn't have been more than a minute. The gunman's hand was outstretched, and the stolen police-issue pistol was about a yard away from it.

Werner knelt by the man. He appeared to be looking for somewhere to take a pulse, but didn't seem to be able to bring himself to touch the body. It was messy; bullet hits apart, the glass had whipped at the gunman like a storm of razor blades. Judging by the look of him, the need to take a pulse seemed academic.

Werner straightened. Other officers pushed past him, and one of them kicked the gun even further away. Werner surrendered his own pistol, and it went into an evidence bag. He seemed dazed but perfectly functional, almost unaffected. An ambulance had joined the crush of vehicles around the remaining sides of the square now.

People were venturing out of the buildings, standing uncertainly, craning to see. Those who saw the body quickly turned away. The square was being taped off, most of the onlookers already being ushered back beyond the lines. Werner looked around himself, as if lost. Then he saw Jennifer, and started over towards her.

He had the surprised look of someone who'd walked through fire and come out without even having been singed. But it hadn't hit him, yet, that was all. Even she could see the signs.

He said, "Well, I suppose now you can go home." He gestured back in the direction of the gunman, who was about to disappear behind folding screens. "I'm sorry I couldn't do better for you than this."

And Jennifer, taking one last look at the body, said, "I'll be with you for a while longer yet, Werner. That wasn't him."

CHAPTER 45

"Why aren't you talking?" she said.

They were at a road stop, about an hour out of town. It consisted of a two-pump petrol station with a house behind it and an open-air grill to the side. About thirty motorcycles stood out front, alongside four big buses backed up with their noses towards the road. It was surrounded by open land where, in the middle distance, a field irrigator was sending an intermittent spray of water high into the air. Beyond that, the fields went on and on until they reached the forested horizon where the ground began to rise. Even more distant lines of woodland cover could be seen further out, painted in finer and more transparent detail as the distance increased.

Ryan was leaning on a stand-up table under the grill trailer's striped awning. The tables were all the same, giant Coke cans on their ends and with wipe-down tops. Perhaps he was wondering how there could be so many vehicles out in the middle of nowhere and yet so few people hanging around.

"You're not talking to me," Marianne said again.

"That's because I can't talk and think at the same time."

"I can," she said.

"Yeah," Ryan said hollowly. "I bet."

She left it awhile, and then said, "What are you thinking?"

"You don't ask people something like that," he said. "It's private."

A while longer. And then:

"What *are* you thinking?"

Ryan looked into his empty paper cup.

"Nothing," he said.

CHAPTER 46

By the time Jennifer got back to the Praesidium building, they'd brought Cadogan over and left him in the second-floor waiting area. Nothing more than a white Formica table and a fixed plywood bench at the corridor's end, it had been set aside for visitors, victims, and witnesses. The wooden bench had been covered with scratched-in graffiti. There was nothing else to look at.

She saw him rise to his feet as he realized that she was approaching. She knew in an instant, from the look on his face, that he'd been told nothing of the situation's outcome.

"False alarm," she said quickly.

He looked as if he'd been drained, and had no reaction left to show. He swayed.

"Better sit down again," she said.

She sat by him, and he listened while she started to explain what had happened. To begin with, the "girl of the right age" in the room of the transients' hotel had actually turned out to be an undernourished twelve-year-old-boy, the son of an unlicensed immigrant worker. Death appeared to have been by natural causes, possibly as a result of untreated viral meningitis.

"The father didn't dare go to a doctor," she explained, "so he was treating the boy himself with over-the-counter medicines. It's fifty-fifty as to what got him first, the disease or the cure."

"Why no doctor?"

"The man's an illegal. *Was* an illegal. He got into a state over the child and then got his hands on a uniformed officer's gun. But not for long."

Cadogan looked at her. "Were you there?"

"Yes."

"Was it really bad?"

"These things are never anything else. The point of it for you is that it wasn't Marianne. So everything's as it was. You can go back to your hotel."

He nodded, and started to get to his feet. He had a beaten look about him now, as if he'd plunged around so much on the adrenaline roller coaster that his body could no longer recognize the differences between the highs and the lows. He moved almost like an old man.

Before the double doorway at the corridor's end, he stopped.

"I made a fool of myself today," he said.

"No," Jennifer said. "I don't think you did."

He considered that.

Then he managed a brief smile of thanks, stuffed his hands into his pockets, and shouldered his way out towards the elevator bank.

Jennifer went into the women's washroom, and ran some cold water into a basin. Her hands were still shaking. She wondered if Cadogan had noticed. Everything was proceeding by the book, here, although the players were close to falling apart. Werner had been smiling when she'd left him, joking with those investigators who'd come along after the event and who were half-seriously complimenting him for having performed a social service even as their hard little eyes watched and assessed his behavior. But there had been a kind of desperation hiding behind the smile, and hiding none too well. He'd seemed to be looking for a way out, and she'd been unable to offer him one.

She felt hot, she felt dry. She scooped up a double handful of the water, and put her face into it.

And as the water poured back through her fingers and into the basin, she spluttered on it and coughed and nearly cried.

But only nearly.

She hadn't been inside the building, and she hadn't seen the child. But from what she'd seen and heard, conditions inside had been dismal. The building was owned and operated by an *Arbeiter-Verleihfirmen*, a recruiting agency specializing in non-Germans who could show neither work nor residency permits. The two had come into the country on a round-trip ticket, the second half of which was unusable. Its only purpose was in being shown at the border on entry, as proof of an intent to return. Labor recruited in this way was sold to big companies through contract middlemen who kept most of the money and paid a minimal wage with no security, no benefits, nothing.

She hadn't been inside. But she'd still been there when they'd stretchered the wrapped body out.

She dried her face on the roller towel. Someone had put a circular sticker on one of the cubicle doors that read POISON GAS around a skull and crossbones. She sniffed, straightened, and checked herself in the mirror. A little red around the eyes, that was all. She wished that it wasn't a Sunday. She wished that the place could have been full of people, their presence a constant pressure to support her self-control.

She went out.

One of the doors across the corridor stood open. She went through into the big central office where the morning briefings took place. It had a green chalkboard and a large conference table with a TV set and videotape player over by the window. It was the room where they kept the refrigerator, the big jar of coffee money, the wall plaques with crests and badges from overseas forces, and the fading color photographs of the departmental football team.

Werner's jacket had been slung onto the back of one of the chairs, as if onto a makeshift hanger. But he'd missed with one shoulder, and it hung almost onto the floor. Werner himself wasn't there.

Nor was he in the next office reached through the interconnecting door, where his empty waistband holster had been slung onto one of the desks before sliding across and off, taking a number of forms and files with it. She picked it up, and went on through.

Werner was two rooms further along. Head down, hands gripping the back of a chair. Fighting the same fight. Only harder.

"Werner?" she said.

"Please go away," he said quietly.

"You don't just shrug and get over something like this," she said. "Haven't they offered you some counseling?"

He didn't look up. "I don't want to talk to strangers."

"Will you talk to me?"

He shook his head.

"Come on, then," she said, reaching around behind him and taking him by both of his arms. "It looks as if someone's going to have to get you home."

For a moment, he resisted.

And then, slowly, like a man learning to walk again, he allowed himself to be led.

CHAPTER 47

After a night on the road, for a part of which Marianne slept on Ryan's lap between rides using her knapsack for a pillow, Monday morning found the two of them in a one-room office service bureau and mail drop above a Düsseldorf florist's. It was hard for Marianne to say what kind of sight they must have presented. She'd seen the counter clerk's eyes stray down to the home-made tattoos across Ryan's knuckles, and heard her falter. Marianne couldn't see the big deal in this, they were only *x*'s and *o*'s like the kisses and hugs that you put at the end of a letter. She'd been inclined to suggest that Ryan should wait outside in the square, but then she would have had to have gone in alone. She needed the sense of him there, even if there was nothing that he could say that would help. That wasn't the point. He was her rock, her courage to go on.

"Ask how they get in touch with her," Ryan said.

"They don't," Marianne said.

"So, what happens with the messages?"

"People call them to check. It's all confidential. That's supposed to be what it's all about."

Ryan looked around the place, and for a moment Marianne was almost afraid that he was going to say *Stuff it* and push through the little swinging gate on the counter to start raking through papers while the two women staffers screamed and ran about.

But instead, he said, "Come on, then," and they turned to go.

Düsseldorf was a low-rise, big-money city of street trams and the kinds of shops and arcades where no one ever seemed to be buying anything but you stood outside, wondering how anyone on the planet could even begin to afford that kind of stuff, and why they'd make a point of coming here for it even if they could. Gold pens with engraved nibs. Alligator-skin Filofax covers. Marianne had never been to this town before, and she wasn't even sure why her mother was there now. They'd no relatives in the area, as far as Marianne knew.

A job, perhaps? Did her mother work in one of these places, selling shirts from Paris or designer bags or antiques from windows that were lit like private museums? She couldn't imagine it.

But then, a few weeks ago she wouldn't have been able to imagine doing what she was doing now, either.

They walked the streets for a while. It wasn't like Hamburg here. It was smaller-scale, fewer people just hanging around. It would be much harder to disappear into, she could tell.

She said, "Why doesn't she want me to find her?"

"Is that what you think?"

"It's how it's starting to seem."

"She doesn't even know it's you that's looking," Ryan said. "People run away from all kinds of things. They hide from all kinds of things, as well. But I really don't think that you're one of them."

They sat on a bench alongside a magazine stand, and they counted the money that they had left.

"Jesus," Ryan said bleakly when he realized how little it was. They'd lost money on last night's hotel because they'd paid in advance and the manager had refused them a refund. Then there had been food on the way. Most of it had been nasty, but it certainly hadn't been cheap.

Marianne said, "Don't forget, it'll all be paid back as soon as we—"

And Ryan said, "I know, I know," waving her down as if it was an old song that he'd become sick of hearing, and then he told her to pick out whatever change she'd need to buy some paper and some envelopes.

She got both from a sale bin in one of the department stores. He'd told her to be sure to pick a bright color for the envelopes. He'd said that the paper didn't matter so much. Then they went into a stand-up grill opposite the railway station, and he told her that she was going to write a letter.

"What about?" she said.

"It doesn't much matter what about," Ryan said, "as long as she has to come out to collect it. It's like bait, see? We'll wait and watch."

Marianne eyed the counter. Behind the glass there were pre-cooked but cold hamburgers and schnitzel, wurst, salads, and raw tuna ready for grilling. Everything came with ribbon fries from the range at the back, shoveled onto the plate and slung across the zinc top.

She said, "I don't think so well when I'm so hungry," and when Ryan sighed she said, "We can't just stand here and buy nothing. And we're going to have to borrow a pen."

He conceded a plate of fries. She negotiated him up to fries and a bratwurst, which they shared. Only, Marianne shared it noticeably more than did Ryan. The clientele around them stood at their elbow-high tables like cattle in their stalls, gazing across the tram lanes to the railway station beyond.

"Fill up on ketchup," he advised. "Come tomorrow, that's all we'll be eating."

And then, after she'd been writing for about ten minutes, he said, "Hey. Not your whole life story."

"I'm telling her who you are," Marianne said.

"Well, don't. She doesn't need to know."

"All right," Marianne said, and carried on writing about him anyway. If first impressions counted most, then she didn't want her mother's first impression of Ryan to come with her initial sight of him. There was no tactful way of telling him this, but to see him and rely on nothing other than that would be to misjudge him. Mrs. Healey was the proof of it, if any was needed. And there was a whole string of people between here and home all ready to back her up, if Mrs. Healey alone wasn't enough.

They dropped the letter in the bureau's box by the flower shop, and went over into the square to watch and wait.

Nobody even came down to check the box until the early afternoon. But then they could see one of the clerks emptying it, and Marianne made two little fists and bounced up and down on the bench with suppressed excitement.

"Don't get too worked up yet," Ryan said. "There's a way to go."

The afternoon slipped by. Children came to the playground behind them, and then they went. And then the two women clerks were leaving the office and locking up behind them, and that was clearly going to be that until the morning.

"Now what?" Marianne said.

"We come back tomorrow," Ryan said.

They walked the streets some more. As the rush hour ebbed, the streets began to empty.

Marianne said, "Are we looking for a hotel, now?"

"I don't think so," Ryan said.

"We could beg, like they do in London. I could hang onto your coat and look really pathetic."

"No," said Ryan. "Give me a while. I'll think of something."

And that was how Marianne came to learn all about how to break into a car.

CHAPTER 48

Ryan had picked the oldest car on the lot, right at the back and only just on the edge of the floodlit area. The sales lot was a concrete yard with iron gates at the street end but almost no security behind, where a building site stood like a landslip. It was overlooked by the balconies of some low-rise housing, but no one appeared to notice them as they lifted the wire and stole through.

The cars were mostly Audis and VWs, angled towards the street in two lines. Theirs wasn't priced, and had no wheel trims or wipers; Ryan took about half a minute to get it open. They took a last look around before they slipped into the back, and Ryan closed the door and moved the seats to give them some leg room. One seat stuck, but he kicked it and it moved.

"As long as we keep our heads down," he said, "we should be all right. Soon as it's morning, we'll have to be out before anyone knows."

Marianne said, "I wonder if the radio works."

"Don't even think of trying it," Ryan said.

They'd walked up out of the middle of town, passing under the railway lines behind the station and ascending into a dusty area of blank-faced apartment buildings and almost no shops. The sun had been setting on a horizon of distant construction cranes. The first used-car lot that they'd found had been crammed with Cadillacs and Pontiacs and Buick station wagons along with two or three big customized American vans. It had also had a dog running loose that looked as if the only food it ever got was torn from the bones of trespassers around midnight, and so they'd moved on.

This would do, she tried to tell herself. It was shelter. It was better than nothing.

But it was still just an old car.

She wished that he'd let her have the radio on. There was a continuous rippling sound from the plastic bunting over the lot as the wind passed through it. The bunting consisted of criss-crossed strings of electric-blue and silver flags, and these were supposed to give the place a carnival atmosphere. But they looked like rats' tails and the sound was like some flock of predators hovering overhead.

"I'm hungry again," she said.

"It won't be a problem after tomorrow," Ryan said.

"And I'm sick of carrying bags around. Mine makes my shoulder sore."

"That won't last, either."

She sighed, and looked out. Because of the floodlighting, it wasn't going to get any darker than this and the back seat wasn't going to get any more comfortable, either. She was going to be squirming all night, she could tell. Ryan had slid down and kind of wedged himself into the corner, and now lay with one hand over his eyes. He looked as if he was ready to stay that way for hours and what was more, he looked comfortable. She didn't know how he could do it. Most people seemed to fret about the way things would turn out, but not Ryan. Ryan seemed to go at life like a big horse dragging a plow in a rainstorm. Whatever was thrown at him, he just carried on.

She could never imagine him as a shouter, or a door slammer. Some people were; her father, for one. Ryan had more patience, and he knew things.

She said, "I wonder if God's watching us, right now."

His fingers opened. He looked out at her. "What?"

"I mean, does he watch everybody all the time? And how does he manage to concentrate if he does? I can't even do my homework with the radio on."

Ryan covered his eyes again.

"Who knows," he said.

She put her chin in her hand and looked out. It was an important point, and she might have known he wouldn't understand. Because if God was watching you all the time, what was he thinking whenever you picked your nose or went to the toilet? It was embarrassing.

Still looking out, she said, "Perhaps he just checks on people. Every now and then. Catches up on what they've been doing."

Ryan let out a long, low groan.

"Because," she said, "that would explain how babies die and people hurt each other, wouldn't it? Because he's always *there*, but a lot of the time he's looking the other way. So bad things can still happen, even though he always finds out in the end."

"Whatever you say," Ryan said.

She looked at him. "Don't you think God's real?"

Wearily, he took his hand from his eyes and pushed himself up a little in the seat. "I didn't say that," he told her.

"Some people don't."

"I know. And you'll notice, they always live comfortable lives. They say that there can't be a God because there's so much suffering in the world, and they're always the people who've never suffered. But go to the bottom of the heap, and there it's a different story. It's like light. You take it for granted. You don't even know it's there until something pushes you out into the dark."

Further down the road, a train went over a bridge in a flickering blur of carriage windows. Its entire length was one long red and white Coca-Cola ad. Marianne would have killed for a Coke. A Coke and a doughnut. A Coke and a doughnut and a warm place to sit.

Ryan said, "I saw an angel, once."

He was looking out the other way and rubbing the bristles on his unshaven cheek as if it was something that he'd had to say but which he knew would make him blush.

Marianne said, "Really?"

"Just the one," he said.

"Where?" She was definitely interested now because she knew that he wouldn't lie about such a thing and she'd never met anyone who'd actually seen a real live angel before. "What did it look like?"

"Now," he said, still not actually meeting her eyes, "that's the problem, you see. You tell someone you saw an angel and they immediately start thinking harps and wings and all that kind of stuff. And then if you say it wasn't like that, it was just this person you saw but you knew at the time you were looking at an angel, then they assume that you don't really mean what you're saying and it's just a figure of speech. Like nurses are always supposed to be angels. Whereas some of them can be anything but."

His face had darkened at this last point. He was silent for a few moments, and Marianne wondered whether she ought to prompt him.

But she waited.

Then he said, "I used to go to this market on Saturday afternoons. Like you, on your Sunday mornings. It was about a mile from where I lived, and the only difference is that when I went, I went on my own. I used to go to the bookstall and look at the second-hand paperbacks. The Saint. Sexton Blake. I liked to read, back then. All the books were in these big old suitcases opened out flat, and there was canvas up above to keep the rain off. When the raindrops hit the canvas, it was like . . . well, there's no sound quite like it. I only have to hear it again and it takes me right back. And I'll always remember, the woman who ran the stall . . . she used to cut a corner off the paperback covers and write the new price in the space. And whenever I bought anything . . . I'd take it home, and I'd make a new corner out of a postcard, and when I'd stuck it on I'd try to paint it so the colors matched." He looked down. "It was silly, I know. But it's what I used to do."

"I don't think it's silly," Marianne said. And then she waited, wanting to hear about the angel.

"I'll always remember this one Saturday. There didn't seem to be anything special about it. But I was there and for some reason I looked up and across all the books, and there was this woman on the other side of the stall. She was looking, but she wasn't really interested. You know how it is. You're just passing, you stop and you turn a couple of things over, you move on . . . you probably don't even remember what it was you just saw. She might have been passing the time, waiting for someone, I don't know. But as I looked up at her, she looked up at me and usually when that happens, you both look away again in the same second. But we didn't. And right in that moment, I knew what she was. And I know she knew it too."

"What did she look like?"

"Blonde hair. Very straight, the way they used to have it back then. Dark mascara stuff around her eyes, but her lipstick was really pale. And she was in white. She'd picked up some book and I could see she had these long, straight fingers with rings on them."

Marianne put her elbow up against the back of the seat, and rested the side of her head on her knuckles.

Feeling slightly disappointed, she said, "What made her an angel, then?"

"Nothing did," Ryan said with a shrug. "She just was. She looked straight at me for a couple of seconds and her face was the only thing I could see in the whole world, and then she moved on. That's all. I never saw her again after that."

"But how did you *know*?"

"I've tried to explain this to people, and it's never yet turned out right. Angels are people. And people can be angels. It's like finding that one little face on a diamond that catches the light and reflects it brighter than any other. You have to be in the right place and looking at the right angle, and someone standing right next to you might see nothing at all. I think that's what happened that day. I've had doctors ask me to say what I saw and so I start to tell them, and they start to write things down, and all I want to do is reach across the desk and grab them and say *Don't write it down, just listen!* because not one of them ever really has. Angels are people. And people are angels. And demons as well. And when they catch the light in a certain way, you can see right into them and what you see then is just as real as everything else. Nothing more than that. Those people who wrote the Bible all that time ago, I honestly think that's all they were trying to say."

"Then why didn't they just say it?"

"You can't say it. You can only try to get people to see it. But they don't, ever, because they don't look at it right. Innocence and ecstasy, any dog's got what it takes. But you know what kind of things people spend their time arguing about? Whether women can be priests or not."

Marianne nodded, as if she understood. Oh, well. As angel stories went, it wasn't exactly something out of *The Twilight Zone*. But on the other hand, she could see that he'd been letting her in on stuff that he wouldn't have told to just anybody.

"You're strange," she said.

"You're not the first one to believe it."

"I don't mean frightening strange. I mean interesting strange."

"Well," he said, shifting in his seat and stretching slightly, "there's a lot about me you don't know. And I think it's probably best if we keep it that way."

"You *have* been in prison, haven't you? That's why people were telling me to stay away from you."

He smiled tightly, and didn't deny it. He just said, "I wish you'd listened to them."

"But if I had," she said earnestly, "who can say what might have happened to me? I know what I said about prison before. But I don't mind. Really I don't." He looked at her. "I don't believe you'd ever harm anyone. I know it, I don't need proof or anything. That's faith, isn't it? That's what you were talking about, and this is exactly the same."

There was a long silence.

Then—

"Oh, Marianne," he said in a tone that was somewhere between sadness and warning. "I wish you wouldn't look at me like that."

"Like what?" she said.

"Like young girls shouldn't look to grown-up men," he said.

And she was left confused and uncertain as he turned his back on her and said, "Try to sleep, now."

CHAPTER 49

It had rained during the night. This had stopped before dawn, but in places the streets were still wet. The air was fresher, as well. It made Marianne shiver and when she tried to stop a yawn, her teeth chattered. Ryan told her to keep on moving and she'd soon warm up. But she didn't, not until the small corner bakery where they bought some rolls hot from the oven. The bag on her shoulder felt as if it had been filled with rocks. And so did her stomach, when the bread was all gone.

"I'm thirsty, now," she said.

And Ryan said, "Right."

"And I need a wee," she said.

And Ryan said, "Right."

They came back into town by a road alongside a parcels yard behind the railway station. Everywhere was starting to come to life, now. There were lights in people's apartments, and as Marianne looked up into the ground floor windows of the older buildings, she could just about see the upper halves of bunk beds and ceiling mobiles and boxed games stacked on the tops of wardrobes. Strange, how the children's bedrooms always seemed to be on the street side. Perhaps they slept through noise more easily than most. She tried to remember what her own German bedroom had been like.

She couldn't recall it. Not one detail.

On the station concourse, they separated. She had to go through a turnstile to get into the ladies' washroom, and her red rucksack almost got her stuck there.

Once inside, she took her time. Over in the men's washroom, Ryan would no doubt be shaving with the disposable razor that he kept so carefully wrapped in a length of toilet paper in his soap bag. When she'd changed in a cubicle into some second-time-around underwear, she came out and splashed her face and then stood there with her eyes closed in the stream of a hot-air dryer.

She was first out. She waited for him.

When he came, she said, "It's only two marks for a locker. We can get both bags into one."

And Ryan said, "Yeah, all right."

They reached the square about twenty minutes before the bureau was due to open. The flower shop was open already, and looked as if it had been for some time. Wire baskets of blooms hung outside, and the pavement in front was dark with runoff water. They settled back to wait on the same bench as the day before.

Ryan told her that this could take some time, and said she could go and mess around in the play area for a while if she wanted to. He'd call to her if anything happened. The play area took up half of the square and contained a few chunky pieces of wooden equipment, adventure-playground style. It was screened by trees from the outside.

"No," Marianne said. "That's just for the little kids."

So the two of them waited together.

The first of the two clerks arrived. She opened up, but she didn't come down again and check the mailbox until at least ten minutes later. Marianne shifted uneasily. The bench seating was of hard wooden slats. Nobody could have accused it of being too comfortable.

She said, "Do you think she'll have phoned them yet?"

"I don't know," Ryan said. He seemed to have settled down into his greatcoat and was peering out of it as if from a warm foxhole.

"Should I go over and ask?"

"No. Look, when she comes, she comes, and that's when we move. Make too much fuss before that, and we might just scare her off."

"If it was me," she said, "I'd check every day. I'd check twice." She paused, and thought some more. "Twice in the mornings, and twice in the afternoons.".

"Right."

"If it was me."

He settled lower. "Right."

She did pretty well over the next hour, considering. She took numerous walks around the red shale path that bounded the square and paid about a dozen visits to the flower shop window, where she became such a familiar sight that the owner stepped out and gave her a rose. It was no big waste, because the rose had a broken stem and was probably too short for use in any display. She took it over to the bench to show to Ryan. He hadn't moved at all.

She said, "I'm going to give her this when she comes." Then she laid it on the bench beside her, and sat swinging her legs for a while. One of the women clerks emerged from the bureau entrance and disappeared around the corner on some errand, cardigan sleeves pulled down over her knuckles to keep her hands warm. Although it wasn't a particularly cold morning, now.

Marianne said, "I'm still thirsty."

"Find a water fountain."

"I'm not thirsty for water."

"Well, that's all we can afford."

"I want coffee instead."

"You're too young to have coffee."

"Why do people always say that?" Marianne demanded.

"Because it's got stuff in it that's like a drug. It makes you all jumpy and irritable. As if you weren't bad enough that way already."

She swung her legs for a while longer. She could feel them starting to go numb.

She said, "I want Coke, then."

"We can't afford Coke, either. We can eat later if we keep it simple. And maybe once more after that. And then that's it."

"Can we eat now?"

"Tonight."

"*Tonight?* I'll have starved to death by then!"

He eyed her without much show of credulity.

"I suspect you'll survive," he said.

After about a minute, when her feet had gone so numb from swinging that she'd experienced an attack of pins and needles the moment she'd stopped and set them down, she said, "I've got some money of my own."

He frowned at her. "Where?"

So then she dug in her coat pocket and, somewhat sheepishly, brought out a handful of change and a couple of bills.

He looked at the haul as if he couldn't quite believe it. "Where did that come from?" he said.

"The lady in the toilets had put a saucer out, and I emptied it when she wasn't looking."

"*Marianne!*" he said, sitting up. She could see that he was shocked.

"I know," she said quickly, "it was wrong. But it wasn't *very* wrong. She hadn't even put any bars of soap out. Can't I get some Coke? We can share it."

He looked around the square. Most of the buildings here were in the continental style, with courtyard entrances off the street. Apart from the florist, there were no other shops visible. She couldn't see what he had to get agitated about. Her lifting a few as-yet-unclaimed pfennigs from a dish was hardly in the same league as his own little catalogue of break-ins.

She said, "There must be somewhere close."

"Go on, then," he said. "But don't go far."

She went skipping away, off up the Hohestrasse in search of a kiosk.

When she got back about ten minutes later, Ryan was gone. Only the rose on the bench remained, to mark the place where he'd once been sitting.

CHAPTER 50

They told a story about a pub called the Admiral Nelson, that had stood out on Broad Street until the last days of the war. A big place, a pub in the old style. Shoulder to shoulder on Saturday nights, fistfights in the backyard guaranteed. Upstairs there was a function room for weddings, where vast working-class families would gather like two clans who'd met to discuss peace but who decided, as the evening wore on, that conflict offered the more lasting entertainment. The Admiral Nelson had taken a direct hit from a German bomb on one such Saturday night during the blitz. Warning sirens had sounded at the beginning of the raid but, in a mood of defiance, everyone had closed the blackout curtains and carried on. An estimated two hundred and fifty people had been in the building. Taking into account those who'd died in the infirmary later, only twelve had survived.

And the story told about the place in later years was this.

If you were waiting at the bus stop across the road from where the pub had once been, and it was late at night, and you were alone, and the all-night service was proving to be about as reliable as it usually was, you might see a little girl. You wouldn't see her coming, she'd just be there when you turned around. She'd be wearing a dusty and torn bridesmaid's dress, and she'd have dark circles under her eyes. She'd ask you for a penny and then she'd go away. You wouldn't actually see where she went to, she'd just be gone. And then, depending on who was telling the story, you could perhaps stand and listen and hear voices singing along with a piano, carried faintly on the wind where there was no other sound.

There had been an old pianola in the Admiral Nelson. And each song on the roll had played for a penny.

Everybody knew the story. Children told it in their school playgrounds. In every case, the teller swore that it had happened to a friend of a friend, someone who could always be mentioned by name but never quite called upon to bear witness.

Only Ryan O'Donnell had ever said that it had actually happened to him; and in daylight, at that.

Most of the area had changed by the time that Ryan was growing up. The shops had gone, the houses behind them were gone, everything. There was just the new road passing over, and then the new flats that could be seen beyond it. Everyone who'd moved in there had been happy, because compared to their old back-to-back houses the flats were like palaces. But within a year they'd become palaces that one had to journey through hell to reach. Buses ran through concrete wastelands. The new grass wouldn't grow. Building foyers were vandalized and the lifts broke down as if on a schedule.

There was nothing left of Broad Street but a rubble-strewn plain, and the road that ran through the middle of it, and the bus stop that now stood in the shadow of the overpass. Kids would persuade Ryan to take them out there and tell them what he believed he'd seen. Afterwards they'd get together and compare notes, and they'd laugh so hard that sometimes they'd fall on the ground and howl. But the smaller children didn't laugh. The smaller children tended to believe without question, and perhaps that was why he'd hung around with them more. Only, they frightened easily. Some parents found out and there were complaints to his mother. One complaint went to the police, and a big officer with sergeant's stripes and a Scottish accent had come around and called him a liar and threatened him with being locked up in a voice so deep that it almost rattled the glass in the windows. Ryan had believed him.

Ryan would believe anything in those days, if only it could be impressed upon him deeply enough.

And the question that would often exercise him in the years to come, when he'd have more than enough time and opportunity to ponder it, was this: If a vivid memory of something coupled with total certainty was no guide to what was actually real, then what was? What could you trust? Where was your firm place to stand? They told him that he'd only convinced himself that he'd seen the child in the bridesmaid's dress, but he could close his eyes and see her still. Every tear, every mark, every smudge on her skin. The pity that he'd felt. The understanding in her eyes.

But then there was what he'd done to Vanessa Mulrooney, the day that she'd asked him to take her out there and tell her the tale; and *that* was the memory that defied belief, that was the nightmare.

A nightmare to everyone but Ryan O'Donnell, who had been there and who knew. Who knew how easy a choice it was to take a life, when the taking offered a moment of utter possession that exceeded any possibility of physical desire; and which passed, devastatingly, leaving only horror and self-disgust and a lingering, seductive whisper inside his mind that, once heard, could never be forgotten.

Do it again.

He would never again deny what he'd done that one time, at least not to himself. He'd tried denial, and it had brought him no peace. But where could he go from here? His journey was one that offered no road home. All the penance in the world couldn't wipe out the deed. Unless Vanessa Mulrooney could rise from the grave and take back her life, he would remain unforgiven.

And it would be without end. For with any relief that he might find, any happiness that he might ever reach for, a soft voice would whisper in his ear to remind him of the debt that would be forever owed, forever unpaid.

It was a voice that could never be stilled. He would hear it, and all of the colors would drain out of his life. Small pleasures would turn hollow. All else would turn sour. He would live at a distance among strangers.

Hell could be a quiet place, in its way. Because that was what it meant, to be damned.

CHAPTER 51

He saw Marianne from the back of the taxi. She was dawdling her way back towards the square, sucking Coke out of a can through a straw and looking at the display in a record shop. He tried to wind the window down and call to her, but he fumbled it and by the time he'd cranked it open, she'd slipped by and was out of sight.

What should he do? Stop the cab and go back? Carry on? He didn't know.

But by then, because he'd hesitated and done nothing, the decision was already made.

He looked forward. The cab they were trailing was two cars in front. He could see the back of the woman's head through the rear window, and that was it. She was looking down. There was a change in sound from the note of the car's tires as they passed over tramlines. Ahead of them, at the end of the wide city road onto which they'd turned, there was an elevated interchange that appeared to be for all routes out of town.

A new worry, now, to add to the others. He looked over the driver's shoulder at the meter.

He knew that he shouldn't have let Marianne go off like that. But what could he do? She'd been wriggling like a basket of snakes and driving him mad, and there had been no knowing then how long they'd have to wait. As it turned out, the woman had arrived by taxi less than ten minutes after Marianne had gone. She'd had a word with the driver and then entered the building just as the clerk in the cardigan had been returning with two containers of coffee and a sandwich bag. They'd gone in together.

Ryan had been on his feet by then, looking around in every

direction. He wasn't sure, but the chances seemed high. On the
young side, perhaps, but she had something of the look of
Marianne and her clothes were quiet and, to Ryan's eye, probably expensive. But what could he do without Marianne here?
If it *was* her mother, then this was her moment.

When the woman had come out a minute later, he'd known.
He'd known for certain because of the pink envelope in her
hand. She was crossing to the waiting taxi and in a moment
she'd be gone, and everything would be lost. Gathering his
nerve in the realization that there was no other way, he'd
started towards her. He'd known that he ought to wave and
call, but there had been something not right. Her face. Her face
had been like stone.

Gray.

Hard.

Set.

She'd torn up the letter and got into the cab and Ryan, fal-
tering, had failed to stop her.

But then, as it had left the square and joined the main street
traffic, he'd followed on foot. There had been a taxi stand
about a hundred yards further on. Anneliese Cadogan's car had
slowed for the lights, which had just about given him time to
get to the head of the line and make himself understood. Then
he'd seen Marianne; and by then, of course, it had been too
late.

The meter was running. They were on a high bridge now,
crossing the river and leaving the city behind. This would be
the Rhine, he supposed. It was wide and calm and slow, with
barges chugging along it and with the green sweep of its flood
plain beyond. Then suddenly they were into a tunnel, and the
tunnel had no walkways.

His heart was sinking. It was all sliding out of his control.
Where was the point in hoping that Marianne might guess his
problem and wait for him, if he was going to get stranded so
far out of town that he couldn't make his way back? Trying
not to let the driver see what he was doing, he pulled out his
cash and counted it. By the electronic display on the meter,
more than half was already spoken for. He couldn't even ask

the driver to turn around and drop him somewhere close to where he'd started.

The point of no return. That was an airman's phrase he'd read somewhere. It referred to the point at which you didn't have enough fuel to get you home, so you'd no choice but to go on. This was the stage that he'd already reached and passed.

His problem now was that he had no idea of the distance to his ultimate destination.

Out of the tunnel, and onto a motorway. They passed a brewery, and then they passed through suburbs without actually touching them. It was here that the driver began to lose the FM station that he'd had playing in the background, so now he had to reach over and resume the radio. He picked up Radio Caroline, catching the tail end of the weather in English.

As far as Ryan was concerned, they were still in the middle of nowhere. The car ahead was showing no sign of stopping. He didn't know what to do. If he bilked the driver, the driver would call the law. They were passing through an area of pleasant, low-rise housing by this time, broken up every now and again by a few acres of market gardening land on which stood long, low greenhouses.

He got ready to lean forward and stop the cab.

The taxi ahead began to indicate a left. There were no other cars between them now.

So he held back as they made the turn after.

Here was a street where money lived. Big money. It was long and it was quiet and it was tree-lined, and back from the trees stood huge detached houses. They were perhaps a step down from being mansions, but it wasn't much of a step.

Ryan said, "I think you'd better stop. My cash just ran out."

The driver hadn't seemed to understand a great deal of English when Ryan had jumped into the car. But he understood that, all right. He braked, hard, and turned in his seat. But Ryan was already getting out.

"This is everything I've got," he said, handing it in through the driver's open window. It was three marks short of the figure that was now showing on the meter.

"Sorry about the tip," he added.

The driver looked him over. Then he made a face of scorn and, without another word, slammed into gear and U-turned around Ryan in the middle of the street.

Ryan didn't watch him go. He was already looking down the street in the direction taken by the other cab. From here it looked like a dead end, with woodland beyond. He started to walk.

The returning cab, empty, passed him a few moments later.

No two houses along there were of the same design. They covered every style from modern and bizarre to staunch and traditional.

Everything seemed quiet. A phone was ringing somewhere, unanswered. In one house, a big dog barked cavernously as Ryan passed.

As far as he could tell, Anneliese Cadogan had been dropped at the last house at the end of the road. This was just before it ran out and became a woodland path. The house was one of the biggest in the row, two-storied but with an extra upper floor of attic-style windows in the high-ridged roof. The walls were pink, the garden well-stocked and cared for, probably not by the owner. There were garages for three cars to the side, and another just visible around the back. The house looked as if it had been extended a couple of times since it had first been built.

Ryan stopped by the gate, flexed his fingers, and then walked up the short driveway to the door.

He was out of place here, and he knew it. He also knew that he didn't dare to look furtive, or he'd be dead on the spot. He rang the bell and then took a step back, hands locked behind him to conceal his tattoos. Most of the time he could forget about them, but this wasn't one of the times. He could hear the bell echoing in what sounded like an empty house, and for a moment he sensed his own doubt. Had the cab dropped her somewhere else, and merely come to the road's end to turn? He didn't think so. He rang again, and then again.

Eventually, she came.

The door opened about halfway, and she was looking straight at him. He knew then that he'd been right; close up she seemed older, the resemblance more certain. She wasn't a tall woman, very slender, her hair in an elfin cut but with the same gray eyes and slightly pointed chin. From a distance she might look almost like a child herself. She was looking wary.

"Why did you tear up Marianne's letter?" Ryan asked.

She tried to slam the door on him, but by then he'd managed to get his foot in the way and it bounced back at her. He followed it in and she backed off, and he said, "Look, I put my neck on the block to get her to you and if you won't even talk to her, then I'm in deep shit. I don't know what went on between you and her father and I can't tell you what to say to her, but I'm on a hook and you've got to get me off it."

They were in the hallway now, a big one that gave onto an open-plan lounge area with a stairway up one side and a gallery above. No one else was there.

And then Ryan said, belatedly, "You . . . you *do* speak English?"

Her gaze was cold.

"Not here," she said. "Come with me."

CHAPTER 52

She turned away and headed for the stairs. He closed the door behind him, and then followed her up. He couldn't help looking around like a tourist. He'd never been in a place like this before . . . pale furniture, real framed pictures on the walls. He'd probably never even been in a place that had cost as much as the *carpets* in here.

Apart from the two of them, the house appeared to be empty. Across the gallery and deeper in they ascended another, narrower stairway to the topmost part of the building. It was sparser up above; it had the look of a place where the servants might live, boxy and echoey and with limited light. But

Anneliese Cadogan didn't have the look of anyone's house-keeper. She went into one of the attic rooms and left the door open for Ryan to follow.

The room was small, square, and bare, with some of its headroom cut off by the angle of the roof. There was some plain furniture and a narrow single divan bed. She seated herself on the divan, barely denting its covers. There was nowhere else to sit. It looked more like a cell than a bedroom. No books, no magazines. And nothing on the walls, not even a mirror.

"Who sleeps here?" he said.

"I do. Now say what you wanted to say. You can't stay for long."

Ryan was still looking around. He'd once lived on a twenty-four-patient ward where the only private space was created by a curtain drawn around each bed. This was about on the same level of intimacy.

He said, "This isn't quite what I was hoping to find."

"Really," the woman said. "I think you'd better tell me what you're doing with Marianne. Why isn't she with her father?"

He hesitated for a moment and then, because he didn't want to stand there explaining himself like a teacher or a priest, he sat on the bed alongside her without waiting for an invitation.

"I'll start at the beginning," he said.

He told her everything that had happened, starting with that day on the beach. From what he'd heard so far, her English was faultless and she seemed to have no problem understanding him; at least, she didn't stop him at any time. Ryan felt awkward. It wasn't often that he was required to perform, and several times he came close to drying up. But a sense of urgency drove him along.

He said little about himself. Nothing he could say on that subject would be of any help. As she listened, Anneliese Cadogan's face in profile gave him nothing in response.

And at the end of it he waited, but she said nothing.

"Mrs. Cadogan?" he said. "Please?"

The woman gestured briefly, as if for a moment she couldn't answer. She clasped her hands before her.

"I can't believe he'd ever make her unhappy," she said. "He always loved her more than anything."

"I know only what I saw, and what she's told me."

She looked at him, then. "And he *beat* her?"

"She had bruises."

Anneliese Cadogan's eyes were now shining and empty and her voice was shot through with bitterness. It was a strange brew of signals and whatever they were supposed to be telling him, he couldn't quite make it out.

"In all this time," she said, "the one thing that I believed was that he'd be caring for her. That he'd help her to forget me and their lives would go on."

He started to rise. "Come on, she'll be waiting."

"I can't bring her here," she said.

"Where, then?"

"You don't understand, Mr. Ryan."

"Please," he said. "She's on her own in the middle of town, she doesn't even know where I am."

There was a sound from downstairs.

It was the main door closing. Someone had come in. Anneliese Cadogan quickly signed for Ryan to be quiet. Rising to her feet, she slipped past him and stood listening at the door. Voices in conversation could be heard from some way down below. Two men, at least.

"He must have come home early," she said, almost in a whisper. "Don't make a sound."

One of the voices, raised, called her name. She stepped out and gave a reply down the stairs, and then she quickly moved back in again and almost closed the door.

With some urgency, she said, "You have to get out of the house. *Now.* You can go down the back stairs and out through the kitchen. Go out across the yard and into the woods. I'll switch off the alarms."

"What about Marianne?"

"I'm sorry," she said. "I can't help you."

He could hardly believe this. But she'd a hand on his arm and she was already starting to reopen the door; Ryan blocked it and said, "Mrs. Cadogan, you're the one who doesn't understand. Listen to me. Listen to what I'm saying. I'm not the most suitable person to be in charge of Marianne."

She stared.

"Oh, my God," she said.

"I haven't touched her. I don't intend to. But I've served time and I've had treatment. I can't put it any more plainly to you, Mrs. Cadogan, but you've got to take her away from me."

"Turn her in to the police."

"She'd think I'd betrayed her. So far she thinks I'm the only person in the world who hasn't. You're what I promised."

"Tell her I'm dead. That wouldn't be so far from the truth."

Ryan looked around, unable to believe that he was getting nowhere like this.

"Let's talk to your new boyfriend. What have I got to lose?"

He moved as if to push by her and head downstairs. But Anneliese caught him as he tried to pass and jerked him back, whispering *"No!"*

Ryan waited.

"You don't know the situation here," she said somewhat unsteadily, as if the feelings that she was keeping under tight control were fighting to get out from under the barrier.

He didn't reply and so she took a deep breath and went on. "Let me put it like this. Marianne's my daughter. I love her, I'd die for her. I'd give anything to be with her. But I'm poison. That's why I've never tried to find her, and why I won't let her near. The life I have now isn't something that I'd ever want her to see."

"You got one thing right," Ryan said. "I *don't* understand."

From down below there came another call. Louder this time, and with a distinct note of tetchiness.

"I have to go down there," Anneliese said.

"I'll come with you."

"For God's sake," she said through gritted teeth. *"Please!"*

Again, Ryan waited.

Finally Anneliese said, "Cafe Heinemann, on the Königstrasse. Ten o'clock tomorrow morning, but come alone. I'll work something out for you, but if she's there, I'll walk away. I mean that."

As she backed out of the room, she made a last finger-to-the-lips gesture calling for complete silence before leading the way down. He moved after her carefully, and made no sound. On the next floor she pointed along the passageway to where the service stairs continued. The men's voices were just below them now. With a final look of apprehension, she turned from him and headed out across the gallery to descend the main stairway into the lounge.

Ryan didn't move. He couldn't make this out, any of it. He could understand her not wanting anyone to see that she'd brought someone like him into the house, but that was about all he could grasp.

The gallery rail was only about a dozen yards away from where he was standing. He could hear her speaking, now. Her voice sounded quite different in German. He wondered what they were talking about.

One of the men spoke again. It sounded like the one who'd called to her, but it was hard to be sure. He asked her about five questions, one after another. All of her answers were one-word replies.

Then the man said something else, and as she answered she moved away.

The gallery had a polished wooden floor with a big Oriental rug across the middle. Ryan took a couple of steps out and then, before he'd reached the point at which anyone below would be able to see him, he dropped to his hands and knees.

Now, stretching out carefully and drawing himself towards the edge, he was able to look down through the banister rails like a child out of bed keeping watch on the grownups.

Two big, luxurious sofas faced each other across a coffee table of polished green stone. Two men sat, one on each and both at ease. The one who'd called to Anneliese was dark and somewhere in his forties. The other was older, a white-haired avuncular-looking teddy bear of a man with glasses. They both wore gray business suits and they both looked as if they had plenty in their lives that they could take for granted. Anneliese herself was no longer in the room.

They were chatting. Nothing remarkable about it. The younger man was doing most of the talking and Ryan's guess, from his manner, was that the house was most likely his. After a couple of minutes the two of them got to their feet with old-world courtesy as Anneliese returned. Ryan couldn't see her clearly at first because she came out from somewhere below the gallery but then, as she came around behind one of the sofas, he saw that she was carrying a tray with a glass coffeepot and china for two.

Ryan didn't know what it was, but he could sense that something wasn't quite right. The older man said something to Anneliese, and she stopped at the end of the table with the tray in her hands. He said something else, and she inclined her head with her eyes lowered.

At which the older man turned to the younger with a look of inquiry and the younger man made an open-hands gesture as if to say *Yes, of course.*

Then the older man turned back to Anneliese and raised his closed hand and, without any change in his manner or unusual show of emotion, he punched her hard across the face.

The blow made a crack like a whip. Her head snapped to the side and the rest of her followed. She spun around and went down in a crash of falling china, dropping to her knees as the glass coffee jug hit the stone table and burst. The black liquid rushed across its surface as the older man shook his hand loosely from the wrist, as if to take away the sting.

He looked at the younger man, and Ryan saw him smile and nod approvingly. Then he looked at Anneliese again, and said something to her.

Slowly, Anneliese shuffled forward on her knees. Then she bent and, equally slowly and painfully, began to lap the spilled coffee from the table.

Ryan was vaguely aware that his mouth was hanging open. He made an effort to close it. The two men moved away from the mess and down to the other end of the facing sofas, and seemed to be carrying on with their amiable conversation as if nothing out of the ordinary had happened. Anneliese paused, picked a piece of broken glass from her lip, laid it to one side, and carried on. By now the two men had both pulled out Filofax organizers and were flipping through the pages, offering dates back and forth. Anneliese, ignored, wiped her mouth on the back of her hand and Ryan glimpsed a thin streak of blood there. Whether it was from the blow or the broken glass, it was impossible to say.

Ryan moved back from the rail. The Oriental rug was thick enough for him to make no sound as he stepped across the gallery and into the concealment of the passageway. It was only here that he dared to start breathing.

One conclusion seemed inescapable.

Despite their respectable exterior, these were not the most decent of people.

He made his way downstairs and through a door that led him into a modern kitchen, large and well-equipped enough to service a small restaurant but with an air of little use. He stopped to check on the refrigerator; there was fruit and there was cheese, though not very much of either on shelves that were mostly empty. He filled his pockets anyway, and then closed the fridge in silence before crossing to the door that led him out into the garden behind the house.

The rear garden was a long, flat lawn, a stretch of immaculately kept bowling-green baize that ran all the way out to a low fence that marked the start of the woodland. He broke into a trot. Whatever he did was going to make him look suspicious to any observer, so there was no point in hanging around. When he reached the fence he scrambled over, snagged his coat, pulled it free, and then made his way through dead bracken to the nearest path.

The woodland seemed almost primeval, untouched apart from the beaten earth of the pathway. The trees were tall and straight and well spaced and there was an almost complete lack of undergrowth, just the same regular carpet of dead leaves and bracken rolling on through. In most woodland, Ryan reckoned, you could never see beyond fifty yards or so. Here it was as if you could see forever, into a forest that ran on without end.

He followed the pathway along the backs of all the houses, looking for some other way out. He saw a woman walking a runt-size dog and a track-suited jogger who moved as if he was struggling through water, and they appeared to be the woodland's only other users right now. There was a wind stirring the trees so that occasionally, far overhead, branches banged together with a sound like an accidental meeting of oars.

Ryan had an entire new set of problems now, and his head was aching with them. He didn't know what to make of what he'd seen. He couldn't understand it and he certainly couldn't begin to explain it. What was he going to say to Marianne?

She'd been alone in town for almost two hours, not knowing where he'd gone or why or even whether he'd return. What must she be thinking? And God alone knew how long it was going to take him to get back across the river to her.

But more than anything else, he found himself thinking of the younger of the two men. Not the older, and that was interesting because he'd been the one who'd struck the blow while the other had stood back. But the master of the house—and, by implication, of its attic tenant—lingered in Ryan's memory in a way that the other did not. It was one of those imponderables, like stage presence or star quality. Some had it and some hadn't, but still it defied definition.

Perhaps it was simply that he'd learned what to look for. Something that was there to be seen by anyone but glimpsed by only a few. It was as if he'd been able to develop some kind of sensitivity to the exact angle on that one little face on the diamond where the truth blazed out.

Sometimes it blazed out as light.

But sometimes, as it had today, it opened onto darkness.

CHAPTER 53

Marianne waited.

She waited for what seemed like the entire day, but then she checked on the time and found that it had been for less than an hour. Then the lunchtime crowd came and went. Sometimes she sat on the bench and sometimes she walked around, but she didn't dare to leave the square. There was her mother to watch for. And what if Ryan were to come back and find her gone? They might never link up again but fall further and further apart, lost souls being swirled away from one another like so much jetsam.

She played games with herself. She sat looking at the ground between her feet and counting to a hundred, determined that she wouldn't look up until she'd finished and with a growing certainty that when she did, it would be to see him walking towards her.

And when it didn't happen she'd think: *Well, not that time, but definitely this.* She counted again, this time cheating and glancing up early. She became angry with herself because she'd weakened and perhaps even prevented it from happening.

The woman who ran the flower shop came out and picked up some litter from around the doorway, then went back in again. She was a red-haired, middle-aged woman. Her neat hair was trimmed short at the sides and she wore a vinyl work apron. She glanced over towards Marianne as she was on her way back inside, but not for long enough to make it worth a wave.

Marianne got up off the bench and walked across the square towards the shop.

It was called *Blumer Rosenthal.* Flowers, ferns, and blossoms stood inside in vases on ranked shelves like stadium seating; it was like stepping into the world's most over-the-top secret garden. The humidity level was high, almost like the tropical house at the zoo. A glass-fronted counter displayed wreaths and ready-made sprays. Beyond the counter was an open doorway through to an inner room, some kind of a workshop area. It was from here that the woman emerged as Marianne was closing the door behind her.

"Excuse me," Marianne said, "but could you tell me the time, please?"

"It's after half past two," the woman told her, closing a computerized order book and laying it on the counter. "That's a long time to spend hanging around."

"I know," Marianne said.

"You've been there nearly all day. What have you been waiting for? Because I can tell you now, nothing much happens around here."

"I'm looking for the man who was with me this morning. Did you see where he went?"

"Was that your father?"

"He isn't my father, he's just a friend. Please, did you see him?"

"I didn't see him go," the woman said, clearly aware that this wouldn't exactly be welcome information.

And Marianne simply said, "Oh."

"You look exhausted," the woman said. "Do you live around here? Where have you been staying?"

"We've been traveling around," Marianne said.

"I'm not sure that it's good for you to be sitting on your own out there for so long."

"I'm not on my own. He'll be back soon."

"How about if I let you wait in here?"

Would that be an advantage? Marianne wasn't so sure. "I might miss something," she said.

"Not if you put a chair in the window. And I'll get you a drink. Something hot? You'd like that?"

The offer of a drink did it.

"Can I have coffee?" she said.

"If that's what you want."

So then Marianne nodded, and the woman went on: "There's a chair in the back room. Go and bring it through."

Marianne went into the workshop area. The room was well-lighted, but sparse in comparison to the jungle out front. There was a big table where the bouquets were made up, where fancy paper could be pulled across from a roll and where string and about twenty different kinds of ribbon hung within reach. An arrangement lay, half made, on the table's surface. There were knives, scissors, a deep bin full of cut stalks and leaves. Apart from Marianne herself, there was no one else in the room.

On the window ledge, an electric kettle stood with mugs and a coffee jar. The window looked out through thin bars onto an inner courtyard. Under the window were a desk and telephone, swamped by a mess of orders and receipts on top of which had been dumped a desk diary so filled with notes that it looked as if it had been used as a scribble pad.

There was only one chair, and it stood at the desk. The chair was straight-backed and heavy, with a red upholstered seat and chipped gilt decoration over dirty white. As Marianne was dragging it through the doorway and out into the shop, the woman said, "Find the spot where you can see best. I won't be a couple of minutes."

She went into the back as Marianne juggled the chair around in the window to find the best position. This was actually a pretty good solution; it seemed as if she'd fallen on her feet for a while, at least. She'd be safe and she'd have shelter, and she could watch both for her mother and for Ryan with equal ease. She might feel like an exhibit sitting in the window this way, but if that was the worst of it, then it wasn't too bad.

Outside in the square, she could see the bench. A mother was sitting there now, lifting her small baby out of its buggy. No sign of Ryan, unless he'd suddenly become a master of disguise.

The woman was going to give her coffee. No one *ever* gave her coffee. She'd tried it once and she hadn't liked it, but that had been a long time ago. She'd grown since then and she was sure that she must like it by now.

Someone outside was coming this way. A well-dressed man, nothing to get excited about. He came up to the door and tried to open it, but the door seemed to be stuck. He rattled it a few times and then, quickly, as if embarrassed, he turned and walked away. Marianne looked back towards the workroom, but in spite of the noise the shopkeeper didn't emerge.

She looked back towards the outside. And it was only then that she noticed that the door had been bolted at the top.

Marianne sensed the signs of warning.

The bolt was too high for her to reach. The shop wasn't supposed to be closed yet—at least, the woman hadn't said anything about it. So, why?

Marianne stood up from the chair, crossed the shop, and eased her way around the counter. She could hear now that the woman was speaking on the telephone in the back. The connecting door had been pulled almost all the way shut. She moved to the doorway and listened.

Well, I don't know, the woman was saying. *Just tell me what the appropriate department is. Child welfare, or whatever.*

Marianne went back and quickly dragged the chair over to the street door. She climbed onto the chair and reached up to work the bolt. The bolt was stiff and difficult. When at last she got it to move, it shot back with a bang.

She could hear the clatter of the phone being hung up in the other room.

Marianne got down and pulled the chair out of the way just as the woman was emerging. She opened the door and dived out into the street.

"Hey!" the woman was calling after her. "It's all right! Don't worry, there's no reason to run away!"

And Marianne was thinking, *You want to bet?*

She kept on running until she reached the wide Königsallee, then slowed to a walk because she'd realized that people were looking. She was breathing hard and her sides hurt. She didn't know what to do now.

She looked for him in the shopping crowds. She couldn't believe that he would desert her. It didn't matter what anybody said or thought, at home or anywhere else. Later on, as the shops and offices began to empty, she looked for his face again. She kept returning to the streets around the square where they'd parted, but the square itself was as good as barred to her now because there was no way of knowing who'd be watching. It started to get dark. She was hungry, but she felt too sick to eat. And then as darkness fell and the city changed gear, she began to feel less and less secure.

The light turned electric. Traffic became a river of beasts, bright-eyed, prowling. She didn't know where she was going to sleep, or what she was going to do next. All she could think to do was to keep moving, and to keep alive the certainty that this next minute, or around this next corner, she'd find him and he'd take her back into his protection and he'd know exactly what to do.

The galleries and arcades began to close. For a while she

hung around in a twenty-four-hour video store, watching the screens until a ponytailed counter clerk leaned over and pointed out the age restriction on the door in a low voice, as if he wasn't actually trying to throw her out but was conspiring with her to help her escape management attention. She was under eighteen, so she had to go.

She kept moving. And eventually, sometime approaching eleven, she looked around and realized that she was lost.

She'd crossed underneath a lighted overpass. Here the pavements were slippery with grit and she seemed to be heading into some dark urban backwater of factory yards and empty warehouses. There was one parked car down here, a battered Opel with its rear end smashed and a widening pool of transmission oil, blacker than the night itself, fanned on the road beneath it. She turned to look behind her, but the way back looked no more promising than the way ahead.

Off at an angle ran a long, dark street with some sign of a fast and well-lighted road at the end of it. Above the buildings in this direction she could see the roof neon of some of the city's big banks and industries. Their offices were empty at this time of night, but at least their lights could show her the way back into the middle of town. She started along the street.

A car went by. She was passing a fenced yard of washing machines and refrigerators, all of them rusting and stacked three and four deep. Now she could hear another car coming up behind and she waited for it to pass as well, but it didn't.

It slowed.

She looked back without actually stopping. It was a yellow Mercedes with a lucky horseshoe on its radiator grille. The effect was like a twisted smile. She turned and walked on, but the car put on a short burst of speed and drew level, pacing her. She heard the sound of an electric window being lowered, but she didn't look.

"Are you lost?" she heard a man's voice call to her. She didn't look up or answer, so he said it again.

"I'm all right," she said.

"You don't look all right. You look as if you need help."

"No thanks," she said, and started to run.

She hid in a narrow alleyway and saw his car go past the

end of it three times as if circling, trying to find her again. Then she left it a good quarter of an hour before she risked emerging. As she waited, she could hear trains in the distance.

Trains.

Their luggage was in a locker in the main railway station, and Ryan still had the key.

It took her more than an hour to find her way back. In the end she took a risk, and rode a tram without a ticket. The tram drew into the plaza before the station where the last five passengers, Marianne included, disembarked. It was nearly midnight, now. In complete contrast to Hamburg at this hour, the Düsseldorf station square had emptied as if under curfew. A couple of the passengers had looked at her curiously, but she'd made a point of meeting nobody's eyes.

There was still some life inside the building. It was as if, here at the day's end, the station had become a magnet for the less well-heeled with nothing better to do. The through-concourse was a vast, noisy, low-ceilinged hangar about the length of two or three football pitches. The lighting was relentlessly dull and flat. All of the bars and kiosks had closed, and everything now concentrated around the all-night waiting room at the heart of the building. Inside this, late travelers dozed or sat looking bleak. Outside on the open concourse, a few teenagers huddled. A bag lady had loaded all of her possessions onto a luggage trolley and sat alongside it, scratching the back of her lowered head. Four thick-voiced and beery men were standing by one of the pillars, drinking from cans and pushing one another and generally exploiting the acoustics.

Marianne crossed the concourse to the side corridor where the luggage lockers were situated. The three banks of metal lockers were like deep, dead-ended passageways with strip lighting above and square-tiled floors. They'd left their stuff in the second row. She couldn't remember the number, but she thought that she'd recognize the locker itself because the door had some graffiti that hadn't been properly cleaned off.

There was a definite smell of stale urine along here. How could people *do* that? she wondered. Even dogs went out of doors. She looked all along the bottom tier. One locker door was missing completely and the space had been stuffed with bottles and rubbish, and she knew that she was close. It was just along by here. It was . . .

It was empty.

She stared. The green flag was up under the coin drop and the key was back in its place.

She heard a sound, a rumbling, and looked up just in time to see a hand-drawn trolley laden with bags, coats, and boxes that was passing the end of the row. She ran to catch up; by the time she'd reached it, the two uniformed railwaymen who'd been pulling it along had stopped and were opening up more time-expired lockers and hauling out the contents.

"Please," she said, "have you got two bags on there? Mine and my friend's? We got separated, and I need to know if he's been back yet."

"Ask at the counter," one of the men said.

"Which counter?"

"The left-luggage counter. If we take it out, that's where it goes."

She was looking, but she couldn't tell. There was a red nylon bag in there, but it didn't look like the right shade and it didn't have green straps like hers. But the rest of it was such a heap that she wanted to clamber on and rummage.

She heard her own name.

She turned.

Ryan was standing there. His own bag was on his shoulder and her red rucksack was in his hand. She started to run and he let both bags fall to the floor as he dropped to one knee to catch her. There was barely a moment for him to brace himself, and then she hit him like a truck.

She wrapped her arms around his neck and held on tight. She was shaking, but he rocked her and smoothed her hair. They were right in the middle of the passageway and some people had to step to one side and walk around them, pretending that there was nothing unusual to notice as they did it.

"It's all right, now," Ryan said. "It's all right. Don't worry. Don't be scared."

"I know," she said into his shoulder. She had two fistfuls of his coat and she was holding on as tightly as she possibly could.

"I'm not scared," she said. "I'm not scared at all."

CHAPTER 54

They met up again after they'd used the washrooms to get themselves fit to face the day. They'd stayed all night in the station, finding a couple of seats in the waiting room. Someone in uniform had come around waking up sleepers at about three in the morning and then again at five, but no one had checked to see if they all held tickets. Marianne felt rough. Dog-rough, to use one of her father's phrases. She looked at herself in the washroom mirror and, for one scary moment, found herself staring at an older stranger. But that passed.

Ryan was waiting when she emerged. She told him, "You don't have to look at me like that. I didn't steal anything this time."

"Good," Ryan said. "Never use the same routine twice in one place."

They'd no money, but they did have breakfast. Ryan dug it out of his pockets. All of it had survived apart from a ripe cheese in some foil that they had to throw away. He hadn't told her where he'd been or what he'd done the previous day, and he wasn't telling her now.

They sat and watched the incoming commuters as they surged up from the U-bahn and headed for daylight.

"I want a shower," Marianne said.

"Me too," Ryan said. "Maybe soon."

And then after a while, Marianne said, "I don't think I'm enjoying this so much anymore."

"It's no way to see the world," Ryan conceded, stretching

out stiffly. "I can tell you that for nothing." Something went *crack,* and then he relaxed.

Marianne looked at him curiously. "Was that you?"

"Old bones," Ryan said. "Now, listen. We've got some developments here, and it means I've got to go and meet someone."

"I guessed that," she said.

"How?" Ryan said, puzzled.

"You're wearing aftershave this morning. It was her, wasn't it? She came after all and that's got something to do with the reason why you disappeared. Aren't I right? Where is she? Where do we have to go?"

"Slow down," Ryan said.

"I don't want to slow down," Marianne said, "I want to see her."

"Well," Ryan said with some irritation, "you can't." And then, seeing the expression on her face, he added, "It's not as simple as you think. I've got to meet someone and work a few things out, and then one way or another I think we'll have it solved. But you've got to trust me. Which means don't ask me lots of questions that I'm not ready to answer, and don't make it any more difficult than it already is."

"But it *is* her, isn't it? She's the one you're meeting? Why doesn't she just come for me?"

"What did I just say?"

She opened her mouth to speak again, but then she managed to stop herself. It wasn't easy. She closed her mouth and pressed her lips together and glowered at him.

"You look like a frog," Ryan said.

Marianne didn't respond, except to compress her lips harder.

"That's the idea," Ryan said. He glanced around the station. "I think you should stay around here. Don't leave the station and if anyone tries to talk to you, go back into the waiting room and stay there until they've gone. If someone comes to you and says that I sent them, ask for the code word. You want to pick a code word now? Make it something we can both remember."

"Rudi," she said.

"Rudi it is," said Ryan. "I don't know how long I'll be but

if it starts getting late, don't worry. I *will* be back and I'll look
for you here. So, do we have a deal?"

"Deal," Marianne said gloomily.

"Good," Ryan said, and he produced one last red apple from
his pocket. "Here's lunch," he said, "and remember. It can
only get better from here."

She watched him go. She'd taken two bites out of the apple
before he'd even reached the doors. He looked back and
waved, and she responded without too much enthusiasm.

She *hated* to wait.

As soon as he'd gone out, she got to her feet. She was
shouldering her red rucksack as she started after him towards
the doors, weaving through the crowd at a brisk pace. She
didn't want to lose sight of him but she didn't want to get so
close that he'd turn and see her, either. This was spy stuff.

Better from here? That sounded worthwhile.

But she'd have felt happier if, on the evidence of what she
reckoned she'd seen in his eyes, Ryan had believed in it just
a *little* more.

As Ryan O'Donnell was stopping strangers in Düsseldorf and
asking the way to the Königstrasse, DI Jennifer McGann was
climbing the stairway of a prewar business arcade back in
Hamburg where a certain private detective's office had proved
to be a waste of time as a mantrap. When Werner had arrived
to set it all up on the Monday morning, he'd found the door
glass punched in and the office open and the tapes from
Schlesinger's answering machine gone. The targets had been,
the targets had flown. Forensics people had moved in and had
sealed off the office, then started to take it apart. Johann
Schlesinger had walked in at four that afternoon, and it had
been a while before anyone had been able to convince him that
his office had not, in fact, been bombed by a dissatisfied client,
of which he had a number.

Werner had been with him for most of the previous day, trying to determine what might be missing from his files and if
there could be any inferences drawn, anything at all about
where O'Donnell and Marianne could be heading.

The first thing Jennifer saw was that the plastic incident tape used to close off the section of gallery had been snapped and now hung as so much litter. The area around the door and even the rail outside were still smudged with white aluminum residue, as if a sticky-fingered child had been playing with talcum powder. They'd lifted several of O'Donnell's prints from around the filing cabinet and the desk, and identified some clear ones from the girl on the telephone answering machine.

The circus had departed now. Only Werner and Schlesinger were inside. Both looked up as she entered.

"The document analysis has come through," she said to Werner. "O'Donnell tore off about five pages after he'd written on the notebook, but they've lifted a trace and enhanced it. Guess where."

"Düsseldorf again?"

"An address in the middle of town. I spoke to one of the office staff there. Someone delivered a letter for Anneliese Cadogan on Monday. It was collected yesterday. They say that's all they know."

Werner was about to reply, and then he stopped. He looked at Schlesinger, and Jennifer did the same. Schlesinger was sitting there without any show of expression. He was a small, squashed-looking man with glasses and brilliantined hair, and his face in repose had the look of someone who'd just taken his teeth out. It wasn't a face that gave much away, either.

Werner indicated to Jennifer for the two of them to move outside, and so they left Schlesinger in his office and went out to stand on the gallery.

Werner said, as if he'd just worked it through in his own mind and couldn't be sure that he wasn't missing some obvious flaw, "This is good, isn't it?"

"What do you mean?"

"He's doing his best to get her where she wants to go, and he doesn't appear to have harmed her yet."

"We don't know *what* he's done to her. And we won't, until we catch them both. Seduction of the innocent, Werner, you lead them by the hand and get them to participate in their own corruption. And if O'Donnell's now managed to link up with the mother . . . I have to say that means greater danger in my book, not less. Josef's making arrangements and I'm heading down there today. Sergeant Moon's still unfit, but I've been told that one of your people will be assigned to come with me. Is that likely to be you?"

Werner looked out over the rail.

"I don't think so," he said.

She watched him for signals but Werner, she'd come to realize, was a harder man to read than he might appear. Josef's description of him as a one-man disaster area was only a small part of the story. As was the fact that on the surface he was easygoing and unhurried, and seemed unlikely to be fazed by anything. There was much more to him, as she'd seen on the night of the shooting.

She'd taken him home in a taxi. His apartment was near the university, in an area of wide streets and big old town houses. Within minutes of arriving there and getting him inside, she'd realized that he lived alone. There was clear evidence of someone having recently, but not *too* recently, moved out . . . the stretches of empty space on the bookshelves, those signs of where a couple of pictures had been taken down and nothing hung in their place. When she'd gone into the bathroom, she'd noticed one or two almost-used-up toiletries that she couldn't imagine Werner, or almost any other man, buying for himself.

When she'd returned to the main room, he'd been sitting there with his head in his hands and she'd sat down beside him and then . . . well, it was hard to describe exactly how it had happened, it had just *happened*. Neither of them had pressed for it and neither of them had done a thing to stop it. They'd just gone into it like a rockslide. Minutes later they were both half-undressed with no system or logic to it, and she'd her legs wrapped around Werner and he was carrying her towards the bedroom and trying to kick off the trousers that he couldn't get rid of because he hadn't realized that he still had one shoe on and, get this: when they got there *it was better than it had ever been in her life before.* It was thermonuclear. Time stopped. It was like an out-of-body experience, five tons of TNT going up on a speeding train. And when it was over and they started to come down and then lay there intertangled and panting like a couple of sprinters, she realized that Werner still had his pants and shorts trailing from one leg like a ball and chain.

She'd known what it was, then. What had happened in the past few minutes couldn't be divorced from what had happened that afternoon. It was death and sex, sex and death—the most potent linkage of opposites imaginable. No one was immune from the association. No one. It hadn't just been good. It hadn't even just been the best ever.

It had been so good, it was frightening.

He was still looking out over the rail. "Werner," she said. "We can't just leave it like this."

"I think we'd better," he said. And he looked at her then. "What's going to happen, Jennifer?" he said. "I mean, seriously. What's the future here? Because I don't see one. So I think it's best if you simply do your job, and then go home to . . . whatever his name is."

"Ricky," she said quietly.

"Whoever," Werner said.

And she knew then that he'd been just as scared and exhilarated as she; that the lid had begun to lift on something primitive and awesome, and it had shaken them both more than either would care to admit.

"Well," she said. "Then I suppose this is thanks and goodbye."

She held out her hand to shake his, but Werner winced slightly as if at some inner pain and waved it away before turning and going back into Schlesinger's office alone.

"I'm sorry to keep you waiting," the lawyers' receptionist told Patrick Cadogan when she'd reemerged from the inner suite of offices and held out an envelope. "This is for you."

Cadogan said, "What is it?"

"I'm afraid it's your account," she said. "None of the partners can consent to further meetings until it's been settled."

Cadogan sighed. He accepted the envelope and held it before him without opening it. "I don't suppose you take Visa."

"Not this time," she said, shaking her head with a faint smile.

"Well, I wouldn't feel too bad about this," Cadogan said, instinct telling him that the woman herself probably had some

sympathy even if the obligations of her job didn't allow her to
do much about it. "It's not your fault. It had to happen."

He flopped into one of the reception area's low leather
chairs, bleak and exhausted. In the past couple of days he'd
started to feel like a test-bed motor being run at speed towards
its own destruction. He could sense himself starting to break
up, but there wasn't anything that he could do about it.

He looked up at the receptionist and said, "They know what
I've been landed with here, don't they? I mean, we're not just
arguing points of law. There's a serious situation."

"I only work for them," the receptionist said. "That doesn't
mean I have to agree with everything they do."

"I know," Cadogan said. "I'm sorry. Look, I don't want to
be a problem for you, but ... just give me a minute to pull
myself together, will you? Then I'll leave."

She moved to the seat beside him and lowered herself to
perch on its edge. "I saw them, you know."

"Who?"

"Your daughter and that man. They came here into the office. Didn't the police tell you?"

"The police don't tell me anything. Relatives of the victim
tend to get in the way. How did she look?"

"I think she was all right. She didn't seem frightened."

"What about him?"

"That was something different. He worried me. And while I
was calling security, he stole some information and the two of
them ran. I'm not saying this just to make it worse for you.
But you ought to know what happened."

"You couldn't make it worse for me even if you tried." He
waved the account envelope which was still in his hand, unopened, and said, "Look, they'd better not hold their breath
while they're waiting for this. But if anything else like that
happens, will you tell me?"

"Assuming I'll know where to find you."

"That'll be one step ahead of my creditors. A vast and
growing army. But I'll keep in touch with you here, as long as
you promise not to send the dogs after me for the bill."

"We'll have to see, won't we?"

He got to his feet. Nothing would have been more tempting

than to let himself drop back into the soft leather and close his eyes, but then he knew that it wasn't an option.

"Thanks," he said. "I'll not come back again. I don't want to give you any more problems."

And then he moved to the door, where he turned.

"But I'll kill him, you know," he said, entirely reasonably. "If I ever manage to get my hands on him before they do, I'll kill him."

And then he left.

CHAPTER 55

The Cafe Heinemann stood alongside a small back-street playhouse, and probably drew most of its clientele from the theatre crowds in the evenings. There was even a connecting door with brass comedy and tragedy masks for its handles, where people could move from one venue to the other without having to go out onto the street. Judging by the photographs outside the playhouse foyer, the current presentation was a farce set in a hotel. But at this hour of the day, the foyer was dark and the cafe was comparatively quiet.

Ryan stood just inside the entrance and scanned the tables. About half of them were occupied, and there were another three people on high stools around the diner counter. The style of the place was a suitably theatrical mix of the old-fashioned and the avant garde, and yesterday's avant garde at that. There wasn't a piece of furniture or decor that didn't have the look of a redundant stage prop, from the dusty overhead chandeliers—unlit—to the puppets and masks and bamboo cages that hung all around. He couldn't see Anneliese Cadogan, but then he was early. He wondered if they'd mind him taking a seat and waiting, or if he'd have to watch for her outside. He'd no cash at all, and so couldn't even ask for a glass of water. In places like this, the water fizzed and cost money.

But then he spotted her.

She was at a table on the far side of the counter, in the deepest and gloomiest part of the cafe. Even so she was wearing dark glasses, and so it was hard to tell if she was looking straight at him or straight through him. She didn't raise a hand, or make any sign. Squeezing through between the tables, he went over.

She didn't look at him as he sat. She'd turned so that the worst side of her face would be away from him. The dark glasses had a graduated tint so that they looked more like a fashion accessory than serious sunwear, but even they and the makeup couldn't disguise the bruise and the swelling and the tear over her cheekbone that looked as if it had been made by the sharp edge of a ring.

Without any preliminaries, she said, "I've had a chance to think. I believe there's a way that all of this can be dealt with."

"Before we start," Ryan said, "you might as well know. I stayed and watched after you went downstairs yesterday."

There was a silence. Then she said, "Oh."

"What was happening there?"

"That's none of your business."

"But you were just putting up with it! Why?"

"Because that's the way it is," she said suddenly and with some irritation. "Don't make judgments about me, Mr. Ryan. You know nothing about the situation. We're here to talk about Marianne."

"You should leave him," Ryan said.

"Please."

"You're going to get hurt," he persisted. "I don't see what's keeping you there. Get out of it while you're still free to move around."

She looked down. "I'm not free," she said.

"Don't you even care what could happen to you?"

"No."

And that, he could tell, was no more or less than the truth. Sitting back, he said, "I just don't understand."

"I don't care what happens to me, because my life is over.

It ended the day that I threw it away. Now Axel has custody of the ashes, that's all. What he does with them is his concern. I go where he sends me."

"You like to be hurt?" Ryan hazarded. "I've known people who do. Is that what it's all about?"

But she was shaking her head, slowly.

Ryan said, "Who's Axel?"

"Please. I don't want to talk about this."

"I've done exactly what you asked. I came here to meet you and I persuaded Marianne to stay away. If you think that was easy, you don't know her at all. So at least tell me what I'm bringing her into."

She drew a breath and looked around, and then it was as if she put a little iron into her backbone. Ryan glanced around as well, wondering if anyone might be sitting too close or taking an interest. The walls of their alcove had been papered with blow-ups of old theatrical posters, set designs, and blueprints for mechanical stage effects. To these had been added extra adornments of cutout paper hearts, life belts, and plastic lobsters.

"All right," Anneliese said. "I'll tell you about Axel Reineger, and I'll tell you a little about me. Then perhaps you'll understand what I'm asking you to do, and why. Axel Reineger is a trader in people, in more ways than you could possibly imagine. Immigrant workers, people without papers, Germans from the east . . . he hires them cheap and he sells them where the work is dirty and where questions would be awkward. Most of what he's paid for them, he keeps. For that he sells their lives, and he sells their health. And sometimes more."

"How did he get hold of you?"

"Oh," she said with a brief wave of her hand as if this was the least important of details, "we met. Socially. He's a very respectable—" And here she hesitated before correcting herself. "He's a very respected man. He seems to know everyone who counts. He was a supplier of contract labor to my husband's company and so, whenever there was some formal occasion, he'd often be there. I saw him looking at me once, and that was all it took."

"You're not going to tell me you fell for him," Ryan said.

"Nothing of the kind, Mr. Ryan," she said quietly. "I'm telling you that I saw the expression in his eyes, and I realized that he knew. He hadn't just looked at me. He'd looked into me, and he knew what I was. But I don't suppose you believe that can happen."

Ryan said nothing.

She went on. "He'd phone me when I was at home alone. That's how it began. At first I thought he wanted me for himself. But that's not his way. When everything finally fell apart, I went to him and he took my life over. Now I go where I'm sent, and I do what I'm told."

"Like yesterday."

"That was just a demonstration. From today I spend two weeks as that man's property. This is the deal that they made."

"Who is he?"

"I don't know. Another respected man. It really makes no difference to me. What happens after that will depend on how long it takes my body to recover."

"Why do you let them do this?"

"Don't imagine I chose this life, Mr. Ryan. This life chose me. We like to think that we're free, but the truth is that we're on rails. We're going where we're going, but we never think there's an end to the line until we reach it. That's when we look back. And we wonder how we might ever have deluded ourselves that it could have ended any other way than this."

"So, where does this leave Marianne?"

"That's the only concern I have left. I'm too dangerous, and you're unfit. I don't care what you promised her. You've got to give her to the police."

"I can't."

"You're very tenacious, Mr. Ryan, and I'm grateful for what you've tried to do. But understand me when I say that I don't want my daughter in your company any longer."

"I can't give her to them because apart from what I promised her, my only excuse is that I was bringing her to you. Without that for a defense, I'm seriously fucked. I've got nothing to prove that I didn't just take her because I wanted to."

"Be honest with me, Mr. Ryan," she said. "And with yourself, as well. Are you saying that was never a factor?"

Ryan looked down and didn't speak.

She laid an envelope on the glass surface before him. Under the glass was a display of old visiting cards, pressed there like a squashed-bug collection. The envelope had apparently been taped somewhere, and then the tape along its edges had been slit to make possible its removal.

"I stole this from Axel," Anneliese explained. "If ever things should go wrong for him, he has an escape route. This is the key to it. With this he can get hold of everything he needs to disappear and then come up again as somebody else. If you'll leave her, then it's yours."

He looked up at her, warily.

"A new life, Mr. Ryan. The past wiped clean. Think about that."

"And what happens to Marianne?"

She sat back in her chair. "She belongs with her father. I know he loved her once. But now that she's older, he probably looks at her and can think only of me and the pain that I caused him. He'll never forgive me as long as I live. Could I be right about that, Mr. Ryan?"

"She's getting to look a lot like you," Ryan said.

Anneliese nodded slowly.

"Then," she said quietly, "that is the problem I shall now have to address."

Anneliese was the first to leave. She went out without even looking back. She was the best-looking woman in the room, the best-dressed, apparently the most self-assured.

All that Ryan could think as he watched her go was: *what a waste.*

He looked down at the envelope in his hands. Yet again, the doors at the journey's apparent end had opened to reveal an entire new gameboard with a new set of rules. It was like being chained to an arcade machine where each screen was tougher than the last and the scoring involved life and death and was for real. The envelope's main contents were a key and a local address. The key didn't look like a door key; it had only two small teeth and resembled a skeleton key more than anything. The address meant nothing to him. Also folded in the envelope

were a small amount of cash and a few well-used work permits
and forged identity cards, mostly for short-term use by illegals.
These, she'd told him, were all that she'd been able to scrape
together out of Reineger's office drawers and compared to
what the key would bring him, they were nothing much.

A new life.

The past wiped away.

Was such a thing even remotely possible?

There was a moment of panic when he realized that she'd
left him with the bill, until he remembered that she'd also left
him the means with which to pay it. He paid at the counter and
then waited for his change, and then he picked up his knapsack
and went out.

The daylight made him wince a little. He looked around to
establish his bearings before starting to make his way back towards the station. It was then that he saw Marianne.

She was on the other side of the street, in a doorway almost
directly opposite. She couldn't have seen into the place from
there, but she'd have been able to observe everyone who came
and went for as long as he'd been inside. She could only have
followed him, and been there all the time. There was no other
way that she'd have known where to go.

A couple of cars passed, and then he crossed over. She was
holding herself, and she looked cold. Her eyes were wide and
empty. The doorway where she'd been standing was a deep recess between a barbershop and a joke shop and deep inside it
was what looked like the rear exit to a bank, with a steel re-
inforced door and armored glass about six feet in.

He stood beside her. Was there a camera over the door? He
tried to glance up without making it obvious, but he saw nothing. After a moment, she looked up at him.

She hadn't been crying but she had that pinched, watery-
eyed look.

She said, "She never came, did she? You were supposed to
meet her here and she never even turned up."

Ryan didn't know what to say.

Marianne looked down. "I hate her," she said.

"Let's go," Ryan said.

She allowed herself to be guided out of the doorway. She

seemed awfully grown-up right now. Young as she was, Ryan wouldn't have wanted to be the object of her anger. She didn't cry it out like a child. She kept it in, and you didn't quite know where or in what form you might see it again.

"Come on," he said. "We've got places to go."

Marianne sniffed with what-do-I-care defiance. She'd recognized no one, in spite of the fact that Anneliese Cadogan had passed no more than a dozen yards from where her daughter had been standing. Ryan wondered if Anneliese had set eyes on Marianne, and if she'd known her. He reckoned that she almost certainly had. Apparently she'd walked on without flinching.

"Don't hate her," Ryan said. "That isn't right."

"I hate them both," Marianne said.

And then she said, "But I'm glad I've got you."

CHAPTER 56

That evening Jennifer arrived at her new hotel in Düsseldorf, alone. Josef was looking for somewhere to park the car in which they'd driven down, and would be joining up with her at the local police headquarters later. And as for Benny Moon—Benny was flying back, at last, to where he could sleep off the flu in his own home instead of in a three-star room on the departmental budget. He wouldn't be replaced until the two-week handover, if at all.

She wondered if anyone had told him that, yet.

"I have two reservations here," the clerk said.

"Just give me the best room," Jennifer said. What the hell. She'd put up with Josef's driving and his conversation for the past four hours. She deserved it.

The room was on the first floor. It was an odd shape, probably in the corner of the building, and the ceiling was high. It was neat and it was forgettably pleasant and it had those few small touches that could give an illusion of luxury on top of what was actually spartan simplicity.

Most important of all, it had a phone.

She checked the piece of paper that she'd been given as she called the Düsseldorf police headquarters building.

"*Kriminalhauptkommissar* Rilke is not in his office," she was told. "Will you leave a message?"

"Please tell him that Detective Inspector McGann from England has arrived. If you can find him and tell him right now, I'll be grateful."

She gave the hotel's name and her room number, and then she hung up the phone and started to unpack. She knew that she ought to feel excited, but she felt despondent. She'd barely been starting to find her feet in Hamburg, and now they'd been kicked from under her and she was having to climb back up from ground zero again. Besides all of that, she'd gone through all of her clothes and she would have to wash them in the bathroom basin and leave them to drip in the shower.

Her notes and files were dumped on the bed to be sorted. On top of everything else, she'd made a bad end of it with Werner and now probably wouldn't see him again to put it right. She was hanging her wet underwear along the shower curtain rail when her room phone rang, and she hurried out with dripping hands to pick it up.

"Inspector McGann?" a man's voice said in faintly accented English. "This is *Hauptkommissar* Rilke."

"Thank you for getting back to me," she said. Was that another mobile phone? It sounded like one. Hurriedly drying her free hand on the bedcover, she said, "I'd like us to meet as soon as possible. If you can tell me where you are—"

"I'm with Anneliese Cadogan," the officer said.

"You've found her?"

"Less than an hour ago."

Jennifer stretched over from the bedside phone to the coffee table, where a notepad bearing the hotel's crest lay barely within reach. She scrabbled it to her with her fingertips and then noted down the address that Rilke gave her.

Leaving her washing half done, she stepped into her shoes and raced out.

The street names had a brutal ring to them. Hellweg. Junkerstrasse. Dieselstrasse. Municipal apartment housing lined the way, five stories high and just about long enough to seem endless. Fast roads cut through on their way to the industrial zone beyond, with its not-so-distant skyline of incinerator plants and power station chimneys and cement works towers. As the car made a turn into one of the smaller residential avenues, Jennifer looked out and saw some teenagers playing football on grass that had been battered into submission by a few too many such games. Others were having shouted conversations with friends up at third floor windows.

Her immediate impression was that they'd entered some kind of a backwater in the shadow of heavy industry. The area had an off-road, unbuttoned feel to it that the center of town didn't have, and there was more greenery around than she might have expected. On one side of the avenue stood apartment buildings, modest in scale and balconied. On the opposite side, overlooked by the apartments, the land had been divided into what appeared to be garden allotments. Shanty huts and mobile homes stood on these, some of them far enough back to be barely visible from the street.

Jennifer leaned forward to speak to the driver.

"Stop at the police line," she said.

She paid him off and he had to U-turn to leave, because ahead of them the narrow lane had been blocked by a large number of police vehicles. Barriers had been set up, and only certain cars were being allowed through. There were people outside on most of the overlooking balconies, watching as nothing much happened; one or two were waiting with cameras, but not with anything that looked professional from here.

She showed her British ID and her temporary Praesidium pass from Hamburg, and was allowed through the barrier. She didn't have to ask where to go; all activity was centered on a low wooden building at the far end of a long, narrow plot. The plot was like a garden haven, the house a retreat at its heart. From the road, the house could barely be seen.

A narrow containment way had been strung up with plastic tape to prevent anyone from wandering off the path and perhaps trampling on evidence. She passed a mailbox by the open gate in the chain-link fence, and started down towards the house. Junior uniformed officers were combing the lawn on their hands and knees. Big floodlights compensated for the fading of the day, throwing long shadows and making the grass seem vivid and unreal.

The house itself had probably started out as a plain wooden hut. But it had been embellished and extended and extended again, with redwood sides and a tarpaulined roof and with cartwheels and hitching rails for a ranchhouse effect. It looked like the fantasy retreat of a weekend cowboy, *Bonanza*-style. As Jennifer approached, the windows lit up with the electronic bursts of flash guns being triggered inside.

The inside was something else.

Instead of the holiday home that she might have expected, it was almost bare of furniture. The walls had been lined with fiberglass insulation felt to a thickness of about eight inches, pinned at two-foot intervals by the use of a staple gun. Where the edges met, they'd been taped. There were heavy swinging shutters on the insides of the windows, their backs lined with the same material. With the shutters closed, the place would probably be as dark and as soundproof as a tomb—which could only make her wonder about the big Grundig ghetto blaster that stood in the middle of the floor.

She asked for Rilke, and a man on a radio pointed her towards a further, inner door.

Jennifer squeezed through. It was standing room only in there, with one exception.

"Miss McGann?" a voice said, and she turned. A pleasant-looking man in a suit, very sharp, eyes dark in color and bright in their expression. He was probably in his forties, but looked fitter and younger. He passed a clipboard to someone else, and held out his hand to her. She took it.

"I'm Rilke," he said. "Welcome to Düsseldorf."

Jennifer looked around. An extra layer of heavy canvas curtaining had been added to the fiberglass wool in here. There were two plain chairs and there was a bed. The electronic guns flashed again. The object of their interest lay unmoving on the mattress, a plastic ligature pulled tight around its neck.

"Anneliese Cadogan?" Jennifer hazarded.

"You really didn't need to hurry over," Rilke said. "There's nothing more she'll be telling us before nine o'clock tomorrow."

PART THREE

DESPERADOES UNDER
THE EAVES

CHAPTER 57

It was a chilly morning. The car that had been sent for Jennifer dropped her outside the mortuary building on the Heinrich Heine University campus just before nine. Rilke was there on the steps just ahead of her.

"Only one of you?" he said.

She hadn't yet had the chance to explain about Benny, and so she said, "Detective Sergeant Moon had to return to England early. He'll be replaced at the end of this week. As I will."

"Let's go inside," Rilke suggested. "It's been an interesting night."

Anneliese Cadogan's post mortem had been scheduled in the basement of the Institut für Rechtsmedizin, the university's forensic pathology department. It was a white, flat-roofed building with a sloping lawn and a cycle rack out front and a pull-in area for collections and deliveries around the back. Rilke pressed the bell, and a woman in an inner office craned her neck to get a look at them before buzzing them in. Once they were inside Rilke led the way to the end of the corridor, where they descended a stairway to basement level.

"What have you found out?" Jennifer said.

"Where to begin telling you is the problem," Rilke said. "The body was discovered when one of the neighbors went over to complain about the noise. Some old song, set to play over and over again. No one had ever heard a sound coming out of the place before. Considering the way it had been fixed up, that's hardly a surprise. The doors and the windows were all open. It would seem that someone wanted her to be found. But not too soon."

"Are you ruling out suicide?"

"We're ruling out nothing."

They emerged from the stairway into a receiving area with a basin sluice and some hanging gowns and a board carrying the names and the details of those dead passing through. The floor down here was of yellowish marble chip, the walls of yellow tile. A door like that of a meat locker stood open and two technicians were bringing Anneliese Cadogan's body out of storage for the autopsy. Beyond them, through the plastic inner flap doors, three other clients could be glimpsed as they awaited their turns without complaint. Each was on a stainless steel table with a drain bucket underneath. They were naked, but they lay on shrouds with their feet towards the door. They were in various states. The skin of one male was swollen and green and dark around the abdomen, pale pink and bruised-looking at the extremities. By Jennifer's estimate, he must have been lying unrefrigerated for about a week before discovery.

They waited as Anneliese Cadogan was rolled by. The shroud had been drawn over to cover her, but not too well. Her clothes and anything else that might have been found with her now sat in a blue plastic sack at her feet.

"We have an interesting connection, here," Rilke said. "The mail bureau couldn't give us an address, but one of the clerks remembered that she'd arrived in a taxi and told it to wait. We checked and found a record of a telephone booking for a pickup and return to a house out across the river. Somebody went over this morning, but there was nobody home. What we *did* establish was that the house is the main home of a local citizen named Axel Reineger. Herr Reineger is also the owner of the cabin where Frau Cadogan was found, although he's tried to conceal the fact with a company name. I might say that Herr Reineger is of considerable interest to us, and has been for a while."

At the entrance to the autopsy room they were handed a couple of disposable aprons in white plastic. There were about half a dozen people inside the room already. As they pulled the aprons on, Jennifer said, "Did this Reineger person know that she'd gone out to the cabin?"

"He claims not."

"And does O'Donnell come into this picture anywhere?"

"Who knows?" Rilke said as they went through the double doors and into the room. "Although she'd seem a little too old for a man of O'Donnell's known preferences."

"Don't underestimate him," Jennifer said. "He's a lot more complicated than most people seem to suppose."

Anneliese Cadogan's body had been transferred to the autopsy table, and her head was being lifted as a curved steel block was slipped under her neck. Apart from the two technicians, it appeared that there would be two pathologists and a stenographer present for the procedure. The others were introduced to her as a state's attorney and a fingerprint officer; altogether they made quite a crowd, and there wasn't a lot of space to move around. The room had one high-up, long window with opalescent glass, but the main illumination came from two bright sets of fluorescent tubes directly above the table. One of the technicians had opened up an equipment closet and was loading a camera with Polaroid film. The other was setting out rows of twist-cap jars and bottles alongside a big weighing scale.

Rilke said, "Something's beginning to open up here, and the more we find out, the more interesting it gets. You saw what the inside of the cabin was like. Reineger had it set up that way for a very specific purpose."

"Meaning what?"

"I'd say it was a perfect design for a torture chamber, wouldn't you?"

"What exactly does Reineger do?"

"He's an entrepreneur of no detectable scruples. Which means that for a man like him, there can be no limits. He claims that Anneliese Cadogan was his housekeeper. Housekeeper! Look at her!"

Unshrouded now, Anneliese Cadogan lay exposed in death beneath the lights. Her eyes were half closed, their lashes dried-out and crusted. She had a pale and wasted look, her ribs showing like those of a starving dog; it was like a teenager's body, hardly developed but showing a terrible mileage.

She was almost hairless, deliberately so, and in the faint stubble over her pubic bone there was what appeared to be a one-word tattoo.

They were given masks. The stenographer took her seat at the low gray desk by the head of the table, and Rilke exchanged a few words with the senior pathologist as the other doctor, a woman of around Jennifer's own age, began a close examination of the body. She began with the hands, lifting them to examine the nails. To handle the body she wore what looked like ordinary yellow kitchen gloves. She gave a running commentary to the stenographer as she worked her way down the length of it, and then she called for help to turn the body over.

"What's she been saying?" Jennifer asked Rilke. "I can't follow."

"The body bears a large number of healed scars and old injuries. She's clearly submitted herself to regular and systematic abuse. The most recent damage preceding her mortal injury was a blow in the face. The cut on her cheek was probably caused by a ring."

Jennifer said, "What does the tattoo mean?"

"This is not a tattoo," the senior pathologist said, moving back to rejoin them as his colleague continued her examination. He was tall and straight, with strong features and a pleasant manner.

"What is it, then?" Jennifer said, and there was a hurried conference over translation between the two men before Rilke said, "A burn. A burning."

"You mean a brand?" Jennifer said with some disbelief. "She was branded? *There?*"

"The word is *Sklavin*," Rilke said. "It means *slave girl*."

Jennifer stared blankly.

"Not housekeeper," Rilke added.

After the examination and the taking of various swab samples, the body was measured and photographed and printed. Then the cutting began.

The ligature around the neck was almost certainly the cause of death. There had been a box of them found at the cabin;

white plastic industrial ties, normally used to hold together cables and piping. Once pulled tight, they couldn't be released.
At a guess they'd been intended for bondage use, but they
could serve a more lethal purpose in the case of an uncon-
scious victim or a determined suicide with sufficient nerve.
Other stuff had been found as well. There had been a trunkload
of off-the-shelf S&M gear up in the loft, along with a few
chains and some industrial grease. There was always the possibility that a game had gone wrong, but she'd been fully
dressed when found.

Looking down at the body, Rilke appeared to be smiling.

"What's the matter?" Jennifer said.

"Axel Reineger," he said fondly, "your empire begins to
fall. Bless you, child. Bless you."

And Jennifer went cold inside.

They stayed for a while longer, but nothing else remarkable was found. In the end Rilke asked the pathologist if
she could keep the appearance of the autopsied body as neat
as possible and then explained to Jennifer, "We're getting
her husband down here to confirm identification this afternoon."

"Who gave him the news?" she wanted to know, but Rilke
couldn't tell her.

They were hosing everything down with the table's
built-in shower head when Rilke and Jennifer left. She was
glad to get back into the open air. She'd probably attended a
couple of dozen post mortems. Enough to have lost count of
them, anyway. It wasn't a part of the job that she'd ever
dodged, but it wasn't one that she felt inclined to seek out,
either. She felt no disgust; her overwhelming feeling now
was one of sadness.

As they were walking out to where Rilke had left his car,
he said to her, "There's one other thing I didn't tell you yet.
When we searched the cabin last night, we found places for
concealed cameras in most of the rooms. I've a suspicion
that the secret of Reineger's untouchability is about to be revealed."

"What does that mean?"

"He didn't use the place himself. Why would he? He'd acquired it for others to use."

"I hate to say this," Jennifer said, "but I'm getting worried, here."

"Why?"

"You're getting all excited about your Axel Reineger, and you're hardly thinking about my people at all."

"Your people?"

"Ryan O'Donnell and that woman's daughter. You've got your head full of your old obsession with this Axel Reineger while they're still out there together. Well that's fine. You're the dog and he's the bone you've always wanted, so go fetch. But don't let an eleven-year-old girl suffer because of it. She's the reason for my being here, and if there was ever any doubt about the kind of danger that she's in, no one can be doubting it now."

He didn't seem offended. He said, "Let me tell you something about the way Axel Reineger does business. He once started a travel agency by selling bogus round-trip tickets to the immigrant workers that he was bringing over."

"I've heard of that kind of arrangement," Jennifer said.

"He took it one stage further. He filled the outward flights with tourists. These were mostly men on their way to arranged liaisons with third-world partners, both male and female. Some of those were ten-year-old prostitutes. Some were even younger. By the time we'd caught up with him, he'd been warned and he was out of it. His hands were clean and there wasn't a thing we could do. That's what always happens whenever we get near."

"I understand what you're saying," she said. "Just don't trample over Marianne Cadogan in your rush to get hold of him, that's all."

"We won't," he said.

Jennifer only wished that she could be quite as certain as he wanted her to be, as they separated and moved down either side of Rilke's silver Scorpio.

He reversed out of the parking slot and headed out along narrow campus access roads towards the street exit, slowing for bicycles at every junction. The university had the look of a high-tech manufacturing plant landed somewhere in the middle of parkland. Rilke ran through what they'd learned so far about Anneliese Cadogan's life in Düsseldorf. She'd been no prisoner, that was for certain; neighbors had seen her come and go with complete independence. She appeared to own a wardrobe of startlingly expensive designer-label clothes and almost nothing else. She held no driver's license, she wasn't registered to vote, her name appeared in no accounts for civic services; she appeared to have no bank, and she'd paid no state taxes. Rilke said that it was as if she'd been invisible. Jennifer had seen a different message. To her it was as if Anneliese had given up on herself; as if she'd considered herself no longer a human being, even, but just a thing to be offered for use. *Remember me when I was happy,* her last letter had said. *Think of me now as one who has gone.*

Dear mama. I am so sorry.

Rilke said, "Did her condition tell you anything?"

"She'd been managed," Jennifer said. "Like an athlete or a boxer. For all the damage she'd taken, she was still reasonably fit and healthy."

"Somewhat undernourished, wouldn't you say?"

"Hardly," Jennifer said, although she'd had the same thought herself. She didn't know why she felt the impulse to defend Anneliese, but she responded to it anyway. "Just lean. I know women who'd die for a look like that."

It was an unfortunate choice of words and she regretted it as soon as she'd realized what she'd said, but Rilke didn't seem to notice.

He said, "It's a condition I've seen before. Women of slight build who starve themselves for a look that's almost childlike, even down to the urchin haircut. They pose for magazines and pornographic films. They wouldn't fool a pedophile, of course, at least not in the flesh. But for your ordinary person with a latent pedophile streak . . . between that look and the hidden cameras, I think we may be close to finding out how Herr Reineger has managed to elude us for so long."

As they slowed for the midday traffic on their way through the middle of town, a radio message came through that she couldn't follow. She'd the impression that some elaborate understatement was being used so that no eavesdropper would be able to make out the exact nature of what was being discussed.

When the caller had signed off, Rilke explained the meaning of the conversation.

"It's started already," he said. "Axel Reineger has produced an alibi backed by one of the most prominent men in town. He's starting out with a show of force. I think that means it's war."

Rilke looked eager for the challenge.

Oh, God, Jennifer thought despairingly.

Unlike Hamburg's modern Praesidium tower, the Düsseldorf police headquarters was a much older redbrick citadel cut off from the center of town by a fast overpass. They grabbed a parking space in front of the finance ministry next door and headed for the entrance, a narrow walk-through past a glass-fronted control point. To reach it they had to go around a long, dark chauffeured limousine that was double-parked at the foot of the steps.

From behind the glass, a leather-jacketed man in his fifties nodded them through. The security arrangements seemed casual, but probably weren't.

They came into a mosaic-floored rotunda with echoing headroom all the way up to the top of the building. A party was descending the wide stairway opposite, and Rilke touched Jennifer's arm. The two of them stopped as the crowd went by. At the center of this buzzing group of aides and assistants walked a man whose thoughts and expressed wishes were clearly the main concern of all those around him. Most people's idea of the embodiment of major-league business success tended towards the expensive Italian suit and the manicure, but Jennifer knew that the reality could be far more subtly marked. In the course of a fraud investigation she'd once been present at the interview—on his own territory—of the head of a decent-size European multinational. Because of his schedule, they'd had to talk to him on the company plane. Jennifer had worn her good gray outfit, the most formal thing that she owned; chain-store bought, but still not cheap. The businessman had worn an old cardigan and a pair of well-worn carpet slippers that his secretary had produced from an attaché case without waiting to be asked. He'd reminded her of somebody's grandfather, surprised by a visit to his garden shed.

This man was of the same type.

A white-haired, avuncular-looking teddy bear of a man with glasses.

She looked at Rilke. *The alibi?* was the question that formed in her mind, and it didn't even have to be asked. Rilke nodded very slightly.

When the group had gone out, Jennifer and Rilke crossed the rotunda floor to the stairway. Right alongside the stairway was something that Jennifer hadn't seen in years—a double-set of Paternoster lifts, the open-sided kind where you could step in and out on any floor but the lifts themselves never stopped. They were running, but nobody seemed to be using them.

She said to Rilke, "That was a hefty-looking set of rings that the big man was wearing, there."

Rilke gave her an interested sideways look.

"Yes," he said. "Wasn't it?"

They ascended to the third level. Away from the rotunda this was a building of long corridors with polished floors, the corridors themselves windowless but with some second-hand daylight getting in through the glass transom above each office door. Here and there, to one side or the other, stood a single straight-backed chair. The place wasn't run-down, but the overall feeling was of drabness.

"What we like to call it is *Kafkaesque*," Rilke told her as he pulled out a bunch of keys to unlock one of the offices.

As they went through, they passed into another world. It wasn't necessarily a better world, but at least it was on a human scale and with human touches. As in Hamburg, each office let into its neighbor and as before there were two or three desks to each room. The decor was the usual mix of potted plants, family photographs, and official notices.

Rilke showed her to a desk that she'd be able to use. It was by a window and it had no phone, but there were phones within reach.

"Settle in," he said. "I've got some calls to make. I'll see you again in a little while."

When he'd gone, she put her bag on the desk. She couldn't think of any other settling in that she could do.

She sighed, and rubbed her eyes. She was homesick and she was travel weary and she'd had enough of hotel rooms and scrounged-up favors. She knew nothing of the ground here and everything she wanted to do, she had to ask for. She'd come out from home all full of piss and vinegar, but now it was getting so that all she wanted to do was hand it over to someone else and go back. At first she'd been determined to get it all sewn up before it was time to go. Then she'd begun to be afraid that someone else would come out and steal the glory after all her work. But now it was getting hard for her to become animated even over *that*.

It was a sick world. And there were no heroes. And for those who tried to be, it was like fighting the ocean with a wooden sword. Marianne was slipping from her, and she didn't know what more she could do.

She looked out of the window. From here she could see down into one of the building's two inner courtyards. The yard was divided by a wall, with two-thirds of it as a vehicle compound and the other area looking like an enclosed exercise yard for the in-house jail.

Somebody was getting out of a car down there, and her heart gave a momentary leap of recognition.

It was Patrick Cadogan. He was looking around himself. He seemed dazed. The car's driver said something to him and he responded belatedly. He looked like a man who'd been sandbagged. They started moving towards the building.

They'd be taking him to identify his wife sometime this afternoon, perhaps even straight away. Not that the timing would matter much, especially to Anneliese. It wasn't to be that kind of a reunion.

She took some papers out of her bag and left them on the desk, to keep her claim on it.

Then she left the office and hurried downstairs, in the hope of being able to intercept the new arrival.

One Week Later

CHAPTER 58

In the bar with the pool table just around the corner from the Kiefterstrasse, the Englishman was back again. No one could mistake him. As before, he seemed to move slowly and stiffly, as if he'd just picked himself up from a hard floor. And as on his last visit he moved from group to group, showing the same pictures and asking the same questions. He was always polite. He never raised his voice. Someone asked him if he was all right.

"Yes," he said. "Yes, thank you. I'll be fine."

Cadogan had been warned about the Kiefterstrasse, but that hadn't been enough to keep him away. It was a long, high, curving street almost medieval in its look and layout, the houses mostly run-down and untouched by modernization. The buildings were squats, their tenants a concentration of the city's young radicals. It was rumored that some members of the Red Army Faction hid out in there and that, by extension and by inclination, those who lived inside might be likely to give shelter to anyone on the run. The graffiti and the banners started at one end of the street, and continued on all the way down to the other. Above the ground-level fortifications the sense was of some long, late, and endless party, with a guest list consisting entirely of gate-crashers.

He spoke to two young men, hardly more than teenagers, in black leather jackets and with headscarves tied Mishima fashion. They were in a corner, with two beers on the table and a box of groceries on the floor between them. They said they couldn't help, but they offered to take him to talk to some of the others in the buildings. Cadogan had been warned about such invitations. He'd been warned not to consider them.

But he went.

From a distance it looked like a war zone, a haunt of glee-ful savages. The upper stories of the houses were like one long, rambling mural of desert scenes, slogans, and political flags and symbols. Down in the street itself there were two or three serious mounds of rubbish consisting of supermarket trolleys, car dynamos, empty cardboard boxes, and assorted trash. Some of the parked cars looked almost as if they'd been firebombed, but still ran.

But not all of them. Some of them were just ordinary middle-market sedans. And on some of the balconies above, children's clothing had been hung out on lines to dry along with the T-shirts and denims. As Cadogan followed the two boys over to where some punkish types dressed in black stood chatting before one of the squats, he felt no apprehension. He felt almost nothing at all. These were people and they could either help him or they couldn't and if they couldn't, he'd move on.

His life had become much simplified, of late.

He spent most of the afternoon there. He spoke to kids in dilapidated mattress-on-the-floor places, he spoke to young professionals in apartments of stylish minimalism. They passed him from one to another, each giving him the intro-duction to the next without which he probably wouldn't have been able to get past the door. He saw a print shop for the un-derground press, he heard sewing machines clattering away in a back room as if in a sweatshop. Some people were wary, some were suspicious, but none openly refused to help. They knew nothing of use to him, that was all.

On foot, as ever, he plodded back towards his hotel at the northern end of town. He was beginning to feel as if he was drowning and that Marianne was being swept away from him by strong currents that he didn't have the strength or the wits to fight. He was doing his best for her, and his best wasn't enough. At one time—it seemed centuries ago—his fear had been that she might be hurt, or die. To that had now been added a more subtle terror, that she might grow and live as a stranger in some place beyond his knowledge.

He didn't know what the police were doing. Their plans

didn't involve him. All that he could do was to press on alone. After what had happened to Anneliese, money was no longer such a problem; notice of her death would release those funds that had been tied up in both of their names. There had been a time when this would have been a matter of intense interest to him, but no more. He sometimes felt as if he'd died, as well . . . but then how could he be dead, if he burned so much inside?

They'd taken him out to the morgue to look at her. An unlikely looking place, until you got downstairs. That policewoman from home had gone along with him, and he'd appreciated her presence among strangers for something so overwhelming. She wasn't around any more; her place had been taken by two hard-nosed coppers who'd made contact only to tell him to keep out of their way. One of them, Somerville, had been his interrogator back at the beginning. He clearly spoke no German, and neither did the other. What great progress *they* were likely to make.

It stank. It all stank. He could trust nobody. But he was controlled about it now, not the way he'd been before. Much of the bitterness had been drained from him when he'd stood in the mortuary and looked down at Anneliese. They'd tidied her up a little, but there was nothing cosmetic about it. And although he'd sometimes gone so far even as to dream of this moment, there was no satisfaction in it for him. Instead, he found himself thinking of something that his old Irish grandmother used to say.

Only the dead, she would say, *can be forgiven.*

Only the dead.

He'd called Anneliese's mother for the first time in years. He knew that phoning wasn't the right way to break it to her, but he didn't want to leave the city now unless it was to get closer to Marianne, and he'd hoped she'd understand. He'd promised to send her a copy of Marianne's photograph, and to bring her to see her when he finally got her back. He'd made it a point to say *when*, and not *if*. Since then, the picture had been reproduced in most of the national newspapers and shown twice on the television news. It had reproduced badly, and they'd had to retouch it. Looking at the printed image of

Ryan O'Donnell, he'd realized with some sense of shock that this was the first time that he'd actually seen the man's face. His own imagined likeness of O'Donnell had been so vivid that it was hard for him to overlay it with this new truth. Doing so had released an entire new set of fears, opening up yet more avenues of apprehension.

A few moments after he'd picked up the key at his hotel, the desk clerk called him back.

"Mr. Cadogan," he said, "there is a message for you." He handed over an envelope that had apparently arrived in the mail.

Cadogan studied it as he waited for the lift to arrive. It carried the imprint of his lawyers back in Hamburg. Perhaps they'd heard about Anneliese and were taking the opportunity to remind him of their bill. Well, they could wait. Everybody who wanted anything from him could wait, until perhaps they'd lose interest and then finally go away.

When he got into his room, he tossed the envelope onto the bed and then went on through into the bathroom. He ran some cold water into the basin and then splashed it onto his face to get the day's dust out of his eyes. As he dried himself on one of the clean towels, he studied his face in the mirror. It was an odd feeling. It was as if he was beginning to recognize himself again, like seeing the face of a brother who'd been away for a long time and returned looking older.

So many things changed with time. At first he'd been thinking of Marianne constantly, a buzz in his mind that would scarcely admit any other input at all. All the time he'd be thinking, What's she doing right now? What does she see? How does she feel? But it was as if that could only go on for so long. He'd started to find ways to function, and each accommodation had carried with it the sense of a betrayal.

It wasn't that he wanted her back any less. But he'd found that, with time, one could adapt to any situation, learning to shut down the demons in the mind so that business as usual could continue even in the shadow of the greatest danger. He'd still be devastated to learn of any harm that might come to her, but . . . it was almost as if, after rehearsing the possibilities in his nightmares so often, a piece of him had already died with her. As if he'd crossed a bridge over which, whatever might happen in the future, there could be no return.

He turned on the TV for company, and dropped onto the bed. There were eleven channels, including cable at no extra charge so that he could watch the same stupid game shows in four different languages on any night of the week. Now, at last, he opened the lawyers' letter.

Two things slid out of the envelope. One was a compliments slip, unsigned. The other was a second, unopened letter.

He looked it over. The envelope was a vivid pink. No return address, the postmark smudged, the handwriting spidery and deliberate and not too well-formed. Not like a child's, more like an older person of minimal education. He sighed as he ripped it open, already gauging the distance to the wastebasket so that he could send it the same way as the other dozen or so crank letters that had managed to catch up with him. He'd had requests for the exact time and place of Marianne's birth in order to cast a horoscope that would pinpoint her and he'd thought, Yeah, and where were all of *you* when I needed reminding of her birthday? There had been one letter typed in capitals urging him to give away everything that he owned and then PRAY, closely followed by another, guaranteeing to find her for 10,000 Deutschmarks typed in exactly the same manner on the same kind of paper.

Whatever this one was going to be, he was pretty sure that it could hold no big surprises.

But this one was different because, to begin with, it was in English.

And it came from Ryan O'Donnell.

CHAPTER 59

"Oh, for Christ's sake, Jen," said Ricky, "you're a million miles away all the time, still. What do I have to do to get your attention, here?"

Jennifer belatedly drew her gaze from the blue-misted range of mountains at the distant head of the dale, and looked at Ricky. He seemed peeved again, and probably not without reason. Ever since she'd arrived home, she'd found it almost impossible to concentrate on the everyday and routine. It wasn't exactly that her mind returned to Düsseldorf and the pursuit that she'd had to leave behind; it wasn't that her thoughts went *anywhere* too specific. They just went, as if to a familiar room which, having found it empty, they were then unable to leave.

"I'm sorry," she said lamely. "I was thinking."

"Well, try thinking about what I just asked you." Ricky waited for a moment and then, when she didn't reply, said, "You don't even know what I asked you, do you?"

"Didn't hear," she said. "Say again."

"I said, they've closed down for a funeral. Where do you want to try next?"

"I really don't mind."

This wasn't what he wanted to hear, although it seemed to be more or less what he was expecting. With a look of weary resignation, he began to descend the wooden steps from the lakeside restaurant. Jennifer glanced at the handwritten notice that had been stuck on the inside of the door glass, and then followed him.

A stiff breeze cut in from the lake. The bay village was pleasant, although not exactly pretty; for that you had to seek out the quieter spots in the side valleys and on the high passes.

But it had been a rush booking, and Ricky had taken the best he'd been offered. She couldn't fault him for that. Couldn't fault him at all, in fact; he'd been patience personified ever since she'd got back. She only wished that she could somehow make a better job of her own part, or at least pretend that nothing was troubling her.

Because, thinking back to Werner and what had happened in his apartment, she knew that she'd be walking on dangerous ground if she didn't.

They started to head back in the direction of the guest house. She took another look behind her, at the valley and the fells. But what she saw was the long, drowned road and the lonely Cadogan house.

"I don't know about a funeral," Ricky said as they walked through the village square, with its parking spaces crammed with tourists' cars and not a single business open. "The entire place seems dead on its feet today." Jennifer said nothing, but then he went on. "This wasn't such a good idea on my part, was it?"

"What do you mean?"

"This entire weekend. It's turning into one of the great disasters of our time, isn't it?"

"Ricky, no!"

"Go on," he said. "You can be honest. It won't be taken down and used in evidence."

What could she say? The fact of it was that he was right, but the fault was entirely hers and it was nothing that she dared to explain.

"I promise," he said. "Just talk to me."

Jennifer said, "There's nothing wrong with the idea at all. But I just spent two weeks living out of a suitcase in hotels, and . . . I'm not complaining, but I'd have been just as happy if we'd stayed at the house."

"If you want the truth of it," Ricky said gloomily, "I've been getting sick of the sight of the house."

"I thought you had this big vision of how you want it to be."

"I know," he said. "But it's endless."

"Perhaps it's time to scale down some of our ideas."

"But isn't that a bit like admitting defeat?"

"Not if you've changed your mind over what it is that you want."

He looked at her as they walked. He looked at her for long enough to make her uncomfortable. Then he looked down.

They passed the church. It was a low, traditional slate building on a rise, surrounded by a hillside cemetery. Some of the stones were centuries old, the slopes around them kept to perfection. The faint air of a hymn drifted over.

Ricky kicked at dust with a few shreds of old confetti in it. "You haven't really said anything about what happened out there."

"Yes, I have," Jennifer said.

"I heard all about what they fed you on the plane and how many towels they put out in your room. What I mean is, was it all worth doing?"

She tried to find the words. "They're all still out there and I didn't bring anyone back," she began. "That's how successful I was. As to whether it was worth it . . . well, Benny Moon, who's never done me a favor in his life and who'd probably complain about the draft if I fell out of the window . . . this same Benny Moon is now whining like a dog because *he* couldn't cut it and I wouldn't cover."

"Is he making trouble?"

"Let's just say that the atmosphere around me at the moment is less than comfortable. But I'm used to that. It's the price you have to pay if you want to break out of peewee corner."

Ricky was blank. "Out of where?"

"It's just an expression," Jennifer said. "What I mean is that if I seem distant for a while, it's not because of anything anyone can help me with. I've just got to crash on through it somehow."

"Will they send you out again?"

"I really don't know. It's a two-week rotation, so if I *do* go out again, it will mean that by then O'Donnell will have been holding her for an entire month. That's not something I ought to be hoping for."

"But some part of you is, isn't it?"

Jennifer had to give a wry little smile of admission.

"I ought to be ashamed to say it," she said. "But yes, a part of me is."

CHAPTER 60

That night, as Cadogan waited in the darkness of the alley beside the opera house, he heard a solitary oboe start up a practice piece in the building somewhere above him. Cadogan thought that he recognized it, although he couldn't have put a name to the tune. He was no big music buff. In the right company he'd admit to being able to sing all the words to "Money for Nothing," and that was about as far as it went. Because it was the first thing that had come along to relieve the monotony of the last hour, he moved along the alley and stood somewhere close under the open window so that he could listen. But the oboe player wasn't performing, he was obviously working on his technique and after a while of stop-start and numerous new beginnings, Cadogan peeled himself off the wall and strolled back towards the road.

He checked his watch. He'd arrived early, but now it was late. He'd give it another ten minutes, and then he'd go.

He'd had the same thought about ten minutes before. But in spite of whatever he might have been telling himself, he knew that in reality he was going to stay here until something happened. Anything. Even if it was only tomorrow's sunrise.

The opera house was a huge building at the north end of a main thruway, six lanes, bright lights—a modern sketch in concrete with the shape and look of traditional baroque but none of the details. Its frontage looked out onto the traffic, while to its side stood an extensive city park. At this hour traffic was light, and the park was deserted.

Hands in his pockets, Cadogan stood by the side doors to the foyer and looked in. Across the warm, polished floor was the cloakroom, where a woman attendant sat and presided over what he estimated to be a gathering of about three hundred fur coats. Otherwise the foyer was dead space, all the life being inside the auditorium.

Jesus, he thought. How much longer?

Once more down the alley and back. It was tarmac for some way—about as far as the street lighting went—and then it was cobbles patched in places with asphalt. A few staff cars were parked down there. Up above were the windows of administrative offices and dressing rooms, some with costumes hung up high. The rooms themselves looked bare and unwelcoming.

At a break in the foliage, he stood and looked out across the park. He could see darkness where the lake was, and then the lights of the road as it carried on northward. He wondered if anyone was watching him from out there, and if they were, why didn't they make some kind of a move? He'd been there for long enough. Nobody could doubt by now that he'd come alone.

He heard a sound.

He started to turn.

And then suddenly, almost before he'd realized what was happening, he was engulfed in a floodtide of people.

The performance was over and the foyer doors were open, and the audience were pouring out all at once like a well-heeled football crowd. They came in the same kind of numbers, and their outward-moving pressure was about as easy to resist. Cadogan was thrown, momentarily disoriented to find himself so rapidly plunged into a sea of strangers; they were all around him, they were coming at him in waves of black ties and sable and jewelry.

And then a hand gripped his arm and held him steady.

"Just go along with the crowd," a voice said close to his ear. "Don't attract any attention."

Cadogan flinched, and tried to pull away. The grip hurt. It didn't slacken.

"Stay calm," the voice said. "Make a signal or anything, and I'm gone. Keep moving."

They were borne along with the crowd, surrounded on all sides. As a form of camouflage, it was ideal; they were moving in plain sight where no observer could fight his way through to follow. And then they were out of the crowd and into the shadows, and then they were moving around the back of the opera house and leaving all of the public activity behind them.

Cadogan was being pushed along faster than he could comfortably manage. He didn't get much of a chance to look back, and when he tried, he got an extra shove by way of a warning.

The voice said, "Did you talk to the police?"

"No."

"That's good. We've got to trust each other here, or we're going to get nowhere."

He'd obviously got this all paced out and planned. Less than a minute had passed, and they were now heading for a lighted stairway that would take them down into the ground for the U-bahn.

"No police," Cadogan said. "Just me."

"That's fine. Because I've been watching you for a while, and I'd know if you were lying."

On the underground level directly beneath the road was an extensive, well-lighted, but mostly deserted plaza. The U-bahn was one level further down, but Cadogan was hustled away from the escalators and across the open shopping floor. By a café with its shutters locked into place, they made an unexpected turn into what looked like an unlighted service corridor.

Cadogan said, "Wait a minute, wait a minute, please. Where have you got her? Is she here?"

"Don't worry about Marianne," the man's voice said. "I've left her somewhere safe and she—"

That was enough for Cadogan. She wasn't here, he had nothing to lose. He stopped and drove his elbow back, hard. There was a gasp as he made contact, and the grip on his arm was released. Now he could reach for the knife. He fumbled inside his coat and found the handle, but then when he tried to pull it out he somehow managed to catch it in the lining; in panic he tried to yank it free, aware now of O'Donnell as a wheezing shadow coming around him, but there was a ripping

sound and several inches of the blade popped out through the
material, and in one of those *oh-shit* moments he realized that
it was now stuck fast. . . .

And at this point O'Donnell, recovering and straightening,
shoved him hard on the shoulder and slammed him into the
wall. Cadogan lost his balance and, panicking as he fell because he thought that he was going to drop onto his own blade,
windmilled away with his free arm before sitting down so hard
that his teeth clicked together.

The blade was sticking out of his coat like a single erupted
stainless-steel tooth. He looked up, and saw O'Donnell a few
yards further on along the corridor. He was standing out of
reach, and looking down at him. Cadogan's knife was stuck
fast and he was sprawling in the night's litter and he felt like
an idiot.

"I'll tell you what," O'Donnell said. "Why don't you stay
right there?"

Cadogan glowered up at him. "You've got a fucking nerve,"
he said.

"I've also got Marianne. So are you going to control yourself and talk to me, or not?"

Slowly, almost contritely, Cadogan began to get to his feet.
But then, as soon as he'd worked the blade free, he let out a
roar and launched himself straight up at O'Donnell; but
O'Donnell took two steps backwards and, reaching out to the
side, quickly drew some kind of a sliding metal gate across the
corridor. It engaged with a crash, and Cadogan hit it with another.

The noise echoed around the plaza for several seconds. The
gate wasn't enough to stop Cadogan completely because he
thrust his knife arm through the bars and took a couple of
swipes at O'Donnell, who was standing easily out of reach. On
the third swipe, O'Donnell caught his hand and held it; and
now Cadogan was pinned in place, completely powerless.

"Be honest," O'Donnell said. "This isn't really your style, is
it?"

Cadogan shook the bars in fury, but could achieve nothing.
He turned to look back towards the echoing concourse, and
drew breath. . . .

And O'Donnell said, "Yell if you want to. I'll just go."

Beaten, Cadogan looked back at him.

O'Donnell released Cadogan's knife hand and stepped away. Cadogan withdrew his arm through the gate. It was hurting where the scissor-hinged metal had pressed. O'Donnell had kept the knife, and was now giving it a close inspection.

He said, "Did you buy this for tonight, or bring it over with you?"

Cadogan tugged at the gate again, with no more effect than before. And then he tried once more, but now his heart wasn't in it. With all the steam running out of him, he gave up.

Then he started to slam his head against the ironwork in frustration, hard enough to make the entire gate shake.

"Hey," O'Donnell said gently. "No. That's enough."

There was a touch on Cadogan's shoulder. It was O'Donnell's hand. Cadogan looked at it, but he didn't make a grab for it.

And after a moment, O'Donnell took his hand away.

"When you're ready," he said.

Cadogan stared bleakly through the bars. Although they'd passed this close once before, at the lineup in the police yard, he gazed at his daughter's kidnapper with full knowledge for the first time. He felt almost overawed.

"And what are *you* staring at?" O'Donnell said.

"You, you evil fucker," Cadogan said.

O'Donnell's face set hard.

He said, "You can call me all the names that you want, but I haven't touched your daughter." He leaned closer to the bars. "I've never laid a finger on her. Not in anger, or for any other reason. You're her father. Can you say the same?"

Cadogan was about to speak, but faltered for lack of the words. It seemed that they both knew what O'Donnell was saying; and for the moment, Cadogan had no answer to offer.

O'Donnell went on. "I finally managed to find Marianne's mother. She wouldn't have her daughter back and that was for Marianne's sake, not for hers. She wanted me to leave the kid to the police, but the way I see it, that's the same thing as giving her back to you."

"Bring her to me, then. Cut the police out of it, if that's the only problem."

"It's not so simple."

"Just bring her back. I won't call anyone. I'll let you walk away after. Just bring her."

"You don't understand. I got a good offer, just to unload her and disappear. But the way Marianne feels about you now, she wouldn't come. And even if I lied and tricked her into coming, she wouldn't stay. So what kind of an answer is that?"

"Do it anyway. It'll be my problem. Not yours."

O'Donnell took a deep breath and looked down, before meeting his eyes again. "You've got all kinds of ideas about me. But do you know what I really am, Mr. Cadogan?" He gave Cadogan no chance to reply, but went on. "I'm a scavenger. I pick up stuff that no one else is interested in, and then I turn it into something that someone might want. You may think that's a pretty low ambition in life, but it was the way I learned to hold my head up again after a long time in the lockup. I'd *love* to dump her and run. I really would. And I'd love to think that I could start up somewhere with a clean sheet, be someone else, and never hear the name of Ryan O'Donnell again. But we're not in one of those films where they keep all the money and run off to Rio. The one thing I know is that whatever you do, it either stays with you or it catches up with you later. If I hand her back to you now, and nothing's any different . . . then everything's been wasted, and Marianne will suffer, and it'll all be down to me. And that's what I'll carry wherever I go."

"It *is* different," Cadogan insisted.

But O'Donnell was shaking his head.

"I never meant to hurt her," Cadogan said. "That was an accident, and she knows it. None of it was what I meant to happen."

"That's exactly what I mean," O'Donnell said. "We've all got something we'd like to be forgiven for, but you've got to be the last one to say you deserve it. Not the first."

And with that, he started to move back.

"Perhaps you should think about that," he added with some sense of bitterness. "Think about it as hard as you like."

It was then that Cadogan realized what was happening: O'Donnell was about to leave. He had some other way out. He was backing off into the shadows of the service corridor, and with the metal gate locked across the way there wasn't a thing that Cadogan could do to stop him.

"You're not just going to go!"

"Watch me," O'Donnell said as he turned and started to walk.

What could he do? Cadogan's mind raced. He had to stop him somehow.

"Anneliese is dead," he called after him. "But you know that already, don't you?"

O'Donnell's step slowed for a second. But he didn't turn, and after a moment he picked up speed again and carried on.

"O'Donnell!" Cadogan screamed. *"O'Donnell!"*

But still, the shadows took him.

After taking the stairs two at a time to the level of the street, Cadogan ran out into the night. O'Donnell had to come up somewhere around here. How many points of access could there be? He turned one way, then another. He felt lost. Stupid. Dazed.

He didn't know what to do.

A few yards away, a car skidded to a halt by the pavement with a long, sliding screech of tire rubber.

"What happened to you?" Somerville called from the car as Cadogan ran over. "We had you in our sights for the whole time, and then you had to go and disappear into the crowd."

"I didn't disappear," Cadogan said. "He was there. He'd planned it that way. And he's still around here somewhere!"

"Get in," Somerville said.

Cadogan jumped into the back of the car. It was moving before he'd managed to close the door, and the acceleration slammed it shut on him. He put out a hand to steady himself. The *Kriminalpolizei* driver was on the radio already, alerting the other cars on backup.

"Tell them to check all the ways out of the plaza," Cadogan said, speaking over him, and Somerville held up a hand for him to wait. Cadogan ignored him. "And tell them he's got hold of a knife." And then he added, lamely, because he'd kept back the fact that he was carrying it, "From somewhere."

Somerville turned in his seat. Outside, the city at night was streaking by in long blurs of neon.

"What did he say to you?" Somerville demanded. "What *exactly* did he say?"

Cadogan held his head in his hands. It felt as if it was getting ready to explode. They'd wanted to wire him for sound, but he'd refused.

He said, "O'Donnell seems to look on holding Marianne as some kind of a mission." He let his hands fall. "And that's about the sanest thought in his head."

She woke in darkness.

He'd come back, she could sense it immediately. She hadn't made him promise to wake her when he returned, because she'd been sure that she wouldn't fall asleep; but somehow she had, and now she'd have to wait until morning to find out what had happened. Morning seemed an eternity away. She was cold and she was stiff. The worn springs dug into her, and where the upholstery had rubbed her skin she felt raw and sandpapered. She tried to turn over. It was like trying to roll uphill, and she couldn't do it.

She lay there for a while. She could hear him breathing. There were lights outside that would burn all night, but they were harsh like the lights of a prison camp. He'd blocked the broken window with some loose Formica sheeting, but the light still got in. He was a big, shapeless mound under his coat. He'd left all of the scrounged-up bedding for her, and still she was shivering. The bedding stank. She felt lonely. Earlier on she'd heard somebody picking around outside and then she'd been scared, as well.

She stared at the dark patterns in front of her, and tried to think of nothing. That worked sometimes. Or so she'd been told.

She shivered again.

And after a few minutes, as quietly as she could, she swung her legs out until her feet touched the floor and then stood. The floor creaked, but he didn't stir.

His overcoat seemed huge. He probably wouldn't even notice that she was there. She crawled under and settled herself down against him, fitting herself into the space between his side and the drop. She'd have to be careful not to roll off. But she felt herself responding to the warmth of shared heat already, and she no longer felt unsafe.

He turned slightly. Seemed to tense, as if he'd sensed her there. But nothing after.

She took a deep, deep breath. Sighed without a sound. Sometimes it seemed to her that sleeping badly could be more wearing than not getting any sleep at all.

She began to drift.

And almost the last thing that she was aware of, as her consciousness spiraled downward into nothing, was the slowly moving pressure of his hand as it slid underneath her.

Ten Days Later

CHAPTER 61

When Jennifer walked back into Rilke's departmental offices after two weeks' absence, it was to find most of the crew in the briefing room and the sense of a celebration in progress. It was somebody's birthday, as far as she could gather. Rilke's immediate boss was there, a woman with very blonde, very cropped hair wearing big earrings and a loose red sweater that matched her lipstick. At a glance, most people would have taken her to be a magazine editor rather than the head of a department whose responsibilities covered a range of operations from missing persons to sexual crime. But then, none of the others tended to fit any known stereotype either. Rilke, over by the window, looked like an unusually sharply dressed company accountant. He was talking to a younger man who wore a tweed jacket over a checked shirt with a T-shirt underneath.

Somebody handed Jennifer some warm Rheinwein in a paper cup. Rilke saw her, and waved. She waited as he drew himself out of his conversation and then squeezed his way over.

"In here," he said, gesturing towards the next office. "It'll be quieter."

They went through, and he closed the door behind them. There was a dartboard on the back of it. The buzz of the party, not exactly loud to begin with, was muted to a low hum.

"So," he said, walking around behind one of the desks. He pulled open a drawer, frowned, and shut it again, then pulled open another. "You picked a good time to rejoin the chase. Ryan O'Donnell joins our list of suspects in the murder of Anneliese Cadogan just as Axel Reineger's alibi falls to pieces. Nothing's certain and there's everything to play for. Reineger

331

ran like a rabbit. O'Donnell left us a print on the cabin door handle but is still out of sight. You ask me, the man's a magician."

"What about the child?"

"There's no word on the child at all."

"Damn."

"The work of two departments has been brought together. We've got more resources and more manpower now. I like to think that Anneliese Cadogan would approve. She was hardly anybody's idea of a happy woman, Inspector McGann. At least this way she does something of benefit to her daughter. Wouldn't you say?"

He found the drawer that he was looking for, and brought out a sheaf of phone memos. There had to be at least a couple of dozen, and they'd been thrown in together in no particular order.

"All of these messages are for you," he said, and he dropped them onto the desk before her. "They're from Herr Cadogan. It seems that you're the only one he wants to talk to, now."

He said that he had something definite for her. They arranged to meet at the open-air tram terminus on Vennhauser Allee in a suburb named Eller. He said they could walk it from there. He said he'd been busy.

Cadogan was waiting for her by the kiosk. People over at the counter were eyeing him a little nervously, but he didn't seem to be aware of it. He was like a boxer, all hyped up for a big fight and unable to keep still. Dark rings under his eyes gave his stare an added level of intensity. His was the sick look and the energy of a man in remission.

He said, "Thanks for coming. Are you in a car?"

"No."

"That's fine," he said. "That's no problem. It's not so far to walk."

"To where, Mr. Cadogan?"

He glanced around, and lowered his voice before he said, "I've found one of the places where they've been staying."

"Who've you told about this?"

"Only you. I promised these people no police. So please, don't even tell them who you are."

He raised a finger to emphasize the warning. Then they started to walk.

His clothes were clean. In fact, they looked new. They looked as if at some time in the past couple of days he'd stepped into a discount clothing store and picked a complete set of working man's wear off the racks, leaving his old stuff in the changing room to be thrown out or burned. His boots were work boots, as well, and still had their shine.

Well, it was one answer to the laundry problem.

Prosperous turn-of-the-century houses gave way to more modern apartment buildings. Then the apartment buildings gave way to wide open land and railway lines. Beyond the lines, the road they were following appeared to run onward and outward into nowhere in particular.

"How far is it?" she said.

"I'll be honest," Cadogan said, "I can't tell you. I've been on the move for so long, I'm losing track. I can't even say what day it is. How were things at home?"

She gave him a stony look, to tell him that he was overstepping the mark.

He shrugged and said, "Sorry."

They took a side road, hardly more than a lane, that ran down between open woodland and an industrial estate. The estate included a garden center and a warehouse yard for building supplies. Their path ran parallel to the roadway now, some distance from it and half-hidden in the trees.

"Down *here*?" she said.

"Just a way," he insisted. "It's not so far, now. Honestly."

They walked on. The path was carpeted with twigs and dead leaves, and seemed to be veering deeper into the woodland as they went on. Jennifer hung back a little, keeping Cadogan constantly in her sights. She'd no reason to rate him as a risk. But one never could tell.

"I stepped onto a scale last night," he said. "I've lost more than half a stone. I've been moving all the time, like a shark. Never stopped. I'll just go through the day, and I won't even remember to eat. Have you ever done that?"

"No."

He was watching the ground as he walked. "I wish I could describe how it feels," he said. "After a while, you don't get tired anymore. You don't feel pain. But colors change. And sounds. Everything's sharper, and brighter. And your mind gets so *clear* . . . so clear that it's scary. Like you've been all the time in a room with this one lightbulb, and then suddenly you can see all the way to where the world ends. And the scariest thing of all is the feeling you have that . . . if you could drive yourself just that *little* bit harder . . . perhaps you'd be able to see just that little bit further."

Jennifer said quietly, "You should go home, Mr. Cadogan. You're right on the edge."

He looked at her. "You think so?"

"Yes."

He nodded, matter-of-factly.

"I think so too," he said.

The path and the lane met up again where a dirt parking area had been set out for woodland users. Over on the other side of the lane there was a wire fence, and beyond the wire fence was what looked like a railway siding.

They went over. In one place, a way had been made through the brambles to where the fence had been cut and rolled back. The hole was big enough to walk through, and they barely had to duck. Ahead of them now, across five rusted sets of tracks on a flatbed of gray flinty stone, there stretched a number of rows of what appeared to be derelict railway carriages.

"What *is* this?" she said.

"Old rolling stock," Cadogan said, "lined up for scrap. People sleep rough, here. The railway police know about it, but they've never been able to stamp it out."

Jennifer picked her way across the tracks behind Cadogan. The carriages didn't exactly look inviting, and the closer she got, the less appealing they became. Along with the half-hearted graffiti on their sides, not one of them had a window intact. In a couple of places the window seals hung out in rubber loops. Interior fittings had been ripped out and scattered onto the tracks; there were luggage nets, seat squabs, carpet, plastic, entire doors ripped from their hinges. The broken shards of toilet bowls crunched underfoot like shells on a beach.

"There's nobody here," Jennifer said.

"They all move around," Cadogan assured her.

Fires had once been set inside some of the carriages on the next row. They'd roared up from the window openings and burned off the paintwork into bands of bare metal. Now the bare metal was rust.

Jennifer saw a face. It ducked out of sight.

"I think this is far enough," she said.

"Trust me," Cadogan said. "It's nothing I haven't done before."

Nervous now, she looked all around. If O'Donnell and Marianne had ever stayed here, it surely couldn't have been for long. There'd be no comfort, and very little sense of security. The overhead lights would burn all night, stadium-style, and there would be a constant rumble of passing trains from the adjacent through-lines.

A rabbit, startled by their approach, darted quickly into the rubbish and disappeared under one of the wagons. Cadogan put two fingers into the corners of his mouth, and whistled. Jennifer glanced at him with some curiosity. This was something that she'd never been able to do.

A face appeared. Then another.

They were all young, all pale. And there was no mistaking the marks of bad food, bad hygiene, and a chronically disrupted sleep pattern. It took young kids like these and it turned them into old people, fast. Cadogan called out something, and one of the kids—boy or girl, it was hard to be sure and that wasn't any gibe—disappeared inside.

A few moments later, a boy in his teens climbed down from one of the wagons and walked towards them. He stopped and stood with his hands in his pockets, head on one side and his eyes screwed up against the light as he listened to Cadogan's explanation.

Then he shrugged, and walked forward.

Cadogan turned to Jennifer. "This is Matthias," he explained. "He's going to tell you what he told me."

They didn't go into one of the carriages. Instead, they went to a railworkers' shelter at the end of the siding. The tracks just ran out here; no buffers, no warning signs, nothing.

The hut was open-sided, like a promenade or a park shelter. They sat on hard wooden seats. Matthias spoke quite reasonable English, with what sounded like a trace of an acquired American accent. He wasn't a hard case, and seemed an almost studious-looking boy. He was soft-spoken, and met nobody's eyes.

He said that O'Donnell and Marianne had been out here together for a few days. Everyone had assumed that they were father and daughter, but nobody had thought that they might be English. It had been assumed that they were maybe *Ossis*, incomers from the Old East, or Poles. They'd tended to keep apart from everyone else, and when anything had been said it had always been the girl who'd done all the talking.

Jennifer said, "What happened to them?"

"Sometimes people come around places like this with offers of work," Matthias said. "Mostly it's nothing, farm work or digging ditches ... long hours and bad money and most of it going into someone else's pocket. This man came around with a piece of paper, looking for people for the harvest. It was just a few weeks' working, a bus to take you there and somewhere to stay. They went. They were the only ones from this place who did."

"Have you ever seen the man before?" Jennifer said.

Matthias shook his head.

"A name, at least?"

A shrug.

As they were crossing the tracks on the way back to the lane, Jennifer said to Cadogan, "They could be just out of town, or they could be on the other side of the country. This is what I was most afraid of."

"It isn't what *I'm* most afraid of," Cadogan said. "Doesn't even run it close."

And when they reached the woodland again, Jennifer said, "First phone I see, I'm getting a cab. I've walked enough for one day."

"Walking's good for your soul," Cadogan said.

"I don't need to worry about my soul. I'm on expenses."

Ten minutes later, they reached the main road again.

Cadogan said, "Sleeping's harder than anything. I'm wound up so tight, I can't sleep. What I have to do is, I go to a cinema late show. I can't concentrate on whatever's running but as soon as I try, off I go. Best night I've had was during a Chuck Norris double bill. Can you imagine that? Sleeping through two entire Chuck Norris movies?"

"I find it hard to imagine doing anything else," Jennifer said.

CHAPTER 62

Ryan stopped what he was doing for a moment, so that he could watch the one who called himself Ganz.

Ryan was at the head of the field by the baling machine, and Ganz was some way downslope. He'd an army-style jerrican, and appeared to be watering down the cut rows of stubble as he walked. Except that what he was throwing around was gasoline, not water, and he was throwing it onto ground that was freshly stripped and tinder-dry. Ryan was pretty sure that nobody had told him to do this. The can was the spare from the baler truck, and when Ganz had come over to pick it up he'd done it openly but with a glance around as if to say, *Let's see if anyone's going to stop me*. The truth of it was, not many of those who were working in these fields were likely to try. They were seasonal help who just did what they were told and then climbed onto the bus at the end of the day, hands raw and backs aching. They'd all been recruited from the towns, and most of them looked it.

And besides, Ganz cut an intimidating figure. He was bigger than Ryan, and broader, and uglier. He looked the way that wrestlers had once looked, before wrestlers had become bodybuilders. During the time they'd been out here, Ryan had come to the conclusion that Ganz probably wasn't his real name and that he'd taken on the work only because it gave him the opportunity to drop out of sight for a while. Unlike most of them, he'd come alone.

Marianne was with a group of the others, raking loose straw into heaps right down in the lowest corner of the field. There was little of it left, and the heaps weren't so big. There were four teenagers on the workforce, but Marianne was the youngest of them all. She always wrapped up her hands and pitched in, but it was hard to say how much real use she was able to make of herself. No one seemed to mind.

Ganz was getting close to the group, now. They'd stopped and were watching him. Ryan glanced around. The farmer had ridden back in with the last trailerload of bales, leaving Rolf in charge of the clearing-up; Rolf was scrawny and middle-aged and almost studious-looking, a one-time production manager in a shoe factory until his factory had been closed, driven out of business by the new competition. He meant well, but he was a fusser. As soon as the boss was off the scene, Ganz tended to ignore him.

Now Ganz was level with the girls. Too far away to act, Ryan could only watch. Behind him the baler's old engine was thumping away but even so, he heard the shriek from the distant group as Ganz made a sudden feint with the jerrican. He saw the streak of gasoline as it caught the low sunlight and then fell to the ground, and he saw Marianne skipping back before it and dropping her rake as Ganz, laughing, moved on.

Ryan took off his gloves, and threw them down by the baler. Then he started off down the field.

He could hear some of the others calling to him from behind, but he didn't look back. Marianne had picked up her rake and the girls were watching him as he approached, uncertainty on their faces. Ganz was further down the field now, almost at the boundary. He was still throwing the stuff around, and he hadn't looked back. If he knew that Ryan was coming, he gave no sign of it.

The baler's engine puttered to an idling halt. That probably meant that the others had stopped and were watching him, too.

The gasoline smell was crude and heavy as it hung over the stubble. It was the end of the day and the day had been hard, but Ryan ignored the fatigue in his joints.

As he passed by the group of girls, Marianne called out to him, "It's all right, Ryan. He didn't get any of it on me."

But Ryan carried on by, and didn't even take his gaze from Ganz. Ganz had reached the end of the row by then, and he turned and saw Ryan.

Ryan stopped.

"Why don't you try that with me?" he said pleasantly.

Ganz was looking blank. Ryan knew that Ganz spoke no English, but he waited, knowing that his meaning had to be pretty clear. From way uphill, Rolf or one of the others was calling his name. It was impossible to tell who.

Ganz looked him over. He didn't seem to think much of what he saw. Ryan stood his ground, outwardly calm but his heart racing with fear and anger so closely run together that it was impossible to separate them. Ganz was grinning.

Then suddenly, he half feinted at Ryan as if to throw the contents of the jerrican onto him. But if he expected Ryan to flinch, he didn't see it happen. Ryan didn't move at all.

And then, slowly, Ganz tipped the jerrican upside down and held it that way.

Nothing came out until, after several seconds, a total of three drops emerged and fell to the ground.

Ganz walked by, laughing loudly. He almost bumped Ryan as he passed too close, moving as if to crowd him in the middle of nowhere, but they didn't quite touch. Ryan turned to watch him go. Ganz was climbing back up towards the idling baler, swinging the can as he went.

In silhouette against the sky at the top of the hill stood the machinery, and the old truck that would pull it, and the half-dozen others who had been watching the standoff. They seemed to realize that it was over, at least for the moment, and they turned to go back to their work. It was cleanup time.

Marianne was standing with the other girls, still holding her rake. Ryan beckoned for her to follow him back as he passed on his return.

"*Did* any of it get onto you?" he asked her.

"Only a little splash," she admitted as she fell into step beside him.

"That's all it would take," Ryan said.

When they reached the baler, Ryan called Rolf over and had Marianne translate for him. Rolf kept casting nervous glances in Ganz's direction. There was a denting clatter as Ganz tossed the empty jerrican over into the open back of the equipment truck.

Ryan said to Marianne, "Tell him he'd better get the children out of the field right now. All it'll need is one spark, and that stubble's going to go up like a bomb and take the girls with it."

Rolf swallowed and nodded, and went to call everyone in. He really looked as if he'd be happier as a bookkeeper or a clerk, anything other than the unskilled laborer that he'd been forced to become. The wind was changing now. The loose hay gathered in from the rows had made up into about another dozen bales, and these had been bound up and stacked behind the cab of the truck in an arrangement that would give everyone somewhere to perch on the ride back down to the farm.

With the last of the tools stowed, they helped each other aboard. Everybody except for Ganz. He'd returned to the empty field, seen from here as a great sloping plain now bared as if ransacked by locusts. As the truck engine turned over, Ganz was striking matches.

Everyone watched from the back of the truck, apprehensive but unable to look away. Ganz was being impatient, dropping the matches that wouldn't light and then fumbling out others in his haste. Some were flaring, but the wind was blowing them out again within moments.

It took even him by surprise.

One of the almost-spent matches must have hit the rising vapor as it fell. Ganz had to leap back as the air above the ground became a rapidly expanding fireball that flashed to earth and lit the gasoline trail like a fuse. The fireball lifted and dispersed even as its heat wave hit those on the back of the truck, but the fire had taken hold and was zigzagging off down the field.

From where Ryan was sitting, it looked as if the ground was

being raked from above with some huge out-of-control laser. Black smoke poured out, so thick that the wind couldn't disperse it fast enough. Having recovered himself, Ganz had begun to pace, fascinated, unable to take his eyes off his handiwork. Only when the truck's driver leaned hard on the horn did he manage to drag himself away.

He came up the field and climbed aboard and then banged loudly on the partition behind the driver's cabin as a signal for them to move. The field was really pumping the smoke out now. His face was sooty and red from his proximity to the heat; it was hard to tell, but it looked as if his eyebrows had been partly singed away. He looked as happy as a kid on the way back home from the fair.

And all the way down the hill, even when the burning field was out of sight, he sat up like a prairie dog and seemed unable to take his eyes from the rising column of darkness that would almost certainly be visible for several miles around.

There was some reaction when they reached the farm. The smoke had been sighted and the farmer and a couple of his family were already on their way out there, but Ryan was feeling too whacked to care. Other stubble had been burned off elsewhere in the local countryside, and they'd seen the results on their way in every morning; it seemed to be only Ganz's pyromaniac methods and his preempting of the landowner that were in any way unusual. The cooperative's bus was waiting and, together with Marianne, Ryan crossed over and climbed aboard. The result of their day's work stood out in the open beyond the farm buildings; what looked at first glance like a collapsed barn was actually a mountain of bales onto which a patchwork of boards and corrugated iron had been lashed to make a low and ramshackle roof. It had the look of an old stilt house whose stilts had been kicked from underneath it.

With everyone finally on board, the bus started out.

Nobody talked much. It was the same every day.

Ryan looked at Marianne. She'd flopped back into her seat and had her eyes shut. She looked exhausted, but she'd yet to complain. He'd forgotten what a child's energy could be like; he knew that when the bus arrived at their billet about twelve miles down the road, her eyes would pop open and she'd be back at full operating power.

Ryan glanced back along the bus. About twenty nodding heads, a few open mouths. Someone snoring already, and it wasn't even late. Ganz would be stretched out across the back seat, as usual. Some would wake when it was their turn to get off. Others would have to be woken.

Their accommodations were scattered among the various individual farms of the cooperative. Each farm was a small unit, some consisting of no more than a dozen cows and the land to graze them on. The farmers had clubbed together to buy equipment, and now they were doing the same with their hired labor. The pay was rock-bottom basic. So were the lodgings, mostly.

The bus passed through a village. The villages around here were small and pleasant, with town square fountains and boarded-up churches and prominent town halls. They went through about five of them every day, never all the same ones and never in the same order.

It had been a fine day, good haymaking weather. But Ryan rearranged Marianne's coat to close up a gap and cover her better.

"I'm not asleep," she said. But she didn't open her eyes.

Half an hour later, the bus pulled to a halt in the middle of nowhere and he touched her sleeve to wake her. She came awake all at once, popping up like a cork.

"We're there," he said, and they both moved to get out.

The bus left them standing by the road and went on, with more miles yet to cover. The way to the Lüderssen farm was hardly more than a dirt track off the road, its entrance marked by a spreading fan of light soil across the black tarmac. Ryan took off his heavy coat and slung it over his shoulder for the climb.

"Damn," he said, looking after the bus.

"What's the matter?"

"We forgot to ask where we'll be tomorrow."

"What are you worrying for? You don't even know where we are now."

They left the road, and started up the track.

* * *

Frau Lüderssen was a widow. She'd a daughter around the same age as Marianne, but her daughter went to school and this cut down on her usefulness around the place. There was no other help. The farm consisted of a neat white bungalow with a sheet-steel barn behind it, a cattle shed that looked as if it had been thrown together cheaply sometime around the year 1400, and several outbuildings in various stages of dereliction. The best of these—actually half rebuilt, getting as far as a new roof and plastered walls before the money had run out— provided their quarters.

"Look," Marianne said, and she nudged him as they approached.

There she was. Frau Lüderssen, all two hundred pounds of her. Cropped blonde hair showing black roots. She was up on top of the silage heap near the house, pitchforking it over. She was wearing a yellow bikini and a pair of Wellington boots.

She stopped and waved as they headed for their outbuilding. Marianne waved back. Ryan raised a hand as well.

"I think she likes you," Marianne said, knowing perfectly well that she was prodding Ryan in a sensitive spot.

"God help me," said Ryan.

Their lodgings were clean but basic. Electricity came via a cable strung across the house. There was a wash basin but no connected water supply. They slept on folding camp beds and their table was an old door across two orange boxes. Marianne had her own room at the back, while the place where Ryan slept doubled as their sitting room. A pinned-up curtain in the doorway separated the two. Frau Lüderssen had given them a radio when they'd first moved in, but its batteries had died after a couple of days.

After about twenty minutes Ellinor, Frau Lüderssen's teenage daughter, appeared with the familiar red casserole dish and set it on the table along with some bread wrapped in a clean white cloth. She was a dark-haired girl, pretty enough but with the beginnings of her mother's build. She had a conversation with Marianne that Ryan didn't even try to follow. As usual she didn't meet Ryan's eyes, and as usual she giggled at his accent when he tried to thank her. When she'd gone, Ryan lifted the lid of the dish and took a peek inside.

Marianne said, "What's in it?"

"I don't know," Ryan said. "You tell me."

There was actually nothing at all wrong with the food, unless one were to count the rubber chicken they'd been given three days before. It was something they always said, that was all. Marianne got the plates out from under the table and served it up, chattering away about nothing as usual. Ryan had more or less acquired the knack of tuning her out. It was either that, or blow some of the valves in his brain simply trying to keep up with the roller coaster that was her train of thought.

"I think it's some kind of fish stew," Marianne was saying. "Where do you think they'd get fish from, around here?"

"The deep freezer," said Ryan.

She seemed happy enough. She was playing housekeeper, just another bright child with a tea party to set out. She'd taken to all of this a lot better than he'd expected, despite the hard work and the long hours. Perhaps it was because she'd had a glimpse of realities much harder than these, and she'd developed an instinct for appreciation. In which case, he reckoned, she'd already achieved something in her short life that many people never manage at all.

Later on, Marianne went over to the main house with her soap bag for the bath that she'd been promised. When she'd gone, Ryan took a big, deep breath and then relaxed. It wasn't that he minded her company. But he was a solitary man by custom and probably by nature as well, and too much of her could make his head spin. They'd been together for so long, now. They'd become almost used to each other and he didn't know whether that was a good thing, or not.

Probably not. He could see that much, at least.

He ferried in some water from the outside standpipe, and used it to cold-rinse their plates and the casserole before refilling the dish and setting it on their electric ring to heat. He'd scrub himself down in here, before Marianne got back, and then he could perhaps take out some of their laundry as well. They'd been told they could use the machine around the back of the main house whenever they needed. It hadn't been work-

ing when they'd arrived, but he'd taken a look at it on the first
night. It was a Bendix, and now it was working again.

As he waited for the water to heat, he went outside to watch
the sunset. In the fields below, the cut hay lay in rows. It had
been drying there for three days, now. All of the windows on
this side of the bungalow were dark except for one, where the
flicker of a TV set lit up the room behind the glass.

What was he going to do?

Whichever way he turned, he'd been stitched up in one way
or another. And by nobody more than himself. It had all got
out of control and gone too far; Marianne now saw her future
with him and with nobody else. What had he been thinking of?

And don't lie this time, he told himself. What *had* you been
thinking of?

Dr. Wallace had finally been the one who'd got him to talk
with honesty about what he'd done to Vanessa Mulrooney.
He'd said the words for the other doctors, told them a lot of
what they'd seemed to want to hear, even come to believe
some of it himself; but he'd told Dr. Wallace the truth. There
had been no voices. Nothing had taken him over. Sometimes it
was easier to say that he'd been driven in some way that he
couldn't control, that he wasn't really responsible.

But none of that was right.

The police had tried to get him to admit that she'd gone out
there with him and listened to his tale of what he'd seen and
then derided him for it, the way that others had done. He was
supposed to have got angry then, and taken it out on her. But
the fact of it was, she'd believed in him. Vanessa Mulrooney
was the only one of them who ever really had.

What he did, he did.

What had he been? Fifteen. But they'd treated him like an
adult afterwards because he'd proved, beyond a doubt, that he
could be as dangerous as one. Her life had gone like a stone
from a bridge, falling off into the darkness, already too late to
recall.

We've all got something we'd like to be forgiven for, he'd
told Cadogan. *But you've got to be the last one to say you deserve it. Not the first.*

He went back inside.

The water was nearly hot enough now. It didn't have to boil, and he didn't need much. Afterwards, he'd stretch out for a while. He wished he had something to read. Marianne had a book with her, there among the possessions that she'd neatly arranged on her bedside box; it was something in German and it had a picture of a lion on it. He'd tried to get her to explain how that worked. Did she think in one language all the time, and then translate it into the other when she had to? She'd said she didn't know. All she knew was that from being a baby, her mother had mostly spoken to her in German and her father in English, and it had never been anything she'd even had to think about. And then she'd accused him of messing up her head, because now he'd got *her* wondering how it worked as well.

It was dark when she returned a couple of hours later. Her hair was damp and dark and her face was shining.

Ryan said, "You smell clean."

"I've been having a good time," she said. "Frau Lüderssen let us watch television. Why didn't you come over?"

"I had a few things to do around here."

Marianne looked around the more or less empty room. "Like what?"

"I like to be on my own now and again, that's all."

"You're avoiding her, aren't you?"

"End of subject," Ryan said quickly. "Besides. You know I can't follow the programs."

"I could have told you what was happening. And most of the rock videos are in English. And some of the people who make them are at *least* as old as you."

"Well, thanks," Ryan said dryly.

Marianne went through into her own room, and they dropped the curtain between. They'd have to rise at dawn in order to get down to the end of the track in time for the bus to pick them up again and take them to wherever in the cooperative the day's work waited. He undressed, switched off the light, and climbed into bed. It bounced a little and creaked a lot, but it was comfortable enough. The light on Marianne's side of the curtain stayed on for a while. Perhaps she was reading. Ryan turned over to face the other way.

How much longer?

And after this, what?

A man named Jansen had fixed it for them. Perhaps, when the job ended, he'd be able to offer them something else. He'd collected them from the railyard in a dirty white van and then picked up a number of others waiting in different parts of the town. Then a four-hour drive to get out here, and then he'd taken everybody's papers away for what he called *registration*. Ryan had handed over the well-used papers from Reineger's desk drawer. Payment would be in cash; no wage slips, no receipts.

From the next room Marianne suddenly said, "We're doing all right here, aren't we?"

Ryan hesitated for a moment, and then rolled over onto his back again.

"I've known worse," he said.

"I mean, it's better than sleeping in old trains."

"You told me you thought that was fun."

"It was. The first night. But it was beginning to look like that was going to be it, forever."

"What do you think this is, then?"

"Well, I know this is temporary, as well. But we're making some money, and then we can do something else."

There was silence for a while. Sleeping out in the wreck of an old railway carriage, using the seats for bunks and with a tabletop jammed across the window opening, had to have been about the lowest point of them all. But even so, she'd endured it. The night that she'd come over and crawled into the cover of his coat to join him, she hadn't even awakened as he'd lifted her and carried her back to her own side of the compartment. Whereas he himself had lain there, wide awake and restless, until daybreak.

Ryan said, "Don't you ever get homesick? Just a little?"

"Oh, no."

But she sounded as if she were trying to sell it to him a little—just a *little*—too hard. And then she said firmly, almost as if in a statement of faith, "I'm having a really good time. Aren't you?"

"Yeah," Ryan said tonelessly.

It didn't sound too convincing, even to him.

But right here and now, it seemed to be good enough for Marianne.

CHAPTER 63

It was already light when Ryan woke.

For a moment or two he just stared at the ceiling, and then he realized what was wrong. It ought still to be dark, or a grainy twilight at the most. He sat up, fully awake and with the sudden panic of the oversleeper.

"Marianne!" he said. "Come on, we're late!"

There was no reply. He scrambled out of bed and into his clothes. As he was buttoning up his work shirt, he called her again. Then he went to the dividing curtain and pulled it aside.

Her bed was empty.

Usually, they'd be awakened by Frau Lüderssen rapping at the door as she left a can of raw milk just outside. The can stood on the table now, but he'd heard nothing. There was one empty bowl with a spoon stuck in it.

Well, so much for his catlike reflexes.

He went outside. Marianne and Ellinor were emerging from the bungalow as he crossed the yard, still shoving his shirttails into his trousers. "What's happening?" he said. "Is there something wrong?"

"Oh," Marianne said, "didn't I tell you last night? Everyone's working here today, so we didn't have to be up in time to catch the bus. I've been helping Ellinor to get the packed lunches ready. I thought I'd let you sleep in."

"Oh," he said.

Ellinor elbowed Marianne and said something. Whatever it

was, she glanced at Ryan as she was saying it and then quickly looked away again.

Ryan said, "And what are you two cooking up now?"

"She says that Frau Lüderssen wants you over in the barn."

"Really," said Ryan.

"Honest," Marianne insisted. "That's exactly what she said."

Ryan looked at her for a moment or two, and with some suspicion. She was wearing a look of exaggerated innocence which could mean either that she was setting him up for something, or she wasn't but was getting some fun out of letting him think that she might be.

As he set off for the barn, he glanced back to see if they were watching him.

They were.

But it was legitimate. Frau Lüderssen had run her tractor into the barn and positioned it under the chain winch that hung from the rafters; she'd unbolted the scoop and left that standing on the ground, and she now needed help to winch and position a three-pronged balesticker in its place. The tractor's engine was idling, filling the barn with a noise like hammers in a bucket. Ryan hauled on the chains as she maneuvered the piece of gear onto the arms, and then he held it fast as she hammered the split pins home. Then she swung herself into the saddle and spun the wheel and backed the tractor out.

The girls were waiting outside by now. The two of them clambered up behind the saddle to ride down into the fields; Ryan waved them on, indicating that he'd walk.

He went back to their outbuilding, grabbed some breakfast on the hoof, and then set out to follow them down.

It had all the signs of another fine day, with warm summer sunshine and a cool summer breeze. The bus was already down there, by the field closest to the road. The gates had been opened up, and the baler was just arriving. Two Fendt trucks and two green-painted trailers followed.

They were having the usual trouble coaxing the baler into life as Ryan arrived. He looked around. He was looking for Ganz; not for any particular reason, but simply for an awareness of whatever he might be doing. He saw no sign until

Ganz emerged from behind one of the trailers, zipping his fly and then wiping his hands on the fronts of his thighs.

Ryan caught Marianne's eye. "I'm glad he's not making the sandwiches," he said.

Marianne translated in a whisper for Ellinor. At this moment Ganz was passing them and there was an uneasy glitter in his eye as if he was aware that something was probably being said about him, but he'd no way of knowing what. Then he pulled out his pale rawhide gloves and put them on and smacked his hands together so hard that dust flew out of them and formed a cloud of motes in the morning sun.

The baler started up with a raggedy roar. The men started to move out across the field.

The day's work had begun.

They went hard at it and had mostly cleared the first field by eleven, when half of the team and the biggest machines went bumping and bouncing along to the next while those remaining—mainly the women, but only by coincidence—stayed behind to finish off. Ryan knew nothing of farming. He couldn't even be relied upon to lay out a garden. But he'd watched the others, and he'd picked up whatever he'd needed as he'd gone along. What they were doing could probably be achieved in bigger farms further west by a couple of drivers and the latest and most expensive agricultural technology; but this was poorer country, and the methods were low-tech and labor-intensive. The machines spluttered and misbehaved, all drive chains and canvas belts and not a microchip anywhere. The trucks had seen better days but had new paint jobs which gave them the air of old men in Sunday suits. Ryan had pitched hay into the baler's maw for half of the morning, and then ridden behind on the following wagon to receive the made-up bales as two of the others heaved them up from the ground to him. It was prickly, itchy, strenuous work.

But no one trailed him and called him names. And at nights, as a bonus, no one was disturbing his sleep by pelting his roof with stones and then running away.

The next field was an odd shape, had an awkward lie to the land, and was dominated at the lowermost end by an electricity pylon in one corner. Three of them had to work underneath this for a while with sickles to clear where the machinery had been unable to go. You could see the nearest village from here, he noticed. Church spire at one end, radio mast at the other.

Everyone broke for lunch at noon; it was the usual bread and sausage, with apple juice and homemade beer. Most of them took it in the shade of the vehicles, sitting on the sloping ground. Ryan stretched out in the sun. The stubble was rough against his back like a bed of nails, but it was easier to put up with it than to move.

"You look like a stiff," he heard Marianne say.

He opened one eye and looked at her. She was standing above him, her figure darkened against a sky of an intense, almost artificial blue.

"A what?" he said.

"A dead body."

"I feel like one."

She lowered herself to the ground and sat beside him. "And when you snore," she said, "you sound like a car."

"Thanks."

They stayed that way for a while, in companionable silence. From some way down the field there came the strange and barely perceptible fizzing that could often be heard around high-tension cables.

Marianne said, "You know, you never did finish that story."

"What story's this?"

"The one about the time when you nearly died."

"There's nothing much to tell. It was just like you can read about in all the books."

"But what *happened*?"

He raised himself up, propping himself up on his elbows. The sunlight was so bright in his eyes that he had to squint to make her out. She was waiting.

He was probably going to have to tell her this sooner or later, anyway. She wouldn't let it go until she knew.

And so he said, "I was supposed to be asleep, but I wasn't. Well, I *was* . . . what I mean is, a part of me was. Another part of me was awake and watching, just like I was somebody else. That's how I knew it wasn't a dream. I could look down into the operating theater and see them working on me. Then I began to turn away and I could hear somebody say *Uh-oh*, as if something had started to go wrong. But I wasn't worried. I wasn't worried about anything. I don't think I've ever felt happier than I did right then. Life's always seemed complicated, but it didn't then."

"Were you dying?"

"I think I was. They said I wasn't. What I really think is, somebody made a mistake and they had to put it right quickly to get me back, and then they kept quiet about it. They didn't know I was watching, you see."

She mused about this for a while. And then she said, "Did you get to see heaven?"

"I don't know about that. I saw something."

"What was it like?"

"A tunnel. It's what everybody sees when that kind of thing happens. A long tunnel with a light at the end. And the closer I got to it, the harder it was to reach ... because by then they'd realized and they were trying to pull me back, I think. Do you remember what it was like on the beach? How we were trying to get up onto the sand but there was this terrific current under the water that kept dragging us out?"

Marianne nodded.

"Well, that's how it was there. I nearly made it. I was nearly at the end and I could see ... it wasn't just one light. It was like a whole city, all made out of lights. But I couldn't reach it."

"And was *that* heaven?" Marianne persisted.

Ryan hesitated. He was thinking of how he could launch into some complicated series of qualifications that would, in the end, only lead him to the same place anyway, and so he simply said, "I think it probably was."

"And is that why you're not afraid of anything now?"

"Who says I'm not?"

"I'd have thought that if dying was the worst thing that could happen to you and you've already seen heaven so you can't be afraid of that, then there's nothing left that can scare you. Is there?"

He scanned the far horizon, where there may have been just the hint of a distant city below the skyline.

"You'd be surprised," he said.

"What scares you, then?"

"Hundreds of things," he said evasively.

"Like what?"

"Big women in yellow bikinis, for one."

A couple of dozen yards away, Frau Lüderssen was rising from the squatting conversation that she'd been having with the haybaler's operator. She crossed over to the wide open gateway, where the gold-colored VW Golf from the next farm had drawn in. Ryan recognized four of the area's farm wives on board the car, the back end of which had been so stacked with boxes that it was half open and held together by a rope. The one who was driving wound down the window as Frau Lüderssen approached.

Ryan said, "I wonder what that's all about."

"*I* know," Marianne said smugly.

"Oh, yeah?"

"Ellinor told me this morning. But you're going to have to wait until later to find out."

"Why?"

"Because it's a secret and I'm feeling mean, so I won't tell you."

The Golf chugged away and labored on uphill towards the farm buildings at the top of the track. As if at some signal, all of the others in the field were starting to rise from the ground.

Ryan got up awkwardly.

At some time in the course of the afternoon, Marianne left the work party. She went up with one of the hayloads and didn't come back; nor did Ellinor. Ryan felt lost without her. Nobody here spoke English, and he could speak nothing else.

There was a big push to get finished as the sun went down. The last bales were loaded and carted by the headlights of all the available vehicles, which crisscrossed the darkening field and turned it into a stage of dazzling beams and giant shadows. There was a sense, when it was ended, of a race that had been won. Everybody piled onto the last wagon. It was moving when Ryan caught up with it, but several hands reached out to pull him aboard. Frau Lüderssen was the last to leave the field, closing the gate behind them as her aging tractor *put-putted* in patient attendance.

When they reached the farm at the top of the track, it was as if the day was draining out of the sky with one last, grandiose display like the painted canvas backcloth of some thousand-voiced opera. Down below, on a more human scale, were the lights of the farmyard.

Lines of bulbs had been strung from the house to the outbuildings and back again. Hurricane lamps stood on the long trestle tables that had been set out beneath. There was more of the beer, there was food for everyone. As Ryan climbed down with the others, he saw Marianne waiting.

"Is there where you disappeared to?" he said. "To help with all this? What's it all for?"

"It's the end of the haymaking," she said. "This is what they do every year when it's over."

Music was started up on a Dansette-style record player that stood on a crate as far out from the barn as its power line would reach. The music was a Paul McCartney album of bootleg quality. Farmers and field hands and farmers' families mingled in the yard, voices were raised, hands were shaken. The crowd was no beauty contest, that was for certain.

As always, Ryan checked around for Ganz.

There he was. He had that same dented jerrican from the equipment truck, and he was filling it from the big tank over by the silage heap. Nobody had asked him to do it, Ryan could be sure of that much. He looked about him, wondering if he ought to tell someone. No one else was taking any interest. He looked for Marianne, but she'd moved off and was conspiring with Ellinor and the others over something new.

Ganz was moving now. From his leaning, slightly staggering posture, he'd filled the jerrican to capacity and was straining at its weight. With a definite sense of purpose, he was heading for the dirt road that would take him back down to the fields of new stubble.

As he glanced around to see if he was being observed, his eyes met Ryan's.

Ryan didn't move.

It was pretty obvious that he planned to torch the land again. Ryan was imagining how spectacular that would be. Seen from here, it would be like a firebomb going up. From close-up in the darkness, it would be like warming oneself before the gates of hell.

Walking on, looking back, Ganz held his eyes. A challenge, perhaps. Or defiance.

Or even a demand for recognition.

Suddenly, the headlights of Frau Lüderssen's tractor had Ganz pinned. He stopped there at the top of the dirt road, blinking, as Frau Lüderssen pulled on the brake before swinging herself down from the saddle and striding towards him. Others had seen him by now. Heads were turning, conversations trailing off; only McCartney carried on as if nothing new and interesting was about to happen. The tractor's headlamps flickered slightly as its engine idled only a notch above stalling.

Ganz was a head taller than Frau Lüderssen, but Ryan still wouldn't have cared to swap places with him right at this moment. She was obviously clued in to what he'd been planning, and she was berating him even as she approached. Still shouting into his face, she took the jerrican away from him with one hand and then, with the other, she clouted him hard.

The sound of it echoed like a gunshot across the open countryside. There was weight and force behind the blow, enough to turn his head and make him stagger.

And everyone in the crowd began to applaud.

She'd walloped him like the world's biggest, dumbest naughty boy, and now he was just standing there with face red and his fists doubled as she walked away from him, lugging the jerrican two-handed back to her tractor. Then, belatedly, he seemed to become aware that he had an audience. He turned his head and stared at them. But then Frau Lüderssen crashed the gears and blasted her horn at him, and he had a choice of either getting out of the way or being run down, and so he jumped.

She left him in the dark. He shouted something after her, but nobody could quite hear what. They could just about make him

out as he turned and squared his shoulders, and started off
down the hill empty-handed. He'd have a long walk back to
his lodgings, five miles or more. And nobody but the dogs
would be waiting when he arrived, because everyone from
there was already here.

It was about the best start to a party that anyone could have
imagined.

There was music, and more music. When everybody got
drunk enough, there was dancing. And when some got even
drunker, everybody sang. The farm cats scavenged under the
tables, moths hovered about the lights. Ryan smiled when anyone spoke to him, but mostly he just moved through the crowd
and watched.

"Look what I got," Marianne said breathlessly from behind
him at one point, and he turned. One of the farmers had made
some small hand-carved wooden dolls, one for each of the
girls. "Isn't it nice?"

"Yes, it is," Ryan said.

She was happy tonight, he could tell. She was back in touch
with a world that was hers, even if the contact wouldn't last.
Some part of her that he would never know, and could never
address. He watched her joining in the songs, unaware of his
attention and completely unselfconscious. She seemed to know
quite a few of the words.

It was then that he realized three things.

One was that he loved her. Another was that he'd never actually loved anything in his life before.

And the other was that sometime soon, regardless of what
might happen, he was going to have to let her go.

Late that night, when everyone else had gone home, leaving
most of the party debris to be cleared the next morning, Ryan
lay in his bed and wished, once again, that he had something
that he could read. He wouldn't even be choosy. Anything,
even one of those hard books full of fine writing where nothing much happened. He needed distraction. Anything that
would allow him to turn away from himself for a while.

From the next room, Marianne tapped on the wall.

"What is it?" he said.

"Are you still awake?" her muffled voice said. "Can I come through?"

"Yeah," he said. "Come on."

He heard her bed creak. Then Marianne pushed aside the dividing curtain and came in. She switched on the light. She was wearing her coat over her borrowed night-dress. He pulled himself up to make room for her as she sat on the end of his mattress.

"What's bothering you?" he said.

"Nothing's bothering me. I've been thinking, that's all."

"What about?"

She took an excessive interest in the dust on the floor in front of her. She said, "We got fixed up pretty well, here, didn't we?"

"No better or worse than most of the others."

"What I mean is, it all worked out for us. We landed on our feet."

He couldn't see where she was trying to lead him. So all that he said was, "I suppose we did."

"We're going to have to stop moving around sometime," Marianne went on.

"If you're going to ask if we can stay here, I don't see how. The harvest's over. They won't need us any more."

"Ellinor says the work's too much for them on their own. And that's all year round, not just now."

"I don't know, Marianne," he said. "I wouldn't go looking for anything too permanent in this."

"What are we going to do, then?"

"I don't know that either, yet."

"Because what I'd really like . . . I mean, if there's any way I could . . . I'd like to go back to school again. I don't mean those schools back in England. I mean, like I used to when I lived here."

"Well . . ." he said, "I don't know. I don't know how we'd manage that."

"Gypsies do it. They go to all different schools, and nobody ever knows where they come from."

"I'm not telling you no. What I'm saying is, I don't know

how to make it happen. We're in a less than perfect situation, here."

"I know," Marianne said gloomily.

Ryan hesitated and then, aware that he was venturing onto delicate ground, said, "Don't you ever miss your father, at all?"

"I always did," Marianne said, "after he turned different."

"What if he came to his senses and you could have him the way he used to be? Would you want to go back to him, then?"

"But then I'd miss you, wouldn't I?" she said lightly, and stood up. No problem there, no case to answer. "Good night," she said, and she kissed him on the forehead.

And then she moved over to the doorway and, just before she disappeared through the curtain, said, "Ellinor told me that if Frau Lüderssen married again, her husband would get half of the farm."

"Forget it," Ryan said flatly.

She shrugged, and went.

A couple of minutes later, Ryan said, "You didn't turn the light off."

There was no reply, and so he said it again . . . and this time the response was a manufactured snore.

"You sound just like a car," he said.

Nothing.

Wearily, he struggled out of his bed and went over towards the light switch by the entrance door. Her own area on the other side of the divider curtain was already dark.

As he reached for the switch, the door burst open.

And before Ryan had realized what was happening, Ganz had slammed into him and was bearing him backwards across the room.

CHAPTER 64

Ryan was off balance, and there was nothing that he could do about it. He backpedaled all the way until they hit the folding bed, where he fell. He crashed down with it as the whole thing overturned. Before he could move or do anything else, Ganz had heaved the bed onto him and then put a foot on it to pin him down. With most of the other man's weight to hold him there, Ryan was trapped. Behind Ganz, he could see others coming in. From the next room, he could hear Marianne screaming.

First through the door was Jansen, the fixer with the dirty white van who'd brought them out here. In one hand Jansen carried what appeared to be a sawn-off shotgun, both the stock and the barrel cut down to a size that could be hidden inside a big enough coat; but it was hard to be certain, because no sooner had Jansen stepped in than he'd thrown the dividing curtain aside and gone through to where Marianne was making all her noise. Ryan tried to heave the bed off him, but Ganz increased the pressure. Ominously, the screaming stopped ... and Jansen came backwards out of the doorway again, with a finger raised to the out-of-sight Marianne as a warning for her continued silence.

The third and last man into the room was a much-tousled, unshaven, frayed-at-the-edges Axel Reineger.

He was wild-eyed and dark. His good clothes didn't look so good. He looked as if he'd gone for a night on the town and stayed out for a year.

He squatted down before Ryan and made some kind of a demand. His voice was harsh and his face meant business and Ryan couldn't understand a word of what he was saying.

Ryan tried to tell him as much, but everyone seemed to be shouting at him at once. He knew that Jansen spoke some English and he tried to direct his words towards the fixer, but he wasn't getting through; suddenly the bed was being thrown off him and Ganz was grabbing one arm while Axel Reineger took the other, and then they hauled him up and dragged him out into the yard. They didn't even give him a chance to get his balance, so he staggered and stumbled and his feet dragged and he tripped on the threshold.

"What?" he kept saying. "What is it? Will you tell me what you *want*?"

The white van was out there. Lights on, engine running. They were dragging him towards it. Over at the farmhouse, a door was opening. Frau Lüderssen stood framed in the doorway, her face a picture of anger that quickly turned to shock as Jansen swung up his gun arm and leveled the sawn-off at her. She dived back, and the house door slammed. Ryan was thrown to the ground before the van. He hit hard and was winded. He tried to rise, but one of them kicked him back down and then he was pinned again.

Someone took his arm, bending it at the elbow and then forcing it to the ground at right angles to his body. Jansen was kneeling on him, holding the bent arm in place with one hand and the gun to his head with another. Ryan was terrified. The gun on its own would have been enough. Axel Reineger was down on his hands and knees on the ground before him, barking the same questions into his face like a dog and to about as much effect as before.

Ganz was climbing into the van, first looking around himself to sort out the controls and then revving the engine. He made a noisy gear change and let out the brake and then, overrevving mightily, began to let the van roll forward.

It was then that Ryan realized what it was they were planning to do.

The nearside tire of the van crunched slowly towards his outstretched elbow. Ryan tried to struggle but Jansen was holding him firm, and Axel Reineger was still screaming at him but now there was the noise of the van's engine added to and drowning out everything else. Ryan was shouting as well, now, and Axel Reineger was beckoning to Ganz up in the driver's seat and guiding him in, and Ryan felt the touch of the tire against his bent elbow and tried to jerk it away and almost succeeded, but only almost. He heard Ganz pull the handbrake on and then start to rev even harder, rocking the van against the brake so that the pressure increased and started to push his elbow down into the hard-packed dirt. The dirt gave but not much, and Ryan's elbow screamed louder than anything else but with a sound that only Ryan could hear.

Ganz was leaning out of the van's window, looking down so that he could judge his progress with more precision. There was a smell like burning metal and oil. Even through the pain, Ryan prayed that the brake would hold. The van was straining like a sled dog against its harness, baying and howling and eager to be away.

Another inch. The crushing pressure on his elbow increased.

Ryan beat his forehead on the hard ground.

And then, suddenly, there was a shout that managed to make itself heard; it was from Marianne. All heads turned to her. The pressure on Ryan's elbow didn't let up, but the roar of the van's engine did.

Belatedly, Ryan managed to raise his head.

Marianne was standing in the open doorway to the outbuilding. She was holding up the envelope that had been given to him by Anneliese Cadogan, back there in the coffee shop when they'd met for the second time.

"This is what they want," Marianne said. "This is what all the shouting's about."

The van's engine spluttered, and stalled.

The gun barrel was taken from the side of Ryan's head, and the pressure from his back a moment later. He pulled his arm free without help.

He saw Axel Reineger walk over and snatch the envelope from Marianne's hand. Once it was in his possession, Reineger took a deep breath and made a clear effort to reestablish his self-control.

It was there. It seemed to settle on him like an entire new personality, filling him and straightening him out.

Ryan didn't know what Reineger said then. But he was

pulled up to his feet, and they all started over towards the main
house.

CHAPTER 65

It was only the second time that Ryan had actually been inside
the Lüderssen house. It was plain and modern, and fairly
sparse. The floors were tiled and the walls were bare. Only the
kitchen was cluttered, and that with the temporary debris of the
party preparations. Axel Reineger had swept the table clear and
laid out a small number of documents on it. These included the
key, and the address that had come with the key, and the false
registration papers through which Ryan assumed that he'd
tracked them down. Reineger was looking at everything with
an air of dismay. He had, it seemed, been expecting rather
more; he'd been expecting to find Ryan in possession of all the
goods to which the key would give access. His emergency
cash, his escape route. When he'd learned that these were in
fact still back in town and undisturbed, he hadn't taken the
news well.

"Are you all right?" Ryan said in a low voice to Marianne.

"I think so," Marianne said, and then she had to fall silent
because Jansen the fixer leaned over and poked her with the
end of the sawn-off. The barrel came within Ryan's reach as he
did this, but Ryan only stared at it dully. He was no hero. You
saw that stuff in stories or you read about other people and you
knew with great certainty how you'd want to behave, but when
the reality came you just sat there and hoped that you wouldn't
have to move again until it was over.

They were sitting in a line on the floor, with their backs
against a plain wall. Frau Lüderssen was nursing a swelling
eye, her head tilted into the heel of her hand as if she was ex-

pecting the wound to bleed even though the skin was unbroken. This had been Ganz's work, carried out within seconds of finding the widow and her daughter crouched in a windowless cupboard in the middle of the house. Frau Lüderssen had been trying to load the wrong size of shells into what looked like an old twelve-bore shotgun, her daughter behind her; Ganz had dragged Frau Lüderssen out and taken the gun and clubbed her with the stock like a seal.

Both of the girls were untouched. They sat between the adults, looking scared.

Ryan shivered. The night wasn't so cold but he shivered anyway and gritted his teeth in the hope that nobody would notice.

Reineger turned and looked at Ryan. Ryan had no idea what he said, but then Reineger looked at Marianne and gave a curt jerk of his head in Ryan's direction, which Ryan took to mean that he wanted her to translate.

"He says we were stupid to think that we could hide from him," Marianne repeated. "He says it was easy for someone like him to find us through the papers that you stole. But what he wants to know is, how did you get hold of them?"

"Tell him I found them," Ryan said.

An exchange, and then: "He doesn't believe you."

"Then tell him that someone sold them to me, I don't know who it was."

"He wants to know if it was a woman. A woman named—"

At which Marianne stopped, and needed to say no more because Reineger had already spoken the name.

There was a silence.

Then Reineger said, *"Und warum würde Sie wohl so ein Risiko für einen Mann wie Sie eingehen?"*

And Marianne replied, *"Weil ich ihre Tochter bin."*

"Did you tell him what I think you just told him?"

"I told him I'm her daughter."

"Oh, great," Ryan said dully.

"But he might know where she is now!"

To that, Ryan said nothing.

With a small gesture, Reineger beckoned to Marianne to go over to him. Ryan quickly put a hand on her arm to stop her from rising, but then he was forced to withdraw it as Jansen the fixer leaned over and tapped him twice, painfully, on the bony part of his shoulder with the barrel of the sawn-off.

Marianne got to her feet, and Ryan looked at the floor. There was nothing that he could do. He was wishing that he'd simply turned her out of his house when she'd appeared with her bruises on the day that the police had let him go. He'd had the same thought at a number of their low points before. But then, it had been for his own sake.

This time, it was for hers.

Axel Reineger had pulled out a chair and sat down, and he had Marianne standing before him now. He was patting her shoulder, and talking to her like an uncle; clearly unsettled by this proximity and uncertain of his purpose, she was giving him stone-faced monosyllabic replies.

Reineger glanced at Ryan, and Ryan realized that this was mostly for his benefit. A man like Reineger would clearly know how to threaten without seeming to threaten. But his technique seemed to be wearing a little thin under pressure. Marianne could sense the wrongness of it; and Ryan, after years of practice, could see further into him still. Ryan could see all the way down.

All the way down to the devil behind the glass, to the mask behind the mask.

"He wants to know why you haven't used the key," Marianne translated.

"Tell him how we went to the house," Ryan said. "Say that whatever he's got hidden there, I didn't find it."

There was a brief exchange, and then: "He says you've got to go back. He says that between you and her, you've caused him serious problems and he'd be out of here and safe by now if it wasn't for you. He says it's up to you to go back there and bring out what he needs."

"He's got the key now ... why doesn't he do it himself?"

"I don't know," Marianne said, "he seems scared of something."

Axel Reineger said, *"Die Polizei."*

"Did you get that?" Marianne asked Ryan.

"The police? What makes him think that my chances are going to be any better than his?"

"He says that's your problem, not his. But he has confidence in you. Wait a minute, he wants me to do this next bit exactly."

Reineger fed her the lines, his glittering eyes fixed on Ryan.

"Because," she said, "if you're caught . . . or if you try to run with what you find . . . or if you fail to come back for any reason at all . . . then Anneliese Cadogan's daughter is sure to prove of even greater value to him than Anneliese Cadogan ever did. He says nod if you understand."

Slowly, Ryan nodded.

Marianne said, "What does that mean?"

"Just tell him that I'll do whatever he wants," Ryan said.

CHAPTER 66

In the hour just before the dawn Ryan, now fully dressed, was escorted out to the barn. Marianne was brought along with them; Frau Lüderssen and her daughter had been returned to the windowless cupboard and a chair jammed under the door handle to keep them there. Jansen had run his white van into the barn some hours before in order to keep it out of sight and also, Ryan suspected, in the hope that a night under cover might improve its chances of getting started.

It didn't.

They waited in the doorway while the starter motor turned over sluggishly. The van coughed, as if this kind of taunting game was about the only pleasure that it had left as it neared the end of a long, hard life. Reineger fanned his face as a stray breeze carried over a reminder of the silage heap, and he made some comment that needed no translation. His other hand was on Marianne's shoulder.

Ryan watched the van dejectedly. It would start, and this would be no reprieve. He could see no way for them other than for him to go through this laid-out course of action like some kind of a puppet. And then?

The van coughed again, and caught, and growled into life.

Ganz hauled back the sliding door on the passenger side and, with a broad smile, gestured for Ryan to climb in. Half doorman, half gorilla. Ryan obeyed. The seat was splitting, its springs all but gone. By the general state of the van's interior, when not moving people around it looked as if it had been used to carry bags of cement and building rubble.

When Ganz had slammed the door on him, Ryan looked out of the open window towards Marianne. Axel Reineger was watching him, and absently stroking Marianne's hair. Making a point.

Ryan said, "Don't worry. Don't do anything that might annoy them, just sit tight and wait for me. I'll go for what he wants and then I'll be right back to get you. Nothing's going to stop that from happening. All right?"

"If you promise me," she said.

"I promise. All right?"

Marianne nodded slowly. And Reineger smiled.

The van backed out of the barn. The chances of anything having been noticed last night were remote. The farm was isolated from its neighbors, and no shots had been fired. Reineger and the others had cut the phone line on their way up the hill. And suppose, just suppose, that there was even one early riser around who wasn't nursing his head or thinking about sticking it into a toilet after the previous night's intake; what was there to see? What to suspect?

Axel Reineger might not be able to sit it out in the Lüderssen farm forever.

But for the moment, and for a man on the run, he seemed to be pretty well placed.

The van bumped its way down the dirt road. There were trees lining it, and each one that they passed created a sound heard through the van's open window like a sharp indrawing of breath. Ryan tried to wind the window shut, but it got halfway and then dropped open again.

Jansen reached across to pull a grubby map from under the dashboard. He dropped it in Ryan's lap.

"Read the way," he said.

Ryan opened the map. It wasn't particularly old, but had been so well used that a lot of the print had been worn off along the creases.

"Starting from where?" he said.

Jansen glanced across and then reached over, the van weaving dangerously from side to side as he pointed to an area that had been marked. Several farms had been indicated with x's but only one had been marked and then ringed with ball-point pen, scored around heavily and several times.

It took Ryan a while longer to find Düsseldorf.

"Why didn't he send you?" he asked Jansen.

"Got no kid for him to hang onto," Jansen said. "Me on my own, I'd take whatever he sends me for and fuck off. I know it, he knows it. Trust your partners least of all. That's business."

"Just suppose I didn't make it back. What would he do with her?"

"Find the highest bidder," Jansen said, as if the answer was obvious.

"For what?"

At which Jansen looked across at him with an expression that seemed to say, *Can you really be that stupid?*

Ryan settled bleakly, and tried to read the map. His hands weren't too steady. Marianne had asked him how he could be afraid of anything if he didn't have to be afraid of dying. Well, perhaps he wasn't, although he'd never really know until the moment came. The hard fact of it was, there was still the journey to be made with all of its prospects for pain and loss along the way.

She'd asked him if there was anything that could be worse.

And when he thought of Axel Reineger's hand on her hair, and remembered the lack of life he'd seen in the eyes of Anneliese Cadogan, he became increasingly certain that there had to be.

CHAPTER 67

They cruised around the back streets, circling in to get there. If there was any police activity still to be found around the area of the cabin, they didn't see it. They passed the place once, but they didn't stop.

Ryan had learned little from Jansen on the long drive into Düsseldorf, other than that the cabin was the place where Anneliese Cadogan had been found dead. Axel Reineger was convinced that the woman's final act had been more of a calculated gesture on her part to ruin him; first she'd removed his escape route, and then she'd turned up the heat. Self-sacrifice? It seemed like it, but Ryan wasn't so sure. Sacrifice meant being prepared to part with something that you didn't really want to lose.

There was another possibility: the fallout for Reineger could have been purely incidental. Ryan suspected that the true targets of her probable suicide might well have been the heart and mind of Patrick Cadogan.

Jansen pulled off the road onto the wide dirt shoulder alongside some chemical plant. Mud and stones had been churned up in ruts by the wheels of lorries that had turned there. Traffic was heavy, but the shoulder was empty and there was nobody walking. They were now at least half a mile from the end of the lane where the cabin stood.

Ryan said, "I didn't spot anything. Did you?"

Jansen shrugged.

So then Ryan said, "Are we going back there, or what?"

"Go right ahead," Jansen said, and settled back in his seat. This was clearly as close as he was prepared to get.

Ryan climbed out of the van, and started to walk. Over inside the chemical works, a couple of big dogs came bounding across to the perimeter wire and paced him along the inside until he'd moved out of range, upon which they started to bay.

He looked back at the van. Jansen had slid down and appeared to be dozing already. Ryan felt physically weary, but as if he'd never be able to sleep again. He envied Jansen. He envied just about everybody right now.

He walked on.

Nothing much appeared to have changed since he'd been out here last. The cabin looked as if it had simply been closed up by its owners to await their return, like every other hut and shanty on the lane. Weekend havens, small and cheap, standing in midweek stillness. This had been the address on the paper that Anneliese Cadogan had provided along with the key. He'd come straight out here with Marianne and they'd looked around, but had found nothing. Finally they'd realized that the key fitted not the house, but the mailbox; but then they'd checked the mailbox and it had been empty. From what he could gather, Anneliese Cadogan had been found inside only a few hours later.

One thing this time was different, apart from the new padlock and chain on the gate and the shred of police tape that still clung to the wire. This time he'd been told what he was supposed to be looking for. He stopped by the gate and glanced around. There were no cars parked on this side of the lane, and there was no smoke rising from any of the stovepipe chimneys that he could see above the surrounding greenery. Across the way, all the balconies of the overlooking apartments stood empty except for one or two where wet washing had been hung out.

The mailbox was fixed to a concrete post just inside the wire fence. The wire links had been cut and folded back to make a gap just big enough for the door on the front. There was a tube for newspapers and magazines below this. With one final glance around, Ryan unlocked the door and swung it open.

The metal interior was empty, as before—nothing but road grit that had built up in the corners and a single, dried-out leaf that the wind must have managed to blow in through the slot.

He brushed the leaf out of the way and then ran his hand around the base. He probed, as he'd been told to. He pushed. He felt something begin to give beneath his fingers.

From under the aluminum paint, he dug out a strip of glazier's putty that had been disguising the edge of a let-in piece of the box floor. As soon as he could get his fingertips under, he lifted it free. The piece came out with a rip, like an old sticking plaster. The recess exposed underneath was exactly the same size as the unmarked padded envelope that it contained.

He slipped the envelope inside his coat, swung the mailbox door shut on the mess that he'd made, and started to walk away.

He had to hold the envelope against his side out of sight, because it was too big for any of his pockets. Getting it out had taken about thirty seconds. Surely no more than that. As far as he could tell no one had seen him, no one had paid him any attention at all. He resisted the urge to look behind him until he came to cross the lane, when he'd have a legitimate reason. And then as he reached the end of the lane and turned onto the main road, he felt as if he'd been lifted slightly.

All of the big problems were still in place. But at least he'd passed the first hurdle. He hadn't dared to contemplate the consequences should a police presence have remained around the building; nor those of returning to Reineger empty-handed. Worse still would be the consequences of not returning to Reineger at all. The man was getting desperate and he'd nothing to make a play with now, apart from Marianne; and Ryan knew that he wouldn't hesitate to convert her into some harder currency at the first opportunity. Ryan now had the envelope and whatever it might contain, but he wouldn't just hand it over. During the journey back he was going to work out some way of making it into an even trade, like when they swapped spies. Jansen might be a problem there. But Ryan wasn't prepared to let him be much of one.

He passed under a big painted mural on the end of an apartment house. It was a human eye, in realistic detail five stories tall; an unexpected flash of imagination among architecture that otherwise showed none. Just a couple of blocks to go, now. He hoped that Jansen had the van's engine turning over. He didn't think that he could handle the frustration of a mechanical breakdown, not at this stage.

It seemed that Jansen did, indeed, have the van's engine turning over.

Because neither Jansen nor the van were in the place where he'd left them.

CHAPTER 68

The long-distance bus was an old dusty vehicle; under the dirt it had once been white, with an orange stripe along its side that almost matched the rumpled curtains at its windows. The luggage that had been lined up in the bay ready to be loaded had been bulging and battered, and most of the owners of the luggage looked pretty much in the same way. Many of the women were in furs that seemed to be functional rather than luxurious. Most of the men wore leather jackets and boots and scarves. One carried aboard a portable color TV set in a box tied up with a string, another a single roll of wallpaper. None looked as if they had any spending power, and all appeared to have been spending with purpose and determination.

The bus was almost full, but Ryan got a seat on his own. It was an eastbound service, its ultimate destination being somewhere that Ryan couldn't even have taken a stab at pronouncing. Those around him were mostly one-occasion-only visitors from the old DDR and beyond, heading for home. Some, like him, traveled alone. He sat with Reineger's envelope on his knees and rested his head against the back of the seat and looked out of the window. Every now and then a burst of Muzak would play over the driver's address system, but it would cut out again after only a few bars.

He'd had three frantic, uncertain hours. At first he'd stayed on the spot where he'd last seen the van and had looked around, bewildered. The two dogs over behind the works fence had been up on their hind legs, making the wire shake as they'd braced themselves on it and barked at him. Same dogs, same scenery, same place; there had been no chance of a mistake. When he'd looked down at the ground he'd seen that the only evidence remaining had been a glistening patch of new oil on the stones, about the size of a five-mark piece.

But there had been no van, and there had been no Jansen.

Ryan had then moved to the side of the road and looked both ways into the traffic, thinking that perhaps the fixer had moved the van to turn it around and was heading back in to pick him up even now. Big lorries and tankers had thundered by, a few cars, more big lorries. Whatever Ryan might try to tell himself, he'd already known the hard truth.

Jansen had clearly spent the journey turning matters over in what Ryan might, with some charity, have called his mind. However the small-time fixer might look at it, the once-powerful Reineger made an increasingly risky business partner and for little promise of return. So, true to his trading principles, it seemed that Jansen had cut his risks and dropped out.

Which meant that Ryan had been left standing with the goods by the roadside, on the wrong side of the country and with no means of getting back, stateless, penniless, wanted by the police of two nations, unable to speak the language, not even knowing the name of the town nearest to where he needed to be, and with Marianne's time rapidly running out.

Someday, he reckoned, he was going to have to sit down and try to work out how one man of modest talents could manage to achieve so much.

His first move had been to look inside Reineger's envelope. As he'd expected, he found cash there. There had also been a Swedish passport in an unrecognizable name but with Axel Reineger's photograph inside it, along with matching credit cards and U.S.-dollar travelers' checks. There were airline tickets as well, with destinations but no dates or flight times, and there was one of those slot-in plastic discs used in computers and computer games, but without a label. He could never have used any of this, and he'd known as much almost from the beginning. He could take some of the cash now to help him get back to the farm, but that was about it. All that stuff about a new life, a new start—he'd have needed to be an entirely different animal, sharp-witted and a compulsive liar with bags of confidence and a heart of ice.

It had been a frantic three hours, but now Ryan was moving in the right direction at last. He'd have to change buses twice and he wouldn't arrive within striking distance of the farm until around midnight. He'd still have the problem of how to cover the last dozen or so miles, but he'd worry about that closer to the time. By then he'd be almost twelve hours overdue.

That was the part that worried him the most.

The bus was slowing, and pulling into a service area.

Ryan snapped awake. Had he been dozing? For how long? The driver was making some kind of announcement over the PA system that Ryan couldn't understand, but it raised an ominous groan from the other passengers. As the bus rolled to a stop and its automatic door hissed open, they were rising to their feet and reaching for their hand luggage.

"Excuse me," he asked one of the younger women, "but what's the problem?"

"The driver says he's been having trouble with the bus," the woman said, lifting down two well-filled shopping bags.

"What kind of trouble?"

"He's going to radio for another. And we're all going to have to get off and wait."

"Did he say for how long?"

But the young woman could only shrug resignedly as she took her bags and pushed her way out into the aisle to join the others as the bus slowly emptied.

Ryan was the last to leave. For a while he simply stayed in his seat, feeling dazed. He'd pulled it together, but it was all sliding apart again. He was powerless, now.

Slowly, stiffly, he climbed down from the bus. The driver was nowhere around. Even if there was another vehicle lined up and ready to go back at base, it would take it at least an hour to get here. He'd miss the first connection. Twelve hours would become twenty-four. Reineger would be gone, and so would Marianne. No one that she knew would ever see her again, and her last thought of Ryan would be of his broken promise.

Numbly, he followed the others over towards the main services building.

He started to become more aware of his surroundings. The thought flashed across his mind that he might steal a car, but a place like this was probably the worst in which to try it. Vehicles stood unattended for minutes, not hours, and pursuit would begin before he'd managed to cover any distance at all. They'd probably nail him before the first autobahn exit. And what use could he be to her then?

The service area had been built for less traffic than it was getting, and was overstretched. Long queues of vehicles waited over by the pumps and a mobile grill wagon, set up in the car park along with a couple of chemical toilets to help with the overspill, seemed to be doing more business than the main kiosk and restaurant. But it was into the latter that most of his fellow passengers appeared to have gone, and so he followed.

The decor included lime-green curtains and cheap wood-veneered furniture. He took a seat and when the waitress came, he asked her if he could have a glass of water. It was a long time coming, and as he waited, he could feel his sense of bleakness growing. It was all unraveling, falling apart. He'd been a fool to suppose that it might end in any other way. Marianne seemed to think of him as a hero, but what was he, after all? A beachcomber, semi-institutionalized and fit for little more. Even to call himself a beachcomber would be to romanticize what he did. He'd been a tinker, a tramp with a rent book and the railways for a landlord. And not even that any more.

For the first time in ages, he started to wonder whether there might be any useful purpose in prayer. Most people did it when their problems got big enough; it was like a reflex, it came naturally. But Ryan hadn't prayed in years. Every Sunday in the hospital chapel, he'd stared forward while others bowed their heads. It wasn't that he didn't believe. There was a God, he still knew that. But prayers, saints, miracles, the walking dead ... these were just special effects. Devices that were supposed to lead people to a truth, but which had become diversions in themselves. He could try it, he supposed, he could always do that. But not one atom or impulse in the whole of existence would alter if he did. To think otherwise was to believe in magic, if only under a more respectable name.

Well, perhaps there were more unlikely things than magic. He put his hand to his head, and looked down. What next? He realized that he'd forgotten how.

A woman's voice said, "Excuse me. I heard you talking to the waitress. Are you English?"

He turned his head. He looked.

She was young, but not a girl. She had dark red hair that had been expensively cut, and it hung straight with a lower edge like a razor. She was dressed all in black, apart from a belt buckle of silver.

"Can I sit with you for a minute?" she said. "Would that be all right? I'll explain why."

He made an uncertain gesture with one hand, and she moved over to his table.

"I'm trying to unload this German hitcher," she said. "A friend introduced him back in Hanover and said she could vouch for him. But he's terrible."

"What's he done?" Ryan said.

"Nothing. It's his questions, they're creepy. What do English women like? What do they like to do? What do they think? He's been driving me mad. I don't think he's completely well."

Ryan's mind was racing. Was there an angle here? Something that he might be able to exploit?

She was starting to tell him something else, and he said, "Take me in his place."

He hadn't meant to put it so baldly; it had just tumbled out. The woman faltered and he saw some of the color drain from her face, as if with the belated realization that she'd walked too far into the wrong side of town and what she'd taken for the lights of home actually indicated the way into somewhere just as welcoming but far more sinister.

Ryan quickly said, "What I mean is, let him see us walking

out to your car. By the time he's realized we're not really together, you'll be gone and it won't matter."

Her expression cleared and she said, "Do you have the time for that?"

"I've got all the time there is."

They got up and made for the door. As they were leaving the restaurant, a man in his mid-thirties was coming in. He was slim, with thinning hair and one tiny gold earring, and when he saw the woman he seemed to be about to speak to her; but she swept on past him and Ryan, following, saw his nonplussed expression as he turned with the unsaid words dying on his lips. Then Ryan had followed the woman out into the open air and they were heading across the parking area, and he caught up with her and said, "Was that him?"

"I daren't look back," she said, not slowing, and so Ryan glanced over his shoulder.

"It's all right," he said. "He isn't following us."

"Is he watching?"

"Only from inside the building. He hasn't come out."

They reached her car, a compact rented hatchback.

"Well," she said as she unlocked it, "thanks."

Ryan shrugged. No trouble. He stood and waited.

She didn't get in.

"Whereabouts is your car?"

"I don't have one," he said. "I was on that bus over there, but it broke down."

"But . . . you *are* fixed up."

He shook his head. Nothing more. *Don't push this,* he was thinking with suppressed excitement. *Push it, and she'll run.*

"Aren't they laying on another?"

"Not soon enough for me," he said. "My little girl's waiting."

She hesitated a moment longer. But the little girl was the clincher.

"I suppose you'd better get in."

Ryan didn't hesitate at all.

He could sense her unease as they rejoined the autobahn, but he didn't know how to put her mind at rest. He sat with Reineger's envelope across his knees. He saw her glance at it, but he didn't try to explain. She asked him if that was all the luggage he had; he said that it was.

Traffic was heavy. There were lorries and bus convoys and road trains and a sprinkling of Trabants and motorcycles. The road climbed towards a wooded skyline, dropping out of sight beyond the cut at the crest of the hill. When she asked him, he told her that he was a salvage dealer on holiday. Well, in a sense it was true. She said that she was a secondary-school teacher and that she was on holiday as well, but it was more like a working holiday because there were people she had to look up. She had a voucher to stay that night in a hotel in Magdeburg. Did he know Magdeburg at all? Ryan said that he didn't.

And then he saw a familiar-looking vehicle going by them in the overtaking lane.

"I don't believe this," he said.

"What?"

"It's my own bus," he said. "The one that was supposed to be out of service."

"Perhaps they managed to fix it."

"Yeah, with rocket parts," he said as the bus swung in front of them and then out again to pass someone else. The driver seemed to be trying to make up for the time that he'd lost. Ryan glanced across at the hatchback's speedometer but it showed the speed in kilometers, which meant nothing to him. "How fast are we going?" he said.

"Fast enough for me," the woman said. "If you don't like it, I'll be happy to drop you off again."

He clasped his hands together on his knees and said nothing. He clasped them so hard that his knuckles turned white.

"What's the matter with you?" she said after a while.

"I'm sorry," he said. He was blowing it, and he knew it.

"You're not in trouble or anything, are you?"

"No," Ryan said. "There's just somewhere I have to be."

"Where?"

"I don't know what it's called."

"How are you going to find it, then?"

"I can find it on a map when I have to."

"You're strange," she said. "No offense."

Ryan looked at the floor.

"None taken."

They went through what must once have been the border, hardly slowing at all as they followed the chevrons winding through the abandoned control buildings. Vehicle standing areas behind hurricane fencing were now completely empty, the row dividers knocked over and weeds sprouting up through the concrete. Overhead road signs had been painted out. The windows in the control tower were broken.

She hit the indicator for the next exit, and Ryan knew with a sinking heart that she was going to dump him somewhere around here.

"Let me have the car," he blurted out suddenly. "I can give you American dollars. Then you can say it's been stolen or I can take it back later, whatever you want."

"Don't be ridiculous."

"I'm not. I really mean it."

"Don't say another word," she said, and he could sense some of the anger that she was controlling. Anger and hurt, as well. She pulled into a parking area with a lot of heavy trucks that was overlooked by a newer and more modest service area; the eastern mirror image of the one that they'd left, their spacing on the road an odd hangover of the frontier that no longer separated them.

She made sure that she took the keys as she opened the driver's door. She backed well away and said, "Please get out of the car."

Ryan complied.

"What's the matter with you?" she said. "Are you in trouble, or something?"

"I can't tell you," he said.

"I've never *seen* anyone so desperate," she said.

"That's probably true."

She watched him for a few moments. Then she said, "I'm not going to take you any further. But I'll give you five minutes to tell me what's the matter and if there's some other way I can help you . . . I don't know. I'll have to see what I think." She turned to walk towards the main building, but then as he started to follow her she looked back. "Not too close," she said.

They climbed a wide brick stairway from the car park to the Mitropa buffet and shop, a long, low, white building with ventilator hoods on its roof and a red plastic awning over a Coca-Cola machine at the front. After the last place, this one seemed more or less empty.

The woman with the dark red hair sent him over to sit at one of the tables while she went to the counter. She came back with a cheap map and a borrowed pen. She pushed them across the table to him.

Then she waited.

He opened the map out. It took him a minute to find the place that he had to mark. His hand trembled slightly as he put in the position of the Lüderssen farm as accurately as the scale would allow. There was no doubt in his mind now that, one way or another, this woman was going to help him and that everything was still there to be played for.

He knew what she was. She might not know it, but he did. What else did you get sent to you when you were down at your lowest and staring evil in the face and could see no way out without help?

She sat back with her arms folded, her body language defensive and impatient. He turned the map around to show her.

"There," he said. "That's as close as I can get it. That's where I have to be."

"And that's where your little girl is?"

She was rising, the map in her hand, studying it thoughtfully.

"Wait here for a minute," she said. And she started to walk away, still looking thoughtful. As she reached the doorway, a couple of truck-driver types moved aside to let her pass.

Ryan sat back. It was working out. It was all beginning to mesh, and it was starting to come out right. The order that he'd always believed in was beginning to make itself shown and it pointed, as he'd always believed that it would, towards the light. There were devils, there were angels; but all were simply people acting out parts in the world's vast drama of good and evil without even knowing who they were or the deeper meanings of anything that they did.

He reached for Reineger's envelope, to draw it closer to him.

A hand reached from behind him and caught him by the wrist.

Uncomprehending, he looked up.

He was looking into the face of the unwanted German hitch-hiker from the previous stopover; the same thinning hair, the single gold earring. He looked a little older close up than he did from a distance, and he said in a cool, almost professional voice, "Stand up, please."

His other hand showed a brass disc. And before Ryan could respond in any way, the two truck-driver types had moved in to either side and grabbed his arms; and then they were hauling him up and bending him forward over the table with rough efficiency, and when they pulled his hands around behind his back he knew what was coming next, and he tried to struggle because it was something that had happened to him before and which he hated but already it was too late, and the handcuffs were on; and with his cheek pressed hard against the table and his head turned sideways he could see out into the car park and there were police cars and uniforms where there had been none before, and people were running towards the building.

They stood him up and pulled him out into the aisle with his hands locked behind his back. He felt incredibly open and vulnerable. They tugged him around a little as they frisked him down. He looked for the German with the earring, but now he was walking out towards the foyer with Reineger's padded envelope in his hand. With a push, Ryan was sent after.

The boy on the hot-dog counter was staring. The few other customers were rising, abandoning their drinks, and moving out to follow. Ryan stumbled, but the grip on his arm prevented him from falling as they went through the doors.

He could see the woman, ahead of them now in the foyer, where she'd stopped and turned. The look on her face was one not of surprise but of great tension now released, and the man was asking her something and she was nodding, saying that she was fine.

As Ryan was being hustled past, the man was saying, "Well done, Jennifer. Well done."

And then as Ryan was being dragged out of the foyer and into daylight, the woman was saying, "Thanks, Werner, but whose brilliant idea was it to let the bus go so early? Because that came bloody close to wrecking everything."

Then Ryan was out and in the open and could see that there was a police car waiting for him right at the entrance in the paved area where no cars were supposed to go, and then he was being pushed down into it and sandwiched between two uniformed men. The cuffs were digging into his back, and he had to lean forward.

Then the doors were slammed, and the car was on its way. Ryan turned his head to look back. The woman was standing there in the foyer of the building with the so-called hitchhiker's reassuring hand on her shoulder.

After she'd picked up the map and walked away from him, she hadn't looked at Ryan once.

CHAPTER 69

It was when he saw the two police vans blocking the way on the back road that Cadogan knew for certain that he was in the right place. It was night, and this was a deeply rural area, and there hadn't been too many road signs. The uniformed men on the barricade waved him down, and as he slowed to a halt, Cadogan leaned out of the window of his hired car and said, "You've got to let me through. I've been called for."

The police *Obermeister* came around and looked him over. "Who are you?"

"I'm the English girl's father. I'm wanted here, don't turn me back."

The man looked for a moment longer, giving nothing away.

"Wait here a moment," he said then, and he returned to his vehicle and his radio.

"Check with the British officer," Cadogan called after him. "She's the one who called for me."

But the uniformed man made a waving gesture, as if to tell him to keep his voice down. Cadogan waited tensely. A couple of minutes later, the officer returned.

"You can go on through," he said. "Go straight into the village and don't leave this road. Use your sidelights only, don't rev your engine, and don't even think about using your horn."

"Exactly how close are we?"

"We're about four kilometers from the farm. Nothing much happens around here at night, so if they hear anything at all, they'll know."

Four kilometers. Close enough to be heard, here in the still of the country night. Cadogan felt tense, wired up; he could feel his heart hammering uncontrollably as he drove on, almost as if he was entering into some overwhelming presence.

She was barely more than a mile away from him now.

He went on into the village. Along the way, he passed a line of vehicles whose only illumination came from their faint interior lights; against this moved a parade of spectral silhouettes making ready like an army for war, drawing on bulletproof vests, easing heads into helmets, hefting weapons high and checking their actions. There were dozens of them, too many to count as he rolled by. And as far as Cadogan could see, not one of them had a face.

He found a place to park in the village square, which was no square at all but a three-sided cobbled area with a fenced pond, and a tree overhanging the pond, and a bench that had been set out under the tree. The buildings all around looked as if they'd been lifted from a fairy tale, unaltered by man but somewhat run down by the centuries. They'd high walls and small windows and gated carriage arches leading to inner courtyards, and they looked down onto police cars, police vans, official vehicles with local *Landes* crests, and a scattering of identifiable incomers. Cadogan got out of his car and crossed the square. One building was the clear focus of everything, a huge barn of red bricks and oak beams that stood behind a much humbler concrete bus shelter. The barn doors were open, and the only light of any intensity came from within. Right alongside, a battered white van had been brought in on a trailer. The van looked as if its entire replacement cost would be rather less than that of a tire change for the Mercedes jeep that had towed it here.

The barn's interior was low-ceilinged and crowded with people. There was temporary lighting and a lot of equipment, effectively turning the main thruway and the cattle stalls into one big command and control center. From the heavy thumping sounds that came down from the boards only inches overhead, the upper livestock level was equally busy.

He caught hold of someone and asked for Jennifer McGann. He got no help, but then he turned at the sound of his own name.

It was her.

She said, "I had to argue for you to be let through. Don't do anything to embarrass me, now."

She was all in black and she looked exhausted. Cadogan said, "Are you all right?"

"It's been a tense kind of a day," she said. "I don't know if anyone's told you, but we've picked up O'Donnell."

No one had. "Already?" he said. "Then, what . . . ?" And he let the question hang, indicating all the activity behind them.

"It's not quite as simple as it was," the policewoman said, and Cadogan could feel his heart begin to sink as surely as that of a man watching his doctor trying tactfully to dress up the worst possible news.

"Tell me," he said.

They moved into one of the stalls, into which containers like empty bandboxes had been dumped. There was straw underfoot, but it was clean. While everything else carried on around them, she explained.

The police search of Axel Reineger's property following the death of Cadogan's wife had uncovered hidden money and a passport—Reineger's escape kit, it had seemed reasonable to assume. These had been returned to their hiding place and the damage made good, and surveillance put on the cabin from an empty apartment across the way. But instead of Reineger, O'Donnell had returned for the bait. They'd grabbed the white van, driven by an occasional associate of Reineger's, before O'Donnell had returned to it. A plainclothes officer in an unmarked car had picked him up and given him a lift to the bus station, where another officer had been waiting behind the counter to deal with him. This way they got an idea of the area that he wanted to reach, but couldn't get a specific location without arousing his suspicions. So then they'd pulled a stunt with his bus and finally ended the game when he'd pinpointed the place where Reineger—and Marianne—now waited.

"I don't get it," Cadogan said. "What's Marianne to Axel Reineger?"

But before he could get an answer there was a rumbling overhead as if a herd had started to move, and over on the other side of the barn there was a play of light and shadow as a crowd of booted legs descended from above. They were coming down a wooden cattle ramp, dropping into sight as they managed the steep angle. They moved like bodyguards or jailers and at the center of the group, face pale and hands manacled before him, hemmed-in and jostled by everyone, came one that Cadogan recognized in an instant.

"O'Donnell!" he shouted, forgetting everything else.

Every head in the place, O'Donnell's included, seemed to turn towards Cadogan for a moment. Then the honor guard grabbed O'Donnell and started to push him onward towards the door.

"Don't let them do this!" O'Donnell was shouting as the sheer numbers of people slowed his group's progress towards the exit; Cadogan had launched off to try to get him, but Jennifer McGann had caught his arm and was holding him back and so were about four others.

"Don't take him away," Cadogan bellowed. "I want him here!"

Everyone was making a racket now, and everyone seemed to be moving into the way to keep the two of them apart. O'Donnell was being half carried by, but he managed to bob up again and yell, "I know what you think of me now, and you're wrong! I made a bargain for her, and they're not going to let me keep it!"

"What does he mean?" Cadogan said to Jennifer McGann.

"They've had me drawing diagrams up there," O'Donnell went on. "They're going to go in shooting. I've looked after her every inch of the way and now *they're* going to get her killed just to reach someone they want more!"

Cadogan looked at the policewoman again. "Is that true?" he said.

"Of course it isn't."

"You don't look too fucking sure."

O'Donnell was being hustled out of the doorway now. "If I don't go back and he gets away," he called, "he's going to sell her like he sold her mother. Talk to them! Make them stop!"

Someone grabbed O'Donnell by the hair and turned his head around, then. Unable to resist, he was carried forward roughly and then out into the night, where a car waited.

Cadogan looked at the policewoman. "How can we stop them?" he said.

"We can't," she said simply.

As they were propelling him towards the car, O'Donnell suddenly braced himself and stopped. It wasn't easy and it took everybody by surprise. It wasn't entirely successful, either, and he nearly fell; but enough of them had their hands on him to insure that he didn't. There was Jansen's van, on a trailer only yards away. Two men were pulling out blocks from under the wheels, preparing to winch it down. The plan was clear to him now; the van would be a kind of a Trojan horse, used to get a strike team within yards of the house and with the idea of taking out the two men in a single surgical sweep. The alternative was containment and negotiation, packed with uncertainties and with three innocent people at stake as bargaining pieces.

But was it the best way? Ryan didn't care how accurate or well prepared they thought themselves to be. All he knew was that there was a firestorm heading for Marianne, and it was because of his failure. Now that they had what they needed from him, they were taking him away. Miles away, right out of the area. No one would even tell him how it had gone. No one would think that he mattered.

He raised his hands before the officer in charge and said, "Can you do something about this?"

The officer looked down. Ryan's wrists were a mess, the skin torn and bleeding where he'd twisted against the manacles.

"Nice try, Herr O'Donnell," the officer said dryly. "But I think we'll get you into the car, first."

When everything was comparatively quiet again, someone brought Cadogan a paper cup of water. He didn't want it, but he took it anyway. He sat on a plastic chair and he set the cup between his feet and put his head in his hands. Jennifer watched him for a while, and then she went outside to be sure that the car with O'Donnell had been sent safely on its way. It had. But now two mechanics were working on the old white van, which was resisting their most skilled efforts to get it started. Two new batteries stood on the cobbles, and the six-man special detail stood all around in their body armor with weapons at the ready, all itching to go. The mechanics were hurriedly tearing off and replacing the van's plug leads.

Jennifer went back inside.

Cadogan looked up at her and said, "I think I know why you wanted me here."

Jennifer didn't answer.

"He's right, isn't he?" Cadogan said. "Or, at least, you think he is. It's pass-the-parcel with Marianne, and everybody's sights swing from her to Reineger . . . so then I'm supposed to turn up like some specter at the feast to remind them she's around."

Jennifer said, "It's coming to an end. You'll have her back within the hour. *That's* why you're here."

Somebody called for quiet. Everyone was gathering around the radio desk at the far end of the barn. Cadogan jumped up at the sound of the name. The paper cup was knocked over and the water shot out across the floor, but he didn't notice. He went over to listen with the others. Jennifer didn't try to stop him; instead, she followed him. They listened to the rest of the message as it came through.

O'Donnell's car had failed to pass through the roadblock. Hadn't even reached it. O'Donnell had persuaded his guards to remove the handcuffs; he was with four stronger men in a locked car moving at speed, two beside him and two in the front, and his wrists were in serious need of first aid. He'd headbutted one officer, broken the nose of another, sprung the eye of a third with a well-aimed jab of his thumb, and choked out the driver in a matter of seconds. The car had gone off the road and turned over in a field, where O'Donnell had kicked out the rear windscreen and escaped.

His whereabouts, as the official jargon went, were now unknown.

Jennifer became aware that Cadogan was looking at her.

"I don't know if that's good or bad," he said.

Jennifer could only say, "You tell me."

She looked towards the doorway, and out into the night. O'Donnell was out there now. Most in his position would take the opportunity to run.

But somehow, she was certain that he would be trying to get up to the farmstead alone.

CHAPTER 70

Ganz was making preparations to torch the Lüderssen place.

No one else knew about this, of course, and the big payoff wouldn't come until they were ready to depart in the morning; but at that time, as they were leaving, his last act would be to light up a rag and toss it back over his shoulder and then watch the fat lady's expression as her home and her business went up with a bang, all at once. After the previous night's humiliation, her face when it happened was the only thing in the world that he wanted to see even more than the fire itself.

Ganz loved fire. He'd loved it for as long as he could remember. As early as the age of thirteen he'd begun to steal cars and then run them down to the stolen-car graveyard by the river outside town. Other kids who took cars went for rides and then abandoned them in fields, but for Ganz it was always straight to the river in the shortest time so that he could pull out the fuel lines and set fire to the engine. The engine would blaze and the windscreen would pop and melt, and after a while the heat would set off the fuel in the tank and that was the most satisfying part of all as the fireball leapt forward through the car and burst out of every seam. Then the slower process of cremation, as everything in the car was rendered down. The body to a blistered shell, the tires to coils of blackened wire. He'd stay around to watch and sometimes he'd stay around for too long; that was how they'd first caught him, at the age of seventeen, when he'd torched a Corvette from one of the American bases and realized a childhood dream.

Axel Reineger knew nothing of what Ganz was doing now. As far as Reineger was concerned he was supposed to be out here keeping lookout, not draining off the farm's oil tank and splashing it around as an overnight marinade for all the foundation timber that he could cover. Ganz was pretty well convinced that neither Jansen nor the Englishman would be coming back. Jansen he knew, and as for the Englishman ... well, why should *he* return? The kid wasn't even his own.

He held the jerrican under the spout, and waited as it slowly filled. There was just about enough light from the single downward-angled flood over the door of the main house. He'd lost count of the number of times he'd done this, now. A dozen, at least. He'd done half of the house and most of the outbuildings and then he'd started on the cow shed.

The spigot was stiff, and his big hand was getting sore from turning it on and off. As the weight of the jerrican increased, he leaned over to look at the transparent indicator pipe on the side of the tank. It was supposed to show the level of oil remaining with a floating ball, but the pipe was clouded over and the ball was probably stuck somewhere in the wrong place anyway.

He shut off the spigot, and lugged the can over towards the cow shed to continue. At least, he thought he'd shut it off, but as he moved away he could hear a spattering behind him like the sound of someone taking a pee out in the open. He looked back; where the escaped oil caught the light from the house, it made rainbows on the cow shit. Ganz contemplated the beauty of it for a while, and was glad that his life had meaning.

Then he went on to the cattle shed.

Although the house was bland and not particularly old, the cattle shed was ancient and rickety. For a while, until it crumbled, it would probably be the centerpiece of his pyrotechnic display. The wood was soaking up fuel like a blotter. The results upon ignition would be amazing. Like a forest fire, or something. He'd seen a forest fire on television once, filmed at the end of a long, dry summer; the trees had seemed to explode spontaneously, one after another, as the irresistible wave of heat had swept along through them. His imagination could hardly wrap itself around the idea of starting something as big as that. You'd need to be everywhere at once, just to appreciate it.

As he sloshed the fuel onto the timberwork, he could hear the cattle inside moving uneasily in their pens. They were probably getting the smell, and wondering what it meant. Well, weren't *they* going to have a surprise. He'd never attempted anything on this kind of a scale before; stray cats and dogs in boxes had been the most he'd ever done, and that had been quite some years ago. He tried to imagine the racket and the panic in there when the building suddenly went up around them. A living barbecue; face it, he thought modestly, you're an artist.

Then he started to think of Frau Lüderssen and whether he dared, just *dared* to contemplate doing it with her trapped inside the house as well . . . he'd miss the expression on her face but he'd probably hear her screams, and maybe if he was to put her on a chain he might catch sight of her dancing around inside through the windows as well.

But he knew that it was a fantasy, a non-starter. Axel

wouldn't have it, for one. Although Ganz had to consider that he was beginning to worry less and less about what Axel might think, because Axel was starting to look more like a losing horse as the hours went by.

They'd met him on the road as he'd been walking away from that stupid party after the fat woman had clouted him in front of everyone. He'd have clouted her back, but then they'd all have been on him; and were he to be honest, it had been unexpected and mortifying and he hadn't been thinking straight right at that moment. Of the two men who'd picked him up, Jansen he knew already; Jansen was the one who always fixed up for him to get out of town whenever his continued presence became inadvisable. This latest occasion involved some antique pistols and was one that he didn't care to dwell on too much. Reineger he knew hardly at all, except as a bigger-fish version of Jansen. The offer they'd made him had seemed pretty good at the time. Better than farm work, anyway. But everything was falling apart, and it all seemed rather more like wild promises now.

The jerrican was almost empty. He started to shake the last few drips onto the wood.

"Hey, Ganz," he heard. *"Come on, shitface, look behind you."*

He didn't understand what had been said, but he'd heard his own name and he spun around. The last of the fuel spattered out in a circle around him.

The Englishman was standing there. Waiting. His coat was open and his hair was a mess and he looked wild. Excited. Hyped up like a junkie on a high. Ganz looked around for Jansen and the van, but there was no sign of either.

The Englishman pointed at him. Then he made a fist, and raised his eyebrows in inquiry.

Then he spat on the ground in front of him, his face making it pretty clear that this was an expression of an opinion, and then he turned around to walk away.

Ganz slung the jerrican aside, and stalked after.

By the time that Ganz had caught up, the Englishman had already gone into the barn. The electric lights came on just as Ganz hit the threshold and he stopped, his night-tuned eyes so dazzled that they hurt, and he had to take a step back. This was the one part of the farm that he hadn't bothered with; sheet steel and a fiberglass roof, there was stuff here that might burn but nothing that would be too spectacular.

His vision began to adjust. The Englishman was heading over towards the far side of the barn, shrugging out of his overcoat. Ganz started forward. This was long overdue. He'd taken against the Englishman from the moment he'd first set eyes on him. He looked rough, and he looked reasonably strong. But he wasn't hard, not the way that Ganz was. Ganz had never been beaten in a fight, ever. He'd been outclassed and he'd been downed, but then his opponents had always made the mistake of turning around to walk away.

Ganz stopped, and stared in disbelief at the ground.

A ring of about three yards across had been drawn in powder—white lime, perhaps, or fertilizer—on the barn's dirt floor. Its edges wavered, betraying the unsteadiness of the hand that had poured it, but it was a ring nonetheless. A boxing ring. What did he think this was, one of those English public schools? Ganz decided then that he was going to hold the Englishman upside down like a wheelbarrow and make him eat it. The moment he put his fists up, Ganz would go for his undercarriage and then they'd take it from there.

Right now, the Englishman was folding his coat with fastidious precision. He seemed to be intending to hang it up somewhere on the wall.

Ganz kicked up the white dust and cracked all his knuckles.

"This will hurt," he promised, knowing that he wouldn't be understood.

The Englishman looked back over his shoulder and saw Ganz there in the ring, swinging his arms to warm up.

"You first," he said with an equal likelihood of comprehension, and he removed a chain from a cleat to make way for his coat.

It was like magic. As soon as it left his hand, the chain seemed to vanish.

Ganz had maybe a second to think about this. He vaguely registered the sound of the tackle spinning overhead and that, if he'd been able to think about it for a few moments longer, might have given him some idea of what was coming.

But then the tractor bucket hit him, and this was all that he knew.

CHAPTER 71

They'd been let out of the cupboard twice that evening, once to eat and once to use the toilet. Otherwise, they'd had to sit there in the darkness. The dust made Marianne want to sneeze all the time, but it didn't happen and that made the feeling worse. There was just enough room for the three of them to sit on the floor, pressed close together with their knees up under their chins, but there was no space for stretching out or changing position. When stiffness became pain, which didn't take long, all that they could do was shuffle around and ease it in a very limited way. In addition to all this, the cupboard was hot and airless.

Ellinor was taking it the worst. She was sobbing quietly, constantly. Frau Lüderssen was silent, apart from the occasional *Shh, shh,* accompanied by a comforting pat on her daughter's back or shoulder. To Marianne she said nothing. Marianne knew that she probably blamed the two of them, Ryan and herself, for everything that had happened in the past few hours.

She wondered what was going to happen next. Ryan had been due back at the beginning of the evening, but he hadn't appeared. The man in the soiled white shirt, tense and watchful all afternoon, had become increasingly nervy as time went by.

Marianne herself was calm. She had no doubts. Ryan had made a promise that he'd come back and get her, and that everything would be all right. He'd never broken one of his promises to her yet, going right back to the time when Rudi had come home just like he'd said.

There in the darkness, she thought about her dog. She thought about all the things she'd once had, and had no more. And as she reflected, she found herself repeatedly going back to keep touch with that central idea.

That Ryan would return as he'd promised, and they'd go on from there.

The cupboard door suddenly opened.

All three of them looked up, blinking. The man in the dirty white shirt was standing there with that ugly cut-down gun in his hand. He reached in, grabbed Marianne by the arm, and hauled her out. Then he slammed the door again on the others. Marianne saw their upturned faces for a moment, and then they were gone.

Her legs were weak and tingling, and could hardly support her as he half pushed, half dragged her through the house. He'd been here only a few hours, and in that short time he'd turned it into a pigsty. They'd been able to hear him having a fit of temper earlier, flinging things around. She wondered where the other man was.

He signaled to her to be quiet. She rubbed her arm. It hurt where he'd gripped her.

He said, almost in a whisper, "It seems your friend is back, and he wants to play games. Unfortunately for him, I'm not in the mood."

She looked around. She saw no one. The man turned her and, with his hand on her shoulder, started to march her forward. She tried to shrug his hand off because it hurt, but he squeezed harder.

He was walking her towards the barn, she realized. There were lights on in there. He had her out in front of him, using her like a shield. The strange gun with the taped handle was in his other hand. He prodded her in the back with it a couple of times to encourage her along.

One of the barn's doors was open. Nothing moved inside. The man pulled her to a halt, and then over her head he called out Ganz's name.

Nothing.

"I think I can see him," she began to say, but his hand clamped over her mouth and silenced her.

He moved her along slightly, changing their angle of view. Now they could see clearly that Ganz lay on the barn's dirt floor. One arm was outstretched. In his hand was what appeared to be a large brown envelope. He looked as if he'd been dropped in his tracks like a bull in an abattoir, but there was no sign of how.

Without any warning, Marianne was suddenly propelled forward through the open doorway and into the barn.

She stumbled, almost falling. There was a flurry of movement in the corner of her eye and she let out a scream as something came towards her; she looked up just in time to see Ryan hitting the brakes and swinging to miss with the length of timber that he'd been about to use to club her down. He twisted. He lost his balance. The makeshift club hit the floor and then the man in the dirty white shirt stepped in from the night and, before Ryan could rise, he slammed him to the ground with a blow from the gun's hardwood stock.

Now the man aimed a kick at Ryan's head, but Ryan managed to take it on his raised arm instead. In fury, Marianne flew at the man and launched herself at him with a running leap; and then suddenly she was flying backwards and seeing stars as he knocked her aside with his elbow. She hit the ground like a sack.

He stood there, the gun leveled as the two of them slowly managed to sit upright.

"What are you doing?" he said. "You're both as mad as each other!"

Ryan blinked, unable to understand. He shook his head as if to get water out of his ears, and then seemed to be sorry that he'd done it. Marianne didn't bother to translate.

Still covering them with the shotgun, the man went over to Ganz and crouched by him. Ganz groaned, but didn't stir. His head was bleeding and he seemed well out of it. The man took the envelope from his hand, at which point the envelope unraveled and revealed itself as a folded strip from a paper fertilizer sack.

"You can tell him that it isn't even the right color," the man said contemptuously, and he tossed it aside.

Ryan glanced at Marianne. "Are you all right?" he said, and she nodded. "What about the Lüderssens?"

"Shut up," the man said. "And stand up."

And he gestured for them to rise.

CHAPTER 72

"Sei ruhig," the man said. *"Und steh auf."* And he gestured for them to rise.

Ryan looked at Marianne again. "What was that?"

"He wants us to be quiet and to get up."

Ryan was of the opinion that the sawn-off gave Axel Reineger a certain natural authority in such matters, so he didn't argue. He clambered to his feet, and helped Marianne to do the same. He saw her looking at the dried blood on his shirt cuffs and the raw skin around his wrists.

As soon as they were standing, he let his sleeves drop to cover them.

Reineger spoke again, and Marianne translated. "He wants to know what happened."

"Tell him we nearly got back here, but the van broke down." He hadn't anticipated having to do this, and it was the best he could come up with in a hurry. The part about the van breaking down had to be credible enough, at least.

He added, "It's at the bottom of the hill, and the driver's trying to get it fixed. He's held onto the envelope and that's why I don't have it here."

Marianne began to translate again, but this time Axel talked across her and she had to break off and say, "I don't think he believes any of this."

Ryan couldn't exactly blame him. "Tell him this, then. The police were watching the cabin. They started to follow me back. Once they knew where I was heading for, they picked me up. They kept the envelope. I got away."

Marianne said, "Is that what really happened?" Ryan nodded. Then she retold it for Axel's benefit.

Ryan could see that this version was being believed. Axel Reineger's eyes went hard and calculating, like a cornered animal's. He glanced out into the night before he spoke again, gesturing them towards the door with the sawn-off.

"He says we've got to walk in front of him," Marianne explained. "Back to the house."

They started to move.

Reineger stayed several paces behind them as they left the barn and started towards the yard light that shone down from the back of the house.

As they walked, Ryan said quietly, "We're not going into the house with him, understand? We do that, and we're just hostages."

Axel interrupted then, and Ryan added, "Say I'm telling you not to be scared."

She half glanced back over her shoulder, and said as much. There was no reaction from Reineger and so Ryan went on. "That's a sawn-off shotgun he's holding. For anything beyond ten yards it's useless; the shot just scatters everywhere."

"How do you know that?"

"I was on a ward with a boy who shot his mother. He used a sawn-off. He'd cut it down himself. He said it scattered so much, the pellets made the shape of her on the wall like a shadow."

"Did it kill her?"

"No." They were more than halfway now, and their options were disappearing fast. He put his hand on her shoulder and said, "So I'll count to three . . ."

"Don't count," Marianne said quickly. "He'll know."

"Yeah, right. I'll do the names of the Three Stooges instead."

"Who?"

"It doesn't matter who they are, it's just a way to count to three."

"Do Donald Duck's nephews, then."

Twenty yards to go.

"I don't *know* Donald Duck's nephews."

"Well, *I* don't know the Three Stooges."

"Forget it," Ryan said. "Let's just go." And instead of heading for the main door, he launched her in the direction of the cattle shed where they could dive down the gap between that and the house and be out into the fields within moments.

There was a shout. They were running now. Ryan could almost sense Axel's aim tracking up his back as the gun was brought to bear, a point of heat like the red dot of a laser . . . and he actually heard the *click* of the double hammers being drawn, and realized they weren't quite going to make it and so he grabbed Marianne by the collar and threw her down onto the ground and landed heavily on top of her just as the blast came, shockingly loud and terrifyingly close. Pellets whistled over them like white-hot birds. Some of them ripped into his coat and penetrated deep into his back and shoulder like driven hail. From under his arm he could see Axel stopping and taking proper aim this time; Marianne was squirming for air underneath him, but he hunched up and bore down in a vain attempt to insure that none of her, no part of her at all, could be exposed to Axel's fire. . . .

And then there was a howl, as of stripping gears. Headlights raked across the yard, and Axel began to turn in surprise. Jansen's white van came up out of nowhere, braking and skidding around so hard that two wheels lifted off the ground and it almost turned over.

Even as Axel turned, the moving shotgun discharged into the ground.

Instantly, the ground took fire.

It ran like a series of detonations, each bigger than the last and all with Axel at their center. Without hesitating at all, Ryan got Marianne up onto her feet and half ran, half carried her before the expanding fireball that the yard had suddenly become. The van's doors had been thrown open and men in spacesuit armor were jumping out, but they were too late; a sequence had started that no human agency could now halt, and instead of attacking they too were running for their lives.

Ryan's last, indelible image was a brief flash-photograph of Axel Reineger leaping at the heart of an inferno; his high, shrill, vibrating scream could be heard as a kind of harmonic to the explosion while his running body in the middle of it was a stick figure drawn in charcoal on a brilliant background.

He propelled Marianne on, away from the blistering heat. But the heat came on after. They were heading for the cattle shed when Ryan remembered how Ganz had been there last with the jerrican, and he turned her away just as it caught. One entire end wall went up, sucking in wind as the flames appeared and then sending it all out again as a belching wave of heat. The cows were bellowing inside, but there was nothing he could do for them.

"Come on," he shouted to Marianne, "stay close to me!"

But she'd her hands clamped over her ears so his yelling went unheard. He probably couldn't have competed with the roar of the firestorm anyway.

They hit the fields, running into their own long shadows. The farm was going up like a beacon that would be visible for miles.

Ryan realized, with some dismay, that he was hurt.

This was at about the same moment that the remaining fuel in the farm's tank reached flashpoint. It sent out a jet of boiling flame that lifted and spread in the air like a napalm burst.

CHAPTER 73

Jennifer's car went up the hill as part of the third wave, following the strike teams and the field ambulances and behind just about everybody else who was essential to the operation. But at least she was getting there; Cadogan had to stay back in the village, and she could only imagine how he'd be reacting to that. The burning farm was lighting up the underside of the sky like some huge diorama, burnt chrome on petrol blue. Even seen from here, it was raging so hard that it seemed to be intent on searing its way down into the earth.

The convoy suddenly halted and for a moment she couldn't see why, and then it was upon them; it was a stampede, a real honest-to-God stampede of panicking cattle coming at them down the hill and not even slowing as they met the cars head-on in the narrow lane. The drivers could only brake as the oncoming wall of livestock divided, just, and then thundered by with a pounding of beef against metal that rocked Jennifer's vehicle on its springs. A wing mirror came spinning and bouncing over the roof of the car in front, and everybody flinched instinctively as it ricocheted off the windscreen and away into the night. A chip flew out of the glass, but the rest of it didn't break; the buffeting continued with nothing but walls of living, moving hide to be seen anywhere and in any direction, and then suddenly the last of the beasts had gone by and the car before them was restarting its stalled engine.

Nobody spoke. Jennifer realized that she'd been holding her breath. She let it out quietly, and straightened in her seat. Werner was looking out of the back window, but there was nothing more to be seen.

They went on.

When they got close to the top, they saw that one of the policemen from the local force was waving all the traffic over into one of the fields. There was no gateway, but an entrance had been made by breaking through the fence and the hedgerow behind it. The scene as she climbed out of the car gave her incongruous feelings of nostalgia and awe; there was nothing in her life that it resembled more than her memories of big public bonfires in the park, with the burning timbers stacked higher than most houses—to her eyes, at least—and the onlookers a ring of people-shaped silhouettes at a safe distance from its power. Something burst, sparks blew. The house was raging now, window openings pumping it out under high pressure. The cattle shed was a skeletal negative in the brilliance, reduced to the thinnest of bones and just now beginning to crumble. The heat was like a wall, even from here.

Rilke had traveled up as part of the second wave, in the company of the local police commander. She couldn't see either of them now, but there was so much chaos that it was hardly surprising. The local firefighters had given up on the blaze and were spraying the trees and the fields downwind, hoping to prevent any spread; sparks flew over their heads, illuminating them like foundry workers. Two ambulances with their rear doors open had become emergency first aid centers where SEK members armed and prepared for one kind of crisis were being treated for the effects of another: burns, exhaustion, smoke inhalation. They'd gone ahead and stormed the burning building anyway, and had dragged out alive its owner and her daughter. Another man had been found in the barn; according to one of the radio messages, he'd suffered a depressed skull fracture but in spite of that he'd been semiconscious, if not coherent. He hadn't responded to anybody's questions, but he'd wept and howled when they'd closed the ambulance doors and he was no longer able to see the fire.

She saw Rilke at last. He was having something pointed out to him on the open ground before the farm where it seemed, impossibly, that even the earth was ablaze. Nobody could get too close, but the burning figure was still recognizable in its general shape. A human being, fallen. Drawn up tight as if in an endless pain that lasted beyond even death, and cooking to ashes. She'd seen the usual news pictures of immolations, of petrol-doused students and monks who burned themselves to death as a public spectacle. But in their cases the cameras always cut away after a while, usually when the life had left their bodies. This went on. And on.

No firm news on Ryan O'Donnell. Nor on Marianne Cadogan.

Jennifer took a deep breath. The air was hot and choking, even standing upwind. Sirens could be heard across the countryside as extra forces headed through the night to give support.

Perhaps they were in there, somewhere. It would be hours before they'd know.

If they were, then it was over.

So Jennifer could only hope that it wasn't over yet.

CHAPTER 74

Marianne watched the sunrise from the side of the road. Ryan was still sleeping in the car, and she didn't want to wake him until she had to. He'd been exhausted, his head dropping forward over the wheel and then snapping back up again just as the car had started to drift. They'd stopped around four o'clock. Now it was almost eight.

For most of the last hour she'd been sitting on the corner of a wooden picnic table on the grass by the *Parkplatz*. She was supposed to be writing, but she'd spent most of the time looking out over the landscape. They were pretty high up here, and the view went on for miles. It was a rolling terrain, a patchwork of fields and forests with a skyline that aspired to be mountainous but which was just a shade too gentle to achieve it. Patchy cloud overhead translated into patchy sunlight that moved slowly across the land, rising and falling with its contours and briefly touching each of its parts into a more vivid life.

She looked back at the car. No sign of activity. Part of her didn't want to break up this moment; she didn't want to be the one who moved things along, knowing now that they could be moving only in one direction and that in it lay some kind of an ending.

It had to end now, didn't it?

She could see that. She'd come to realize that the future she'd imagined them building was a future made out of a child's bricks, brightly colored and with no sharp edges. The reality was darker and more complex, and would be far less susceptible to any one person's control. In realizing this she supposed that, perhaps, she'd started to grow up. She hadn't ever wanted to, but it was happening to her anyway. The loss that she'd once feared so much had become a reality now, and it had stolen upon her without even being noticed. You stopped being the dream, and instead you became the dreamer; and when the dream was no longer you, then you could only watch as it started to die.

She climbed down from the picnic bench and walked over towards the car. Ryan had reclined the driver's seat as far as it would go and was lying there now, having half turned onto his side. He'd curled up as much as he could and was holding his coat shut over his face, his big tattooed fist clenched in the material like a baby's. She'd tried to tell him that he ought to get into the back and rest properly before they went on, but he'd insisted that he was only going to close his eyes for ten minutes. That had been almost four hours ago, and he was sleeping still.

She watched him for a while. She shivered slightly. She watched him until he started to stir; he looked up and saw her through the door window, and then she went around the car and climbed in to sit beside him.

He said, "How long was I asleep?"

"Not long."

"Have you seen anybody?"

"No."

He looked out of the back of the car, with its view of the long and mostly empty road.

"We've lost them, then," he said, yawning and starting to rack his seat back up into a driving position. "We can still work this out. Everything's going to be fine."

"I know," Marianne said.

She smiled back at him, but it wasn't easy for her to do. She saw him grimace as he reached under the dash for the hanging wires to restart the car. She knew that he'd taken some damage back at the farm, but he was doing his best not to let it show.

"You're still bleeding," she said. Apart from the obvious places where his coat had been shredded, the only outward signs of injury were the specks of blood that had smeared on his neck like free-running shaving cuts.

"I know," he said. "I don't know why it won't stop. It's really nothing."

The Golf sparked and the engine turned over a few times, and then it caught. It was the car that had brought in farm wives and supplies on the last day of the haymaking; they'd taken it from the next property while everyone had been around the other side of the buildings, watching the fire.

They pulled out onto the road. He didn't look until it was too late, but there was nothing coming anyway. He could do all the mechanical stuff and he could make the car go, but he didn't seem to be much of a driver. Marianne doubted whether he'd ever had any lessons or taken a test back home, let alone held a license.

"I wish you'd stayed behind," he said suddenly.

Trying to keep the tone light, Marianne said, "Who'd look after you?"

But he was shaking his head.

"It's changed again, Marianne," he said. "And every time it changes, it gets more difficult to carry on. Now we've got to start looking for a way to end it. You understand that, don't you?"

She didn't answer. They were passing through another red-roofed, oak-beam-and-redbrick town with a clock tower and a church and a bridge over its river, the newer houses like little Monopoly pieces in white on its outskirts. There was almost no traffic, so that even a driver like Ryan would be hard pressed to find something to hit. So many of these places looked the same, but somehow . . . well, it was hard to say for certain, but somehow Marianne was sure that they'd passed through this one before.

When she saw some cleared land and a closed-down transit drivers' clubhouse no more than five hundred yards beyond the edge of town, she became certain that they had.

"When did we eat?" Ryan said abruptly. "We haven't, have we? What've I been thinking of?"

There was nowhere to stop for a while, but when they'd picked up a bigger highway and came to a moderately busy service area, he turned in. They'd passed a police car by the side of the road about ten minutes back, blue lights flashing a warning and its officer in attendance on a red sedan. The sedan had one wheel missing and its rear end down on the ground. The uniformed man hadn't looked their way. Marianne wasn't even sure whether Ryan had been aware of the vehicle, let alone its driver.

They entered a parking area overlooked by an old-fashioned and quite sizable motel. Beside it was a long, low building with a corrugated asbestos roof, and that was a mini-supermarket. Over by the road and under the trees there was a circular snack kiosk like a fairground ticket booth. Among the trees were roofed picnic benches, only one of them occupied. There were big plans for the development of the area—a new twenty-foot billboard in front of the hotel said so—but nothing much seemed to be happening yet.

When he'd stopped the car, Ryan carefully went through his pockets. She knew that he'd no papers and nothing much in the way of money, because the police had taken everything. What he got together was all of his loose change, which he handed to her.

"Take this," he said. "See what you can get for yourself."

"What about you?"

"I'm not hungry," he said. "Really." And then he said, "I think I'll just go and be taking a look in the shop."

He didn't actually push her out of the car, but the feeling was the same. Once out she took a step back and watched him, wondering if this was some pretext to dump her and drive away. But he held onto the wheel for a few seconds as if gathering his strength, and then seemed to kick himself into gear as abruptly as if he'd just engaged the energy of some dangerously free-spinning inner flywheel.

He got out of the car.

"Go on," he said to her. "I'll see you back here."

The tiny weeping cuts on his neck had leaked down. The collar of his shirt was stained. But then he turned up his coat, and the vivid flash of red was hidden.

The kiosk had a radio playing loudly through a couple of speakers on a shelf outside. There was a blackboard listing the usual schnitzels and wiener and *fischbrotchen*. Counter service was by a teenage girl in a white blouse and with long, dark wavy hair. There wasn't much that Marianne could afford, but she picked what she could from the menu. It wasn't an expensive place. There was a dispenser by the service window that looked like a bubble-gum machine and was selling real wristwatches at a Deutschmark each.

As she was waiting for the food, Marianne looked back across the parking area. Right over at its far end were a number of travelers' vans, and the small children playing on the asphalt nearby looked as if they might be genuine ethnic Gypsies. Then a movement caught her eye.

It was Ryan. He was shambling around uncertainly and looking lost. She threw down the money, gathered everything up, grabbed some paper napkins, and then went over to him. He was wandering up and down the rows of cars, unable to find their own.

She took his arm.

"Over here, Ryan," she said. "It's this one over here."

She steered him towards the Golf. She wondered whether they were being watched by the girl from the kiosk, but she didn't dare to look. There was something that had been shoved inside his coat, and she wondered if he'd been shoplifting. If he had, she hoped that he'd picked up a first aid kit, because she couldn't imagine anything that they needed more.

They got into the car. Marianne climbed into the back so that she could spread everything out on the seat and then hand stuff forward to him. It was the usual cheap bread, cheap sausage—not much else.

He unbuttoned his coat. From inside it, he pulled out a soft toy.

"I just remembered," he said. "I got you this."

"What is it?"

"It's supposed to be a lion," he said, holding it out. "Like the one on the front of that book you take everywhere."

He meant *Der König von Narnia*. Her copy was back at the Lüderssen farm, probably reduced to ashes by now. She wasn't even aware that he'd noticed it.

"At the farm the other night, I realized that I've never given you anything."

"You don't have to," she said.

"It's a present anyway. Is it the kind of thing you like?"

She nodded.

"Take it, then."

She took it.

They started to eat. Marianne sat with her fluffy and barely recognizable lion, but found that most of her attention was taken by Ryan. He was picking the food apart, making attempts at it like someone who was only just beginning to learn.

She said, "What's the plan, now?"

"We just keep moving. If we can keep moving, it'll come to me."

She didn't know how to reply. They couldn't keep moving forever. The needle on the car's fuel gauge was hovering close to empty as it was, and they'd no money for more. They wouldn't even last out the morning.

And then, without changing his manner but with what seemed like a sudden flash of lucidity, Ryan said, "Listen. However this turns out ... whatever becomes of me ... you *will* tell them how it really was, won't you?" He looked at her then. "Because, you and me ... we're the only ones who really know."

"I'll tell them," she said.

"Promise me."

"I promise."

"And we don't break our promises, do we?" he said.

And she could only shake her head.

She could see that a police car—perhaps the same one that they'd passed some way back on the road—was making the turn into the parking area. It slowed momentarily as one of the Gypsy children ran across in front of it. Ryan had his back to the windscreen, and hadn't seen it at all.

She waited until it had passed out of sight before she gathered some of their waste paper together and slid out over the passenger seat and through the door. "Wait a minute. I've got to get rid of this."

He didn't object.

Marianne looked around her as she walked towards the motel. She could see the police car beginning a slow cruise of the rows from down at the far end, but she tried not to panic. A battered yellow box streaked with rust stood beside the billboard. As she was feeding the papers into this, she kept looking back. It may be routine, she was thinking; they'd come so far that perhaps no one around here knew to be looking for them or their car.

But how far *had* they come, really? They'd been circling a lot, she knew that much. Ryan seemed to be under the impression that he'd been heading for freedom like an arrow, but the truth of it was that they might not even have left the area. Marianne had no sure way of telling.

The car was cruising their own row, now. She hesitated. She wondered if this might be it. It was the same feeling that she'd had all that way back on the sandbar, kneeling there and hugging Rudi and knowing that whatever might happen to the two of them that afternoon, the dog's days were numbered and there was nothing, no human agency or force of will, that could reverse the process of his departure. It might have been that day or it might have been the next; but the certainty was that it would happen, and soon.

The grownup thing to do would be to end it now. There was only one way that this could go, and even Ryan had shown that he knew it, deep down. She could flag down the *Polizei* car and it would be over within a minute. Quick. Clean. Kind.

Kind as a bullet, or a lethal injection.

She couldn't help remembering how they'd dealt with him back there in the lane as they'd marched him out of his home. Their faces, already set in judgment on what they handled. That hand on his head, roughly thrusting him into the car. She'd promised that she'd tell them. But she couldn't promise him that they'd listen.

The green-and-white passed the Golf. Ryan had closed his eyes and slumped down in his seat for a moment, and the driver didn't seem to see him. As soon as the car had gone, she ran over.

Ryan's eyes opened as she jumped into the passenger seat.

"A police car just went by," she said.

He straightened up and looked around in surprise. "Where?"

"Don't panic. He only seems to be driving around. I don't think he noticed you."

"Where is he now?"

"Down at the other end," she said. "We can be gone by the time he comes around again."

So Ryan reached down for the wires and restarted the car.

CHAPTER 75

By the time that daylight had arrived and it had become obvious that the search was going to have to be widened once more, they'd already begun to relocate the command center from the village barn to the main *Polizei* building in the next big town. At any other time, the facilities that Jennifer saw would have a certain antique charm about them. Like a telephone system that had been installed in the 1920s and had stood largely unimproved ever since. Or a fleet of heavy, underpowered Ladas that could knock down brick walls but would be useless in a pursuit. Rilke was working in close cooperation with the local police chief but was, strictly speaking, under his authority—as were the SEK men, equivalent to a SWAT team or a Tactical Support Unit, that Rilke had brought with him. They'd a special order permitting them to work outside their usual area. Jennifer's status, as previously, was that of observer/advisor and nothing more.

Her last sight of the barn had been of a place stripped of equipment but still a center of activity, with night-shift police and firefighters gathered there to wind down. The fire had threatened to spread beyond even where they'd been able to damp down, and they'd had to recruit volunteer beaters to work over a wider area; when the buses had come back from the fields at dawn, it had taken Jennifer a few moments to realize that Cadogan was among them, smoke-blackened and accepted. She'd watched him chatting with the others for a while, the barriers between police and civilian lowered, and she'd had no doubt that he was scratching around for whatever information he could find. Well, good luck to him, she'd thought, and then she'd moved out to where her car had been waiting to take her on.

So, this was to be the new operations center. It looked like some preserved war room—maps, antique telephones, and all. In a cleared space on one of the desks, bagged up and relatively uncharred, were a shotgun and shells that had been taken out of the farmhouse along with Frau Lüderssen and her daughter. There was the burned ruin of a sawn-off, as well, similarly bagged.

Rilke was standing there with his hands in his pockets, looking at them. His suit jacket had gone, probably smoke-stained and ruined. He was wearing a dark military-style pullover instead.

Jennifer said, "What's the problem?"

"The guns and those shells don't match," he said. "Whether that means there was another gun in the farmhouse, I really don't know."

"Why don't you just ask the woman?"

"I did. First she said yes, then she said no, now she's saying that she can't be sure. Her husband had five shotguns altogether, but his brother took the best ones after her husband died. We're going to have to assume that O'Donnell could be armed."

"Armed and dangerous?"

He looked at her with eyebrows raised.

"Well," he said, "I think he's answered that one for us already, don't you?"

Two rooms away, Werner was watching the newly installed fax machine and wondering if, this time, the completed message would make it through. There had been a number of transmission errors, but from what he'd seen already, this was material that would pull the investigation to an early conclusion. He'd already sent someone to find Rilke. As he was waiting for the machines to reconnect, he looked through the pages that had arrived so far.

They weren't easy to decipher. Apart from being handwritten, they seemed to consist of a number of scraps and paper bags, and these had been covered with scrawl in a hurry. As far as he could make out, it was the kidnapped girl's own account of what had happened—rushed, compressed, unreadable in places, but with certain essential specifics like the make and the number of the car in which they were traveling.

Rilke appeared behind him. Werner handed over what he had. Others were coming from the machine now. They'd been photocopied for transmission; the originals were on their way over by motorcycle.

"Where's this from?" Rilke said.

"A rest area on the main north-south highway," Werner said. "Somebody pushed it all into a mailbox there. The sorting office thought it was rubbish, nearly threw it away."

He handed the final page to Rilke. This part appeared to have been written with difficulty on a paper napkin. He'd glanced through it only once, but already he thought that he could recall it word for word. *Er ist ein guter Mann. Er hat sich und mich gekümmert und mich beschützt. Er hat nichts falsch gemacht. Bitte tun Sie ihm nicht weh.*

He is a good man. He has looked after me and protected me. He has done nothing wrong. Please do not hurt him.

Rilke made a tight fist, a restrained punch-in-the-air of victory. *Yes.*

"Let's go and get him," he said.

CHAPTER 76

"Can we stop?" Marianne said.

"I don't think that it's a good idea," Ryan said. He seemed to be leaning forward oddly, too close to the wheel. As if it hurt him to sit back, but the fact hadn't actually registered in his mind yet.

"Just for a minute? I'm not very good in cars."

He looked at her for a moment too long. "Really?"

"I'm all right for a while and then I start feeling sick. I just want to walk around and get some fresh air."

"Open the window," he said. "I'll stop as soon as I see somewhere."

They'd been climbing steadily for a while, into hill country as densely wooded as rain forest. Every now and again, a castle would seem to rise with abrupt suddenness out of the greenery on one of the peaks. They were many-spired, and built of yellow stone. Fantasy creations, and far beyond reach.

They came to a place where the roadside had been cleared as if ready for construction work, raw dirt pushed back around the edges and the tracks of a bulldozer still visible on the ground. Ryan slowed, and turned off onto it. Out here in the middle of nowhere, Marianne couldn't imagine what they could be planning to build.

She waited until Ryan had stopped the engine before she got out of the car. She was really beginning to worry about him now. As far as she could tell, he was just heading onward for the sake of movement; going nowhere, running like a wounded stag until only exhaustion or the pursuing pack would bring him down. She'd tried to steer the conversation around to it a couple of times—to their situation, that was, and their rapidly

411

narrowing range of options for getting out of it—but both times she'd met a wall. He'd go deaf, or he'd change the subject. Her one big fear was that it was all a blind and that he was actually going to start looking for the opportunity to take off without her. He'd be doing it for her safety, of course. But if that happened, she didn't even want to *think* what they might do to him when they finally caught up.

His best insurance was to have her along. His only insurance, as she saw it now. She wondered if her account had made it to the right people yet. Once they'd realized how it really was, they'd have to look at him differently.

Until then . . .

She stood at the edge of the cleared area and looked down. Before and below her was the great vista of the river valley that they'd left behind, the river uncoiling in a ribbon of mirrored sky along its floor. Here and there, following the rise of the land, it was possible to glimpse the road wherever it turned.

And from here she could see that two or three bends back, following about a mile behind them, there came an army.

Truck after truck, car after car, motorcycle outriders as well. They came into view and they passed out of sight again, each briefly glimpsed as they took the curve. Seen like this, they were like an endless and otherwise well-hidden parade. The convoy was moving slowly, steadily, pacing rather than pursuing.

She started to try to count them, but there were too many.

"Oh, my God," Ryan said dully from behind her.

He tried to get back to the car ahead of her, but Marianne was faster and was already in her seat by the time that he was climbing in.

"Look, Marianne," he said. "This is all way out of control. Stay here and let them pick you up. Please."

"Only if you stay here with me."

"I can't. I can't go through all that again."

"Then wherever you go, I go with you too. They won't hurt you if I'm in the way."

She reckoned that he ought to know her well enough by

now to understand that she meant it. He started to try to argue, but time was limited and the arguments weren't there.

Marianne looked at the gauge as Ryan, with a helpless gesture of resignation, restarted the car. The gauge had been reading empty for most of the last half-hour.

They bumped over the ruts and back onto the road.

"What do you think you're going to do?" Marianne said.

Ryan had no answer.

Marianne saw the car before he did. It was an ordinary-looking van with a lone male driver, but the radio antenna gave it away. He came up behind them slowly, and then hung back. Ryan told her not to stare and to face forward, and then he kept an eye on the mirror.

"He'll be like a scout," he said. "They've sent him on to have a look at us and we're not supposed to know."

The scout car matched their speed for a while, and then started to overtake. Marianne glanced at Ryan. He was pale, and he was sweating. The van drew level and, as it passed them, Marianne got a look at its driver. He'd short, cropped hair and he was wearing dark glasses. He didn't look in their direction once, but pulled in ahead and then started to accelerate.

"There were others in the back," Marianne said.

"Really?"

"They were keeping right down, but there were at least two of them. What do you think they'll do now?"

"I don't know. Yes I do. They'll have the road blocked, further on. That's why the rest of them are hanging back. Because they've already picked the spot where it's going to happen and I'm supposed to be the last one to know."

The scout car reached the brow of the hill and then dropped out of sight. Before the brow a turnoff came up, signposted for some small town or village about two kilometers away.

Ryan took it.

CHAPTER 77

Cadogan had been trailing the others in his hired car like the unofficial last man in the convoy; he'd tagged along without invitation or authority, but as long as they were moving on public roads, there wasn't a lot that they could do to prevent him from following. He knew that something had gone wrong when he saw the leaders suddenly U-turning in the road ahead.

He might have known it. They'd all been so confident. Cadogan was of the opinion that a little humility in respect of the madman would have brought a result long before any of this had become necessary. Now the well-drilled, well-spaced formation of vehicles was suddenly braking and shunting and trying to turn around on itself; Rilke's car came dodging and weaving through and Cadogan had to brake with the others as it shot by, Rilke's driver leaning on the horn to force the way.

Then came the SEK, three men to a car, backwards and at top speed. Once clear of the pack, they spun around in their own length and followed Rilke. The outriders and some of the slower Russian-made sedans came after, the vans last of all.

Cadogan managed to get himself positioned somewhere in the middle, and he clung to his place until one of them almost rammed him off the road where the once-missed turnoff came. There he had the sense to wait, and to fall in behind them again.

The side road was narrow, descending through fields that were largely unfenced. It wound, following the contours of the land. Then the fields gave way to houses, and the houses to walls, and then the reformed and somewhat less well-ordered convoy was entering the town.

Two of the vans had blocked the road ahead, and they were

414

letting only police vehicles through. Cadogan slowed, and wound down his window. He recognized the officer who was controlling the traffic; they'd worked side by side in the smoke and the windblown sparks only a few hours before.

"I'm sorry, Herr Cadogan," the officer said. "But this time you can't go through."

"Can't you at least tell me what's happening?"

"He's still got her, that's about all we know for the moment. He had to abandon the car and they ran into the workings down there. The marksmen are going in after them."

"For what?"

"Please don't worry. They're the best there is."

Cadogan wasn't impressed. "I saw how well they controlled the situation last night."

"I'm not saying that you still can't get accidents. But they *do* know what they're doing. And most of them have families of their own."

"I should be there," Cadogan said, but the officer was shaking his head.

Cadogan said, "Do you have daughters, at all?"

"Don't ask me this," the man said. "I can't."

"Look the other way."

"No."

So then he had to slam the car into reverse, turn it around, and head off down a side street into another part of the town.

Hirschberg was a factory town. Half of its central area consisted of narrow, cobbled, winding streets with closely packed houses and a town square and much of the aura of a nineteenth-century village. The other half, separated by a high wall and covering at least as much ground, was a huge and rambling leather works built into the side of the hill.

Cadogan managed to leave his car in the parking area around some buff-colored municipal apartment houses, and he made his way down on foot to join the crowds. There were several vantage points from which the works could be observed, and people were gathering there for the free show. Most of them were men, and many of them were in two-piece blue coveralls as if they'd just left a shift, or had been pre-vented from starting one.

He eased his way through to the front, and looked down over a parapet of stone.

It was all laid out before him. The *Polizei* had set up a cor-don that included not only the factory but the road alongside it and several of the buildings adjacent to the road. Armed men were at the fence and on the ground, poised like snipers and watching the buildings over the barrels of their high-powered rifles. The central structure was like one great fortress with a clock tower and more glass windows than it was possible to count. There were high chimneys from the tanning sheds be-hind, railyards upslope, goods yards downslope.

The clock in the tower began to strike. It was answered, af-ter a lag of about a second, by another somewhere in the town.

At a guess, the place was working at only a fraction of its original capacity. The chimneys stood cold. All of the yards and the open working areas seemed to be disappearing under greenery. Weeds grew between the railway tracks. The *Polizei* appeared to be clearing the place for safety, but the column of workers and clerks hurrying out of the entrance tunnel under the main building wasn't exactly great in numbers.

She was somewhere inside.

Almost directly below him were the iron gates of the upper railyard. They'd been pushed inward by six feet or more, mak-ing a gap big enough for a person to get through. The gold-colored VW Golf that had rammed them was still in place, doors open and hood burst upward. Police in flak jackets were searching it, while others with machine pistols covered them.

"Is there anyone here who works in that place?" Cadogan said aloud to the people around him.

There was a slamming sound from down the street. Every-one turned to look. On the roof of a big, square, windowless building that faced the factory, police snipers were running across and taking up positions behind wooden ventilation tow-ers that resembled oversize beehives. This was the *Kulturhaus*, the factory-sponsored concert hall and best visible vantage point for observing the upper floors of the buildings opposite.

"Does anybody know their way around?" Cadogan said

loudly. "Somebody talk to me, please. A man's taken my daughter in there. I don't believe that he's going to hurt her, but I seem to be the only one who thinks so."

Most of them were looking at him now, with some curiosity.

"I don't have much time," he said.

"I work there," one of the men said. "Most of us do. What do you want to know?"

"I want to know how I can get past the police and get inside," Cadogan said.

CHAPTER 78

"Ryan!" she called out.

It had been getting darker and darker, the further they'd gone. Now it was as if the light had been withdrawn altogether. She'd stumbled over something; it felt like a rail, but it was impossible to see. She put out her hand and felt around. It *was* a rail, part of one of those narrow-gauge tracks that they used for pushing wagons around in quarries and mines. They weren't in the factory. They were in the tunnels under the factory, and these appeared to have been driven deep and extensively into the hillside.

She called his name again, and it echoed off down the shaft. There was no response. She began to panic then, because she thought that he'd taken the chance to abandon her in the darkness; but then she felt his grip on her arm, and he was helping her to rise.

"It's all right," he said, a disembodied voice from somewhere by her ear. "Just step carefully. You'll be all right."

"We can't keep going on this way," she said. "It's pointless. We're just going deeper and deeper."

"I know," Ryan said. "But don't you feel anything?"

She hesitated for a moment. She felt nothing other than his hand on her arm, and the pain in her knee where she'd scraped it on the rail.

"What?" she said.

"Clean air," he said. "That's how you tell there's some other way out. There's a breeze coming through, and it's got to be coming from somewhere."

She still felt nothing.

"Don't leave me alone in the dark," she said.

And Ryan said, "Don't worry."

CHAPTER 79

For a scratch operation, Rilke had been thinking that it hadn't come together too badly. They'd cleared the works and contained the situation, and now they controlled the area within which O'Donnell and his victim moved. It wasn't a perfect setup—the works was too big and too rambling—but at least it was better than what they'd had at the Lüderssen farm, where it had been impossible to throw an efficient cordon across open countryside in darkness with the number of men that had been available. This place had ways in and ways out, but all of them could be covered. O'Donnell might hide, but in the end he couldn't get away; the next move had to be the occupation of one section at a time until the two of them had been cornered and negotiations could begin.

Always assuming, of course, that O'Donnell lasted so long.

The man was unstable, and he was violent. He'd shown that he was capable of aggressively protective feelings towards the girl, but Rilke drew no comfort from the fact. Rats ate their young in response to the same kind of impulse, didn't they? And under the same kind of pressure, as well.

Rilke had a feeling that negotiations with such a man were unlikely to proceed along rational lines. O'Donnell hadn't impressed him much in the one meeting that they'd had; at least, not in the same order as the impression that he'd made on his four escorts at the time of his escape, or on Axel Reineger back there in the farmyard. Nothing much had remained of Reineger beyond a handful of teeth and a dark stain on the dirt.

It seemed that O'Donnell wasn't only deranged. He could be pretty damned thorough, as well.

After a few words with one of the SEK commanders, Rilke crossed the factory yard to the communications truck. The works manager was at the back of the wagon and was going over blueprints with two of his officers; the squad in the woodland beyond the complex was having some problem in locating the old and overgrown emergency exits from the tunnels. These had been dug for some purpose during wartime and never completed, and the tannery had been using them for storage ever since. Rilke saw little cause for worry, here. The one major exit had been blocked, the lane that served it vanished through disuse. And of only two vertical escape shafts, one was supposed to have collapsed while the other had never even made it through to daylight.

A careful visual search was being made of all levels before the controlled invasion began. Rilke listened to the messages coming in for a while, and then he said, "Let's see if we can't get the power turned on and some lights working in there. If they *have* moved down below, I'm not going to send my men into the dark where there's a wild animal waiting."

It was at that moment that he glanced out of the open back of the truck, just as several radio transmissions all started to come in at once. They cut over and canceled one another, and were joined by yelled warnings from several points overlooking the yard outside.

Patrick Cadogan was running from one of the outer complex buildings towards the main block.

He shouldn't have been able to get past the perimeter, but somehow he had. He was moving at speed, head down, arms pumping, and he seemed to know where he was going. At least a dozen gunsights had to be following him now, perhaps even more. Rilke held his breath. Would someone overreact? Fail to recognize Cadogan? Maybe take it upon himself to bounce a warning shot off the cobblestones before the running figure and, inadvertently, trigger a volley that would throw him around in one last frenetic dance before dropping him onto the ground?

No, Rilke said. But quietly, and to himself.

Cadogan hit a door. The door bounced open before him, and then he was inside.

The door closed slowly after, under its own weight.

A sense of relief could be felt throughout the limited space of the command vehicle.

"Tell them, well done, everyone," Rilke said to the radio operator. "This changes nothing. Watch out for Cadogan, but proceed as before."

There was a sound.

It came echoing along the tunnel, like a pebble rattling down a drain. There was no way of saying exactly what it was, or from how far away it had come. The only thing it signified for certain in Marianne's eyes was that they no longer had the place to themselves.

Barely a minute later, the lights came on.

She had to cover her eyes with her hand for a while; it was like being hit full in the face by the sunshine when someone— her mother, probably—had jerked open her bedroom curtains on a schoolday morning. There was the same sensation of being dumped, painfully and abruptly, from one world into another. Only this time, the feeling was more welcome; instead of being pulled from the security of her dreams, this was more like being rescued from the terror of a nightmare.

The pain went. The popping sensation in her vision diminished. She lowered her hand.

She'd been imagining that they were in some kind of a grubby mine shaft. But the tunnel was a plain-walled, even arch with a clean floor and a lot of pipes and cables running along it just above head height. The sides had been rendered, and the rendering painted white. The regularly spaced lighting that stretched on into the distance gave it an effect as ribbed and hollow as a throat.

"It goes on forever," Marianne said.

"The further it goes, the further away we can get," Ryan said, and he released his grip on her arm.

It didn't go on forever. It went on for about two hundred yards, and then another tunnel met it at an angle. Before they made the turn, Ryan wiped his nose on the back of his hand and she thought, for one moment, that she saw a thin streak of red across white. But then he wiped his hand on his coat and plodded on.

There were side branches, partitioned-off sections, entire suites of dusty and unused rooms. At one point there was a complete washroom, with all the doors unhooked from the toilet cubicles and rust stains on the bathing trough down its center. Barred gates blocked the way into unfinished excavations where enlargement of the complex appeared to have begun and then been abandoned. As they moved along, their own footsteps echoed around them with no sense of form or direction; surely, Marianne was thinking, surely any pursuer would have an easy time in tracking them down. He'd only have to stop, and listen, and then follow.

Then there was machinery. Big machines on concrete bases, cold furnaces and stilled pumps and air recirculators that resembled Victorian prototypes for the jet engine. Strange words and groups of figures had been stenciled onto their sides. Pieces of them were missing, so that lengths of duct hung emptily in the air. There were stacks of rails, stacks of wood, scaffolding, broken clay pipe. Marianne suddenly had the sense that they'd descended to a place that no human eye had ever been meant to see—that they'd come down into the workings of the world itself, of the engines that drove the planet, that pumped the air and drove the winds and moved the backcloth that they called the sky.

She said, "Ryan, I've been thinking."

"Well done," he said.

"No, I'm serious. I want to do a deal."

He looked down at her. "What kind of a deal?"

"I know you want to get rid of me now. You think it's for

my own good, but I won't go. So what I'm suggesting is, we keep on trying it your way just a little while longer, and if it doesn't work out . . ."

"Then, what?"

"Then you let me take you back to them."

He carried on looking down at her. He seemed tired now, his face gray and his eyes growing heavy-lidded. Then he started to shake his head slowly, not so much saying no as trying to show his regret that he couldn't say yes.

"That's not going to work," he said. "I'm sorry. It just isn't."

"You don't even know what you're doing."

"I can't go back," he said. "No one's ever going to understand."

"But I've told them," she said. "I've told them everything."

He seemed puzzled, then. He made as if to say something. But then he stopped himself, still trying to work out what it was she meant.

"While you were sleeping," she said, "I wrote the whole story down. About how it happened, and everything you did for me. I put it in the post box when you thought I was getting rid of the rubbish. And I know they've read it now, because I told them about the car and which way we were going and that's how they found us. I'm sorry I lied to you. Except I didn't lie, not really. I just didn't tell you. I think I did the right thing, Ryan. I know you may not think so. But I think I did."

He closed his eyes, as if in pain.

Then he turned unsteadily and started to walk away.

"Ryan!" she said, and ran after him.

She tried to get him to stop, but he only forged onward. She tried to get in front of him so that he'd have to stop and say something to her, but he sidestepped and left her standing, catching her as he passed and almost making her stagger.

They turned a last corner. Twenty yards ahead, the tunnel came to a dead end.

The wall was of concrete, with two bulkhead-style doors placed side by side. These were metal, painted gray, with massive hinges. Instead of a conventional handle, each had a wheel. It was the kind of wheel that could be screwed down to make a door airtight. To Marianne they didn't look as if they'd been moved in years, but with something that was almost a snarl Ryan fell upon the nearest and threw all his weight into trying to turn it.

Please, God, Marianne was thinking. Please don't let it move. Please let's end it right here.

Slowly, fractionally, the wheel began to move.

Ryan seemed to get new energy for his efforts. He needed it, because the action of the wheel didn't seem to get any easier. Blue-faced, straining, looking as if he was about to burst, he got it through a slow quarter-turn. He was like a man trying to lift a safe. But it was as if he'd sensed his last slim chance of freedom, and he was going to reach for it or kill himself in the attempt.

"Ryan, look!" she said.

He almost didn't listen. But he was regathering himself for his next big push, and he couldn't help but see where she was pointing.

At the lower edge of the door, water was starting to run.

It was brackish and green. It was coming down in about a dozen parallel rivulets and, even as he watched, the rivulets widened and merged and became a steadier trickle.

Higher up around the seal, a single tiny jetspray sprung out like a fountain.

Ryan stood there, holding onto the wheel for a minute or more. Water was streaming down around the door by now. The one arcing jet had become several, playing and shimmering like chains of silver. There was a shining pool on the floor, and it was spreading.

He released the wheel, took several staggering paces backwards, and sat down heavily with his back against the tunnel wall. He seemed utterly spent.

With some hesitancy, Marianne crouched by him.

"Ryan?" she said.

Slowly, he turned his head to look at her.

"Let's go now," she said, and she held out her hand.

He stared at her hand for a few moments, as if it was a strange thing whose significance he wasn't quite able to grasp.

Then he reached out with his own and took it. Her small fingers almost vanished within his.

Wearily, awkwardly, he began to rise.

CHAPTER 80

Cadogan had grown hoarse from calling her name. He'd been shouting both entreaties and warnings, but then he'd finally lapsed into silence after realizing that his words were no longer making any sense. Far-off phones kept ringing. Steam hammered in the pipes. The ventilators sucked wind. The works had been evacuated, all the plugs pulled and the engines stalled and the pumps shut down, but it was almost as if its hindbrain still housed a spark and its slow heart kept on ticking in defiance of all medical opinion.

It was vast. He'd never been in a place like it. He'd visited a number of Masako's assembly plants back when he'd worked for the company, but they'd been high-tech and comfortable whereas this was almost medieval. Raw animal hides down near the yard, piled high and stinking of the abattoir. Dipping vats that stank worse. Rolling plant and drying rooms and cutting shops and row upon row of piecework stitching machines. Offices where they still used high stools and ledgers, and where the daylight was like dirty water. Worksheds where there was no daylight at all.

And there were idle areas, as well. Huge and high-ceilinged galleries where the only evidence of use was in old oil stains on the floorboards where the shapes of missing heavy equipment could be made out like stencil cuts. Stairways that echoed like a prison's, and in which he could hear the faint strains of an abandoned shop-floor radio.

But of Marianne and Ryan O'Donnell, not a sign.

They'd warned him about the tunnels. If your man *is* dangerous, they'd said, don't follow him down there because he could turn around and have you. Better to stay outside and wait. He'd have to come out in the end; there had only ever been one other exit, and that was through a trench in the woodlands that had long been flooded and inaccessible.

All of which had pressed Cadogan to consider, as he'd been making his hasty search. What was he really afraid of, now? Once it had been an easy question to answer. His child was in the hands of a beast, end of story. But it was almost as if, while O'Donnell had grown more monstrous in the eyes of those others who pursued him, Cadogan's stark understanding of the picture had blurred into a less distinct pattern of grays. Beast he might be, but Marianne had chosen him. And what had he done to her? What, apart from his inadequate best to keep her safe?

Cadogan was still afraid for Marianne, that went without saying. He missed her, although it had taken him a while to distinguish this feeling from the others and to recognize it. But he had to admit that his biggest fear was not now of O'Donnell himself, but of the firepower that he was drawing towards the two of them.

He stopped.

For a moment, he wasn't sure why. One of the disused galleries was before him, almost big enough and high enough to put a ship inside. The windows stretched from waist height almost all the way up to the ceiling, and threw a slanted grid-pattern of sunlight onto the floor. Dust motes bobbed around in the rays.

He took another step, uncertain. One of the boards creaked, and the noise seemed shockingly loud in the empty space. He looked towards the windows. They didn't appear to have been cleaned in ages, unless with a dirty rag. Through them he could see the line of the perimeter wall across the factory yard and beyond that, the silhouette of the *Kulturhaus* roof.

Up on the roof, nothing appeared to be moving. With some care, he began to take a step back in order to remove himself from the building's line of sight.

A doubtful, not-quite-believing voice said, *"Daddy?"*

Cadogan turned.

They were standing there, at the far end of the gallery. His daughter, and her dancing bear. His daughter looked blank, astonished to see him at all. O'Donnell seemed unsteady beside her ... so big, so rough-looking, so much of everything that she wasn't. She was holding O'Donnell's hand—but not like a prisoner, more as if to lead him along.

She started forward, making as if to speak.

Cadogan waved and shouted, *"No!"*

He saw her stop, puzzled. And then she made as if to move forward again, uncertain this time, but now O'Donnell held her back.

"What is it?" O'Donnell said.

"They're watching the windows," Cadogan said, raising his voice to reach the two of them across the floor. "They're watching everywhere. If either of you takes another step, it might be the last thing you ever do."

He saw O'Donnell look towards the windows. O'Donnell's hand touched Marianne's shoulder and then, like two people who'd just realized they'd begun to enter a minefield, he guided her backwards almost into the shadows again.

"Just stay calm," Cadogan said. "That's the only way we're all going to be able to walk out of this."

And although it was hard to be certain over the distance, he felt sure that this got a wry smile out of O'Donnell.

Nobody spoke for a few moments, and then O'Donnell broke the silence.

"Well," he said. "Here we are again."

"It seems that I have to keep asking you for my daughter back."

"Like the last time?"

"No," Cadogan said, remembering the empty shopping plaza and the way that he'd banged his head pointlessly against the bars of the slide-across gate until O'Donnell's touch and his quiet word had helped to bring him down.

"No," he said. "Not like the last time. You've done what you said you would. I still think it was wrong, but I think I understand why. Now I want her. Please."

Marianne was staring at him.

"I'm asking you to come home with me," he said to her. "I want to tell you some things about your mother. I'm not going to tell you everything, not yet . . . but I'm not going to lie to you, either."

Then he added, *"Bitte komme mir mit. Und versuche mir zu vergeben."*

He saw her look up at O'Donnell.

"I don't know what to do," he heard her say falteringly.

"I think you do," O'Donnell said.

She looked at Cadogan again. But Cadogan switched his attention back to O'Donnell and went on. "There's a way out of this. Let me get Marianne to somewhere that I know she'll be safe, and then we'll walk out together. Whatever they try to do to you they'll have to do to me. I'll talk to everyone they've got out there. I'll tell them what a mess I made of everything, and what I started. I'll stick with you all the way through. I won't say that you haven't done wrong. But I'll tell them why you did it."

Marianne said, "I don't want them to hurt him."

"I won't let them," Cadogan said.

Everything depended on how O'Donnell would react. There was no point in pretending that everything was going to be fine, because it wasn't. The joy had gone out of the joyride a long time ago, now; too many people had been hit or hurt along the way. But from here it could be played straight or it could be allowed to run off and onward into disaster, and the balance of it lay in this moment.

Marianne was looking up at O'Donnell, almost as if she was waiting for him to advise her on what to do.

"Go on," he said, and with a movement of his head he indicated for her to go towards Cadogan.

But still she hesitated.

"Go *on!*" he said almost impatiently, and he gave her a slight push to start her off.

She looked at him almost in disbelief, but he waved her away. This time he wouldn't meet her eyes.

Cadogan held his breath as Marianne took her first step into line with the windows. They'd see her clearly now, looking down from their positions on top of the *Kulturhaus*. How many of them? He hadn't counted. Marksmen, all. They'd see that she was alone and they'd be holding their fire, but only someone else's patience and concentration and a centimeter's travel of the trigger finger stood between his daughter and the impact of a high-velocity bullet.

She'd come about one-third of the way. She looked back towards O'Donnell for reassurance, but O'Donnell was looking down. He didn't seem right, somehow. Cadogan couldn't put his finger on why. But then he saw the glint of an eye as O'Donnell glanced in the direction of the window, and knew that Ryan O'Donnell was a long way from being out of it completely. He might not have seen what was out there in the way that Cadogan had, but he probably had a pretty good idea of what he might expect.

Marianne hesitated.

Cadogan said, "Don't stop now. Please."

"What if they won't listen?" she said.

"They'll have to. I'll make them."

"But what if they won't?"

"What can I tell you?" Cadogan said desperately. "Keep walking. We'll sort it out."

But Marianne was shaking her head.

"They'll kill him," she said. "They're going to blame him for all kinds of things that weren't his fault."

She was starting to back off. Oh, God, she was starting to back off.

"Marianne," he said, "come on . . ."

"I've got to stay with him," she said, and she started to turn around.

O'Donnell reacted belatedly. He'd been rubbing his brow and seemed to have his mind on something else, but when he looked up and saw her beginning to head towards him again his face cleared with sudden alarm and he said, "No!"

He stepped forward with a cutting gesture to stop her. It wasn't more than one stride, and he probably wasn't even aware that he'd taken it until it was too late.

But it appeared that one stride was enough.

It might have been two shots, it might have been three. It was hard to be sure of anything, because everything seemed to happen in the wrong order. Ryan was staggering sideways even before Cadogan heard the glass being blown out of the windows. The distant crack of the rifles seemed to come an eternity later. His big coat seemed to be plucked this way and that, even as the rounds struck into the floorboards with a series of bangs like a nail punch. More dust rose into the sunlight, drifting like corn chaff. Ryan stumbled backwards into the shadows and the firing stopped.

Cadogan was already moving. As he grabbed Marianne, he could feel that he'd caught her on the point of starting forward and so he spun her around, hustling her away and in the direction of safety before the echoes of the volley had even begun to die out.

He tripped and he almost fell, but he didn't release his hold on her. Only when he was sure that they'd moved well out of range did he give in to her struggling and allow her to look back, and even then he didn't let her go.

O'Donnell hadn't fallen. For a moment, Cadogan wondered if he'd actually been hit. But then he could see that every ounce of the man's strength was being poured into the effort of staying upright, and it was a fight that was slowly being lost.

Marianne said, "Ryan?"

With a tremendous effort, O'Donnell seemed to manage to regain both his balance and his composure. He squared himself. He even managed a shaky but confidence-inspiring smile for her.

"It's all right," he said thickly. "Don't worry, I'm fine." Then he looked from Marianne to Cadogan. "Do something for me, can you?" he said.

"Ryan," she said again, this time with a sense of pleading and apprehension that came out almost like a whine of annoyance; but it was as if he was deliberately ignoring her now. The bond had been broken forever. She'd been passed from one man to the other like a trapeze flyer between two catchers; only Cadogan's grip on her betrayed a true awareness of the long fall that lay below.

Cadogan said, "What do you want me to do?"

"Take her away," O'Donnell said. "I mean, right away from here."

He said no more than that, but his meaning was clear. It wasn't just, *Take her away*. It was, *Don't let her see what's coming*.

"I know this isn't going to sound right," Cadogan said. "But thank you."

Ryan O'Donnell gave a single, almost gracious nod of acknowledgment. But then he coughed, and quickly clapped his hand over his mouth. He held it that way for a moment, as if waiting to see what would happen next; then he took his hand away and swallowed hard, and then he cleared his throat a couple of times.

"Go on," he said quietly.

Cadogan lifted Marianne clear of the floor and, before she could begin to protest, he started to carry her towards the corridor that would lead them down towards the main works entrance and the way out.

She struggled, but only to keep O'Donnell in sight. By the time they'd reached the doorway, he'd turned and was gone.

She hung on, bouncing against Cadogan as he started to run. She turned her face into his shoulder and buried it there. She was no baby any more, but for him she was weightless. Holding her close, he banged open the safety bars on the first exit that he saw and sent the double doors flying outward. Then he was out on the cobblestones and running again, only this time he was heading for safety and he wasn't alone. His lungs were filled with the scent of her. His head was light with it. She clung so hard that it almost hurt.

He was only vaguely aware of the police line towards which they were now heading. People were running towards them. There was a series of reports, and a clutch of missiles went arrowing overhead. Tear gas. They were firing gas grenades in through the windows and he tried to shout for them to stop, but there was too much noise and he couldn't make himself heard. He could hear more glass breaking. A misfire bounced and skittered back across the yard, pouring out smoke in a furious stream. He put his hand on the back of Marianne's head and pushed it even harder into his shoulder as the cloud enveloped them; his eyes were stinging in an instant and both of them were spluttering, but he kept on going.

Men in body armor and gas masks, heading by. They passed either side of him in the fog like ghost troopers, anonymous and inhuman, bug-eyed and shiny black with their weapons at the ready. His eyes were burning now. He had to get her out of this. The wind blew, the gas cloud thinned, and then it was around them again. There was the sound of a shout, of a door being kicked in somewhere behind them.

A car appeared out of nowhere, sliding backwards to a halt only a few yards away. Someone grabbed him by the shoulders, speeding him towards it as the doors were flung open. Someone else tried to lift Marianne from him, but he pulled her away and held on.

Then the car was off, doors slamming, and somehow they were inside it. They were heading out through the factory gates, away from the area of the operation and out of the scene altogether.

O'Donnell was getting his wish.

And Cadogan had his. He'd got her back. She was safe. She was whole.

If there was anything else in his life that mattered to him right then, he wasn't even going to try to think what it might be.

CHAPTER 81

Ryan was back in the tunnels.

Ryan had a plan.

He wasn't about to start writing himself off—not yet. But this was so difficult. Even as he moved, the energy seemed to be running out of him and he had the unreal sense that he was getting closer and closer to the floor. Any moment now he was going to plow on into it like one of those slow-motion films of some awkward bird making a bad landing. When he came to rest, that would be it. Plugs out, lights fading behind all the dials.

But then, in a strange way, it was as if he reached the bottom of the arc and began to swing up again. The weight was lifted from him, and he began to rise. Where before each step that he'd taken had seemed to slam down and shake the ground, now he was starting to fly along with almost no effort at all. Any sense that this might be some kind of a delusion was knocked out of him when a couple of times he lurched into one of the tunnel walls, whereupon he was racked from head to foot by the most terrible pains. This earthed him somehow, and reminded him that it was real.

But still he bounced onward, and with every step that he took he became more and more certain that he could yet come through.

Here were the rails, where Marianne had stumbled.

Marianne, whom, for both their sakes, he would never see again.

What had they ever planned to *do* with all this space down here? It was the kind of place where an army could have hidden. Some of those side workings, their ends barred and gated, were big enough to serve as dormitories. At the far end of each was another set of bars and, beyond the bars, a further lighted passageway identical and parallel to this. No one seemed to use any of it now, and a slow deterioration had been long under way. The white walls had leaked in certain spots, stained with runnels of red oxide like dried blood from a wound. Overhead, some of the cables had come unfixed and hung down in long loops.

He made the turn where another tunnel cut through. He could see now that he wasn't alone.

Ahead of him stood the little girl in the bridesmaid's dress. He recognized her dated clothes, her shell-shocked eyes, her stringy hair thick with the dust of a falling building. Her arms were thin and there were cuts on her hands. If she'd lived, most of her life would have been behind her by now. Instead she'd become this frozen thing, waiting uncertainly and forever at the door that had been closed in her face. He wanted to speak her name, *Vanessa*, but already she was sliding by.

He was only vaguely aware of some far-off sounds that probably came from the complex way back above ground. They were coming in with more confidence now, but that had been inevitable. It wouldn't matter in the end. They'd still have to find him.

Nothing could stop him now. And nothing could hurt him. He was beginning to believe that he'd somehow broken through a barrier and been transformed into a being of no more substance than thought and air. It was exactly at this point that he pitched forward to fall heavily and without warning.

He was jarred by a spasm of intense agony that went almost as suddenly as it appeared. Now, when he started to get to his feet again, it was as if his body had become like a great weight that he was trying to drag along through water. Even those echoing sounds from the tunnel behind had become dragged out and slurring.

But no matter. No matter. The leaking door lay ahead.

He fixed his eyes on the wheel at its center. Everything else weaved and bobbed around like on a ship at sea, but the wheel stayed rock solid. The floor at the end of the tunnel was partly awash, but most of the leakage so far seemed to have run off down the sloping floor to collect at some lower point elsewhere.

Ryan got his hands onto the wheel. He braced himself and stood ready for the pain, if there was going to be any. Then he put all of his strength into the effort of turning.

The outside edges of the door had rusted seriously, the metal beginning to lift and flake in several layered skins all at once. It had the look of old, wet cardboard, if not the texture. So there was water on the other side. So what? If he let it out, he could get through. And if there was more backed up out there than the underground system could take . . .

Well, what did he really have to lose?

The wheel moved an inch. His body sang with the thrill of achievement and he tried even harder, although the blood was thundering in his ears and his vision was narrowing as if he was watching himself on a TV screen that had experienced a sudden drop in voltage.

The stream became a spurt.

The spurt became a jet.

And the jets became many, and then they started to merge. . . .

And the wheel came out and pushed Ryan in the chest, swinging him back but just stopping short of slamming him against the wall as a high-pressure column of water burst through the doorway and roared out into the tunnel. It was six feet high, door-shaped, and solid. It came out like a cavalry charge and it deafened with its thunder. Where it hit the floor and the walls, it exploded into white foam.

Ryan tried to hang onto the wheel. But the force as the swirling level rose was too great, and his grip was broken as he was pulled away.

He hit his head a couple of times. That much he was aware of. As for where he was and where he was going, he was being tumbled and battered around too much to guess. He didn't know how long it went on for. It couldn't have been as much as a minute, although it did seem much longer. All that he knew was that he came to a stop against a wooden door at least two hundred yards back down the tunnel from the place where he'd lost his footing.

He lay there for a few moments, looking up at the light overhead as it stuttered on-off, on-off, and felt sure that he'd never seen anything quite so remarkable and revealing as the pattern of light and darkness that it made; and if only, if *only* he could make that little extra effort, he might understand what it meant and have the key to everything, *everything* that he'd ever felt or reckoned that he needed to know. . . .

And then the lights made up their mind and finally shorted out, and he was left in the shadows with the feeling that some kind of ultimate knowledge had just escaped him again, as it seemed to have in his moments of greatest intensity so many times before.

Something had changed, though.

There was light—literally—at the end of the tunnel.

He struggled to his knees. He was panting. His head was ringing. The bulkhead door stood wide open and daylight was pouring in, so bright in its contrast that it looked as if it had been cut out of darkness with a razor. Where the light was reflecting from the tunnel floor and sides it was gray, almost opalescent.

Ryan made it up onto his feet. Water was still streaming down the floor and past him now, like the sea from the flanks of a risen submarine. There was a stench of something long-held and finally released. He started to splash his way towards the door.

God, he was tired.

He was soaked and his clothes were heavy, and he was beginning to wonder with sudden panic if he'd be able to manage the distance to the doorway at all. With every step, he seemed to weaken. The closer he got, the harder it seemed to be to make any progress.

But somehow, he forced himself onward.

Something seemed to be draining out of him even as he moved. But something was replacing it, too. A sense of the light. A sense of power. His body wouldn't fail him, if only he'd refuse to believe that it could. He was Ryan O'Donnell. Cut his hand or do worse and he'd bleed; but he'd be no less Ryan O'Donnell whatever the damage.

He reached the doorway, and managed to remember to raise his leg in time to step through. His other foot caught on the threshold just as his shoulder clipped the frame. He staggered and managed to keep his balance, but otherwise he didn't notice.

He'd been here before.

He looked out into his city of lights.

They moved, they blurred, they shifted like the sunlight through the trees. He was almost blinded by them. All around him, water sluiced and poured and ran. He stood as if on the deck of a ship newly raised from the deep. The familiar was strange again. The strange had the air of having been known to him all his life.

There were figures out there, in the light. They were gathering, descending, moving towards him. And he realized, with a sense of terror and joy, what it all meant.

He took a step forward, and another. He'd been here once, and had turned away. He didn't want to be afraid. He didn't want to, but how could he help it? He was sure they'd understand.

He wished he weren't so dazzled. He wished he could see their faces. One was coming down towards him, ahead of all the others.

Wait a minute.

Wait a minute . . .

As she came closer, he saw bars. Heavy bars that stood between them, showing up against her outline where her shape was holding back some of the blinding effect of the rays. There was a final hurdle, then. A few yards yet to go before he could hope to relax.

But he was falling, now. He was on his hands and knees, and there seemed to be nowhere left that he could reach into for the strength to make that one final effort.

She was crouching. She'd put her hand through the bars. She was holding it out to him.

Reaching for it, he fell. He fell, but then he squirmed and he crawled and he dragged himself along until he could raise himself up and stretch out his own hand. He looked into her eyes once again; once again after all this time, connecting with that unforgettable moment of recognition across the market stall so many years before. Their hands touched, and the circuit of his life was complete.

Hers folded around his like a mother's around a child's, and he knew that he was home.

CHAPTER 82

Others were descending now, with greater care. As the water level in the hollow had dropped, it had revealed what had once been a makeshift stairway of wooden sleepers and shale. After years of immersion these were now weed-covered and rank, and all around her was like the newly uncovered bed of some deep and long-forgotten ocean. The *Obermeister* who'd gone back for the bolt cutters was picking his way over, holding them high and making faint sounds of disgust as each stride sank him into mud that came up to his knees.

Someone just by Jennifer said quietly, "I think he's gone. You can let go of him now."

"Yes," Jennifer said. "Yes, I know."

The rusted-solid padlock a few feet away from her was sprung with a sound like a bell as the *Obermeister* fixed the cutters in place and put all of his weight onto them. Three of the others started to work on the gate, rocking it back on its equally rusted hinges.

"I will," Jennifer said, although nobody was now listening.

But she held on tightly, and didn't let go.

At least, not until one of the officers gently disengaged her hand so that they could lift O'Donnell away.

Coming in October 1995
to bookstores everywhere!

RED RED ROBIN

by Stephen Gallagher

Published in hardcover by Ballantine Books.

Read on for a sneak preview of this
thrilling novel . . .

The Barclay Hotel stood on the corner of Rittenhouse Square. In most people's minds Rittenhouse Square stood for Old Money, although as a rule the old money was a memory and the buildings around it were now high-rise commercial property just like everywhere else. At the heart of the square was a public park, and at the heart of the park stood a large and classy-looking canvas marquee. It had been raised there only hours before and it was encircled by a ring of private security to hold out the curious. It was a warm evening, and there was music drifting over from it already.

Ruth took a deep breath as she entered the Barclay from the sidewalk. Her heart was beating like a bride's. Ridiculous, but it was. The lobby was long and white, and lit by chandeliers that mellowed it all down to cream and gilt. Faced by it, she hesitated.

"Are you Ms. Lasseter?" a voice behind her asked.

She turned and saw that it came from a uniformed concierge at his desk by the door. "Yes," she said.

"Your guest is waiting for you in the cocktail lounge."

"And where would that be?"

He indicated for her, and she followed a baronial passageway that led off the lobby and around into the bar. She was a few minutes later than she'd planned, but she didn't rush. Not in these heels, buster. She checked herself over in a big mirror as she passed it.

The cocktail lounge was deep in darkness, the main illumination being from a night-light candle in a glass at the center of each table. Twenty beads of light, one overall dim golden glow. The walls were paneled with Chinese scenes, painted in gilt on dark canvas and stretched on wooden frames. The only bright splashes were the red jacket of the bartender, and the baseball game that he was watching on the TV behind the bar. The colors of the field were vivid and wonderful. Ruth wondered why sports fields on TV sets in bars always looked vivid and wonderful.

There was only one other person in here. He rose to his feet as soon as he saw her.

"Mister Hagan?" she said, as she made her way through the tables toward him.

"I'm Tim," he said. "You're Miss Lasseter."

"Ruth."

"Thank you for choosing me." He moved out to meet her and took her proffered hand in a gentle clasp, holding it for a moment before letting it go.

My God, she was thinking. What have I done? He's so *young*.

In this light, and probably in any other light as well, Tim Hagan looked even younger than his twenty-three years. A well-groomed, fit-looking boy in a tuxedo. But no schoolkid. He wore it too well for that. He was broad-shouldered and clear-skinned, and he had a razor-sharp haircut and the wide, clean-lined jawbone of a male model.

He was even better than his picture. He was utterly, utterly unbelievable.

And Ruth thought again, What *have* I done?

She said, "I've got a few things I want to run through with you before we go over."

He stepped back, so that she could go ahead of him to the table where he'd been waiting. There was a tall glass with what looked like mineral water in it, apparently untouched.

He said, "Can I get you anything to drink?"

"This won't take that long," Ruth said.

He glanced at the bartender and shook his head briefly as they sat. The bartender returned his attention to the game. Tim Hagan looked at Ruth attentively, hands folded on the table before him.

"Don't do that," Ruth said, half amused and making a brief waving-away gesture.

He looked anxious, as if he'd been tripped in a detail. "Do what?" he said.

"You're making me feel like a schoolteacher."

He moved his hands from the table.

"Sorry," he said.

"I don't know how much the agency has told you."

"I had a briefing from Mrs. Carroll."

"Did she seem to disapprove of anything?"

He seemed politely puzzled. "I don't understand."

Ruth said, "She couldn't exactly contain her dismay when I phoned to make the final arrangements. She all but pleaded with me to reconsider."

"Mrs. Carroll said nothing about that to me."

"She didn't say anything about . . . an age difference?"

"What age difference would that be?"

She watched him. Nothing changed. She gave him the chance to falter or smirk, but it didn't happen. His gaze was steady and it held her own.

Ruth let through a slow smile.

"I think this is going to work out fine, Tim," she said.

"I hope so," he said.

There was a perceptible sense of relaxation then, as if they'd swapped passwords and agreed on their ground and no longer needed to be quite so much on their guard. Over at the bar, the head waiter from the adjoining restaurant came through and started to ring up a drinks order for his diners. Ruth was beginning to think that she could happily have spent the evening right here. The candles across the tables were like a field of stars reflected in a still pool.

But how realistic would that be? How long before they ran out of small talk and the true size of the gulf between them was uncovered?

Don't even dream about it, she told herself.

She said, "I don't know how much Mrs. Carroll already told you. But I'm going to save both of us a lot of embarrassment and say that you don't have to fake anything tonight. I'm not saying you should tell everyone that I hired you. But trying to pretend we're something we're not is just ridiculous. We should act like friends who've hooked up for the evening because it's expected. You know," she added, a little lamely, "like when movie stars take each other to the Oscars."

"I understand," Hagan said. "You don't have to tell me anything more."

"Well, what do you say? Shall we go over?"

They rose, leaving his drink still untouched.

They walked out of the hotel and across the park toward the open-air ballroom which, like some magic garden in a story, had appeared out of nowhere and would vanish again in the morning. The main canvas had been raised over the fountain at the heart of the park, and side awnings covered the approach walks in each direction. Across each path stood a wooden barrier with the words POLICE LINE on it, and behind each barrier stood a gray-jacketed security person. Outside the barriers, early evening park life went on more or less as normal. People strolled, their dogs met and tumbled, the homeless staked a claim on their benches for the night. The last rays of the sun were gliding the upper floors of the high-rise blocks above them.

The entranceway at the southeast corner was lit up like a fairground booth and was overstocked with flowers. Ruth and her guest were checked off the list, and then they made their way up a red carpet to the receiving line to be greeted by members of the board and the owning family. The latter, an elderly couple and their even older brother, looked as well-bred and frail as rare violins. The chairman of the board was impressive. He remembered her, or at least he was completely convincing in appearing to. As she moved on down the line, she could hear him being equally convincing with someone else.

After the logjam of the receiving line, everyone emerged into a courtyard area around two sides of the fountain that was like a holding pen. It was the cocktail hour, and drinks were being served. Four men in dinner suits, one with a ponytail, were running the free bar at a long and well-stocked table.

All the male guests were in black tie. The women were in more brilliant plumage. Ruth didn't, as yet, see too many that she knew.

Glancing around, Hagan said, "I didn't get much time to prepare. I looked through some books on modern art last night and learned a few names."

"You shouldn't have worried," Ruth told him. "These are finance publishing and society people, not an art crowd."

"I already forgot most of the names anyway," he admitted. "Except for Mark Rothko. Is he likely to be here?"

"Not *too* likely, Tim," Ruth said. "He may be modern, but he's dead."

He was relatively unfazed.

"Someone's waving to you," he said.

She turned to look. A woman was squeezing by in a dress that was sequined like fish scales, but then as her line of sight cleared Ruth could see Jennie and her husband, Bill. She'd met Bill a number of times and she knew, beyond a doubt, that this was not his kind of occasion. It had probably taken a big bribe or some serious blackmail, first to get him into a rental suit and then to come along.

Jennie was in something ankle-length with frills down the front and a ruff at the neck. It gave her a look like a waitress in some chain of southern-style restaurants, or a plantation house guide. She gave the once-over to Ruth's tight black little designer number and said, "Well, look at you! I'd die to be able to fill up a dress like that."

"You could fill it right now, kid," her husband said from beside her, hands in his pockets as he scanned about the crowd. "The problem is what we'd do with the overflow."

Ruth reached for Hagan and drew him forward slightly. "Jennie, Bill," she said, "this is Tim. He's a friend of mine, and he's my date for tonight."

Jennie turned to look at him, holding out her hand. Ruth waited for the shock wave. It came, with a built-in delay for disbelief.

"You are?" she said, and then it hit so hard that she all but took a step backward. "You *are*."

"I'm very pleased to meet you, Jennie," Hagan said with just the right note of formality. "And you, Bill."

Jennie was still a little dazed, but she was recovering fast. She said to Hagan, "Have you . . . known each other long?"

"You know," Hagan said, "I really couldn't put a time on it. Sometimes you just click with someone and right away it's like you've known them your entire life."

"Well," Bill said, not looking at anybody in particular, "that's not unfeasible."

Ruth couldn't be certain, but she was fairly sure that Jennie kicked or somehow distracted him at this point. Under the adjoining marquee the band started to play and a singer started to sing.

Hagan turned to Ruth and said, "Perhaps you'd like to dance?"

Jennie looked as if she needed the recovery time. Ruth said, "See you both later," and then she allowed Hagan to guide her off through the crowd.

"I said you didn't have to lie," she told him as they eased their way through. Ahead of them there was a youngish man in a flamboyant white dinner suit, billowy as a sheik's pajamas, who breezed onto the dance floor tugging his girlfriend by the hand like so much cargo.

Hagan said, "Why do you assume I was lying?"

"Oh, Tim," Ruth said with a smile as they stepped out onto the wooden deck. "You'll go far. Can you dance to this kind of stuff?"

"Please," he said with a pained look. "I'm a professional."

They danced.

The band was a six-piece outfit, old-time musicians with a lot of mileage under their belts. They did nothing showy and they didn't lay a note out of place. Right now they were playing Cole Porter.

"You're good," Ruth said after a while.

"I know," Tim said simply.

That cracked her up, and she started to enjoy herself.

She started to recognize more co-workers and a few clients. The event began to take on an atmosphere. Colored lights were being played over the underside of the marquee, and as flying insects darted through the beams they seemed to be momentarily afire. She thought she saw Alicia and then, next time around, she confirmed it. Alicia was dancing with her husband, Frank. Ruth didn't exactly catch her eye, but she knew that she'd been seen and recognized. Alicia had a stunned look, as if she'd just been struck by something and was waiting for a puff of wind to blow her over; her husband said something to her that she didn't seem to hear.

Ruth looked around for Gordon and Mimi, but she didn't see either of them. They'd be around somewhere by now, perhaps back in the courtyard where the canapes were being served. Maybe Gordon had seen *her*.

She moved closer to her escort. They fit together almost in interlock.

When the band stopped playing, taped disco music took over. Everyone applauded and the numbers out on the floor dropped by

443

about half. Ruth looked around again. Damn it, Gordon, she was thinking, you should see this. He was paying for it, after all. And wouldn't *that* just get under his skin?

But instead of Gordon she spotted another figure, one that she hadn't expected to see. There was an instant in which she recognized him but couldn't make that recognition absolute, a kind of finger-snapping moment in which obvious connections refused to be made; and then it came together and she realized that it was Aidan Kincannon again. He was in an ill-fitting dinner suit with a drink in his hand, glancing around after watching the dancing; there was a kind of pleasant, open look on his face, as if he was trying to broadcast a general signal to anyone who might have been interested that he didn't feel at all uncomfortable, not really. If ever Ruth had seen a fish out of water, Aidan Kincannon was it. He worked for the building's people and not for the company, so there had to be some special reason for his being here.

"I think they're serving champagne," Hagan said as they ducked away from the disco.

"How do you know?"

"I heard the corks being pulled. Would you like some?"

"Yes," Ruth said, "I rather think I would."

"Will you be all right if I leave you for a minute?"

"Of course I will."

Hagan moved off, and Ruth took aim through the crowd for Aidan Kincannon. She took the opportunity to exchange greetings with one or two people along the way, but she didn't stop for anyone.

Aidan seemed to become aware of her belatedly. He smiled, and didn't quite seem to know what to do with his hands as she covered the last few yards.

"Hello, Aidan," she said. "I almost didn't know you out of uniform."

"That's what everyone's been telling me," he said.

"I hadn't realized you were going to be here."

"Somebody stuck an envelope with an invitation in my locker yesterday." He made a wry face. "I've been given to understand that it's some kind of a reward."

"I saw what you did to earn it. I think you deserve more than this."

"Don't tell me," he said, "tell the boss. Who's your friend?"

"Just a friend," she said, playing it down for the first time all evening.

444

"Well," Aidan said, pointing with his glass, "he's looking for you."

She looked over to the other side of the room and there was Tim Hagan, a champagne flute in each hand and scanning for her. She waved, and saw that she'd caught his eye.

"See you later," she said to Aidan. And Aidan nodded, pleasantly. She felt awkward about abandoning him again, but she wasn't sure what else she could do. Except maybe to feed a poisoned hors d'oeuvre to Bill, and to give Jennie a hard push in Aidan's direction.

Hagan handed her a glass and said, "I've heard your name being whispered three times in the last five minutes."

"They can talk all they want, Tim," Ruth said happily. "Let's circulate."

They circulated.

There was an art to keeping a conversation going in circumstances like these. No tale was ever completed, no story reached its point. New people were always drifting up, and new introductions were always being made. Jake brought over some clients with whom she'd dealt by phone for two years but whom she'd never met. Others, she sought out. Hagan stayed by her side throughout, there when she needed him to be, taking a step back when she didn't.

"You're doing well," she told him after a while. A buffet had been unveiled in a side tent and there had been something of a stampede, leaving them alone with some empty tables where they could sit for a minute and recharge. The tables were draped with a bronze-colored cloth, the seats upholstered in red and gold to fit in with the general decor of open-air opulence. Floral displays were like hanging gardens, suspended above each. The effect, upscale though it undoubtedly was, seemed to Ruth like the world's most expensive carousel art.

Hagan inclined his head with a smile and said, "Thank you. I'm enjoying it all."

"But it's not the kind of evening you'd choose for yourself."

"How do you know?"

"Well, what is there here for you?"

He made a show of thinking it over, of running through the options. "There's you," he said.

"Thank you," Ruth said, knowing that she'd done no more than ask for this. "Enough."

"You don't think I'm serious," he said

"I'm going to change the subject. Where are you from?"

"Try to guess."

She had no chance. Ruth had come to the conclusion long ago that she had no ear for nuance in speech. "You're a southern boy," she said. "I can hear that much, but that's about all."

"And I thought I'd lost the accent."

"How long have you lived in Philadelphia?"

"Not very long."

She shook her head. He had a half-mischievous look that suggested he could lead her on like this all night, if she wanted him to.

She said, "You don't give much away, do you?"

"No," he said.

Ruth knew a going-nowhere streak when she saw one.

"Let's go and eat," she said.

The society columnist from the *Inquirer* was there. Ruth had seen him earlier; he'd arrived on a bicycle, wearing a bowler hat. He was leaving the buffet table just as she and Hagan arrived and joined the line. The food had been presented with an artistry that even the thorough wolverine rout of the last ten minutes couldn't obscure. There was crabmeat on the shell, chicken on a skewer, teriyaki on a bed of lettuce; there was a chef out of sight somewhere in the back, but all of those handling the service looked as if they were in their teens. The girl on the salad bar wore a brace on her teeth.

As they passed down the table, the woman in front of Ruth suddenly turned to her.

"It's Ruth, isn't it?" she said. "We haven't met before. I'm Mimi Parry."

Ruth felt as if she'd been caught out. For a moment she didn't know what to say. Gordon's wife was a character who'd lived in her imagination for some time now, someone with a changing image and an almost cartoonlike personality. Mimi the dragon. Mimi the fire breather. Mimi of the five-times-a-year sexual appetite.

This woman didn't look like *that* Mimi Parry at all.

Ruth said, "How are you, Mrs. Parry?"

"Nice to know you," she said, and they managed to shake hands while still holding their plates. Ruth saw Gordon look back and see them doing it and then look again, startled. She'd been within a couple of yards of him and she hadn't even known it. Seen from the back in the line, he was barely distinguishable from all the other slightly balding middle managers. So much for the bond they were always going to share.

"Gordon?" Mimi said. "Get us some paper napkins, will you?" And she drew Ruth away from the table as if there was something pressing that they had to discuss.

"Yes, Mimi," Gordon said hollowly as they left him behind.

With a glance toward Hagan, who was still back in line getting his plate loaded, Mimi said, "Don't tell my husband, but I'm seriously thinking of trading him in for a model like yours. The problem's going to be finding someone who'll have him."

Ruth smiled weakly.

"Good luck," she said.

"Where'd you get him?"

"From Boys 'R' Us. His name's Tim."

Mimi laughed out loud. A couple of people looked. "Pardon me," she said, as if she'd belched. What Ruth knew of Mimi was that she was a working woman herself, a lawyer in a midtown office. She'd risen in her profession, and it showed in her manner. She seemed to be practiced at putting people at immediate ease and making them feel interesting.

"We're going to have to meet and chat properly, someday," she told Ruth; and then Hagan came over to join them, his plate laden as if he was stoking up before a siege, and Mimi said, "Hello, Tim. We've been talking about you."

"Really?" Hagan said pleasantly.

"We've been talking about you, too, Gordon," Mimi added dryly as her husband arrived with the napkins.

Gordon had a hunted look. "Saying what?"

"Nothing you'd want us to repeat."

Mercifully, some old friends came over and howled with delight and fell upon Mimi and Gordon, and that was effectively the end of the exchange. Ruth backed off with a relief that she hoped wouldn't be obvious. She felt as if she'd just crossed a narrow plank above an alligator pool.

Hagan seemed to get a sense of her feelings, and asked if anything was wrong. She said that there wasn't. But she gave him a mental mark for his show of concern.

After the food they switched on the address system and there were some speeches, a couple of presentations, and then a prize draw based on coatroom numbers. Ruth could only marvel at the spectacle of people in thousand-dollar outfits digging their tickets out and squinting at them like bingo players, all for the sake of a

447

big stuffed teddy bear that was going to take up so much house room and pick up so much dust that it would inevitably come to be detested over the years. It was won by Becky from the Subscriptions Department, whom Ruth reckoned probably deserved it. After that the company president, looking older than God and much better-groomed, took the mike and thanked them all for coming and sent them forth to enjoy themselves. He handed the mike to the singer, and the band struck up again.

"Back in a couple of minutes," Ruth told Hagan.

"Are you sure there's nothing wrong?" he asked her, but she reassured him again.

The ladies' powder room was in one of two white tents at the quiet end of the area. Just about everybody was either on or close by the dance floor now. Staff down at this end were picking up trash and bagging it.

Inside the powder room, facilities were basic. One transportable chemical toilet in a booth, one table with mirror and chair, and a basketwork bowl of complimentary sachet wipes.

Rosemary was there before the mirror, making a few repairs to her hair and makeup. She seemed slightly flustered.

"Are you all right, Rosemary?" Ruth said.

"I got a little overheated out there," Rosemary said. "Did you hear about Alicia?"

"No. What?"

"She left early. She wasn't feeling well."

"What a shame," Ruth said.

She hadn't meant it to carry any weight or to sound at all sarcastic, but somehow a note of that must have crept in. Or perhaps Rosemary thought she picked up a shading that simply wasn't there.

Turning from the mirror, she said, "Do you know what you're *doing*, Ruth?"

Ruth looked her straight in the eye. "For the first time in a long time, Rosemary," she said, "the answer is, not entirely."

"It may not be my place to say it, but . . . you could have been his mother."

"That's something I *think* I would have noticed. If a forty-year-old guy turns up with a young woman on his arm, you can't hear yourself talk for the sound of his friends slapping him on the back. I spend the evening with a younger man and suddenly I'm Elvira, Mistress of the Dark. He's just a nice boy, Rosemary, and he hap-

448

pens to be my escort for the evening. He also has a life of his own."

"Well," Rosemary said lamely, "I'm only saying."

"Thank you, Rosemary. I promise you I'll bear it in mind."

"You may not realize how vulnerable you could be."

"He's my escort, Rosemary. That doesn't mean he's got his hand in my pants."

"There's no need to be coarse about it, Ruth," Rosemary said; and the hurt in her eyes was so great and so genuine that Ruth was beset with an almost overpowering sorrow. But what had been said could not be unsaid.

"Excuse me," Rosemary said. She went on out of the tent, leaving Ruth alone.

Back in the midst of the party a few minutes later, Ruth scanned the crowd for Hagan. For the moment she didn't seem to be able to see him. Then somebody bumped into her from behind and she turned and saw that it was Laura, Jake's wife. Where Jake tended to be perpetually harassed and depressive, Laura was the complete opposite. Ruth liked her a lot. She had a sheepish-looking Aidan Kincannon in tow and was hauling him toward the dance floor. She was lightly tanked-up and totally unconcerned.

"He went thataway," she said to Ruth, and pointed out toward the gardens. "Come on, cowboy," she then said to Aidan, pulling on his arm.

"Thanks," Ruth said.

"Excuse me," said Aidan Kincannon as he was yanked on past her.

The party was moving into its later phase now. The champagne had done its work and the music had moved up-tempo. The dinner suits and gowns were unwinding and starting to frolic. There was even some sedate and comparatively tasteful jiving going on.

"Look at them all," she heard some man say as she eased herself around the periphery of the crowd. "That's how it was, back when Dinosaurs ruled the Earth."

Aidan Kincannon was happily dancing with Laura, his necktie undone. There was no sign of Jake anywhere, which wasn't too much of a surprise. He was probably clearing up what was left of the food. When it came to fast living, Jake was a slow trailer hitched up to Laura's Ferrari.

She found Hagan outside of it all, out in the shadowy no-man's-land between the light and the movable barrier across the path. Behind Ruth, the canvas glowed like mother-of-pearl from

449

the bright lights within. There was a photographer now working somewhere inside, and every now and again the marquee was further illuminated as if by the flash of a bumper car's pole.

Hagan was seated on a low wall, looking out across the darkened square with a half-empty glass in his hand. He appeared to be deep in thought, and didn't seem to be aware of her approaching.

"I apologize if it seemed I'd abandoned you," Ruth said.

He looked around and started to rise abruptly, but she put her hand on his shoulder and pushed him back down as she sat beside him.

"Were you looking for me?" he said. "I'm sorry."

She took his drink from him, sipped from it, and handed it back.

"What are you thinking?" she said.

"How unlikely it all is," he told her, looking down into his glass. Straight orange juice, so far as Ruth could tell. "How you can plan the things you do but you can never plan the way you'll feel."

"Have you been reading my mind?" she said.

Out beyond the barrier, about fifty yards away, a mounted park policeman went by in the night. His horse was huge and dark, and his helmet caught a glint of the perimeter lights as his mount carried him by with loose and free-flowing ease. A hint of the beast in the stillness of a city night. Horse and rider made no sound.

Hagan said, "That man back in the food tent. The one who's married to the lawyer. He's the one, isn't he?"

"How could you tell?"

"I was reading your mind."

"I'm serious," she said, and she nudged him playfully with her shoulder. They were close enough for that. "What gave it away?"

"I saw you look at him," he said. "And your eyes went kind of sad. As if you'd already decided to let him go. Have you?"

Ruth breathed deep.

"I don't know," she said. "But I didn't realize I was hiding it so badly. That's something I'll have to watch." She smiled faintly in the shadows, and looked down at the ground. "I'm glad I picked you, Tim," she said. "I'm glad it wasn't anyone else."

"So am I," he said.

She'd a sense that there were a thousand things that could have happened right then. More than a thousand.

450

But they stood, to go back to the party. She linked her arm through his as they moved.

Somebody had come up with the bright idea of building a champagne fountain without actually taking into account the fact that they were using the wrong kind of champagne glasses, and the crash that followed almost drowned out the band. The bread-roll fight was another low spot. Some of the senior management people were out there after that, hard-eyed and cruising and making their presence known; not overtly taking names, but there to give the signal that they'd be damned well ready for it if things went any further. Couples with babysitters to relieve started to make a line for their coats. The free bar closed and the dance numbers turned slushy. A few people talked about going on to a club. All too soon, for Ruth. She felt tight and light, as if she'd been breathing in some thinner, purer kind of air. She didn't want to go to any nightclub. But she didn't want to end this yet, either. She felt like a runner, only just beginning to find her stride and her rhythm as those around her faded and fell away.

There were a couple of people that she still had to seek out and talk to, but when she checked around she learned that they'd already gone. Hagan stayed politely at her shoulder as she inquired. He seemed aware of the room but whenever she turned to him, his attention would return to her and was complete. It wasn't like having a boyfriend along. More like an eye-on-the-ball and attentive bodyguard. She wouldn't have imagined that she'd have liked the sensation. But she found that she did, rather.

Maybe it depended on who it was. Ruth didn't give of herself easily. She didn't like to let anyone under the ropes. Mostly, she'd allow them in and only then find out what they were really like, which was never quite as she'd expected. Or else, she reasoned, you let them in and then that changed how they thought of you, so by the very act you made them different.

In which case you couldn't hope to win, ever.

"What do you want to do from here?" he said.

There were guidelines to be followed, at this point as at the beginning of the evening; nothing special, just a version of the simple precautions of a first date with a stranger in the here-and-now. Meet in a public place. Avoid misunderstandings. Part like a couple of fencers, guard still up and protective layers intact. Take separate cabs or, if sharing, be dropped off last and don't risk being overheard when giving the address.

"You'd better get this for me," she said, passing him her coatroom ticket. "Then I'll drive you home."

"I could get a cab. It's all included."

"We don't need a cab."

As well as the line for coats, there was another for taxis that was moving just as slowly. Waiting close to the exit for Hagan to return, Ruth found herself side by side with Gordon as he was reaching the head of it.

"Congratulations," he said in a low voice and with a peevish streak in his tone that he wasn't quite managing to conceal. "There isn't a woman in the place that you haven't managed to shock, scandalize, or make green with envy."

Ruth knew that he was exaggerating. But she also knew that, in a more limited way, he wasn't wrong. Her actions tonight had been the neutron bomb of bad behavior, blasting the targets that she'd wanted to hit while leaving the major structures undamaged. Half the women here wouldn't even have known her name. The other half would probably have to struggle to forget it.

She said, "Which category includes Mimi?"

"For some reason, Mimi seems to think you're wonderful. It's a shame I couldn't have brought the two of you together in some other life. You'd probably have a lot in common."

"You mean, besides you?"

"Ruth!" he said under his breath, not daring to turn and look around.

"Here's your cab," she said. "Where's your wife?"

Mimi Parry was right behind her.

"Good night, Ruth," she called out pleasantly as she passed.

Tim Hagan brought her wrap and put it around her shoulders. They walked out into the square. There were still a few late strollers at the barriers. They were chatting easily to the security people, pointing things out, asking questions. But nobody paid the two of them much attention as they passed. She took Hagan's arm again and leaned against him. She could do that, couldn't she? What the hell, she'd hired him. It was a fine summer's night and it felt good to share the sensation of being alive. No more than that. And it was clear he didn't mind, because he put his hand over hers and pulled her in close.

They'd no more than a hundred yards to walk to reach the allnight attendant parking which stood, along with three or four other neon-lit facilities, in an alleyway between two modern buildings on the square. They waited at the yellow line for her car to be driven up.

"Thank you for tonight," Ruth said. "I hope the evening wasn't too much of a strain."

"No strain at all," Hagan said. "I think I learned a few things about myself."

"Like what?" she said. But the attendant brought her car then, so she never got to find out.

He wasn't even going to get in until she insisted, and then he gave in with grace. It only occurred to her as they were emerging from the end of the alleyway that he might feel awkward. She looked at him, but she couldn't read him. He was looking out into the night and was stroking his jaw with his hand, as if absently checking the closeness of his shave.

And what, she wondered to herself, did *you* learn about yourself tonight?

"So where to, Tim?" she said.

He gave an address out in Society Hill. Which was a surprise. She'd been expecting University City, maybe, or somewhere across the river. Society Hill had been something in its day, and wasn't exactly the barrio now. It stood some way south of the Old City, where she lived; but whereas much of the Old City had been reclaimed from a run-down waterfront zone, Society Hill had always been a prestigious residential area. She'd checked out its prices when she'd been looking to move, and had backed off fast. It was a district mostly of colonial town houses, the very same streets that often made her think of home. A postcard of home, an idealized dream of home; the home they reckoned you could never go back to, because in truth it had never been there.

Now she was curious. Whatever impression she'd formed of Hagan, projecting her guesses into the gaps left by his good-humored evasions, money had never been a part of it. Poverty, yes. She could see him as a poor boy with one good suit and his wits and a drive to rise. Making contacts, working his way; she couldn't imagine any other scenario that would put him onto the agency's books.

But that was just a kind of groundless romanticism, she realized now. The kind of impulse that made sad women on ocean cruises dream about the lifeguards at the pool. She was no virgin, and he was no Gypsy. Life, it seemed, had an endless capacity to frustrate one's expectations.

453

She drove around Independence Square and down through the main tourist quarter, where the city had bulldozed the ground around a handful of key historic buildings to leave them standing in parkland like rock plugs on a volcanic plain. A few late visitors were peering through the glass of the Liberty Bell pavilion, but otherwise the sector was floodlit and quiet.

It didn't take her long to find the address. It was a low-rise building amid the row houses, designed to blend in. Three stories with attic space above, cellar windows at street level, bars on the cellar windows. The street was short, and tree-lined, and quiet. They'd offset the east-west streets when they were laying out this part of the city, deliberately misaligning the ends so that young men wouldn't be able to race their carriages along them. There was a big van close behind her, and it was too narrow here for Ruth to stop. She had to circle around the adjoining streets a couple of times before she could find a space to pull in.

"Is this where you live?" she said.

"It's where I've been staying," Hagan said. And then, abruptly, almost blurting it out as if he'd been trying and had finally failed to hold it back, he said, "Come home with me."

"What?"

"Don't do anything you don't want to do," he said. "But I don't want it to be over yet. I'm asking you to stay with me awhile longer. Just to talk."

She was lost.

"Tim," she began, "I—"

He held up a hand and shook his head. He was avoiding meeting her eyes. There was a hint of a stammer when he spoke now, in complete contrast to his easy manner throughout the evening.

He said, "Don't answer. Take a minute to think. I'm going to run ahead and check on a few things. I'll leave you in the car. If you're gone when I come back, then that's entirely your choice. You won't see me again. You won't even have to explain."

He got out of the car, then, and crossed the street to the house without looking back. She watched as he let himself in, first through an iron security gate and then through the main door beyond. The Pontiac's engine was running.

There was no question of her going with him. It couldn't happen. But even though she knew how it had to be, her inner reaction was a strange mixture of ecstasy and dismay. Dropping like a weight, soaring like a bird. To know that she dare not. But know that she could. This was the high point of the evening and there

was nothing that could happen from here, *nothing*, that could be anything other than the start of a downhill roll. So best to cut it clean, and go out high.

She'd be gone when he returned. That much was certain.

Lights came on in the second-floor apartment. She could see up to plaster moldings and stripped woodwork, and a turning fan that cast a giant and ominous shadow across the ceiling of the room. She couldn't see Hagan from here, but she knew that she couldn't stick around any longer because he'd come down and find her waiting there and get entirely the wrong idea.

Ruth wondered what he'd run ahead to do. Tidy the place? Make sure that someone hadn't come home without warning, a girlfriend maybe?

Or his parents?

Oh, *God*. His parents. Wouldn't that be terrible? So terrible a thought that it was almost exquisite. It occupied that strange, strange ground between torment and bliss.

Now she'd better go.

But he was standing in the doorway with the hall light behind him. A backlit silhouette, watching, waiting. Ruth switched off the engine and got out of the car.

As she reached him, her eyes met his. He stepped back, by way of invitation, and she went on into the hall. As she started to climb the thickly carpeted stairs, her legs trembled so much that for a moment she was afraid that they might give way under her.

The apartment door stood open. No bare little garret, this. And not his, either, even though he closed the door behind them and moved across to the kitchen with a clear air of familiarity. She could tell at a glance, the style wasn't him. Not the glass coffee table, not the expensive rug it stood on, not the green porcelain dragons nor the dried-flower arrangement in the fireplace.

Whose, she couldn't say. It all looked immaculate, unlived-in. From over in the kitchen area he said, "I can offer you an espresso or a cappuccino. There's a machine that does both."

Ruth said, "What am I doing here, Tim? If you can give me an answer to that I'll be happy because, God's own truth, I really don't know."

Hagan moved out to stand before her. He took both of her hands in his own.

He said, "Your hands are shaking."

"So are yours. Look at the two of us."

He leaned forward and down, and she raised herself to the kiss.

It wasn't perfect, but it was powerful. He dropped her hands and their arms slid around each other, and when they broke off they continued to hug, fiercely, her face turned into his neck. Ruth didn't know if the sensation running through her was the hammering of Hagan's heart or the echo of her own.

"I think I'm going to explode," she whispered.

"Good," he said.

Out of all the details betraying the place as not his own, those in the bedroom spoke louder than any. Lights came on to reveal lush fabrics and deep gold, more like a luxury stateroom than a young man's place.

He was only passing through. Gypsy after all.

Now he was standing behind her. She could see herself and him in the ornately framed mirror across the room. Its glass had an amber tint, so that anyone looking in it would be flattered as if with a tan. It was head-to-toe, a full-length dress mirror. He placed his hands on her back and slid them outward, slipping the thin straps of her black dress over her shoulders. The dress glided down and hit the floor in one rapid cascade. Ruth saw it go, reflected in the glass. No catches, no snags, not even a wriggle.

Let's see Alicia do *that*, she was thinking with a fierce and almost demonic sense of pride . . . it would probably catch on her hips and hang there, like she'd stripped to the waist for a wash.

There she was. Hair up, no bra, the most expensive silk underwear that Gordon could afford. Black stockings and pumps, all the power of her sexuality turned and aimed like a loaded gun.

She turned to Tim Hagan and placed her hands on his shoulders. He was as tight as a wire. He could hardly bring himself to look down.

"Don't be afraid," she said.

Hagan swallowed, hard.

"I want to be," he said.

Ruth picked up her clothes and dressed in the living room while he slept. The lights were off and the drapes were still open. Above her, the ceiling fan was still. The only sound was the rustle of silk on skin and the occasional passing of a car in the street outside. She could see the room around her in shades of gray. Full of grain, like film pushed to its limit.

456

She was breathless, even now. She was high. There was an elation within her that just wouldn't let her come down.

Carrying her shoes in one hand, she tiptoed back in and crouched by the bed. She could see him by the faint red light of the display on the bedside alarm. He was facedown, sprawled, his head turned aside and half buried in the pillow. The pillow was satin, and carried a shine. His face was completely open as he slept, like a child's.

"Tim?" she said. "Are you awake?"

She'd barely breathed it. He stirred a little, and she thought that his eyes opened a fraction, but he wasn't really there.

It was enough. "That was better than wonderful," she whispered, talking as one might to a patient in deep coma; not expecting to be heard, and yet believing that the words would somehow bypass all the barriers of consciousness and reach down to settle in some important place. "But we've each got a life, Tim, and I'm not part of yours. I won't forget this. But never again."

He stirred a little more and then turned over and she froze, waiting to see if he was going to haul himself all the way up into wakefulness. She was hoping that he wouldn't. Anything more that might be said out loud right now could only serve to bring down the moment.

He breathed in. Held it. Then let it out slowly, as if he'd turned from wakefulness in the last instant.

She straightened up and backed off, through the door and across the darkened sitting room. Halfway over she tripped on the phone cord, and the clatter of the handset as it leaped into the air was like the sudden startling-up of a bird. She grabbed at it, fumbled it, dropped it with even more racket onto the hard surface of the coffee table.

Holding it still, she waited.

Then, moving carefully, she righted the handset and replaced the receiver. As an afterthought, she picked it up and checked it. No sound came from the earpiece. No tone, no static, nothing. She wondered if she'd broken it, but then, it hadn't landed all that hard. Maybe it wasn't connected. She laid the receiver on the table alongside it, as kind of an indication.

Did she have everything? She did. She let herself out of the apartment and eased the door shut behind her with a faint click. Her shoes were still in her hand. She didn't put them on until she reached the place downstairs where the carpet ran up to the front door.

Ruth found that she couldn't get out into the street. She got the door open, but it was the barred security gate on the other side that was the problem. It needed some kind of an electronic release from the inside, and she couldn't see where it was.

She sighed. She was going to have to wake him after all. But what a lousy arrangement. What if they had a fire?

She went back down the hallway and, instead of climbing the stairs, continued toward the rear of the building. A swing door let her through into a much plainer service corridor with dim but constant emergency lighting. At the end of it was a solid-looking door with a vinyl sticker on it, red on white and reading FIRE EXIT. It had a crash bar that was secured with a pin on a chain, like a grenade.

When Ruth pulled out the pin and leaned against the bar, the door popped open easily. As it swung out into the night she belatedly wondered if she was going to set off an alarm and bring every resident in the place downstairs in their skivvies, but nothing happened. She stepped out into an alleyway behind the row, with some parking garages opposite and beyond them the high walls and razor wire of another row's yards. There was a faint moon over the rooftops, marbled behind cloud, and yellow sodium security lighting over the garages. The door closed behind her, and she heard its bolts drop.

This wasn't a good time to be out in the open, even in an area like this. But her car was only around the corner.

And being honest with herself, she felt untouchable. Not stupid enough to believe it, but it was the way that she felt. She stepped out through the shadows. The alleyway was paved with herringbone-patterned brick, and was a little uneven.

Hell on the kind of heels she was wearing, but Ruth didn't mind. She was fireproof.

She hadn't put a foot wrong all night, and she wasn't about to start now.